LEGACY OF GLASS

KINGDOMS OF LEGACY WORLD

KINGDOMS OF LEGACY

Legacy of Roses: A Beauty and the Beast Tale (Book One)

Legacy of Glass: A Cinderella Tale (Book Two)

Legacy of Thorns: A Sleeping Beauty Tale (Book Three)

Legacy of Gold: A Rumpelstiltskin Tale (Book Four)

Legacy of Locks: A Rapunzel Tale (Book Five)

Legacy of Ice: A Snow Queen Tale (Book Six)

TETHERED HEARTS

Ties of Legacy: A Companion Novel

LEGACY OF GLASS
A CINDERELLA TALE

KINGDOMS OF LEGACY BOOK 2

MELANIE CELLIER

LUMINANT PUBLICATIONS

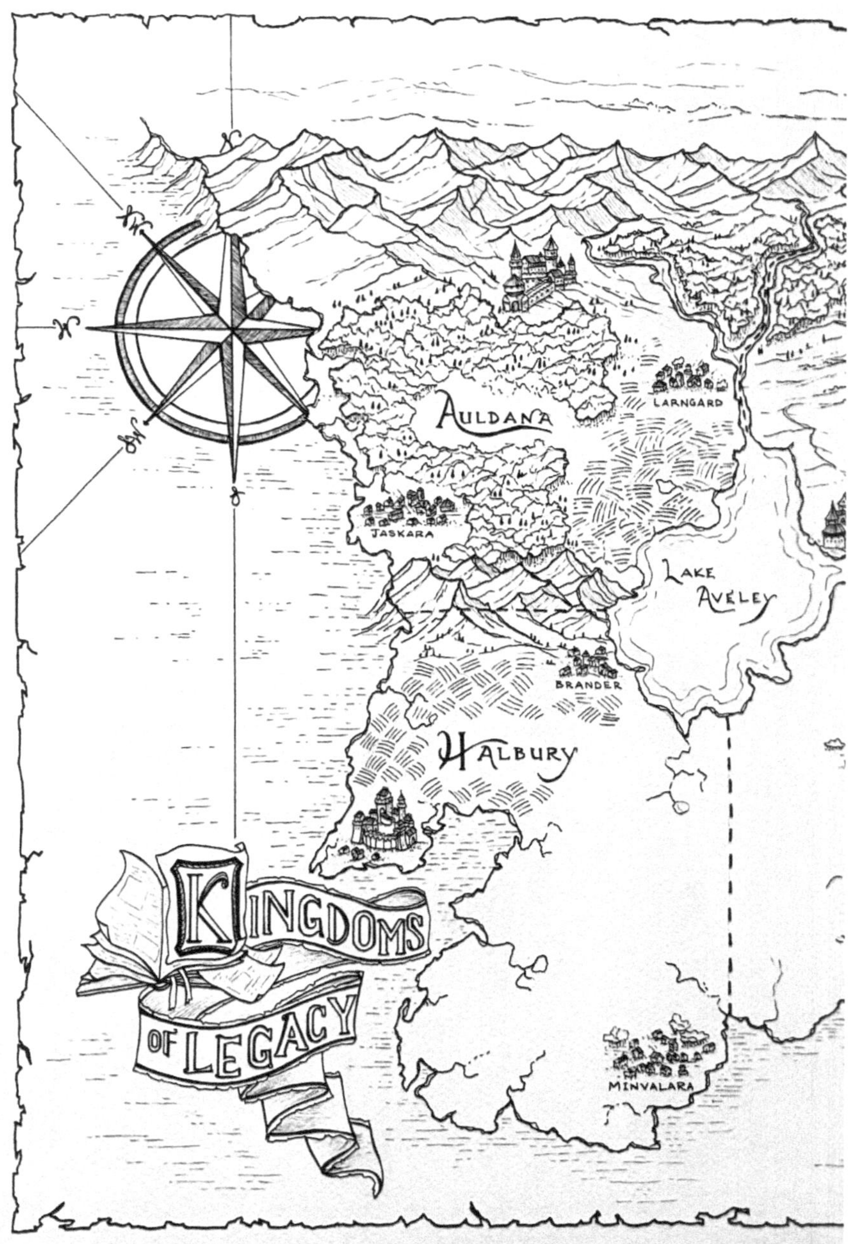

AULDANA
LARNGÅRD
JASKARA
LAKE AVELEY
BRANDER
HALBURY
MINVALARA
KINGDOMS OF LEGACY

MOUNTAIN COMMUNITY
BOLIVERE
GLENALTA
THEBARTON
STONYFELL
GLANDORE
KLYMPTON
ETHELSON
MARLESTON
OAKDEN
SOVAR
HENTON
MIRANDAR

CHAPTER 1
OLIVIA

Olivia dipped her head toward the colorful, fragrant pile in her arms and breathed deeply. Nothing made her quite as happy as a bright sun in a blue sky and the smell of wildflowers. She loved summer.

Squelch. Her left foot landed in something soft, and she froze. She couldn't see what it was through the bundle of flowers in her arms, but she couldn't imagine it was anything pleasant.

Drawing a deep breath, she twisted her arms to the side and peered downward. Mouse droppings.

Her eyes widened. The mice in Sovar were larger than those in other kingdoms, but she had never seen such a large pile of droppings. And placed just there, as if waiting for her. With the flowers obscuring her vision, she had stepped fully into it, her shoe almost totally subsumed.

She let out a wail. The Legacy might have forced her into becoming a servant for her relatives, but this was going too far. Was it really too much for her to be both clean and fragrant for *five minutes*?

She stared at her ruined slipper and groaned. She had overreached. She shouldn't have gathered flowers the same day she was wearing new slippers. It was just inviting trouble.

"Olivia!" A girl in the distance called her name, waving wildly.

Olivia looked up, but with her arms full, she couldn't wave back. And with her foot stuck in mouse droppings, she couldn't go to her friend either. With a grimace, she pulled her foot free. The slipper stayed behind.

Olivia laughed. She couldn't help it. It was such a ridiculous situation. And it was just like Marigold to arrive at precisely that moment.

She took several steps away from her abandoned shoe, wondering uneasily if she should rescue it. It was a new slipper, after all. But would any amount of scrubbing actually make it clean? She shuddered.

"Olivia!" Marigold reached her friend and threw her arms around her neck in greeting. "There you are."

"Were you looking for me?" Olivia's mind was still on her slipper.

"I'm *always* looking for you," Marigold declared in her usual dramatic way.

"I'm not that hard to find," Olivia said mildly. "I'm not sure I can even remember the last time I left my aunt and uncle's manor."

"That would be today." Marigold gave her a cheeky smile. "If you look around, you will see blue skies and green hills. You're currently located on the hill behind both our family manors. If your aunt and uncle are trying to claim this territory, I will fight them to the death." She assumed a dramatic pose, one arm raised in the air as if she was brandishing a sword.

"Ha!" Olivia shook her head. "I heard one of Uncle Walt's business partners claiming your father has more influence than the king. I'm pretty sure my aunt would gift you this entire hill in exchange for one dinner invitation."

Marigold collapsed on herself, letting out a disappointed sigh. Taking Olivia's elbow, she dragged her toward the nearest tree.

When they reached it, Marigold threw herself on the ground, her back against the trunk. Only then did she properly look at Olivia, still with her arms full of flowers.

"Why are you only wearing one shoe?" she asked.

Olivia glanced over her shoulder back toward the enormous pile of mouse droppings. "The other one had an unfortunate accident."

"An accident?" Marigold straightened and followed Olivia's line of sight. When she spotted the abandoned slipper nestling among the droppings, she threw her head back in laughter.

Olivia reluctantly smiled as she carefully deposited her load on the grass and took a more cautious seat facing her friend. Somehow it was impossible not to smile when Marigold laughed. Marigold had that effect on everyone— her presence was magnetic, if a bit chaotic.

"It's not my fault," Olivia protested halfheartedly. "Unless you count the foolishness of wearing the slippers at all. I should have foreseen trouble. The Legacy doesn't like me being too clean and well-dressed—and even you suffer from the issue of losing shoes. One at a time, of course."

For some reason this speech only set Marigold off into another round of laughter. Olivia eyed her. Marigold had never been the focus of the Legacy's power—not in the way Olivia had been since leaving her home town and moving to the capital to live with her father's relatives.

Marigold finally subsided, wiping at the moisture gathered in her eyes. "Thank you for that," she said on a sigh. "I needed a laugh."

Olivia winced sympathetically. "Your mother?"

"Actually it was Father this time." Marigold straightened. "But I don't want to talk about that. Let's talk about something else." She eyed the pile of flowers beside Olivia. "Where in the kingdoms did you find those? I was sure the hot spell had dried out every flower within miles of the city."

Olivia shrugged. "I was skeptical as well, but I wasn't going to argue when Aunt Helen sent me out to gather flowers. I think it's her way of giving me an afternoon off." She rested her hands on the ground behind her and leaned back, tipping her face up to the sky and breathing deeply. "And it turns out there were more surviving pockets of flowers than I expected. Although I nearly toppled over the cliff retrieving one of them." She shuddered at the memory. She was usually more careful of the small cliff that lurked at the back of the beautiful, grass-covered hill.

"Do you know your problem, friend?" Marigold asked in a reproving voice.

Olivia didn't bother to open her eyes. "I'm sure you're about to tell me."

"You're too good at your job. How can your aunt resist

turning you into a glorified servant when you cover the roles of four paid ones, and make it look easy?"

Olivia wanted to glare at her friend, but the afternoon was too nice for her to muster anything but mild irritation. Besides, any day felt more lively and exciting when Marigold was present. Olivia could still hardly believe that the noble girl from the other side of the wall had chosen to befriend her. Apparently she'd never shown any particular interest in either of Olivia's cousins.

"It's because you're different," Marigold had told her once. "I knew the moment I saw your face that I was going to like you tremendously and that we would be best friends. I'm never wrong about that sort of thing."

To be fair, Olivia's cousins seemed to view Marigold with unease. Hattie had once confided to Olivia that she didn't know which of Marigold's dramatic pronouncements could be believed.

If she was objective, Olivia could understand her cousin's confusion. If you didn't know her, Marigold's manner could easily come across as insincere. But Olivia had a method of testing people's sincerity, and Marigold's heart was true beneath her over-the-top manner. Olivia just didn't want to tell her cousins how she had first gained confidence in her new friend—not when the information would make it back to her aunt.

Not that her aunt was a villain. Olivia had confirmed that using the same method. Just as her cousin's uncertainty about Marigold was unfounded, so was Marigold's concern about Olivia's situation.

She straightened and sighed. "Do you think I haven't tried being worse at my tasks? It's harder than you'd think."

"Ah, to be blessed by the Legacy," Marigold said with a grin. "Do you think there's any way I can convince the Legacy that it should assist me with my harp playing? I don't mind performing for my parents' friends—" Olivia snorted. Marigold never minded performing. "But I loathe all the practicing," Marigold finished. "It's so tedious."

"Let me guess." Olivia finally realized the reason for her friend's appearance on the hill. "You're supposed to be practicing right now."

"Obviously," Marigold said without a hint of shame. "It was an unexpected bonus to find you here. I thought that so-called aunt of yours would have you locked away somewhere, working."

Olivia didn't bother to protest Marigold's disparaging description of her relative. It was true that Walt and Helen weren't really her aunt and uncle since Walt was her father's cousin, not his brother. But they were a generation above her and had claimed her as a niece on arrival, something Olivia had no issue with. Marigold, however, liked to take issue with anything and everything done by *Aunt* Helen. She was a very loyal friend.

"I think she sent me out to gather flowers because she felt bad about my working through the heat the last few weeks," Olivia said. "It's not as if she hates me. She isn't half as bad as you always make her out to be."

Marigold poked Olivia with her toe. "You are too forgiving. Your supposed aunt and uncle wrote to your parents about their successful business and said they would happily provide a job in said business for any of their cousins' children who might like to move to the capital. *In said business.* Not as a servant in their home."

Olivia sighed. It was hardly the first time she and Marigold had gone over the issue. "I know that, obviously. I'm the one who told you. But you make it sound like it was some underhanded plan. They really did mean for whoever came to work in the business. But they were expecting one of my brothers." She gave Marigold a look. "One of my many brothers."

Marigold gave a dramatic groan and flung herself back against the tree. "Don't talk to me of many brothers. Not today."

Olivia raised her eyebrows. She and Marigold had first connected due to their overabundance of brothers, and Marigold often complained of hers. But something in her tone sounded different this time. Perhaps something of significance had happened after all.

But Olivia didn't push her friend to say more. Whatever it was, knowing Marigold, she wouldn't be able to hold it in for long.

"I'm not saying Aunt Helen and Uncle Walt are unwilling to employ females in their business," she continued instead. "Or that they were unhappy it was me who came. Nell and Hattie were certainly delighted I was a girl. But if I'd been one of my brothers, the Legacy wouldn't have been a factor."

"What does it matter if you're a girl?" Marigold asked fiercely. "It shouldn't matter!"

Olivia rolled her eyes. "It doesn't matter to any of us. That's what I'm saying. But you know it matters to the Legacy. It wasn't a boy who was forced by his stepfather into becoming a servant, only to eventually go to a ball wearing glass slippers and dance with a princess. It was the other way around."

"More's the pity," Marigold said darkly. "We would all have been saved a deal of trouble if it was the other way around."

Olivia threw her another curious look. Something was definitely going on with Marigold. Other than her staunch defense of Olivia, she had never shown any particular animosity toward the Legacy on her own behalf before.

Sometimes when Olivia was cooking or cleaning, she thought about the long-dead Queen Ella, only the second queen her kingdom had ever had. Had Ella realized during her lifetime the profound impact her life would have on the kingdom she helped rule? All the founding royal families of her generation had fallen prey to enchantments that had reshaped their lives. But had they realized those enchantments were also reshaping their kingdoms—seeping into the fabric of the kingdom itself and affecting everything from the plants and animals to the crafts that were possible within each of their borders?

Surely the Legacy had already begun to make itself felt before Queen Ella's passing from old age? The history books said it had started then—exerting its mindless force, binding those born within Sovar's borders to their kingdom and pushing the kingdom's inhabitants to follow the elements of Ella's own history whenever possible.

Of course no one got to live her entire fairy tale-worthy life. The unpleasant parts would be far less of a burden if you were guaranteed the happily ever after at the end. But as Olivia knew only too well, the Legacy mimicked elements from the original history wherever it could, regardless of the outcome.

For someone like Marigold, that mostly meant she had

trouble keeping track of a matching pair of shoes. For Olivia, it meant she was currently stuck as a servant in her relative's home.

It was the Legacy that ensured Olivia was far too good at her job to be employed in any other capacity. Her mistake had been entering her relatives' home without finding out more about them first. If she'd known her father's cousin had two daughters a similar age to herself, she would have been more cautious. Once she arrived in the household, how could the Legacy resist forcing her into the role of servant?

But if she could go back in time and make the choice again—this time with all the information—would she have chosen differently?

Her new life in the capital hadn't turned out how she had imagined, but that didn't mean she wanted to return to her old life. She could still easily call up the frustrated, trapped feeling that had permeated her days in Henton as she approached eighteen.

When a roving merchant—one of the few people who could comfortably travel between kingdoms, unbound by any Legacy—had appeared in Henton, it had been the most exciting event in her whole year. Olivia had confided her dream to leave her small town and seek adventure in the capital, and Avery's encouragement had been enough to decide her—even before Avery's gift. But that gift—one that allowed Olivia to see a person's true emotions—had provided the final bit of confidence.

How could Olivia have stayed stuck in boring Henton after that—where nothing ever changed and nothing of excitement ever happened? Even if she could go back, she would still choose to experience the capital and gain a friend like Marigold.

In that moment—sitting with her friend in the sun, with the scent of the flowers still in her nose—it was easy to see that it was all worth it. But she might feel differently next time Cook asked her to peel a pile of potatoes nearly as tall as Olivia herself.

A soft squeaking made her twist to look behind her, a welcoming smile on her face. A soft gray mouse appeared, unremarkable except for its size.

Marigold, distracted from her sour mood, stared at it. "Olivia, your pet got bigger," she said. "You can see that, right?"

Olivia laughed. It was hard to see the changes day to day, but she couldn't deny that when she had first encountered the lone creature, the mouse had been the size of a cat. She was now the size of a medium dog. Although she still didn't seem large enough to account for the unfortunate droppings.

"Mildred's not my pet," Olivia said. "She's more like a friend." She smiled as the once-wild mouse scurried up to her and pressed against her side, letting Olivia run her hand over her soft fur. "I think the Legacy is making her smarter as well as larger. She was my first friend here—even before you."

"I must be losing my edge if there's any competition between me and a *mouse*," Marigold muttered.

Olivia ignored her. "I do feel guilty about her size, though. All the changes in her must be my fault. She's been with me for nearly a year now and growing slowly bigger all that time. It's going to be hard for her to hide herself soon."

Growing up in a small town in the middle of the kingdom, Olivia was used to seeing cat-sized mice, usually found with equally large lizards. But she knew most of them had been driven out of the capital long ago—a fact that had been confirmed by Marigold's astonishment and distaste the first time she had encountered Mildred.

It must have been hard enough to stay hidden before, but it could only be getting harder as Mildred kept growing—something that was rumored to happen in areas where the power of the Legacy was strongly concentrated. And Olivia knew it was her fault the Legacy was pouring its power onto those around her. If Mildred had never befriended Olivia, she might never have started to grow.

"Only you would worry about a mouse," Marigold said with a laugh. "You really are too kind for your own good. It's too bad you—" She froze, her eyes widening.

She had clearly been hit by an idea, and Olivia's heart sank. Marigold's ideas had a way of sucking Olivia into their orbit, and they were rarely what you might call sensible or realistic.

Marigold seized her hand, confirming her fears. "Olivia," she breathed, her eyes shining. "I have the best idea!"

Before Olivia could either protest or express curiosity— she still wasn't sure which was about to spill out of her mouth—the sound of shouting reached them from the bottom of the hill.

Marigold dropped Olivia's hand and leaped to her feet. Olivia scrambled up after her, peering down at three servants wearing the livery of Marigold's family. She bit down on a grin. It wouldn't do to express sympathy for the poor men sent to find and fetch the missing Marigold.

"Oh, drat," Marigold said. "I was hoping it would take

them longer to notice I was gone. I'll have to run or else they'll catch me, and then I'll be practicing all the way to the evening meal."

"Or maybe your father is just concerned about you," Olivia suggested. "He is both wealthy and influential. If you keep sneaking off alone, you might find yourself abducted one of these days. You'd be a juicy ransom target."

"Ha!" Marigold grinned. "I'd like to see someone try." She threw Olivia an affectionate look. "You do have an odd idea of life in the capital if you're worried about that."

Olivia shrugged. "One of my cousins confessed that she doesn't like going into the market alone out of fear of such a thing, and my uncle is much less important than your father."

Marigold snorted. "Pure chicken-heartedness. You should tell your cousin not to worry. I've snuck away on my own hundreds of times, and no one has ever tried to abduct me. I've never even heard of a noble youngster being kidnapped, so I'm sure they're not going to come after her."

"If you're truly not worried, you might want to hurry." Olivia watched the men toiling their way up the hill. Marigold didn't have long to get moving if she wanted to outrun them.

Marigold spun, poised to take off when she hesitated and looked back at Olivia.

Olivia raised an eyebrow and waited.

"I really have had the most fabulous idea," Marigold said. "Meet me back here when it's dark, and I'll tell you all about it."

Olivia didn't have time to agree before Marigold was off in a swirl of shrieks and racing feet. The men struggling up the hill changed direction, heading after the fleeing heiress and leaving Olivia alone with only Mildred for company.

The mouse had sat down beside her, leaning her head on Olivia's leg, and Olivia patted her absentmindedly. Mildred usually avoided people, but she had grown used to Marigold, and even the girl's exaggerated actions and noises no longer sent the mouse running. She really was an unusually intelligent creature.

"Is it all thanks to the Legacy?" Olivia wondered aloud. "Or were you always a remarkable mouse?"

Mildred squeaked and burrowed her head harder against Olivia. But a moment later, the mouse froze. Her ears twitched, and she surged back to her feet. With a single flick of her tail, like a farewell wave to Olivia, she raced in the direction of the hidden cliff.

Olivia would have been afraid for her, but she knew Mildred was an expert at survival and familiar with every inch of the local area. So she rose unhurriedly to her feet and carefully gathered her flowers back into her arms. Mildred's departure was a clear indication that someone was approaching, and it might be someone from her aunt and uncle's household—possibly even Aunt Helen herself. It was time Olivia was returning anyway.

But she had barely stepped away from the tree when the newcomer strode into view. Tall, young, and broad-shouldered, with dark hair and light eyes, the strange man approaching her was certainly not Aunt Helen.

CHAPTER 2
JULIUS

Julius strode up the grassy incline, enjoying the pleasant warmth of the sun and the slight breeze. The recent hot spell had made venturing outside the palace grounds an unpleasant prospect, and he had been starting to feel cooped up. It felt good to be free again, if only for a single, stolen hour.

He could have left the palace for longer, of course, but then he would have had to tell his parents. And if he'd done that, his mother would have insisted he take guards with him. Usually Julius didn't mind being trailed by guards, but the itchy feeling beneath his skin demanded true solitude.

His father had dedicated his life to serving the Sovaran people, and the royal family was popular as a result. Julius had never felt unsafe in the environs of the palace, and he had picked his direction based on the likelihood of solitude. He didn't need guards on this occasion, and he certainly didn't want them.

He knew his duty, and he didn't mind fulfilling it, but it was exhausting to fill a role every second of the day. They'd had a visiting delegation for the last two weeks which meant Julius had been on constant show—needing to play a perfect, charming prince day and night.

The Legacy helped, of course—along with a lifetime of training on what it meant to fill the role of Sovar's crown prince. But usually he was able to regularly clear his head with a brisk gallop somewhere talk wasn't needed—something he hadn't managed to do for two straight weeks and hadn't even been able to manage that day. But Julius at least wanted a brief window when no one expected him to be charming.

But as he crested the hill, he realized he wasn't alone after all. A beautiful girl stood frozen mid-step, her arms full of colorful flowers and her wide eyes fixed on Julius. He could see little of her clothes behind the profusion of blossoms, but if she was wandering the hill behind Manor Row in the middle of the day, she wasn't likely to be a servant or tradesperson. But neither did he recognize her from court, despite her memorable face. Perhaps she was the younger daughter of one of the nobles, too young to have yet attended any court functions.

He sighed internally. There was no hope of getting away without polite conversation now.

But to his surprise, the girl wheeled around and hurried away from him, almost as if the encounter was equally unwelcome to her. Worry gripped him. Was she afraid? Of the crown prince?

If he could only speak to her for a moment, he was sure he could reassure her. But perhaps it was shyness, not fear, that drove her away. She needn't have worried on that front, either. Not only did Julius have the Legacy to aid him, he had been trained in social interaction since he first learned to talk. He was equally as skilled at drawing out a hesitant conversationalist as he was at shutting down or redirecting presumptuous or dangerous lines of talk—all without causing offense, of course.

He watched her retreat with a frown, hating the thought that his presence made her uncomfortable. His presence never made people uncomfortable. And she was even limping slightly. He should offer his assistance and ensure she left the hill with a good impression of him.

He hurried after her, collecting several dropped flowers as he went.

"Excuse me," he said, and the deep sound of his voice made her start and drop several more flowers.

When she tried to lean over and retrieve them, she only succeeded in losing even more.

Julius chuckled. "Allow me."

He fetched each of the fallen blooms and gathered them into a rough bouquet, presenting them to her with a flourish and a light grin. She was looking back at him with narrowed eyes, as if she found him at fault rather than charming. Perhaps she blamed him for making her drop the flowers in the first place.

His smile fell, and he tried to tuck the ones he was holding into her arms without upsetting any more or accidentally touching her. It was a tricky task, but he managed it and stepped back.

"You appear to be injured. May I assist you back to..." He trailed off and gestured generally toward the row of houses below them, waiting for her to clarify which was hers.

"Injured?" Her slight hostility melted into confusion.

"What do you mean?" She twisted slightly, trying to glance down her body without upsetting the carefully balanced load in her arms.

His eyes followed hers and finally alighted on her feet. One was shod in a slipper, the other was bare.

"Oh." He flushed slightly and took a small step backward. He should have considered that possibility. Even his own mother wasn't exempt from losing a shoe at awkward moments.

The girl laughed. At his mistake? At his obvious discomfort? Both? His discomfort grew.

"Are you even Sovaran?" she asked in a pretty, lilting voice. "Surely you recognize the national one-shoed limp?" She laughed again.

Julius stiffened. She didn't recognize him? He wasn't sure if that had ever happened before, and it put him immediately off balance.

"My apologies," he said, unused to the stilted note in his voice. "Forgive my intrusion."

"Goodness, you're a barrel of fun," she muttered under her breath, but Julius caught every word, his ears burning.

Where had his famous charm gone? He had initiated the interaction hoping to put her at ease, and somehow he seemed to be doing the opposite. What was wrong with him?

His mind raced, trying to think how to salvage the situation. The thought of abandoning the encounter didn't even cross his mind. Putting others at ease was his job, and he had always been excellent at it.

Luckily, she had a problem that he could help fix. The entire population of Sovar had an issue with losing shoes, but Julius alone possessed the opposite skill.

"Please wait a moment and allow me to look for your missing slipper." He attempted his most charming smile. "I have something of a knack for finding them."

"Find my shoe?" The girl stared at him as if he'd demanded she hand over all her coin instead of offering to help. She glanced back up the hill, her face turning red.

To Julius's chagrin, the soft flush of color that warmed the girl's cheeks only served to make her even more appealing, while apparently he was failing utterly at redeeming himself. He had seen plenty of beautiful women at court, but somehow this fresh-faced girl had turned him into a bumbling fool. It was a new experience.

"Yes, it will likely only take a moment," he said, trying not to let his emotion show.

Her eyes widened. "No!" she said firmly. "Absolutely not."

Julius's jaw dropped.

"You don't want me to find your shoe?" He could hear the grating note in his voice, so unlike his usual self, but he couldn't seem to stop the words. "Why ever not? Is there something wrong with it?"

He bit back the addition, *Is there something wrong with you?* So far he seemed to be the one behaving all wrong.

The girl's brows drew together, and she shot another look at the top of the hill, as if she already knew where her shoe could be found.

Julius drew back. Was she playing some sort of game with him? Was that why he couldn't find his footing with her? Was it possible she did know his identity after all, and she had some sort of agenda?

He narrowed his eyes, scanning her face for some sign of

calculation or duplicity. If she was trying to draw him in, she'd chosen a strange way to go about it. And yet he couldn't deny that she'd already gotten under his skin. He couldn't remember the last time he had participated in such an awkward conversation.

The girl straightened in response to his scrutiny, her expression turning haughty. "I have no desire to retrieve my shoe," she said with formality. "And I don't need assistance to reach my home. Have a good day, sir."

It was clearly a dismissal. He stiffened instinctively. He'd never been dismissed in such a way in his life. But he fought the feeling back and merely inclined his head in her direction. Restraint was a familiar friend, and it was far better for him to utilize it now. The entire interaction had been a disaster from start to finish, and the best he could do was retreat as promptly as possible.

"I apologize for discommoding you," he said stiffly. "I intended only to assist."

Turning, he hurried in the opposite direction to the girl, walking almost blindly in his haste to get away. He had always prided himself on fulfilling his role to perfection and seeing himself fail so badly shook him to his core. He was the crown prince of Sovar, and he could not afford to behave more bumbling than a newborn fool.

"Stop! Wait!" the girl called suddenly from behind him, her voice tense.

He increased his pace. All he wanted was to get far away from her. He couldn't imagine why she would want more stilted, awkward conversation, but he certainly didn't. Just the memory of it made the itchy feeling beneath his skin flare back to full life. He sincerely hoped he would never run into her again.

"Stop!" she shouted again, but he powered on, his head facing forward although his mind was on the girl behind him.

When he heard running footsteps, he wavered. She must already have a poor impression of him. What was more likely to make it worse—further conversation or his obvious flight? The very question hurt his pride, and he couldn't bring himself to turn and look back at the face that had managed to strip him of his most defining attribute.

He increased his speed. He just wanted to get away and forget the whole interaction had ever happened.

The girl's cries turned into a scream as his next step landed on uneven ground and slipped away from him. He tried to pull back, one foot extended into empty air as he finally saw what was in front of his eyes. The land in front of him fell away abruptly into empty space, the gentle slope of the hill cutting off in a sheer cliff.

His whole body teetered dangerously as he tried to recover his balance. He tipped the wrong way.

Two small hands clamped around his arm and jerked sharply, pulling him backward. His center of balance shifted, and he collapsed away from the cliff, falling to the ground and taking the unseen person with him.

He gasped, his heart racing at his near escape. He was unfamiliar with the open ground behind Manor Row, and he should have been more cautious. He knew the treacherous nature of the Sovaran landscape.

The girl—no longer holding any flowers—scuttled away

from him and scrambled to her feet. Dusting herself off, she stared down at him.

He rose more slowly, his mind struggling to think clearly. He knew he needed to thank her—without her quick intervention, he would likely have gone over the edge. But what explanation could he offer for walking straight off a cliff? Or for ignoring her shouts of warning? His face warmed, and for once in his life, he struggled to find any words.

"Unbelievable," the girl pronounced slowly, shaking her head. She picked up steam. "You're truly unbelievable! Do you have a death wish?"

"I—" he managed to say before she shook her head and cut him off.

"No, never mind. You're alive and unharmed, and that's good enough. I'm late back as it is, and now I have to retrieve all the flowers."

Julius glanced back the way they had come. Flowers were strewn in a long path between the cliff edge and their previous location. She had clearly shed them as she hurried after him with increasing urgency.

The girl was turning away, shaking her head, but she paused, looking at him with a creased brow. "Will you be all right to get back to...wherever you came from? You won't walk off any more cliffs?"

His flush grew deeper at how obviously incapable she thought him. He now hoped desperately that she truly didn't know his identity. "I can assure you it was a momentary aberration. I'm not usually in the habit of walking off cliffs."

The girl raised her eyebrows, as if she wasn't entirely sure she believed him, but after a moment, she inclined her head politely and hurried away.

Julius watched her go, his heart still not returned to its normal rhythm. He was unsure if it was residual fear or humiliation fueling its thumping.

He knew he should hurry after her and offer proper thanks for the rescue. But he remained where he was, paralyzed by humiliation and indecision, until the girl hurried through the back gate of one of the mansions in the Row and closed the door firmly behind her.

He started at the sound of its closure, finally coming back to life. But it was too late to go after her. He couldn't possibly barge into the house of one of Sovar's noble families and demand to see the girl who had been carrying the flowers. Someone in the household would be sure to recognize him, even if the girl did not, and then there might be ramifications for his family. He'd already failed in his role badly enough. He didn't need to continue bumbling around, making it worse.

The best thing Julius could do was get back to the palace as quickly as possible and pretend he'd never left. With any luck, he would never see the girl again. Without her flowers, he'd gotten a better look at her clothes, and while she wasn't dressed in a servant's livery, her clothes weren't expensive enough to indicate she was one of the nobility.

She was a mystery he was never going to solve, and he was content to have it so.

But as Julius hurried toward home, he couldn't shake the encounter from his mind. The more he relived it, the less he could understand his own missteps. What had come over him?

He moved faster and faster at the uncomfortable possibility that occurred to him. The girl hadn't known his identity, so he had been interacting with her as Julius, not as the crown prince. Did that mean the Legacy had deserted him in that moment?

He had always known the Legacy aided him to play the charming role required of him, but he had thought of it as a subtle influence, providing a final gloss to his own efforts. But now he found himself questioning all his assumptions. He had given his life to his role, but perhaps he was far less suited to it than he had ever imagined. And if it was possible for both his own skill and the Legacy to desert him so completely, when might it happen again?

He tried to push the thought away. It hadn't happened before in twenty-one years, so there was no reason to think it would happen again. He had met countless people in his life, and this girl was the only one who had ever discomfited him so.

The solution was simple. He just had to make sure he never encountered her again. Since she hadn't appeared to be a noble, he didn't need to fear meeting her at court. And he would make sure that was the last time he ever walked behind Manor Row. If he was fortunate, that was the one and only time he would ever see the girl with the flowers.

CHAPTER 3
OLIVIA

Olivia polished the enormous mahogany dining table with lackluster movements. And yet the warm wood shone in the wake of her efforts. She looked down the remaining length—stretching along the entire cavernous room—and sighed. Even with the Legacy's help, it was a tedious and time-consuming task.

"It's a lovely piece, is it not?" her aunt asked happily, mistaking the meaning of Olivia's sigh. "It's a good thing the previous owner was eager to sell us so much of the furniture along with the house. I don't think this table would fit through either of the room's doors!"

Olivia glanced from the door near her to the one at the other end of the room and had to agree. She didn't feel the glee about the sale that her aunt seemed to feel, though. Olivia couldn't help feeling sorry for the family who had given up their home to strangers, although she knew nothing about them.

"Who was the previous owner?" she asked her aunt, who

was busy arranging the flowers Olivia had gathered into a formal arrangement for the center of the table.

"The man who sold it to us was a merchant. Of course, he wasn't the original owner since all the houses in Manor Row were originally built by noble families. I suppose he must have purchased it from one of them at some point, after he grew wealthy enough."

Aunt Helen paused and looked up from her work, her nose wrinkling slightly. "He isn't wealthy any more, which is why he sold the house." She tsked, and her expression softened. "From what I've heard, his wife was always sickly. And she managed to bear him only a single daughter. So when she finally succumbed to her illness and passed away..." She shook her head.

Olivia's sympathy for the unknown man grew. "The Legacy must have tried to throw every Sovaran widow with two children that it could find at his head."

"Of course," her aunt said. "But the silly man refused to even look at any of them! Can you imagine?"

Olivia could easily do so. He must have loved his wife very much.

"So naturally his business failed, and he was forced to sell the house and all its contents and move to a much more modest dwelling on the other side of town." Aunt Helen gave a disapproving sniff. "He should have thought of his daughter."

On that they were in agreement, although Olivia was inclined to think he had been thinking of the girl.

"Perhaps they wanted to move," she suggested. "Perhaps this house reminded them too much of their missing wife and mother. With only two of them, they might be much happier in a smaller home in a different part of town."

"Happier!" her aunt cried, horrified. "What nonsense are you talking, niece? Do you know how few properties on Mancr Row have ever come up for sale? Only the most successful and influential families of business have ever had the chance to purchase one." Her chest puffed out as she spoke, her expression glowing with pride.

Olivia looked quickly down at her polishing, not wanting her aunt to read her expression. It was true that Uncle Walt had become much more successful than Olivia's family back in Henton had dreamed. But she hadn't seen any sign of his apparent influence. His own wife and children rarely listened to him.

Her aunt swept on, oblivious to Olivia's wry amusement. "If that merchant had known what was good for him—and his business—he wouldn't have flouted the Legacy in such a way."

Olivia polished a little harder, barely keeping a rein on her tongue. Her aunt was talking as if the Legacy had ruined his business as a punishment, but the Legacy wasn't a sentient force. It didn't punish anyone—even if it sometimes felt like it to those who experienced its less pleasant effects. Besides, ruining merchant businesses sounded more like the Glandore Legacy than the Sovar one. Perhaps it was the man's absorption in his grief that had wreaked such havoc. Either way, she felt sorry for his daughter and hoped she was living a happier life in her small house.

"And that," her aunt concluded, with a swift glance at Olivia, "is why it's never wise to flout the Legacy."

"That doesn't mean we have to blindly follow its whims,"

Olivia ventured, unable to stay entirely silent. "My cousin in Glandore says they work hard to avoid falling prey to their Legacy—at least to its negative aspects. Their royal family always has lots of children so as not to risk being left with a single prince like in their original history."

Her aunt gave another sniff. "The *Glandorians* are welcome to do as they please. In Sovar the royal family are careful to only have one son because they understand the importance of the Legacy. And we would all do well to follow their wise example. The Legacy's forces must be harnessed and directed if we don't want to suffer ill effects. Our predecessor should have merely taken the time to select a kind widow, and then the whole matter would have ended there. It's not as if the Legacy forces anyone to live out the whole history. He really should have looked to King Robert for guidance."

Olivia rolled her eyes and once more focused her efforts on the wood beneath her polishing rag. Her aunt spoke as if living on Manor Row gave the occupant unfettered access to the king. But as far as she knew, neither her uncle nor aunt had ever even spoken to the man. Unless it was in the formal receiving line of the annual royal ball—the one that was open to every Sovaran in the kingdom.

"It sounds more like appeasement than harnessing the Legacy to me," she muttered, but she kept her voice too low for her aunt to hear.

She already knew it would be fruitless to get into an argument on the topic. The city-dwellers seemed much more attached to following the Legacy's path than the villagers of Henton had ever been, perhaps because the Legacy's power was so much more concentrated within the city. And Aunt

Helen was even less likely to be convinced to buck the Legacy than most, considering it would be against her own interests to do so. She knew her niece hadn't come to the capital to be a family servant, and respecting the Legacy was the excuse that kept her guilt at bay for placing Olivia in such a position.

Olivia soon reached the end of the table and turned to work her way up the other side. The Legacy had forced her into her current position, but it also made her workload lighter than should have been possible.

"What an excellent job you're doing, Olivia," her aunt exclaimed happily as she finished with the flowers and surveyed the table. She smiled warmly at her niece. "You always do such an excellent job."

Olivia smiled back weakly. Her aunt wasn't an evil woman at heart, and she seemed to have genuine affection for her niece. It was an impression confirmed with Avery's gift. Her aunt didn't hate her, and she didn't wish her ill. Aunt Helen was just extremely good at convincing herself that whatever was convenient was also justified. And in this case, she had the authority of the royal family to back her up. The power of the Legacy had to be respected.

"You know," her aunt said, turning her full attention on Olivia, "I've been thinking about the ball."

She didn't have to clarify which ball. In the capital of Sovar, in the middle of summer, there was only one ball that mattered. The royal family's annual Midsummer Ball.

Like all Sovarans, Olivia had grown up hearing tales of the spectacular event—stories full of women who shone brighter than their jewels, dancing the night away. The doors of the ball were open to every person in the kingdom with only one caveat—every woman who crossed the threshold must come in glass slippers.

But while crafting flexible and practical items from glass —some with quite fantastical properties—was the specialty of Sovar, glass slippers remained difficult to craft. It was a much debated aspect of the Legacy, that it granted those inside Sovar's borders the ability to manipulate glass into impossible creations, but it ensured that slippers would always be a highly desired item.

Only a couple of families in Henton had ever had the spare funds for such a frivolous purchase. Especially when the slippers were of no use unless extra coin was spent to travel to the capital for the Midsummer Ball. Glass slippers longed to dance and had little other practical purpose.

The slippers were passed down from mother to daughter, with most of the fortunate daughters getting only one Midsummer journey to the capital, usually around their eighteenth birthdays. But one of Olivia's friends had gone as young as fourteen—when it became apparent that her feet would soon outgrow her grandmother's dainty slippers. She had come back full of tales of the palace, her gown, the food, and especially the dancing.

She had even claimed to have had a dance with Crown Prince Julius, though Olivia had always privately doubted the truth of that particular tale. The prince couldn't possibly have had time to dance with every girl who attended the ball, and it was unlikely that a fourteen-year-old from the country would have made it onto his list.

She didn't speak her doubts aloud, though, because the whole tale was so enchanting. Olivia was just as prone as the other village girls to dream of the day when she might be lucky enough to attend such a magnificent event.

If she was honest, those dreams were part of what had lured her to the capital. But as much as she wanted to attend the ball, she cared about her cousins more. Nell and Hattie were sweet-natured, hard-working girls—even if they enjoyed the luxury of working in the city for their father's business rather than being confined to the house and its chores. Olivia enjoyed their company, and they had welcomed her from the first day of her arrival. And it was for their sake that she hadn't been able to bring herself to mention the ball to her aunt.

Before arriving in Henton, she had imagined asking to borrow her aunt's slippers, just for one ball. Olivia certainly didn't have the money to purchase her own, and it would be a foolish use of her funds even if she did. She had high hopes of eventually saving enough to leave her current situation and properly establish herself in the capital. But her aunt, on the other hand, had always lived in the capital and had wealth at her disposal. So she not only had a pair but had been to the Midsummer Ball many times. It wouldn't be a great sacrifice on her part.

Aunt Helen probably would have agreed, too, if not for her daughters. She was as softhearted and romantic about the Midsummer Ball as most Sovaran women, and she would probably have welcomed the chance to indulge her niece, especially after maneuvering her into the role of a servant.

But it was only natural that her aunt would consider her own daughters first, and that year was to be Nell and Hattie's first attendance at the ball. Obviously their mother wanted to attend with them.

If Olivia had arrived a year earlier—or even a year later—she would have been accommodated. But there was no point asking her aunt to present her niece along with her own two daughters at their first ball. Even if Aunt Helen initially felt pressured into agreeing, she would eventually convince herself of some reason or other why it couldn't be thought of that year.

Olivia's cousins weren't exactly magnificent beauties. At sixteen and seventeen, Nell and Hattie had yet to fully grow into their features, and Olivia knew her aunt had been a little dismayed by her niece's face when she first arrived on their doorstep. In Henton, Olivia had been considered a beauty, but everyone agreed that while her figure came from her father's side, her looks came from her mother.

Not that Nell and Hattie were like Queen Ella's caricatured stepsisters by any means. Their sweetness granted them a prettiness of their own. But Olivia had to admit that if all three of them were dressed up in formal style, she was likely to attract a great deal more attention than her younger cousins. When combined with the expense of purchasing an extra pair of slippers instead of borrowing a family pair, it put the ball completely out of her reach for that year.

Originally, her aunt had planned to wait before taking Nell and Hattie to their first ball. But both girls had pleaded so fervently to be allowed to attend that year that their mother had eventually relented. Even Olivia, who spent most of her time sequestered in the manor, had heard talk of an upcoming betrothal for the prince, and she could understand her cousins' desire to attend the ball while there was still an unattached prince who might ask them to dance. It was part of the dreamlike appeal of the whole event.

Eventually they had worn their mother down, and having decided that her daughters were to make an appearance at the Midsummer Ball, Aunt Helen had thrown herself fully into the preparations. And while nothing had been said outright about the reasons for Olivia's exclusion from those plans, several comments had been dropped about Olivia's attendance at the ball the *following* year. Olivia hadn't needed the hint, but she had received it loud and clear.

But despite everything, Olivia couldn't help a swell of hope at her aunt's mention of the ball just after her warm compliments for Olivia's work. Perhaps Olivia had been wrong in all her assumptions.

She dropped her polishing rag and looked at her aunt hopefully.

"I've been thinking," her aunt repeated, "that you should complete the final adjustments on the girls' dresses instead of the seamstress. You're handy with a needle, and I'm sure that once you start working on them, you'll come up with some improvements you can make to the designs." Her voice gained enthusiasm. "With you to funnel the Legacy's power, the girls will be the best dressed at the ball!"

Olivia bit her tongue to keep her disappointment from showing. With a couple of blinks, she pushed back the threatening moisture in her eyes. She should have known her aunt wouldn't be rethinking her plans for the ball. She probably thought she could easily make up for it by taking her niece the next year. But Olivia doubted she would still be living with her relatives by then.

"Certainly, I can put the finishing touches on their dresses, if the girls would like it," Olivia said dully.

Her aunt clapped her hands together. "They would love it best of all things!"

Olivia's spirits lifted marginally. If she could help her cousins look their best, it would make the extra effort worth it. She knew Nell and Hattie would have liked to include her if given the choice.

Her two cousins burst into the room at that moment, and their excitement at Olivia's agreement was so infectious that her spirits lifted even further. She even agreed to work on the dresses immediately.

As her aunt had predicted, Olivia had barely begun to pin one of the hems before her hands were flying, not only making the necessary measurements for the final fitting but pinning all sorts of other adjustments as well.

By the time they were finished with the session and sitting at dinner, she was almost convinced she was a true design genius. It wasn't like the Legacy could control people's thoughts, so maybe she'd been the one to make such impressive improvements to the dresses?

But by the time they had reached the final sweet course, she'd laughed the idea away. The Legacy couldn't control people, but it could sometimes influence them in small actions. Her cousin in Glandore—where they grew enchanted roses—had told her how strong the compulsion to pick the roses could become.

She wasn't a design genius, but she was stuck working on the gowns after the evening meal. And unfortunately, the task, so focused on the upcoming ball, made it impossible to put her own disappointment out of her mind. As she finally escaped the house to climb the hill in the near dark, she sighed.

"Olivia!" Marigold abandoned her pacing and pounced on her friend, tugging her toward the same tree from earlier in the afternoon.

Her manner was full of nervous energy and excitement, but her face dropped when she got a good look at Olivia's expression in the moonlight. Marigold's life always seemed so large, but it was one of her endearing qualities that it never caused her to overlook Olivia's own ups and downs.

Olivia made a face in response. "It's nothing. I'm just being sour and envious, which isn't a flattering look. I'll recover in a moment."

"Is it that aunt of yours?" Marigold grasped Olivia's arm. "Should I march down there right now and give her an earful?"

"Please don't!" Olivia was already laughing again, thanks to Marigold's presence. "I'm not sure what effect your lecture would produce, and I don't want to find out. She'd want to know how we became friends for one—and probably demand I recount every word that's ever passed between us."

Marigold laughed as well, releasing Olivia. "As if either of us could remember! I talk far too much for that."

"Besides, I don't really mind working on Nell's and Hattie's dresses," Olivia said, emotions rising in her again as she spoke until her final words burst out of her. "I just wish I could go as well!"

"To the ball, you mean?" Marigold's eyes widened, and she seized Olivia's arm again, this time with both her hands. "Of course you have to go to the ball!"

In anyone else, the dramatic nature of the simple pronouncement would have sounded ridiculous. But Marigold never looked ridiculous.

"Unfortunately my aunt doesn't agree with you," Olivia said wryly.

"Why does that matter?" Marigold asked fiercely. "Everyone in the kingdom is invited."

"Yes, but I can't afford the glass slippers on my own. I haven't earned enough yet, and I couldn't justify spending my hard-earned money on such a frivolity anyway. Not if I want to move out on my own soon."

"Move out—?" Marigold cut herself off. "No, never mind that. Glass slippers?" Her head cocked to the side, and she regarded Olivia in confusion. "You're not going to the ball because you need glass slippers?"

Olivia nodded, wondering if her friend had finally lost the plot.

"Yes," she said slowly. "You know—the glass slippers that are required in place of an invitation in order to gain entry. Remember those?"

Marigold laughed suddenly. "But you're friends with me!" She peered down at Olivia's feet, which were now back in her old, worn-out slippers. "And your feet look much smaller than mine. I've been to the Ball every year since I was thirteen, and I've needed at least two new pairs of slippers in that time because I kept outgrowing my old ones."

Olivia tried not to let a bubble of hope well inside her for a second time. "But surely you don't still have the old slippers that no longer fit? You must have sold them by now."

Marigold snorted. "Have you ever seen the back of my closet?" Her nose wrinkled. "No, of course you haven't, since you've never been inside my house."

Olivia didn't reply, conscious that neither she nor Marigold had ever suggested she visit. They didn't talk about it, but she knew it was because neither were sure how Marigold's parents would view their friendship. But she didn't find it hard to believe that Marigold's closet might be a chaos of old shoes and garments. The noble girl had probably forbidden the servants from touching her things. Marigold found careful order boring.

"This is perfect!" Marigold jumped up and down on the spot. "It's all decided!"

"Wait, wait, wait," Olivia said. "Nothing has been decided. I'm not even sure what we're talking about."

"That you're going to come to the ball, of course," Marigold said.

"But, I can't—" Olivia started before Marigold jumped in.

"You'll come with me, wearing one of my old pairs of glass slippers. I'll loan you a dress too! It's actually what I wanted to talk to you about tonight anyway." She fixed Olivia with a piercing stare. "You have to go to the ball. Please promise me you will! You can't abandon me!"

Olivia shook her head, feeling a little dazed. There had to be reasons why Marigold's plan wouldn't work, but she couldn't think of them. Not from her side, anyway. If she went to the ball with Marigold, she could avoid Nell, Hattie, and her aunt completely. And Olivia certainly wouldn't have to worry about overshadowing Marigold. At Marigold's side, few people would even notice Olivia was there. She would be free to enjoy the evening to her heart's content.

"Surely your mother wants you to go with her, though," she said, considering the matter from Marigold's end. "I can't imagine she wants me tagging along."

But Marigold was already shaking her head before Olivia had even finished speaking.

"No, she's making me go on my own this year." Her words were far too despairing for such a mild discomfort as attending a familiar ball alone.

"How awful," Olivia said dryly. "A short carriage ride alone before you arrive at a party full of friends and acquaintances."

"No." Marigold took Olivia's hand and held it in both of hers, meeting her eyes with the most earnest expression Olivia had ever seen from her. "I won't have any friends there unless you come. You're my only true friend."

Olivia's eyebrows rose. She found that hard to believe, but she was also flattered enough not to protest.

"Promise me you'll come," Marigold repeated, and Olivia grinned.

"You don't have to keep begging me. Did you really think it would be hard to convince me to dress up in a pretty gown and go to the biggest celebration of the year? Every girl back in Henton dreams about attending the Midsummer Ball at least once in her life." Her brows creased as a thought hit her. "But is there something else going on to distress you? I hope you know you can tell me anything."

Marigold shook her head, her face lit up with a beaming smile as she looped her arm through Olivia's. "Now that you're coming to the ball everything is perfect. We just have to plan what you're going to wear!"

CHAPTER 4
JULIUS

Julius jumped down from the back of his horse, still breathing heavier than usual as he handed the reins over to a stable boy. A second horse cantered up beside him, coming to a stop a few feet away.

An elegantly dressed young man with windswept hair slid to the ground and handed his own reins to a second stable boy. He watched the boy and horse retreat before turning to the prince with a raised brow.

"What's gotten into you today, Your Highness?" he asked.

Julius threw him an irritated look. Cade knew it annoyed him when his oldest friend used his title while they were alone. Which was why Cade did it, of course.

Cade laughed and clapped Julius on the back. "See! You're not usually so easy to rile."

Julius grunted in response, and Cade's brows drew together, his voice lowering. "Is it about the ball? Don't tell me you're having second thoughts?"

Julius laughed wryly, finally goaded into speech. "I don't have the luxury of second thoughts, do I?"

Cade's eyes widened, and he cast a swift glance around them to ensure they were still alone. Shaking his head, he murmured. "Not out here."

He strode toward one of the back doors of the palace, not looking to see if Julius was following. Julius hesitated for a moment before sighing and catching up with his friend. Even if he'd kept his mouth shut as he had intended, Cade would have only kept needling him. Julius had given too much away with the frantic pace of their ride. But he'd been desperate to drive out thoughts of the coming ball—and a certain face that kept haunting his mind and preventing his usual mental peace.

As soon as Cade shut the door of Julius's private sitting room firmly behind them, Julius threw himself into one of the chairs by the row of windows. Cade just stood in the middle of the room, looking at his friend with an expectant expression.

Julius ran a hand over his face. "What do you want from me? Second thoughts? It's not as if I ever had a choice to begin with. Sovaran princes always have arranged marriages. This is my duty, and I always do my duty."

Cade winced sympathetically. Arranged marriages weren't a normal fixture of the Sovaran nobility. Only Julius got to receive that particular gift.

"Your mother consulted with several of us, you know," Cade said after a silent moment. "And she confided her final choice in me."

Julius looked at him, his brows raised. He hadn't known

that. His small inner circle of friends—all young men from noble families—had kept quiet about it.

"Do you want me to tell you a bit about the girl they've chosen?" Cade asked hesitantly.

Julius held up a swift hand to stop him. "You know the rules. My long-ago ancestors decided that the Legacy's power will be more potent if I'm taken by surprise by my future bride."

"I wasn't going to tell you her name," Cade said in a rush. "But surely I could tell you a couple of minor things about her without doing any harm? Just to ease your mind."

Julius considered for a moment before shaking his head. "What's the point?" he asked morosely. "Better not to risk it. And I don't want to get you in trouble either."

"Fine, but you won't help anything by worrying about it. Your chosen bride is —" Cade hesitated briefly, something passing over his face that Julius couldn't read. Cade quickly cleared his throat and continued. "I just mean to say that your parents were thinking of you when they made their choice. I don't think you'll be disappointed."

Julius wanted to believe him. He might even have done so if not for that suspicious pause. There was clearly something about his chosen bride that Cade didn't want to tell him. Was she significantly older than Julius?

He sighed. Did it even matter who she was? Even if she was beautiful and clever and kind, he still resented being the only person in the kingdom who couldn't choose for himself.

"It's not really the ball anyway," he said without thinking about his words, his eyes focused out the window. "I've always known it was coming, so that's nothing new. But I met a girl, and I want her out of my mind!"

Cade froze halfway through lowering himself into a chair, his eyes widening. "Is she beautiful?"

"Very," Julius responded before his eyes snapped to his friend. "I mean, no. Drat it! That's not the point."

Cade sank slowly the rest of the way into his chair, his expression strained. "This is bad." He flung up his hands. "Who is she? We already know all the girls at court, so how have you met someone new? And without my knowing anything about it!"

Julius tried not to let his guilt show on his face. "I went for a walk a couple days ago. After the heat wave broke."

"A single walk?" Cade leaned forward, his voice serious. "Julius, you aren't in love with a girl you met on a single walk. Your emotions are playing tricks on you. It's just a form of rebellion against your coming engagement. Your mother warned me to keep an eye out for something like this."

"In love?" Julius repeated in tones of revulsion. "I should think not!" He looked back out the window, afraid his face might be too revealing. "It's not butterflies I'm feeling in my stomach—it's nausea!"

"Nausea?" Cade leaned back in his chair, his concern clearing only to be replaced with confusion. "Did the girl seem threatening in some way?"

"Threatening?" Julius surged to his feet, staring at his friend incredulously. "Hardly."

Cade put up both hands in a placating gesture. "I'm just trying to understand. You don't fancy yourself in love with her, and she didn't make some sort of threat against the crown...so why is she so hard to forget?"

"Because I—" Julius broke off, but Cade continued to watch him expectantly. Julius finally groaned and collapsed back into his chair. As briefly as possible, he related the story of his meeting with the girl on the hill, forcing himself to include every point of his own bumbling, ridiculous behavior.

Cade remained silent until Julius finished speaking at which point he let out a loud crack of laughter.

"Priceless!" He wiped moisture from his eyes. "I would have paid money to see you stripped of all charm around a member of the public. I thought I was the only one permitted to see that side of you. The mighty Julius, felled by a child."

"She wasn't a child." Julius tried not to sound defensive. "I did think she might be a younger daughter from one of the noble families, but I don't think she was."

Cade raised an eyebrow. "Not a child, and 'very beautiful'. Are you sure embarrassment is the only reason you can't get her out of your mind?"

"Of course," Julius said stiffly before groaning again. "I can't believe I was such a fool. I always thought myself socially capable—I've had more than enough training. Tell me the truth. Has everyone been lying about my charm to my face and laughing behind my back all this time?"

Cade went into a fresh peal of laughter. When he finally subsided, he shook his head.

"You have your moments, sure." He grinned at Julius who threw a pillow at his head.

Cade caught it, and his voice turned more serious. "Truly, I've only ever seen you drop the charm when we're alone. Sometimes I've worried about what a strain it must be to so rarely be free to be yourself."

Julius frowned. His friend was trying to comfort him, but his words did the opposite. Julius had never thought that his personality was so very different from the role he was forced to adopt—but his friend talked as if they were entirely separate. Was he the only one to have seen the real Julius? The incompetent, unworthy person behind the royal mask?

"You're too hard on yourself," Cade said with a sigh, almost as if he could read Julius's thoughts. "You've always been like that. I wish your parents had broken with tradition and given you some brothers and sisters. If you weren't alone, you might not go around with the weight of the kingdom on your shoulders at every moment."

Julius shrugged. "I'd still be the heir."

"I suppose so." Cade sighed. "But honestly, if you're looking for official permission to let this go, I'm giving it to you. We've all of us had moments we're less than proud of. I've never seen you do less than an excellent job as crown prince, and a single awkward conversation doesn't change that. Honestly, I wish you had more opportunities to freely be yourself."

Julius shook his head. Cade was a good friend, but he didn't understand. Julius's parents—and the entire kingdom —relied on him to do his job properly and ensure the well-being of all of Sovar. With everything he had already sacrificed—and would be called upon to sacrifice after the ball— he couldn't afford to falter.

But he still appreciated Cade's efforts. Having one person he could confide in had always helped to lift Julius's spirits when he felt overwhelmed.

"Thanks, Cade," he said quietly, keeping silent about his ongoing doubts.

Cade grinned. "What else are friends here for? It's your job to be prince and mine to make sure you don't drown in all the duty. If you like, I can solemnly pledge to remind you of the incident any time you start to think there's nothing to you but your crown prince role. I could even enlist the others to help in that noble task."

"No, thank you," Julius said firmly. "Telling you was bad enough. I just want to forget the whole incident ever happened. Didn't you say I have official permission to do that now?"

"Absolutely." Cade sprang to his feet. "Now I just need to go wandering those hills behind Manor Row so that I, too, can meet a *very beautiful* girl."

Julius also stood, his insides tightening at the thought. The last thing he needed was for Cade to end up meeting the girl with the flowers. He would no doubt end up revealing Julius's identity if that ever happened.

"The ball is tomorrow, so I think we both have more important things to do," he said.

"As you command, Your Highness," Cade said, with a knowing grin.

Julius ignored it. "I, for one, am going to wash up."

He had ridden hard, making the most of the opportunity to escape all the preparations for the ball. He just hoped the ride and the talk with Cade would be enough to prevent him dreaming of the girl again that night.

CHAPTER 5
OLIVIA

Olivia felt as if she'd strayed into a dream over the next few days. Marigold's frenetic energy was poured into planning Olivia's outfit for the ball, and she was constantly popping up to discuss this or that detail.

Olivia had assumed her friend would select one of her old gowns and give it to Olivia in advance so Olivia could adjust it to her much smaller stature and frame. But it quickly became apparent that Marigold was having a dress made specially.

Whenever Olivia tried to protest, Marigold brushed her words aside.

"I've always wanted to design a dress for a petite, golden beauty like you," Marigold assured her. "My own height and wild curls can be useful for certain dramatic styles, but there are other styles that are off the cards completely. Not unless I want to look ridiculous."

Olivia frowned. "But surely your mother doesn't want to pay your seamstress to make a dress for *me*."

Marigold cackled, and Olivia realized with a sinking heart that Marigold hadn't told her mother the dress was for Olivia.

"Before you start protesting again," Marigold said quickly at the look on her friend's face, "remember my overflowing closet. I don't need another dress, and I wouldn't have agreed to a new one for the ball if I didn't want it for you." She smiled reminiscently. "It's actually been surprising fun watching the seamstress's face as I demand feature after feature that would look terrible on me."

"Is your mother just letting you have whatever you want?" Olivia asked dubiously.

Marigold snorted. "She thinks it's my attempt at defiance, and she's placating me by letting me have my way. She seems convinced it will somehow all come together to look presentable. At least that's what she keeps telling the dismayed seamstress. I suppose she's relying on the Legacy." Marigold wrinkled her nose, but Olivia nodded.

Having worked on her cousins' dresses, she was inclined to think Lady Emerson might even be right. The Legacy seemed to surround anything related to the ball with extra potency. It made sense since the Legacy was the whole reason for the ball in the first place.

Holding the event was a way of both respecting the Legacy's role in the kingdom and also seizing control of it. As long as everyone was wearing glass slippers, the Legacy's power couldn't focus on any one girl too strongly. The royal family might revere the Legacy, but they didn't want to be controlled by it.

In the end, Marigold smuggled the dress to Olivia the day before the ball. Olivia wasn't concerned about completing it on time—the Legacy would help with that. But she felt a final pang of uncertainty as she accepted the stunning creation of pink and gold silk from her friend.

"Will it really be all right for me to wear this?" she asked Marigold. "I know your mother won't be at the ball, but if she finds out…"

"Don't worry," Marigold said hurriedly. "I intend to confess everything to them afterward. I'll take all the blame. I won't even tell them your name!" She grinned at her friend. "They won't have any trouble believing this was all my doing."

Olivia smiled reluctantly back. After eighteen years, Marigold's parents must have become used to their daughter's outrageous stunts.

"I'll pick you up from your aunt and uncle's door," Marigold promised, clearly seeing no impediment to carrying out her plan.

"I'll have to leave after my cousins," Olivia reminded her. "Since I'm not planning to mention my attendance to my aunt, I'd rather not create a scene."

"Absolutely," Marigold agreed with a gleam in her eyes. "You know I always believe in seeking forgiveness rather than asking permission."

Olivia grimaced. "With any luck, my aunt won't spot me at the ball at all, and I can avoid any unpleasantness completely."

"I'm not sure there's much chance of that," Marigold murmured.

"What?" Olivia asked, eyeing her askance.

Marigold raised a challenging eyebrow. "Have you seen

this dress? You're going to look like a dream. No one will be able to keep their eyes off you."

Olivia laughed. "You're forgetting I'll be at your side. You'll be the one stealing all the eyes."

She was far from insecure about her appearance, and she was already half in love with the dress her friend had ordered for her, but Marigold had a vibrancy that made other people fade by comparison. If Olivia had been seeking to draw attention, she wouldn't have attended the ball in her friend's company.

"Are you sure you don't mind being late?" she checked a final time. "And your mother isn't going to mind either? We'll miss the receiving line, so we won't have the chance to meet the royal family."

"Stop worrying." Marigold pushed her gently away, laughing. "Don't you know me at all? I have no desire to wait in a receiving line. Everything is going to work out fine."

Olivia finally let herself stop worrying and embrace the beautiful reality. The following evening, she would be entering the famed ballroom of the royal palace of Sovar.

In the privacy of her bedchamber, she examined every inch of the stunning dress, as she considered the best way to take it in. Her fingers moved over the material, folding and tucking as ideas came to her. But clearly the seamstress used by Lady Emerson was more skilled than the one employed by Aunt Helen because there was less room for improvement than there had been on her cousins' dresses.

When a knock sounded on her door, she hurried over to check who it was, only opening the door a crack. But as soon as she saw one dark-haired head and one light-haired one, she opened the door all the way, ushering an excited Nell and Hattie quickly inside.

"Oh!" Hattie cried, clasping her hands to her chest as she saw the dress laid out on Olivia's bed. "It's beautiful!"

"And more importantly, it's perfect for you," Nell added. "Now hurry up and try it on."

Olivia smiled affectionately at her cousins as they helped her slip the gown over her head. She had taken them into her confidence as soon as she'd realized she would need help with adjusting the dress. She couldn't do it entirely on her own when she needed to be both model and seamstress.

Once the material was settled in place—draping comically on the floor as if Olivia was a child playing dress up in her mother's gown—she began issuing instructions. Her cousins worked diligently to follow them, pinning the dress everywhere Olivia directed.

When they'd finally finished, they helped her ease the dress off again, only pricking her twice in the process. Once Olivia was back in one of her own dresses, she gave both girls a warning look.

"Please do be careful and don't blurt anything out to your mother," she pleaded.

"I'm sure she wouldn't forbid you from going," Hattie assured her quickly, clearly distressed at any suggestion that Olivia was being mistreated.

"She can't forbid her even if she wanted to," Nell declared. "The ball is open to everyone, and she's neither Olivia's mother nor her slave master. But that doesn't mean Mother would like it."

"No, you're right," Hattie said with a sigh. "We'll all—

including Mother—be much more comfortable if she doesn't know anything about it."

Nell slipped her arms around Olivia and gave her a hug. "I wish we could get ready together." Before Olivia could respond, she hurried on. "I know we can't, but at least I'll be able to see you at the ball. You'll look magnificent."

Olivia returned her cousin's hug affectionately. She had been fortunate that Nell and Hattie had turned out to be the sweetest possible relations.

When she waved them off from the front steps of their family's mansion the next evening, she was proud to see how well they both looked. Their excitement gave their faces animation as well as sweetness, and she hoped they would have just as wonderful a time as they dreamed. But she didn't linger to watch the carriage rumble down the street. As soon as it was properly moving, she flew back inside and up to her room to start her own preparations.

She managed to put up her own hair, but as she shimmied into the dress, Olivia realized she was going to need help fastening the gown. It wasn't the sort of simple design that could be done alone. She ran through the options in her mind, trying to think who among the servants would be the least likely to report the whole incident to her aunt.

She was still considering the matter when her door opened forcefully. She whirled in time to see Marigold strike a pose, her hand over her heart.

"I'm struck silent by your beauty, great lady!" she proclaimed.

"Demonstrably untrue." Olivia laughed with relief at the sight of her friend. "What are you doing here? I thought we were meeting in the carriage outside."

"It occurred to me that you might need a little help," Marigold said. "Given your planned subterfuge." Her eyes twinkled as she said the word.

"Thank you," Olivia said with relief. "It's foolish of me, but I only just realized that fact for myself. I'm impressed you remembered the location of my room, though. You've only been in here once."

"I have an excellent memory. And besides, I had to give you these." Marigold produced two shoes from behind her back, holding them out with a flourish.

Olivia sucked in a breath at the way the light shone through the glass slippers and sparkled off the small heels. She took them carefully from her friend, and Marigold twitched up her own long skirts to show she was similarly shod beneath the layers.

Olivia grinned and slipped the glass shoes on. They were cooler than a normal pair of shoes, but not uncomfortably so. She turned, the glass bending with her movement just like a normal shoe, and presented her back so Marigold could fasten her dress. Marigold wrestled with it, clearly not having much experience with the task, but she eventually succeeded. Stepping back, she surveyed the finished effect and pronounced her design efforts a triumph.

"You look incredible," she said in a more sincere voice. "I'm so pleased."

Olivia peered down at herself and smiled. "I think the Legacy deserves most of the credit, but I'm delighted. It's just like my friend back home said—I really do feel like a princess going to a ball." She beamed at her friend, who smiled back even more broadly, if that were possible.

"Perfect!" Marigold pronounced, clapping her hands

once, and the two girls hurried out of the house, giggling all the way.

Since Olivia's uncle and the other servants were all occupied with the evening meal in a different part of the house, the two ballgoers escaped unseen. Marigold's coachman grumbled at their late arrival, but a look from Marigold silenced him.

"Oh dear," Olivia murmured once they had both squeezed themselves into the carriage. "I didn't think of the coachman. I hope we're not in for a bumpy ride given how displeased he looked."

But Marigold shook her head, clearly unconcerned. "I already had to bribe him shamelessly to get him to ignore my mother's orders and bring me here before going to the palace. He has nothing to complain about."

"Marigold!" Olivia stared at her. "Did you really?"

"Yes," Marigold said, clearly not in the least bothered by her own actions. "But there's no need to look so horrified. It's not as if I stole my mother's favorite jewels to do it. I used my own allowance." She peered at Olivia. "And don't start feeling bad or moping about it. I've always had a far bigger allowance than I need."

Olivia swallowed her instinctive protests. Since Marigold's actions were already done, she might as well enjoy the experience. She would just have to dedicate herself to making sure Marigold had a good time and enjoyed the ball despite her pessimistic outlook on the event.

"I'm now realizing another reason my aunt didn't want me to accompany them," Olivia said instead, trying to rearrange her skirts. "It's hard enough fitting two enormous gowns in here. I'm not sure how my aunt and cousins fit three, but they certainly couldn't have fit a fourth!"

She eyed Marigold's gown, which was as large as her own but didn't appear as fancy. Her heart sank. Marigold must have thrown on one of her old dresses without touching it up, so it was a creation unassisted by the Legacy.

"Do you really not mind me wearing this dress?" she asked.

Marigold stared at her for a moment before breaking into giggles. "Can you imagine me in it?" she asked through her laughter.

Olivia glanced down at the material and style and then back at her friend and her wildly clashing hair.

"No," she admitted with her own chuckle. "I'm shocked your mother let you order it." Her humor subsided after a moment, however. "Didn't your mother comment on it when you came out dressed in a different gown?"

"She probably would have been relieved given how that one turned out," Marigold said lightly, turning her head to gaze out the carriage window. "But she had already departed for the evening before I was dressed."

There was an odd note in her voice when she said it, and Olivia fell silent, guessing her friend didn't want to discuss her mother. Whatever other engagement was occupying Lady Emerson, it must be the reason she wasn't attending the ball. And perhaps it was something Marigold had also wished to do, instead of being forced to go to the palace.

Olivia, however, was thrilled to be approaching the palace at last. She had used her days off to explore the capital, but she was still far from familiar with the large city. And she had never had the chance to enter the palace grounds, although the structure itself was a familiar landmark, able to be seen from every corner of the capital. The white stone towers and turrets, with their aquamarine roofs, soared far higher than any other building, their color reminding Olivia of the ocean.

Coming from an inland town, she still hadn't overcome her awe of the sea or stopped enjoying the faint hint of salt that hung in the air even far back in the city. Manor Row was located near the palace, rather than close to the wharves or the beaches that stretched to the north and south of the city, but the water was still her favorite place to visit whenever she ventured on a longer excursion.

But for once her thoughts were turned firmly inland, her glass-shod toes already tapping to unseen music, reminding her that glass slippers loved to dance. Before she knew it, they were approaching the blazing lights of the palace, their carriage traveling along a path lined with elegant lanterns.

A soft sound of excitement slipped out of Olivia, and she looked across at her friend. "This is so exciting!"

Marigold grinned back, but the light in her eyes had edged from impulsive pleasure into something more feverish. So it wasn't entirely a surprise when Olivia stepped down from the carriage with the help of a royal footman only to hear a ripping sound behind her. She turned to peer back through the door of the carriage.

"How clumsy of me." Marigold grimaced down at the voluminous layers of her skirts.

"I'll help you," Olivia said quickly. "Do you have a needle and thread stashed in the carriage somewhere? Or in your purse, perhaps? I'm sure I can have it sewn up in no time."

Marigold shook her head. "Leave it to me. It's in a somewhat sensitive position, so I daren't climb down until it's fixed, but if you try to climb back in, there won't be any room for either of us to maneuver."

Olivia silently acknowledged that her friend was right about the difficulty of effecting repairs with both of them crammed into the carriage. "Take your time, then," she said. "I don't mind waiting."

Marigold thrust her head out the far window and peered around before pulling back in and turning to Olivia.

"Don't bother waiting for me. I can already see another vehicle coming along the carriage path behind us, and we need to clear the spot so its occupants can alight." She grinned. "And don't think about lurking here, waiting for me. You might be happy to wait, but I doubt they will be. You'll just make everyone uncomfortable. Please just let the coachman know that he should pull around until he can find an out-of-the-way place to stop. I'll have the tear fixed in a flash and then he can circle back around." She fixed Olivia with a stern stare. "Just promise you won't linger awkwardly somewhere waiting for me. You're already late enough, so go inside and enjoy every moment of your big night."

Olivia considered protesting, but the approaching carriage had nearly reached them, so there wasn't time for an argument. "Very well," she said with a sigh. "Although I feel terrible leaving you. I'll keep a close eye on the entrance and join you as soon as you make it into the ball."

Marigold nodded, gesturing for Olivia to hurry and pass on her message to the coachman. She did so, faithfully repeating Marigold's instructions. The man must have still been irritated because he merely grunted before signaling to the horses to begin moving.

Olivia watched the carriage roll off, feeling a little lost. She had expected to enter the ball at the side of someone who had been many times before, not alone. But the next carriage was arriving, and the footman who had handed her out was waiting for her at the foot of the long, shallow flight of stairs leading up to the palace entrance.

He gestured for her to approach, so she drew a deep breath, grasped her skirts in both hands, and hurried toward him. Despite her fears of tripping over her dress and tumbling head over heels, she made it safely to the top of the stairs, the footman's light support beneath her elbow ensuring her smooth arrival.

As soon as she reached the palace doors, the footman disappeared, running nimbly back down the stairs to help the next arrivals. Olivia was late so there wasn't a constant stream of carriages, but another one had appeared at the distant gate, rolling toward the one that was currently disgorging its passengers. Knowing she wasn't the only late-comer lifted her spirits a little.

The enormous double doors of the palace were thrown open, and Olivia stepped into the echoing stone entrance-way. To her left, the lights and sounds of the ball spilled out through another set of double doors, these ones also propped open. But unlike the front doors, the ones to the ballroom had a ceremonial guard standing to attention on either side. Olivia once again gripped her skirts, ready to twitch them aside and display her glass-shod feet in order to gain entry.

But neither guard moved nor gave any indication of having seen her, and after a momentary hesitation, Olivia approached the ballroom. The footman must have seen her glass slippers as she climbed the stairs. Perhaps his true role was to screen out attendees who didn't meet the requirement.

As much as Olivia had been longing for the moment she would arrive in the grand ballroom—had been dreaming of it since childhood—now that the moment had come, she felt hesitant. Her heart beat fast, and she had to stop herself from wiping her sweaty palms on her dress. It would have been much more comfortable to enter the ballroom beside Marigold.

She glanced back over her shoulder hopefully, looking for a glimpse of the Emerson carriage with its gold crest circling back around. But she could see no glimpse of it. The only people in view were the two ladies and the gentleman currently climbing the stairs as their carriage rolled away to make way for the next.

Olivia drew a deep breath. As little as she relished entering the ball alone—and possibly making an embarrassing misstep in the process—she didn't fancy the idea of trailing in behind a crowd of strangers either. She had imagined herself as a princess, attending a royal ball, and she should act the part.

Straightening, she raised her head and swept across the entranceway to stand at the doorway of the ballroom. Four steps led down into the main room, giving her just enough height to glance across the whole room.

It was even larger than she had imagined, spanning the entire length of the palace. Glittering crystal chandeliers sent light sparkling down on the throng below, the bright colors of the women's gowns contrasting with the gold accents of the room and the green of the potted trees and creeping vines that festooned the walls.

Olivia gave a soft gasp, taking a moment to admire the scene before her. A dance was underway, and couples twirled across the room in each other's arms. She knew no one who might ask her to dance, but for a moment she allowed herself to swell with the hope that she would soon be among them.

As she stepped forward, lifting her skirts so her foot could safely reach for the first step, a trumpet fanfare sounded. She flinched and fled down the stairs as quickly as possible. If the people entering behind her were important enough to receive a fanfare on entry, she was doubly glad she hadn't lingered.

But when she glanced back at the doorway from the safety of the crowd below, the three people behind her hadn't yet reached it. She looked around the room, frowning, but now that she was on the ballroom floor, it was no longer so easy to see. Too many of the ball guests were head and shoulders taller than her.

She could, however, see the orchestra, on their raised platform, and she noted with a frown that it had no brass section. Nowhere in the room was there any sign of the trumpeters who had miscued their arrival announcement. But the noise couldn't have come from the air.

Olivia was still craning her head, trying to see more of her surroundings, when the crowd around her rippled. Movement swept in her direction, a wave of people and a rush of murmurs.

She caught a few of the whispered words, "The prince," and, "Prince Julius!" among them.

Olivia tried to melt backward along with the people

beside her, but somehow the space around her emptied, and she found herself standing in a circle of clear floor, facing a tall young man.

He was bowing politely, apparently in her direction, his movement obscuring his face. But from the top of his dark, carefully groomed hair, to the resplendence of his black suit, with the deep purple and gold sash across the chest, he looked every inch a prince.

Combined with the whispers around her, she could come to only one conclusion. She was facing Crown Prince Julius of Sovar.

He spoke, still with his head partially bent.

"Will you dance with me?"

Her mouth dropped open in response to his words. And when he finally lifted his head and met her eyes, the polite smile on his face faltered as well.

Olivia's jaw snapped shut. "You!" she cried.

CHAPTER 6
OLIVIA

It wasn't the prince standing in front of her at all. It was the young man she had met on the hill after the slipper-incident-that-must-be-forgotten. Olivia stared at him, the silent horror she was feeling reflected in his eyes.

But as the silence stretched out, she once again noticed his clothing, and the way the crowd hung back, circling them and whispering. Surely the odd man from the hill couldn't be the crown prince of Sovar. She pitied the kingdom if so. He had nearly walked straight off a cliff!

"It can't be you," he finally murmured in a hoarse voice, almost too quiet for her to catch. "It's impossible."

Olivia's back straightened, her nerves fading as her anger rose. She had as much right to attend the Midsummer Ball as any other inhabitant of the kingdom—perhaps more if she really had saved the life of Sovar's only prince. Was a little gratitude too much to ask for? He hadn't thanked her then either.

"I don't know what you mean," she said in her iciest tone. "But by all means, feel free to walk away."

She hoped he would listen. Half the room had been staring at her for far too long already.

Unfortunately, he remained in place. But it was obvious from his expression that only his royal training kept his mouth from dropping open as hers had done earlier.

"Walk away? Are you serious?" he asked, again in a voice so quiet she could barely make out the words.

She glanced nervously at their fascinated audience. The prince—for it must be him, as little as she wanted to believe it—seemed more aware of the crowd than she was, and it put her on edge. She had no idea what game he was playing, but maybe it wasn't wise to antagonize the crown prince.

But what should she do? What did he want from her? He just stood there—still staring at her—while the crowd waited as if in eager anticipation of a spectacle. If the prince wasn't willing to walk away, did he expect her to turn around and leave the ball? Why!?

She drew a breath, ready to defend herself, only to realize she had no idea what argument to make. Was she in trouble for arriving late? But there had been two other carriages behind her!

Her mind scrambled to remember every scrap of royal protocol she'd ever heard. She wanted to simply melt away and lose herself in the crowd, but would it be treason to ignore the prince? Was she even allowed to turn her back on him?

In desperation, she threw him a pleading look. He had initiated the confrontation, and he should be the one to indicate what was supposed to happen next.

He met her look, and to her astonishment, his cheeks

reddened slightly. He bowed again, more stiffly this time, and held out his hand.

"Dance with me?"

It was worded as a question, but he was already turning slightly, anticipating her acceptance. Everything in Olivia longed to reject him. Not only did his strange manner and cold assurance irritate her, but the last thing she wanted was for all the eyes to keep following her—if her aunt hadn't seen her yet, she would soon.

But she couldn't muster the courage to reject him so publicly—not when she couldn't remember any detail about royal protocol. She should have grilled Marigold ahead of time. What if the women who chose to attend the ball were obligated to dance with the prince if asked? She didn't want to misstep and bring royal disfavor on her family and their business.

Julius glanced back at her, his brow furrowed, apparently in confusion at her hesitation. She reluctantly placed her hand in his. Now she only had to worry about making a literal misstep.

The prince led her away from the door toward the center of the dance floor, the path before them clearing. For a moment, Olivia felt a flutter of excitement in her chest. Despite the strangeness of everything that had happened since she'd arrived at the ball, she couldn't entirely deny the magic of the moment. She was at the Midsummer Ball in a gorgeous gown, and she was about to dance with the prince.

He pulled her close, putting one hand on her waist, and the brief moment of excitement was washed away by nerves. Since she hadn't planned to attend the ball, she hadn't joined her cousins' dancing lessons, and the dance was new to her, although it resembled one she knew from Henton. For the first strains, she could focus only on following the steps and attempting not to step on his feet.

Only after she had relaxed into the rhythm of the movement did she finally look up and meet Prince Julius's gaze. He was staring at her.

Olivia would have liked to imagine it was an admiring gaze—it would have fit her girlish dreams of dancing at the Midsummer Ball. But the only emotion she could read on his face was incredulity. She wanted to give him a piece of her mind—why ask her to dance if he disapproved of her so strongly? But she remembered he was the prince and stopped herself in time.

Instead, she tried to ignore him altogether, fixing her eyes to one side of his face and focusing on the movement of the dance and the swirl of her skirts. The glass slippers were even more comfortable to dance in than she had imagined, and at times it felt as if they were the ones matching the correct moves rather than Olivia herself. Their assistance allowed the dance to flow smoothly, despite Olivia's inexperience, and she released the last of her worries about taking a wrong step. Instead, she released herself to enjoy the whirl of the movement.

A smile grew on her face as the magical feeling returned. Would any of her old friends in Henton believe her if she described the evening? They would probably think she was exaggerating, just as she had suspected her friend of doing. But no claims had exaggerated Prince Julius's skill at dancing. He moved fluidly, his steps confident as his strong arms clasped Olivia close to his chest.

When he spun, he took her with him in a dizzying whirl

of movement. Her eyes slid over his face and caught there, lingering on his expression. He was blinking at her, his arrested expression harder to read than the previous one. It was almost as if he was seeing her for the first time.

Olivia's joyful smile faded, warmth rushing to her cheeks as the weight of his identity hit her anew. The silence between them made it easy to forget his erratic behavior and notice only the attractive combination of dark hair, blue eyes, and chiseled jaw. He might fall short in manner, but in appearance he fulfilled every possible childish dream.

"Thank you," he blurted out, breaking the moment.

He had the looks of a fairy tale prince, but he lacked the suave charm. Why did rumors claim that Prince Julius was a match for his ancestor—the one who had first earned the nickname Prince Charming? Olivia had seen no sign of any similarity.

Olivia stared at him, trying to make sense of his words. Surely he couldn't be thanking her for dancing with him. The ballroom was full of women who would have loved to take her place.

The prince cleared his throat, clearly uncomfortable for some reason Olivia couldn't fathom. He stiffened, his muscles tensing beneath her arm.

"My apology comes late, but I hope you will forgive my earlier omission." He grimaced. "I'm most grateful for your quick action, although I think I was in too much shock at the time to acknowledge it. I should have been paying attention to where I was walking."

Comprehension broke over Olivia. He wasn't talking about the ball at all.

"Oh," she said, aware she sounded as socially inept as he

seemed to be. She tried again. "It's a dangerous spot for those unfamiliar with the area. I'm just glad you weren't hurt."

The prince's face tightened even further at her response, and his voice grew rougher.

"I'm afraid I did not appear to best advantage during any part of the encounter, and I can only hope you will forget it completely and allow us to begin fresh." He inclined his head in her direction, the movement as close to a bow as their positions would allow.

Olivia gasped softly. Was she in a dream? Was that why everything was so strange? Surely the crown prince of Sovar couldn't be bowing to her, Olivia of Henton. It somehow seemed even more outlandish than him dancing with her.

"I hope you will forgive me and believe that I'm not usually so poor-mannered," he continued when she didn't speak.

He met her eyes, though it was clearly a strain, and her heart softened. An arrogant prince was hardly a surprise, but one with the humility to apologize—especially to someone as insignificant as her—was unexpected.

"Of course I forgive you," she said with a warm smile. "Your lack of gratitude was a little startling, but I should have considered the effects of shock. No harm was done to either of us, so I see no reason why we shouldn't put the matter behind us."

The prince relaxed immediately, his whole bearing changing. When he smiled down at her, she felt the earlier flutters thrill through her. She was far more comfortable in his arms now she knew why he had asked her to dance—he must have recognized her and had wanted to apologize and offer belated thanks.

The music wound down, and their movements slowed. Despite her initial trepidation, Olivia felt disappointed that the whirlwind experience was coming to an end.

But the musicians launched immediately into another melody, and the prince's arms never loosened around Olivia. Seamlessly, his steps shifted, moving into a new rhythm that was close enough to the old for her to effortlessly follow.

Her mood soured. Prince Julius hadn't even bothered to ask if she wanted to dance again. Did he think her grateful acceptance was so certain? Was she supposed to be flattered because he was the prince?

Slowly his speed increased, until they were spinning around the ballroom fast enough to make Olivia dizzy. The lightness that had come over the prince after her acceptance of his apology whirled away with the movements of the dance. She could feel the muscles of his arms tightening and jumping.

"Who are you?" He fired the words at her.

She nearly stumbled. "I'm Olivia." It seemed an incomplete answer, but she wasn't sure what else to say.

"Olivia," he repeated, his deep voice making her name sound rich and full. But his brows furrowed as he said it, and he was still pulling them through the dance so quickly she could barely keep up.

Anger and defiance sparked inside her. She planted her feet and pulled them both to an abrupt stop. They stood, surrounded by swirling couples, still clasped close together, their chests heaving with the recent exertion of the dance.

"But who are you?" The quiet words exploded out of

Julius, despite their low volume. "Who are your family?" She could both hear and feel his frustration.

Olivia hesitated. Her parents' names would be meaningless to the crown prince.

"I…I live on Manor Row," she said, feeling the need to say something, but unsure if she might be causing trouble for her aunt and uncle if she named them.

Julius's brows drew together. "Yes, I saw you there. But I can't understand your appearing here. Of course I've wondered who would show up at the ball—I've imagined all sorts of possibilities. But I never considered the possibility of a stranger. Why would I? I know every family of the court—I've even met the other royal families, although they were unlikely choices. It doesn't make any sense."

The prince was the one not making sense. Would it violate royal protocol for Olivia to say that aloud?

She decided she didn't care.

"What are you talking about?" She tried to wrench herself out of his arms, but they had become bands of steel around her.

"Not here," he hissed through his teeth, his eyes widening. "That isn't how this is supposed to go."

Panic surged inside Olivia, reaching for her throat. Had she strayed into a fever dream?

Just as her self-control was about to snap, the prince released her. She stumbled back half a step, still staring at him with widened eyes.

He put on a smile that didn't reach his eyes and offered her his arm. "It is tiring work," he said at a much louder volume than their previous whispered exchange. "And the room is hot. Allow me to escort you to the refreshments."

Olivia wanted to turn and run, but his words had clearly been aimed at their audience. Her momentary panic subsided as she realized he had been restraining her for the sake of the watching eyes. She was even a little grateful that he had prevented her from becoming the girl who made a scene in the middle of the Midsummer Ball.

But that didn't mean she appreciated his high-handed manner. Everything in her wanted to turn on her heel and storm off. But the tight expression around his eyes reminded her that it would be better for both of them if they waited to part ways somewhere less conspicuous.

Reluctantly, she placed her fingers on the crook of his arm and started in the direction he indicated. The prince immediately drew her hand all the way through his arm, pulling her tightly to his side just in time to prevent a collision with a couple spinning past.

Olivia had intended to pull away as soon as they left the dance floor and whisk herself off. But somehow Prince Julius maneuvered them straight into a small alcove between two of the glass doors that lined the exterior wall of the room.

While Olivia was blinking and trying to work out what had happened, he collected two glasses from a passing waiter and positioned himself so they were at least partially blocked from the eyes of the room. Reluctantly, Olivia accepted the offered glass, her resentment building.

The prince obviously had as little desire to be in her presence as she had to be in his. So why wouldn't he leave her alone? Was his pride stung because she wasn't falling all over herself to dance with the prince?

He downed his drink with a single toss of his head, his

expression as he looked at her reflecting her own frustration and irritation.

"Do you have to make this so difficult?" he asked with a slight head shake. "It isn't as if this was a situation of my choosing."

"Well it certainly isn't one of mine," Olivia snapped back, finally losing her patience completely.

The prince had been the one to approach her. All she had wanted was to enjoy the event from the sidelines, out of notice of the important members of the court and her aunt.

She almost groaned at the reminder of her aunt and tried, unsuccessfully, to peer over Julius's shoulder. Even if Aunt Helen had missed Olivia's dramatic arrival, she couldn't possibly have missed her two dances and abrupt departure from the dance floor. And that meant she was probably making her way toward them at that very moment. She wasn't likely to miss the opportunity of inserting herself into Olivia's conversation and forcing an introduction between the prince and her daughters.

And what of Marigold? Olivia wanted to shake herself. She hadn't even been looking for her friend. Marigold must surely have arrived by now, and Olivia had promised to be watching for her. How had she so entirely forgotten herself for half an hour or more?

She pushed forward, stepping sideways to get out from behind Julius and gain a better view. She couldn't see far into the crowd and could find no sign of Marigold or Aunt Helen. But she couldn't fail to notice how many people were looking in their direction. No one approached them, but everywhere small knots of people were talking, their gazes constantly flicking to the prince and Olivia.

Heat rushed over Olivia. Coming to the ball had clearly been a mistake.

She took another step away, intending to head straight for the ballroom doors, but Julius seized her wrist, stopping her. She immediately pulled free of his grip, but the furious expression on his face made her freeze.

"Who are you looking for?" he asked in an ice-cold murmur. "If it's a lover, I'm warning you now that I will walk away from all of this. I'm willing to sacrifice much for Sovar, but I have my limits."

Olivia's mouth dropped open. She didn't even know where to start. Sacrifice for Sovar? *He* had his limits?

"A lover!?" She fought to keep her voice as quiet as his. "Would I have been dancing with you if I was here to meet a lover? Are you trying to insult me?"

"I'm trying," he said, frustration dripping from every word, "to have a plain conversation. From where I stand, it appears that you are the one trying to insult me."

"Me?" Olivia wanted to protest further, but something kept her mouth shut. She had to be missing something—but what?

She wished Marigold would appear from the crowds. Unlike Olivia, Marigold had grown up as one of the court, never more than a stone's throw away in Manor Row. She understood the palace and its inhabitants in a way Olivia didn't. Perhaps she could act as interpreter between them because it felt as if they were speaking a different language.

She took a step back and tried to gather her thoughts. Storming off seemed like a dangerous option when she clearly didn't understand what was going on.

When Julius stepped in front of her again, she could only

think of all the interested eyes trained on them. This time his tall frame felt like a shield rather than a barrier.

But when her eyes caught on two figures sweeping across the ballroom floor toward them, Olivia realized that even Julius's shoulders weren't going to be broad enough.

"Their Majesties," she said through numb lips.

Julius glanced swiftly over his shoulder, his face shifting to relief at sight of his parents.

"About time," he muttered. "Maybe I'll finally get some answers."

Olivia stiffened, but the spear of anger at his unreasonable words was welcome, driving out her momentary nerves. She had done nothing wrong and had nothing to fear. She straightened her spine and lifted her chin, ready to greet the king and queen.

CHAPTER 7

OLIVIA

As Julius turned his back on her, Olivia caught a glimpse of a charming smile on his face, aimed toward the crowd and his approaching parents. The bravest part of her wanted to step forward and meet them at this side, but her courage failed her, and she remained tucked away, mostly out of sight.

"Father." Julius gave the king a quick half bow. "You look beautiful tonight, Mother."

The warmth and sincerity in his voice almost made Olivia soften, but she steeled her spine. His words were probably a show for the crowd, just like his smile. The people around them were standing back at a respectful distance but were still close enough to overhear words spoken at a normal conversational volume.

"We've been sequestered down the far end of the ballroom," King Robert said, "discussing an urgent issue with Lord Strathmore. But we heard the excitement at her arrival." The king nodded at the empty glass in Julius's hand. "I presume everything has gone smoothly?"

"Of course it has," Queen Elsinore said in satisfied tones. "I arranged it all myself."

"Not as smoothly as I would have liked," Julius said through his teeth, making both his parents frown.

"Come, Julius," his mother said in a whisper. "I made sure to choose a girl who is both beautiful and lively. I'm sure you can have no cause for complaint."

Julius cleared his throat, the back of his neck going red. "Her beauty is not the issue." He kept his voice lowered.

King Robert sighed, his voice equally quiet. "I thought you understood your duty, son, and were ready to play your part. As I did mine when I was your age."

"And look how happily it turned out for us." The queen put her hand on her husband's arm and beamed up at him.

A growing sense of foreboding crept over Olivia. She still didn't understand what they were saying, but it was increasingly clear that she wasn't supposed to be privy to this conversation. She wasn't supposed to be a part of whatever was happening at all.

She glanced to either side, considering the chances of slipping out of the alcove without being noticed by either of the monarchs. They didn't seem good.

A note of indulgent amusement came into the queen's voice as she stepped past her son. "But I'm surprised you're staying so quiet,—"

She broke off abruptly, staring at Olivia.

Olivia stared back before coming to her senses and dropping into a deep curtsy. "Your Majesty," she murmured, relieved her voice came out steady.

"But who are you?" the queen gasped, clearly struggling

to keep her voice low enough not to be overheard by the crowd.

"I'm Olivia," Olivia stammered for the second time that evening as the king also pressed forward to get a proper look at her.

"Julius, what you have done?" the queen wailed in an under voice while the king turned on his son with a threatening growl, his words all the more menacing for being quietly spoken.

"What is this?"

"What do you mean—?" the prince asked indignantly from behind his parents before cutting himself off and casting a lightning quick glance over his shoulder.

"Olivia is overheated," he said in a louder voice, although Olivia could see the strain in his face. "Why don't we step outside for some fresh air and proper introductions?"

A silent hand gesture brought two guards forward from further down the wall. Before Olivia knew what was happening, the men had the doors to her left open and were bowing the party of four outside.

Prince Julius gave the taller of the two a significant look and received a reassuring nod in return. The man closed the doors firmly behind them and took up post inside the ballroom with his back to the glass. His mien must have been stern enough to keep crowds at bay because the faces Olivia had been expecting to appear at the glass failed to materialize.

She turned slowly to face her three companions, gulping as she realized she was alone on the long stone terrace with the king, the queen, and their only son. The king and queen were faced off against Julius, clearly furious about something, and for the moment, none of them were looking at her. But being ignored only served to make clear who was the true outsider among them.

Where had everything gone so terribly wrong? One minute she was on her way to fulfill her dream with her friend at her side, and the next she was alone with the entire royal family.

The king and Prince Julius were still talking over the top of one another, but the queen turned to look at Olivia, regarding her as if she had destroyed all their carefully laid plans.

Olivia dropped into another curtsy for good measure. "I think there's been some sort of misunderstanding."

"Oh Julius, how could you?" wailed the queen, cutting through her husband and son's stream of words. She seized the prince's arm. "I don't care how beautiful she is! How could you?"

Olivia flushed, unsure if she was being complimented or insulted.

"What do her looks have to do with anything?" The prince carefully kept his eyes away from Olivia. "And why are you shaking me? I don't understand why you're both so upset. You're the one who chose her!"

Cold washed over Olivia from her crown to her feet. What was he talking about? She was certain the queen hadn't even known of her existence until a minute ago. She certainly hadn't chosen Olivia for anything.

"Chose her?" the queen gasped. "I did no such thing!" She turned to Olivia, her eyes narrowing. "Who are you, child? And where is Lady Marigold?"

"M...Marigold?" Olivia stumbled over her friend's name,

the ice down her spine turning to heat that flooded her whole body and set her trembling. She was glad her long skirts hid how close her legs were to collapsing. "I don't know. Her dress—"

But the queen was already walking toward the glass doors and the guard beyond, a martial light in her eyes. "Someone has made a grave error," she said. "And I want to know where Lady Marigold is."

She pulled the door open and spoke to the guard beyond. Olivia didn't hear every word, but she did catch "fetch" and "footman." She swallowed. She had traveled to the ball in Lord Emerson's carriage, but she hadn't made any false claims when she arrived at the palace, so if they had mistaken her for her friend, that was hardly her fault.

But how could such a mix-up happen? The royal family knew Marigold. It didn't make any sense.

When Queen Elsinore finished speaking, the guard shut the door again, and the queen returned to them, her eyes on Olivia. But before she could speak, her son interrupted.

"Lady Marigold? You chose *Marigold*? What were you thinking, Mother? She's erratic, temperamental, unpredictable, and has no self-restraint. She would make a terrible queen!"

Olivia could barely make sense of his words, but loyalty toward her friend sent another spear of anger through her, once again helping to keep less welcome emotions at bay. Defensive words hovered on her tongue, but she retained enough sense not to speak them.

"Peace, Julius," King Robert said, echoing her thoughts. "This is hardly the time."

He gave his son a stern look, his eyes flicking to Olivia

and away, and the prince subsided, muttering to himself, "I'm going to kill Cade. *Not going to be disappointed?!*" He shook his head.

Olivia's mind finally caught up with everything the prince had said, circling around and around the word queen. Was Crown Prince Julius betrothed to her friend? Was Marigold the future queen? Olivia's hand flew to her mouth, her eyes widening. How could her friend not have mentioned such a momentous thing? Was it possible she didn't know about the planned match herself?

But a betrothal only made the mystery of the apparent mix-up all the more strange. Clearly Julius knew Marigold, so he couldn't possibly have mistaken Olivia for her friend. He certainly hadn't talked to her as if she was Marigold.

Olivia waited for the queen to speak up in Marigold's defense—given she had apparently been the one behind the betrothal plans. But Queen Elsinore didn't seem able to meet her son's eyes, her gaze sliding sideways and her lips pursing slightly.

Olivia's heart sank, any potential excitement for her friend withered before it could grow. Was it worth becoming a princess if it meant her friend would have to join a family where she was so poorly valued? Clearly Marigold had been chosen for her father's wealth, influence, and power rather than her personal qualities.

Marigold might been dramatic, but she had a good heart. She deserved better.

"That isn't what's important right now," the queen said, turning back toward Olivia. She reached for her dress, and for a terrible moment, Olivia thought the queen meant to rip her billowing skirts.

But she merely tweaked them aside to reveal Olivia's feet, shod in the required glass slippers. Olivia looked back up at the queen, relieved, but the queen had turned pale, a fresh look of horror on her face.

Olivia felt her own face pale in response.

"What is the meaning of this?" Queen Elsinore demanded.

Each turn of the conversation only made matters more confusing, and Olivia had no explanation to give. But before the queen could demand an answer a second time, the doors to the ballroom opened, and the footman who had welcomed her to the palace walked outside. The doors closed behind him, and Olivia felt a pang of fellow feeling for the uneasy look on his face as he crossed the terrace and bowed low before the king and queen.

"How may I be of assistance, Your Majesties?" he asked.

"Your instructions were clear!" the queen said in a low voice, her eyes narrowed. "What is the meaning of this?"

She pointed dramatically at Olivia, and the footman's eyes followed her gesture. The two of them gazed at each other with looks of equal bewilderment. Clearly he had no more idea of what was going on than she did.

"I checked as instructed, Your Majesty," the man said carefully. "She was wearing the glass slippers."

"Exactly!" the queen said, as if they were the ones talking nonsense instead of her. "Why was that girl permitted to enter the ball wearing glass slippers?"

Olivia stared at her. What was she talking about? Wearing glass slippers was the one requirement of attending the Midsummer Ball. Everyone was wearing them...Weren't they?

Now that she considered it, she hadn't actually seen anyone else's slippers, except for Marigold's. But then she hadn't been looking at anyone's feet, and the long dresses of the ladies covered up their footwear most of the time.

"My instructions were to watch for the daughter of Lord Emerson," the footman said. "I saw the crest on his coach clearly, and only one girl got out. Her."

All four of them wheeled to stare at her. Olivia bit her lip.

"It's true that I came in Lord Emerson's carriage," she said. "And that I got out alone."

"Treachery!" the queen cried, clasping at her heart.

"You may leave," the king said quickly to the footman, and the man bowed and hurried away, clearly relieved to escape whatever was unfolding on the terrace. Olivia wished she could flee as well.

"We mustn't jump to conclusions," King Robert said heavily with a warning look at his wife. "Lord Emerson is a long-standing ally of the throne and a personal friend. I do not believe that he would—"

"Oh no," Olivia said quickly, all while her heart sank lower and lower. "It isn't Lord Emerson's fault. He never knew I was inside the carriage at all. And I know I got out alone, but I wasn't in there alone. Lady Marigold was with me. But she tore her dress as she moved to alight and had to fix it. There was another carriage behind us, so she circled around and came into the ball after me."

"But why are you wearing glass slippers?" the queen demanded.

"Am I not supposed to wear them?" Olivia asked, trying to keep her voice steady. "I grew up in the country, and I've always been told that glass slippers are required at the Midsummer Ball."

"Well, yes, of course, usually they are," the queen said with a dismissive wave of her hand. "But not this year."

Olivia's brows drew together. That made no sense. Every girl who had ever gone to the ball from Henton had taken a pair of slippers with her.

"I'm sorry," she said, a small tremble slipping into her voice. "I think there's been some sort of mistake. I can assure you, I never meant to—"

"You entered alone, late, and wearing the slippers?" the king asked in a sharp voice, not waiting for the answer before turning to his son. "And you greeted her on her entrance and asked her to dance? It was at least two dances, if I recall. And then the two of you went for refreshments together?"

Prince Julius, who looked pale, nodded. "I got a glimpse of the slippers as she stepped into the ballroom. And the fanfare sounded! You must have heard it. I thought she was the one."

"But where is Lady Marigold?" the king asked. "We must consult with her at once. Find her and bring her here to explain this situation."

The prince hesitated before nodding and returning to the ballroom. Olivia watched him go with trepidation. Earlier she had longed for him to walk away and leave her alone, but now she felt like running after him and clinging to his side.

He had barely shut the doors behind him when the queen spoke again, her voice urgent. "If the fanfare sounded, the number of dances is the least of our worries! The most important point is who are you, girl?"

"I'm Olivia," she repeated, although she was sure that

wasn't what they meant. "I'm a friend of Lady Marigold. I live next door to her in Manor Row."

"A noble girl?" The queen's head tipped to the side, and her eyes narrowed. "I don't recognize you."

"No, not a noble," Olivia said quickly. The last thing she needed was to create further misunderstandings. "I live with my aunt and uncle. My uncle runs a successful business and recently purchased a manor on the Row."

"Your aunt and uncle..." The queen nodded. "They must be very wealthy. I suppose you're a treasured and pampered niece. Perhaps they took you in because they have no children of their own?" She sounded hopeful.

"Ahh..." Olivia didn't like to say anything that might sound like a criticism of her relatives.

"If he's recently bought a house on Manor Row, your uncle must be Walter," the king said. "Most of those houses have been in the same family for generations."

"Yes, that's right," Olivia said softly.

King Robert exchanged a look with his wife. "Doesn't Walter have two daughters? We met them in the receiving line tonight. Their first ball. They must be about the same age as this girl."

The queen gave a horrified cry and stumbled back a step, her hand once more flying to her heart. "Two daughters?! No! It can't be!" She turned back to Olivia. "How do they treat you, girl? Are you like another daughter to them?"

Remembering her resolution to ensure no further misunderstandings, Olivia reluctantly forced herself to speak.

"They don't mistreat me. I didn't come as a guest, after all, but to work. So I'm more...more like a servant than a daughter." She said the final words in a rush, but she lifted her chin as she spoke. She might not like her work, but there wasn't anything shameful about it.

The queen opened her mouth as if to cry out again, but no sound emerged. She looked so pale that her husband put a hand beneath one of her elbows.

She looked up at him with a blank face, as if Olivia's final words had overwhelmed her completely. "A servant, Robert," she whispered. "The girl is a servant to relatives with two daughters of their own. We are all doomed."

The king rubbed at his temple with his free hand. "It certainly seems our hands are tied," he said after a heavy pause. "We will consult the histories, of course, but for now, we cannot flout the Legacy, or we may risk more than we can afford to lose."

"The...Legacy?" Olivia asked cautiously, her mind connecting dots she didn't want to connect. "What does the Legacy have to do with any of this?"

"Tonight was the night of our son's betrothal," the queen said in despairing tones. "But you're the one wearing the slippers, so the Legacy fanfare sounded for you. It means *you* are his betrothed."

"What?!" Olivia stumbled backward toward the doors into the ballroom. "I'm not betrothed to a prince. Did you hear me say I'm just a servant? You're looking for Marigold. She was just behind me. I'll...I'll find her for you. Just wait a moment, and I'll help the prince find her. She'll explain everything."

Not waiting for the king and queen's reaction to her tumble of words, she thrust open the doors and fled into the crowd.

CHAPTER 8

JULIUS

Julius didn't want to leave the terrace and return to the ballroom. He wanted to be part of the conversation and maybe finally get some proper answers. But his father was right. The girl from the hill had said little of help so far. Lady Marigold was the one to provide answers. Clearly her hand had been involved in the evening's disaster, and he wasn't in the least surprised.

How could his mother have selected *Marigold* for him? And how had Cade dared to look him in the face and say he wouldn't be disappointed!?

Except he hadn't looked him in the face.

"I knew it," Julius muttered under his breath. "I knew he wasn't being sincere." He should have taken more warning from his friend's weak praise. Maybe even tried to talk to his mother before everything was completely locked in.

Except it wasn't locked in even now. He bit his tongue on a louder, stronger exclamation. He had stood ready to sacrifice even his own future, and yet everything was still a mess.

He strode through the ballroom, ignoring all the people

who tried to speak to him. Thankfully, ignoring all attendees at the ball except one was part of the tradition for that particular Midsummer Ball. He only hoped his wandering the ballroom alone wasn't causing too much comment. The chosen girl should have been at his side. The last thing they needed was for everyone to know something had gone wrong.

They needed a solution before the problem was exposed. And for that they unfortunately needed Lady Marigold.

He gritted his teeth and pushed on, circling around the dancers as he tried to scan every whirling couple. Where was the outrageous girl? This was exactly why she was the worst possible choice of queen.

Well, worst except for one. He had been comfortably telling himself he would never meet the girl from the hill again, never dreaming she might turn up like this. He had been struggling to contain his horror ever since the crowd parted, and he got a proper look at the face of the girl in the glass slippers.

It was almost enough to make Marigold seem like a good alternative. She might be rash and unsuited to a life of protocol and restraint, but at least she had never pierced the charming façade that duty required Julius to wear. No matter how much she irritated him at times, she had never made him fail in his duty or caused him to question his sense of self. Even Marigold would be a more comfortable life companion than the girl currently outside with his parents.

The girl from the hill—Olivia, she had said her name was Olivia—was anything but comfortable. Marigold might behave poorly, but Olivia somehow caused *him* to behave in a way unfit for royalty, which was even worse. The sooner she was sent on her way the better, and that meant finding Marigold as quickly as possible.

Except, no matter how hard he looked, he couldn't see her anywhere. And with her bright hair, she should have been more obvious than most. If only the crowd wasn't constantly shifting. It was impossible to be certain he had seen every person present. She had to be there somewhere— Olivia had said they arrived at the ball together.

As he circled the room for the third time, his eyes fell not on the flaming hair of Marigold, but on golden hair above pink silk. His insides clenched.

Olivia. What was she doing in the ballroom and not safely shut out on the terrace with his parents?

He shouldered his way toward her, keeping her locked in his sights. She had come to a stop against the far wall, looking panicked, and hadn't yet seen him.

The crowd had noticed both his passage and his quarry, however, and people began to melt out of his way with soft sighs and giggles. Their false assumptions irritated Julius, although he knew he should be relieved. If they thought he had been searching for his dance companion, it would explain his solitary passage through the ballroom as well as his abstraction.

The other ballgoers had left space around Olivia, so she stood alone in a bubble near the wall, still clearly lost and confused. But as he watched, a footman approached and bowed to her.

At first, Julius thought his parents must have sent a servant to fetch her back and felt relieved. But the man offered her a small silver tray, a single letter resting on top.

Even from a distance, Julius could see the red seal, and

while he couldn't make out the shape of it, he knew his parents wouldn't have sent her a sealed letter from the terrace. He frowned and picked up his pace as Olivia accepted the letter, still obviously confused.

Her hands were visibly trembling as she tore it open, and Julius strode more quickly through the ballroom, although he couldn't explain his sudden need to reach her side.

"What is it?" he asked in a low, rough voice as soon as he reached her side. His eyes jumped from her white face to the page in her hands.

"It's…Oh, it's…" She looked up at him, lost for words. "It's Marigold," she finally managed to choke out.

"What about her?" He lost patience and rescued the letter from her shaking hand.

But he retained enough decency to pause, giving her an inquiring look and waiting for her nod of permission before looking down to read the words scribbled across the page.

He had never seen Lady Marigold's handwriting before, but he had no trouble believing it was hers. The words were scrawled, running together as if written in a hurry by someone who thought they had better things to do than use care in their penmanship.

By the time he had made it to the end with the looped signature that clearly read Lady Marigold, the only clear thought in his mind was that they both needed to be out of sight of the rest of the ballroom. Looking about him, he found the last of the closed doors to the terrace.

Seizing Olivia's hand, he pulled her toward it. Opening one of the doors, he almost pushed her through.

He heard a loud sigh and an audible whisper of "So romantic" as he stepped through himself and closed it behind her. He clenched his teeth as he tugged Olivia further from the door and any prying eyes.

At least the abrupt movement and fresh air seemed to have snapped Olivia out of her shock. She was looking at him with wide eyes, but she no longer looked incapable of thought or speech.

"I couldn't find any sign of her in the ballroom," he said grimly. "I suppose there's no question Marigold wrote this?"

Olivia gasped. "I didn't even think of that! I couldn't find her either, but it didn't occur to me that she might have been abducted."

So Olivia had been in the ballroom looking for Marigold as well? It was odd of his parents to send her to do such a task after already sending Julius, but he was too consumed with his own shock to think much about his parents.

"I hardly think she's been abducted. You do know her, right? Know what she's like?" He raised an eyebrow at Olivia, who was clearly grasping at straws.

When she didn't respond, he pushed harder. "Have you seen her handwriting before? Does it match?"

Olivia looked down at the letter still gripped in his hand and bit her lip.

"Well?" he asked when she still didn't answer.

Reluctantly she nodded. "It does look like hers. It's a... rather distinctive style."

Julius almost snorted. That was one way to put it.

"But perhaps she was coerced into writing it!" Olivia exclaimed. "If she was seized by someone after she left me, then—"

"Why are you wearing glass slippers?" Julius asked abruptly.

Olivia looked down at her feet, currently hidden beneath her skirts. "Why does everyone keep talking about that? I thought everyone had to wear glass slippers to the Midsummer Ball. I must have heard it discussed a hundred times over the years."

"Usually that's true," Julius said grimly. Apparently Olivia was even more clueless than he'd suspected. "But one year in every generation is different. The royal family always has only one child, and the Legacy ensures it is always a prince. So when the prince reaches adulthood, the king and queen host a special Midsummer Ball. And that year, at the ball, no one is permitted to wear glass slippers except the girl chosen by the king and queen to be their son's betrothed. The prince—along with the kingdom—discovers the identity of the chosen bride when she enters the ballroom to a fanfare provided by the Legacy."

"What?!" Olivia gasped. "No, that can't possibly be right. My cousins would have mentioned..." She trailed off, looking to the side.

Julius watched her, trying to work out the meaning of the emotions that flittered over her face.

"Well?" he asked, unable to help a sardonic note in his voice. "Did your cousins mention it?"

Olivia turned a soft pink. "I thought I couldn't go to the ball with them because I didn't have slippers, but I'll admit I knew there were other reasons they didn't include me." She sighed. "And maybe I avoided talking to them about the ball much. But I talked everything over with Marigold, and she never said anything about this ball being different. She was wearing glass slippers too. She—"

"Precisely," Julius said in clipped tones. "And that is the

proof that this isn't some abductor's ruse." He shook the letter. "Lady Marigold clearly planned this from the beginning. Would her letter be so apologetic if all she'd done was leave you to attend the ball alone? She set you up to take her place!" His hand clenched into a fist, crushing the letter. "How dare she! This is the future of Sovar, not some child's game."

Olivia gaped at him. "You're telling me this year's ball was an elaborate drama designed to trick the Legacy?"

Julius shook his head impatiently. "Every ball is an appeasement to the Legacy. This one is just...more complicated. Even my parents can't do anything about the existence of the Legacy. We're all saddled with it, so of course it's my family's responsibility to do what we can to ensure it benefits our people rather than harms them."

"But I came in wearing the slippers," Olivia said slowly, as if piecing the last of it together in her mind. "So the Legacy turned all its focus on me." Her words sped up. "And then you approached me, and we danced together, and that only confirmed it. And now everyone in that ballroom thinks I'm your betrothed, and..." She broke off the hurried words, slicing her arm through the air in a gesture of repudiation.

"No!" she exclaimed. "This can't be happening. I don't care what the Legacy thinks. Your parents may be king and queen, but they can't demand I marry you because of a *misunderstanding*!"

Julius's stomach clenched, his whole body tensing.

"What?" he demanded in low tones. "What did you say? My parents want to go ahead with the betrothal? With *you*?" He shook his head. "You must be mistaken."

"Thank you for the compliment," Olivia said, her tone ice

cold. "I can assure you I have even less desire to marry you than you seem to have to marry me. This whole thing is a farce. They can't be serious."

Julius wanted to assure her they weren't, but brutal honesty prevented him from doing so. His family had been controlling the Legacy for generations with the Midsummer Balls. He had been raised to know they played a significant role in the well-being of the kingdom. Was he sure his parents wouldn't insist on the betrothal?

But no. He shook his head again. It was madness. They couldn't do so. Olivia was a total stranger. They knew nothing about her. They couldn't make her queen!

"What exactly did my parents say?" he asked, trying to stay rational.

But Olivia turned away from him, crossing to the edge of the terrace and back again, apparently taking his sudden calm as a bad sign.

"This is outrageous!" she exclaimed, pacing back for the second time. "The Legacy is a mindless force. It doesn't know what's best for the kingdom! Why should it be allowed to control our lives? First it makes me a servant, and now it's making me a princess—and I get equally little say in either fate." Her voice dropped. "I never should have left Henton."

"A servant?" Julius stared at her in horror. "You're a servant!?"

Olivia's eyes narrowed, her fury turning on him. "Do you have an issue with servants, Your Highness?"

Julius frowned. "If you mean do I have an issue with their existence—of course I don't."

"No, I imagine not," Olivia said contemptuously, gazing out at the vast manicured gardens shining in the moonlight, before turning to look at where the warmer light of the ball-room spilled through the glass doors.

Julius stiffened, his manner becoming formal. As usual, Olivia had gotten under his skin, causing him to behave unlike the charming prince he was trained to be. He had lowered his guard and forgotten himself. He needed to be more careful.

"You seem to be laboring under a misapprehension,"

he said. "I have no objection to the lower-ranked members of my kingdom—I wouldn't even object to falling in love and marrying one of them."

Olivia's eyes snapped back to him, her brow creasing.

"But I did not fall in love with *you*," he continued, frustration creeping into his formal tone, despite his efforts. "I agreed to an arranged marriage because it would bring wealth and influence to the crown—wealth and influence that could be used for the good of Sovar and all its people. If I'm going to marry someone without a single resource or material advantage to her name, surely I should at least be able to choose her for myself!"

Olivia looked taken aback, and he expected her to erupt again. But instead her gaze dropped, her expression thoughtful rather than offended. Perhaps even she was forced to concede he had a point.

"You talk about not having a choice," Julius continued, driving the point home. "But pray tell, what choice do I have? If my parents are demanding we go through with a betrothal, you could refuse them. You could turn your back on their wishes and return to Henton, leaving this whole farcical situation behind. I have no such luxury. I must stay here and do what is best for Sovar."

He built up steam despite his resolution to remain calm. Why did Olivia have that effect on him?

"You must have had the same choice about becoming a servant," he added. "If you don't like being a servant, you could leave and find another job. You've always had a choice."

Her chin rose, and she stood facing him, her eyes flashing, apparently undaunted by their comparative ranks. Clearly he wasn't the only one who let his emotions get the better of him when they were together—yet another reason why a betrothal between them was a terrible idea.

"So if we refuse a betrothal, it could cause untold damage to the kingdom?" she demanded, her voice quivering with anger. "So much damage, that you couldn't possibly refuse your parents' wishes. And yet I am free to walk away? Do you truly believe only princes have any sense of responsibility? Do you really think I would feel free to go home and leave countless others to suffer for my decision?" Her voice calmed and turned cold. "I may not have been born to rank and wealth like Marigold, but apparently I have at least one advantage. Their Majesties seem to think I'm an excellent funnel for the Legacy's power, and if I need to use that for the kingdom's benefit, then I will do what needs to be done."

Julius had been listening to her with narrowed eyes, his stance rigid. But at that, his eyes widened.

"Of course," he breathed.

He had been too distracted by his own personal perspective. He should have seen the full significance of her being a servant at once.

He strode over to the edge of the terrace, stopping at the stone railing that ran along its length. No wonder his parents were contemplating betrothing him to a stranger. It wasn't just the glass slippers or the attention he had given her at the ball. If Olivia was a servant, she was far too perfect a fit for the original Queen Ella. The power of the Legacy must be pouring into the palace already. What would happen if they flouted it and turned her away?

But even so. Making a stranger into Sovar's future queen was going too far. He gripped his hand into a fist and pounded it once against the railing.

CHAPTER 9
JULIUS

"Julius!" His mother's voice pulled him from his thoughts, and he turned to see her rushing down the terrace toward him, his father at her heels.

"There you are!" she exclaimed. "But where is Lady Marigold? And where is Olivia? She ran off before we could stop her, and we didn't want to make a scene in the middle of the—" She stopped as she caught sight of Olivia. "Oh, there you are, child. But where is Lady Marigold? We've just spoken with her parents, and they claim to have no idea."

"But Lord and Lady Emerson aren't here," Olivia said, sounding confused. "That's why Marigold was coming on her..." She trailed off, presumably finally realizing the truth.

Marigold's parents already being at the ball and Marigold traveling there alone was all part of the tradition surrounding that particular Midsummer Ball. He was sure they had regretted the necessity given their daughter's tendency to outrageous behavior. But even they couldn't have imagined...

Julius clenched his jaw and passed his mother the

crumpled paper in his hands by way of explanation. She took it and read quickly, his father reading over her shoulder.

"What?" she exclaimed before she had even reached the end. "In love with someone else? Doesn't want the betrothal? What is this nonsense?"

"Lord Emerson said nothing of this to me," his father said in dark tones.

Julius winced, wishing he could give Marigold an earful. His parents had been trying to form a closer alliance between the throne and the Emerson family—and now her actions might drive a wedge between them instead.

"At least we know Lord and Lady Emerson had nothing to do with this outrageous behavior," he said. "And given we've all known Marigold since she was a small girl, we really shouldn't be so surprised."

He gave his mother an exasperated look. The daughter of Lord Emerson or not, his mother should have known better than to choose Marigold of all women.

His mother, however, still seemed bewildered. "But I don't understand it. How could anyone not want to marry you?"

Julius couldn't help darting a glance at Olivia. Little did his mother realize she was in the presence of a second girl who found the idea of marrying him equally horrifying. And Olivia didn't even have the excuse of already being in love with someone else.

Or did she? His gut churned anew. She had denied coming to the ball with a lover, but that didn't mean her affections weren't already engaged. Which was just what he needed to make the whole situation worse. There was going to be scandal enough without the court watching his bride pining for another man.

His hands clenched back into fists.

"Clearly Lady Marigold is the one at fault here," he said, trying to get his thoughts back on track. "She sent a servant in her place and didn't even have the decency to tell her replacement what was happening! You cannot be serious about going through with the betrothal under these circumstances—to Marigold or Olivia!"

"Given the girl's circumstances, I'm afraid we have no other choice," his father said heavily. "At least until we can work out another way out of the situation. For now, we will appease the Legacy, but I have hope we will find another solution before anything irrevocable happens."

Hope. Julius wanted a stronger assurance than that. If they began the engagement and didn't find a way out, they would only find themselves even more locked in.

"Olivia doesn't want to be tied to me," he blurted out, desperate. "In either betrothal or marriage by the sound of it."

All three of them turned to look at her, and her eyes widened, her throat moving as she swallowed. He instantly regretted being so ungallant as to turn his parents' attention her way. But she responded with a clear voice, despite her obvious discomfort.

"Yes," she said. "The prince is right. I—"

But his mother was already talking over the top of her, her motherly affection blinding her to reality.

"Nonsense," she said. "Lady Marigold is the most eligible girl in Sovar and is well known for eccentricity besides. But when it comes to any ordinary girl, she would be delighted to have you. What girl doesn't dream of attending the Midsummer Ball and dancing with a handsome prince?" She turned to Olivia. "Isn't that right, dear?"

Julius expected a fiery denunciation, but instead Olivia turned delightfully pink, the color only emphasizing her golden beauty.

"Ah, well…" she stammered. "I suppose…"

"Mother!" Julius exclaimed, trying not to think too hard about the possibility that he had starred in Olivia's dreams. If he ever had, she must have revised her opinion after their various disastrous encounters.

She was the girl he had hoped never to encounter again, and yet somehow he had found himself standing on the moonlit terrace, arraying himself at her side against his parents. How had everything gotten so twisted?

He reached for a new strategy, hoping it might have a better chance of reaching his mother. "Supposing a girl had dreamed of attending the ball and dancing with me, wouldn't that just make it worse? It would be cruel to announce her as my bride and a future princess, only to snatch it all away again." He carefully averted his eyes from Olivia. "Do you want to be responsible for that sort of heartbreak?"

An indignant snort from Olivia was thankfully too quiet to be heard by his parents. If she wanted his parents to abandon their plan as badly as he did, she should stay quiet and look as lovelorn as possible.

The queen looked crestfallen, compassion filling her eyes. "Oh, I hadn't thought of that," she said softly. "How could she help falling in love with you?"

She rushed up to Olivia and took both the girl's hands in

hers. "I'm so sorry to ask it of you, child. But we must think of the good of the kingdom! You must resist my son's charms —as impossible a task as that is—and I promise we shan't abandon you at the end. There are many nice men at court, and we will arrange another marriage for you when this is over." She looked across at Julius. "You can introduce her to all your friends, my dear. The court always seems to be overrun with young men, and she may well take a fancy to one of them."

Julius's mouth fell open. "You want me to become engaged to Olivia and then start trying to pair her off with my friends? Some friends those would be if they showed interest in her!"

"Well, not quite so far as that, of course," his mother said, oblivious. "But if any of them should happen to take a liking to her—and her to them, of course—then it would be just the thing."

"Just the thing for one of my friends to take a romantic liking to my future bride?" Julius asked, only growing more incensed.

"Naturally, nothing along those lines can be thought of until the betrothal is broken," his father said in a dampening tone, throwing his wife a stern look. "But certainly we can reassure the girl that we will look after her when this is over."

"Her name is Olivia," Julius muttered, earning his own dampening look from his father.

"To be clear," Olivia said, sounding a little dazed, "you're asking me to enter into a public betrothal in order to appease the Legacy and the expectations of the kingdom? And you truly believe that is necessary or else Sovar will be harmed?"

"That is correct," the king said solemnly. "Your kingdom needs you, Olivia of Henton. Surely you will not turn your back on it."

Olivia looked shaken by his words, but she continued. "But it isn't a real betrothal, right? I'm not actually going to become a princess?"

Julius turned on his father, using a hard tone he had never directed toward the king before. "Don't say yes unless you can guarantee it." He held his father's eyes until the king gave a slow nod.

"My son is right. I cannot guarantee that our experts will find a way out of this situation. But for the sake of Sovar, we must proceed."

"I..." Olivia looked from Julius to his parents. "I suppose there's nothing for me to say, in that case. I will do my best—and hope your scholars find a solution quickly."

His parents both nodded, but Julius could read the lingering surprise and unease in their eyes. Clearly when they'd considered all the problems of this unexpected situation, they hadn't anticipated the possibility that Olivia might refuse to go along with their plans.

But given her earlier remonstrance—which was still ringing in his ears—they needn't have worried. He had been wrong to assume she lacked the sense of responsibility he had been raised with. Olivia would do what was needed for the sake of Sovar, no matter how much she disliked him personally.

"What now?" he asked, wondering for the first time what hour it was. The last thing he wanted was to be forced into returning to the ball and playing the part of a besotted man for the rest of the night.

He had barely finished the question when the loud toll of a clock reached the terrace. At the Midsummer Ball, there was only one hour of the night that rang out loudly enough to be heard outside. He breathed a sigh of relief.

"I think we can all be grateful for that," the king murmured, hearing the same sound. "We've all had enough shocks tonight, and the last thing we need is any further mistakes. Everyone will be expecting Lady Olivia to leave now, and I see no need to even pass through the ballroom again. She can leave directly from here."

He frowned. "But if I understand matters correctly, Lady Olivia will need a ride home since her original carriage has abandoned her." He glanced toward the letter which his wife had allowed to fall to the ground.

Olivia followed his gaze and retrieved the piece of paper, folding it and securing it in a hidden pocket. No one protested. The letter had been addressed to her and was hers by right. Julius imagined she was going to have some angry words for her friend when they next met.

"I'll call for a carriage to be brought round." The queen moved toward one of the doors further down the terrace. "You can circle the outside of the palace and meet it by the front steps without needing to go inside at all. The official announcement of the betrothal always happens the day after the ball, so nothing more is needed for now."

Olivia nodded her assent before looking at the king. "You called me Lady Olivia, but I'm not one of the nobility. I'm just an ordinary girl."

Julius could hear the shock and overwhelm in her voice. She was clearly as unable to believe the events of the evening as he was.

"Consider it a courtesy title," his father replied. "You are betrothed to the crown prince now, after all. And while you will only become a princess on your marriage—if it ever occurs—it doesn't seem right to introduce you as merely Olivia."

"I...I don't know if I'm comfortable with that," Olivia said hesitantly.

Julius wanted to sigh. Did she have to fight them on everything, no matter how small?

But his father showed more patience. "If you're concerned about what will happen if the betrothal is successfully broken, we won't ask you to give up the title in the future. My wife can be overenthusiastic at times, but we will certainly provide for your future one way or another."

"Very well, then," Olivia said in a small, dignified voice. "It's all very strange, but I will manage the best I can."

"And we will assist you, of course."

A footman appeared around the palace, and Julius's father threw him a look. In his role as Prince Charming, he still had one final duty before he was allowed to finish for the night.

Forcing a smile, Julius offered Olivia his arm. She looked from it to his flat expression, clearly wanting to refuse. But then she glanced at the king and placed her fingers lightly on Julius's arm.

Something in the soft, almost trembling, touch made him soften. Neither of them wanted their situation, but they were stuck in it together. Earlier, in the ballroom, he had been the only one acting a role, but now they would be acting it together.

They rounded the building, leaving his father behind.

"They do believe I knew nothing of Marigold's scheme, don't they?" Olivia asked quietly, her brows tight with worry. "Can I trust their promises to me, or do they just need my compliance?"

Julius stiffened, the fledgling warmth freezing over. "My parents are people of integrity. They are not liars."

"I'm sorry," she said quickly. "I meant no offense. I'm new to the capital and know little of you or your family."

Julius closed his eyes briefly, drawing in a long breath. She was not only unfamiliar with court but unfamiliar with everything, it seemed.

They reached the carriage, and he handed her in. He went to close the door more forcefully than necessary, but a sudden memory made him pause. Pulling it back open, he held out his hand silently.

She stared at it as if he was holding out a dagger instead of offering an open palm.

"Your slipper?" he prodded, trying not to let the frustration and impatience sound in his voice.

"My slipper?"

She continued to stare at him blankly until her eyes suddenly widened, and she gave a start. Removing one of the glass shoes she wore, she placed it tentatively into his hand.

Julius sighed, a headache building behind his temples. "If you know so little, it might be best if you don't speak at all. Try not to talk of tonight if you can possibly avoid it."

He heard her outraged gasp as he stepped back and finally closed the door of the carriage, signaling to the coachman to move off. He watched the carriage depart with a stoic countenance, hoping the surrounding footmen couldn't read any of the frustration in his eyes.

Once again he had apparently managed to offend her. But she would be home for a single night, and it was already late. Was it really too much to ask her to refrain from gossiping about the disaster until they could all work out the best story to make public?

His parents claimed a betrothal was the only safe way forward, but did any of them really know what they were getting into?

CHAPTER 10
OLIVIA

Olivia fumed as her carriage rolled away from the palace. But not even the heat of her anger at the insufferable prince could last for long. She was too overwhelmed and stunned to maintain her irritation. Nothing about the night had gone as she had expected.

Not only had Marigold completely disappeared, but instead of enjoying a night of food and dancing and fun with her friend, she was now betrothed to the crown prince.

She let out a crack of laughter. There didn't seem any other possible response to such a ridiculous situation. Part of her was still expecting to wake up in bed and find it had all been a dream. Except she wasn't sure her imagination was capable of coming up with such a scenario.

What would her aunt and uncle think? What would her parents and younger brothers back in Henton think? She burst into fresh laughter, tears running down her face. She couldn't even imagine their faces when the news reached them. Just the betrothal was bad enough. If the king and queen didn't find a way to dissolve it, Olivia's family would have to travel to the capital to attend their daughter's royal wedding. It was completely incomprehensible.

But as she considered her aunt's reaction, her mirth quickly subsided. Aunt Helen was going to be delighted. Uncomfortably so.

She might briefly bemoan that it had been Olivia to befriend Marigold and not one of her own daughters, but she had never expected either of her girls to marry the crown prince. Like everyone else, she must have been expecting to see a girl of substance and position arrive in the glass slippers. Apparently, only ignorant country girls with no experience of the Midsummer Ball could have been unaware of the once-in-a-generation arrangements at this particular ball.

Olivia raked through her memory, trying to find any instances where she had missed the obvious. With so much added context, she could understand a number of comments more clearly in retrospect. People had been abuzz with talk of the prince turning twenty-one and his parents finally arranging a marriage for him. It had often been mentioned alongside the ball, but she hadn't understood the connection. She had imagined that the ball was special merely because it was the last opportunity to dance with the prince before he was wed.

She shook her head at her own foolishness. If she hadn't avoided the topic of the ball with her cousins out of jealousy, she might have eventually heard enough to piece together the truth. And then she wouldn't have landed in such a quagmire.

Fresh outrage filled her as she thought of the true cause of her present predicament. How could Marigold have betrayed her so?

It wasn't only conversation about the ball that seemed obvious in hindsight. Her friend had been bothered by something—a conflict with her father—and it was now easy to guess the cause of the conflict. Marigold's father had informed her of her betrothal to Prince Julius, and Marigold had begun plotting a way out. Olivia had even seen the fateful idea hit Marigold and had feared it would be outrageous. But not even her past experience with Marigold had prepared her for how outrageous.

Her friend's motivation for gifting Olivia with a custom gown and glass slippers was now glaringly obvious. Olivia just wished she had questioned Marigold further beforehand.

But even if Marigold had sent Olivia in alone to confound the king and queen's plans, how could she then abandon Olivia to the unfolding situation? Had she truly thought sending a letter was enough? Marigold had taken the blame in it, but what if the king and queen hadn't believed her written words? They might have blamed Olivia and punished her or her family for Olivia's role in the charade. The circumstances that had forced the royals into continuing with the betrothal might have been the only thing staying their hand.

And even without any blame being assigned to her, Olivia felt the betrothal was its own punishment. She could only imagine what the members of court would think of her for thrusting herself on them. She wasn't likely to have an easy time of it. And if the worst happened, she might find herself tied for life to the man from the hill, of all people.

She had always imagined that she would marry one day, and that when she did, she would find not only a lifelong love, but also someone to work beside her and support her.

She had pictured the two of them as a team against anything life might throw at them, just as her parents had always been. But her betrothed had just suggested she stay silent and out of the way to avoid inconveniencing him or his family. If it came to a wedding, she would end up stuck in a position she was ill-equipped to fill with no one to support her.

Tears welled in her eyes, slipping out and running down her cheek. For a few moments, the ball had seemed as magical as she had dreamed, despite its strangeness. The prince had even apologized to her. But that had all been part of an act.

Everything he had done after she arrived at the ball had been part of a role he was playing. He had thought she was his bride, chosen for him by his parents. No wonder he had wanted to start fresh and make sure she didn't repeat the story of his foolishness to members of the court.

The tears broke the hold she was barely keeping on her emotions, and within moments she was sobbing without restraint in the back of the carriage. But she didn't have the luxury of a private breakdown. All too soon the carriage stopped, and she heard a groom dismounting.

Choking back tears, she wiped at her face just as he pulled open the door and let down the steps. Keeping her head bowed, she murmured polite appreciation and fled from the carriage into the haven of her aunt and uncle's home.

But even the manor wasn't guaranteed to provide privacy for long. How soon before her aunt and cousins arrived home? And would they dare to come into her bedchamber if she was already in bed when they appeared?

And what of Marigold? Olivia wanted to go straight next door and demand to see her friend, but despite everything, she couldn't bring herself to pound on Lord Emerson's door in the middle of the night. Even if she tried, she would likely be sent away by a haughty butler, with the end result that she would run into her aunt and cousins when she returned home, unsuccessful. Abandoning the idea, Olivia took the stairs at a run, slipping into her room and locking the door behind her, just in case. She needed a few hours to compose herself before facing her aunt's shock and joy.

Her thoughts were whirring too quickly for easy sleep, but the emotions of the night had exhausted her, and she did eventually fall into a slumber deep enough that if her aunt knocked on her locked door, she never heard it.

~

When she woke the next morning, it took Olivia a full minute to grasp that the strange memories in her mind weren't tangled remnants of her dreams. When the night before came flooding back in full detail, she gasped and slipped straight out of bed, rushing to dress herself as quickly as possible.

Now that daytime had arrived, she had to find Marigold and make her explain herself. Surely there was still a way for Lord Emerson to fix everything.

She flew along the landing, not even thinking of breakfast or her normal morning chores. She nearly bowled Hattie over as her cousin stepped out of her room, barely catching herself in time.

"Olivia!" Hattie squealed, and Olivia winced at the volume.

"Sorry!" she called back, continuing toward the stairs.

If she stayed for a proper apology, Nell and Aunt Helen would appear, and then she might never get away.

"But—Olivia!" Hattie called after her.

Olivia still didn't slow. She took the stairs two at a time and dashed through the house to a door that led into the walled garden at the back of the manor house. She could move even faster outside, and she soon reached the outer garden wall that gave access to the hill behind Manor Row.

Once actually on the hillside, however, she paused. In her mad dash to get to Marigold, she hadn't considered the issue of how to approach the Emerson manor. She certainly didn't have free access to it, never having been inside before. She and Marigold usually met on the hill, either by chance or prior arrangement.

Despite everything that had happened, she didn't know if she had the courage to march up to their front door and demand admittance. But neither could she return to her own home without making some effort to find her friend. After what Marigold had done to Olivia, Olivia wasn't going to allow her to hide in her room and let Olivia sort it all out on her own.

After another moment's hesitation, Olivia approached the outer wall of the neighboring manor. As with her uncle's manor, a door gave access between the rear of their garden and the hill. In all Olivia's time with her aunt and uncle, she'd rarely seen it used by anyone but Marigold.

Feeling bold, she tried the door but found it locked.

Shrugging, she rapped on it three times—loudly but not too loudly. And then she waited.

When a minute passed and no one came, she grew too impatient to remain still and knocked again. This time using five raps.

A clang sounded on the other side of the wall, making her straighten. If she had to guess, it had sounded like someone dropping a shovel onto a stone path. Her straining ears caught the further sound of footsteps and then the scrape of a bolt being drawn back.

She tried to calm her expression, putting on the best smile she could muster as the door was pulled open a crack and a face looked out at her.

The boy, hovering on the edge of manhood, had the appearance of a gardener's apprentice, and he wore a look of caution. But when he saw Olivia, his expression changed, an admiring light springing into his eyes.

"Did you knock, miss?" he asked. "I haven't heard anyone knock here before."

Olivia tried to look as innocent and appealing as she could. "I'm looking for Lady Marigold. She's a good friend of mine. Could you send her a message to let her know that Olivia is waiting to meet her on the hill?"

The boy's face lit up—this time with the familiar light of someone bearing news that was too exciting not to share.

"Can't do that," he said breathlessly. "Lady Marigold isn't here."

"She isn't at the manor?" Olivia frowned. It was still early in the morning by Marigold's usual standards. "Then where is she?"

"That's just it." The boy leaned forward and lowered his voice slightly. "Don't think anyone knows. Not with the way the house is buzzing. Like an upturned beehive it's been since late last night. The senior gardener has been here for forty years, and he says he's never seen Lord Emerson so angry. Furious, he is. Threatening to disinherit his own daughter and everything." The boy shook his head, clearly delighted at so much excitement overtaking the usually orderly manor.

"If you ask me," he continued, "I think she's run away." He declared this opinion with aplomb. "I couldn't tell you how many times I've seen her sneaking out this back door."

Olivia was too shocked to speak, and the boy hesitated. But after looking at her closely, he regained his confidence and continued.

"I've seen her out here with you sometimes. When I was on my break," he hurried to add. "Is it true you work next door?"

Olivia blinked and nodded, not quite sure what she was agreeing to. Marigold wasn't at home? From the sound of it, she had never returned after leaving for the ball. So where was she? Had she really run away?

With a sinking feeling, Olivia acknowledged it was a possibility. Her friend had dramatically declared her intention to disappear many times, and Olivia had long ago stopped taking her seriously. But Marigold must have known she had gone too far this time and caused more trouble than even she could handle.

"I see," Olivia said slowly, trying to think of something she could ask the lad that might give her a clue to Marigold's whereabouts.

But before she could come up with anything, an older, grizzled voice sounded from behind the boy.

"Oi!" it called. "What are you doing, boy? Latch that door and get back to work!"

The boy winced. "That's my master!"

His words were apparently explanation enough because the door closed with a soft thud, the scrape of the bolt once again reaching Olivia's ears.

She blinked at the solid wood. Clearly there was nothing to be gained by knocking again. And even less to be gained by trying the front door. Having heard the state of the household, she was relieved she hadn't tried it at the start. Who knew how Lord and Lady Emerson would have reacted to the sight of her? They might even have blamed her for the whole thing.

But as she walked slowly back to her own home, she couldn't think of a single other positive. Marigold was gone, and Olivia was on her own. There was no one who could get her out of her quagmire.

She felt suddenly unanchored, listless without a goal. What was she supposed to do now? Go back to her usual chores?

She laughed, despite herself. Would the royal family be offended if they discovered the girl betrothed to the crown prince scrubbing floors?

An insistent squeak made her swing around. She still had one friend who hadn't abandoned her.

But the sight of Mildred wiped the brief smile off her face. The mouse was no longer the size of a medium dog. She could now easily be ridden by a small child.

Olivia ran forward to pat Mildred's silky fur, tears in her

eyes. "What have I done to you?" she whispered. How was Mildred going to keep herself hidden now?

More than anything, the physical changes in her furry friend made everything real to Olivia. She was caught in the Legacy's web with no easy way out.

"Olivia!"

The shout made Mildred squeak again and run for the edge of the hill. Olivia wanted to call her back, but whoever was looking for her in the manor garden would soon turn their attention to the hill.

Sighing, she slipped into her aunt and uncle's garden. She had barely closed the door in the wall behind her when her cousins leaped on her. Nell seized one of her arms and Hattie the other, the two girls dragging her toward the house.

"Where have you been?" Nell exclaimed. "Look at you!"

Olivia gazed down at herself in bewilderment. She was wearing a crumpled dress and had made no attempt to fix her bedraggled hair, but she was decently covered. The gardener's apprentice hadn't seemed to find fault with her appearance.

"What does it matter what I look like?" she asked. "That hardly seems like the biggest issue right now!"

Nell stared at her with enormous eyes. "It seems big enough!"

Hattie broke into sudden giggles, as if her emotions needed some escape, and she didn't know how else to release them.

"The crown prince is waiting for you in our drawing room! The crown prince, Olivia! Surely your appearance matters a little."

"Prince Julius is here?" Olivia gasped. "Right now? But why?" She stared around the garden as if it could provide answers. "Why is he here so early? They only sent me home a few hours ago!"

"Of course he's here," Nell said. "*You're* the one he danced with last night!"

"Why do you think I tried to stop you this morning?" Hattie asked reproachfully. "Why did you run away when you must have known he was about to arrive?"

"I can't believe you didn't tell us you were the chosen girl!" Nell added without giving Olivia time to respond. "Mother would have been delighted for you to come with us if she'd known. She would have ordered you a new dress too, although the one you wore was stunning. But how did you meet the prince? How did he convince his parents to choose you? Everyone knows the crown prince's marriage is arranged by his parents." She gave a long sigh. "It's so romantic!"

"It certainly isn't!" Olivia cried. "Don't talk nonsense about romance to me."

"But Olivia, what do you mean?" Hattie asked. "They usually choose a girl from a rich and influential noble family, so Prince Julius must be madly in love with you if he managed to convince his parents to choose you."

"Is that what everyone is thinking?" Olivia cried in alarm. "Of course he isn't in love with me. He doesn't even know me. How would I know the crown prince? The whole thing is a terrible misunderstanding. I didn't know this ball was different, and I thought I was supposed to wear glass slippers."

Both her cousins gasped in horror. They exchanged a look across Olivia before Nell spoke in a tone of dismay.

"You already had the Legacy's interest—it pushed Mother into treating you more like a servant than like family—so it must have been at full power last night."

"Prince Julius danced with you because of a mistake?" Hattie sounded bitterly disappointed. "Then why is he here this morning?"

"Because of all that Legacy power," Olivia answered dully. "The royal family think we have to go through with the betrothal now."

"So you do get to be a princess?" Nell asked with returned excitement.

"Not just a princess," Hattie said in a dreamy, breathless voice. "She also gets to marry Prince Julius."

Olivia wanted to set them straight about her feelings on the matter, but she wasn't sure the royal family would appreciate her frankness. They might approve the narrative that she had been chosen at Julius's request. If so, they wouldn't thank her for spreading stories about her own dissatisfaction.

She was also, admittedly, relieved to be able to leave Marigold out of the conversation. Both her cousins seemed willing to accept that the Legacy's power was enough to explain the misunderstanding, and neither had yet asked about the actual chosen girl. Apparently, their determination to see her situation as a romantic fantasy was too overwhelming.

"If you didn't know this was the prince's betrothal year, does that mean you don't know about this morning, either?"

Nell asked suddenly. "Is that why you ran off and haven't even dressed properly?"

"If you mean, did I know the prince would turn up at our house first thing, I certainly didn't," Olivia said with spirit.

She still thought it was ridiculous that Prince Julius would be hounding her so soon. Wasn't she even allowed to catch her breath?

Nell and Hattie gave a second pair of synchronized gasps. It was usually a trait Olivia found endearing, but she was too tightly wound to appreciate it that morning.

"It's tradition!" Nell cried. "The chosen bride has to leave the ball early and go home—that's part of the original story —but they condense the timeline for the rest. It's not as if the prince needs to search every household to find where she lives. So he always comes first thing the next morning to collect his betrothed and take her back to the palace. If you don't hurry, you'll be late."

"Late for what?" Olivia tried to ignore the sinking sensation in her gut.

"For the betrothal announcement." Hattie dragged Olivia through their front door. "It's at the palace this morning."

"Quick," Nell said, trying to tug her toward the stairs. "We need to get you properly dressed before…"

Her words died as Prince Julius stepped out of the front sitting room, clearly drawn by the sound of their arrival. Olivia swallowed at his appearance. His attire was much closer to the magnificence of the ball the night before than to the well-made but practical clothing he was wearing the first time they met.

He stopped abruptly at sight of her, a strange look on his face, and she was suddenly conscious of her own appearance. No wonder her cousins had been so concerned about how she looked.

The prince cleared his throat. "You're not ready," he said, his deep voice catching her off guard.

She flushed. "Since I wasn't expecting you, no, I'm not."

His eyebrows rose. "Not expecting me?"

"Please accept my apologies, Your Highness." Aunt Helen came out of the sitting room behind him. "I must take responsibility for my niece's ignorance regarding the traditions surrounding your betrothal. I'm sincerely sorry for the mistake." She cast a swift, assessing eye over Olivia. "If you will grant us just a few minutes more, I will ready Olivia for departure. My daughters will keep you company in the meantime." She sent Nell and Hattie a silent command, and both girls curtsied deeply.

"Departure?" Olivia tried to protest, but her aunt already had her by the arm and was starting up the stairs. "In minutes? But—"

Her aunt shushed her, throwing a warning look back down the stairs. She didn't speak until she'd bustled Olivia into Nell's bedchamber and shut the door behind them. Olivia braced herself for a scolding, but it didn't come.

Instead her aunt embraced her, a beaming smile on her face.

"My dear, dear niece," she said. "I don't know how you managed it, but I should have put more faith in the machinations of the Legacy. Even so...You've done very, very well, Olivia dear."

Olivia blinked at her. She had expected her aunt to be happy, but not until after a barrage of questions and perhaps some blustering.

"No, don't try to explain the circumstances," her aunt said, although Olivia had made no attempt to speak. "There isn't time."

She pulled open Nell's wardrobe and rummaged through the gowns inside. "Thankfully, while you have your mother's coloring and face, your figure comes from your father's family. You and Nell could be twins in that regard since she grew those last two inches."

She emerged from the wardrobe, a triumphant smile on her face. "Thank goodness we negotiated a deal with the seamstress by buying several dresses at once. I was planning for Nell to wear this to the royal wedding, so it's unworn."

She held it up to Olivia, who hadn't seen the soft blue gown before. It was hard to take in what was happening, but she couldn't deny a pang of appreciation at the elegant fall of the skirt and the intricate embroidery on the bodice. The material was luxurious, but the style was more understated than her aunt's usual taste.

"Quick!" Aunt Helen said when Olivia didn't move. "Undress as fast as you can, and I'll help you into it."

As she fastened the dress into place, she chattered away. "Of course now that the royal wedding will be a family wedding..." She stopped to chuckle happily. "We'll be able to secure the services of the most sought-after seamstress in the capital. I'll have something even more lovely made for Nell before the big event."

She stepped back and admired Olivia in the dress. "I must say, you look lovely. I'm a fair woman and can admit the dress looks far better on you than it would have on my Nell." Her eyes lifted to Olivia's hair. "We'll have to do something about that, though."

She whisked Olivia into the chair in front of Nell's dressing table and began brushing out her hair. The feel of her hands and the tugging of the brush reminded Olivia so forcefully of her own mother that she had to blink back tears.

Her aunt's movements slowed. "What's wrong, dear?"

Her tone was so gentle that it only made the tears harder to fight. Olivia met her aunt's eyes in the mirror, but she didn't know where to start. She stayed silent.

Her aunt put the brush down with a clack and began twisting Olivia's hair onto her head in a far more expert manner than Olivia had expected.

"You listen to me, Olivia," she said, quietly but fiercely. "I'm not going to pretend it's not a great benefit to our family for you to be crown princess and one day queen. It's beyond anything your uncle or I ever imagined. But we're your family. And that means we're on your side. That prince has his parents and the whole court behind him, but don't you go feeling like you're on your own. You've got us, and if they mistreat you, we won't stand by, royalty or not. There's more than one way to exercise strength, you know."

The tears spilled over Olivia's cheeks, and she sniffed and quickly wiped them away.

"Thank you, Aunt," she managed.

Her aunt put the final pin in her hair and stood back. "There! You look beautiful, my dear, and I'm sure anyone would expect a few emotions from you on a day like today."

Olivia smiled weakly and wiped the last of the moisture from her face. If she was about to face the court, she didn't want to look like she'd just been crying.

She didn't want to face Prince Julius looking like that either. Her aunt had just reminded her that if she wanted to hold her own among the royals, she needed to be strong. And knowing she wasn't as alone as she had felt out on the hill helped.

"Thank you, Aunt Helen," she said when she stood up and surveyed herself in the mirror. "I didn't know you had such skill with hair."

Her aunt grinned. "We weren't always wealthy the way we are now. I did my own hair for years before I could afford a personal maid. But you'd better hurry downstairs as fast as you can. The prince has been waiting long enough."

CHAPTER 11
JULIUS

It took all of Julius's self-control, honed from twenty-one years of royal life, not to pace the entryway. He was barely listening to the chatter of Olivia's cousins. Where was the girl? How could she have been totally unprepared for his arrival? It seemed incredible that she really knew nothing about the traditions for the morning after the ball. Her cousins seemed convinced of her ignorance, though, and they seemed like artless girls.

The sound of footsteps on the stairs made him turn. Something clenched in his chest at the sight of Olivia descending alone, the picture of royal beauty in a light blue dress that emphasized her figure and elegant bearing.

She had already taken him by surprise with her earlier arrival. As someone who had always had to present a polished image, he had expected to find her disheveled appearance and general uncooperativeness off-putting. Instead, he had been knocked off balance by how beautiful she looked without any adornment or effort. In the short hours of their separation, he had already forgotten her beauty.

But that moment had been about her natural beauty. Descending the stairs, she was stunning on a whole different level. Seeing her dressed for their betrothal made it obvious why half his kingdom was convinced he had fallen in love with her. She looked every inch the princess, in both appearance and bearing.

That didn't make the rumors easier to stomach, though. If anything, it made them worse. Apparently he had been besotted by a pretty face.

His hands clenched into fists, but he forced them to relax. Even after the terrible errors of the ball and the discovery that he had to go forward with a betrothal, he had thought his parents would quietly let it be known that a mistake had occurred. So he had been dismayed to learn that, instead, they expected him to do and say nothing to contradict the public's impression of a passionate romance.

The whole business was humiliating. After a lifetime of putting duty to the crown first in all things, Julius had supposedly thrown all of that aside and begged his parents to accommodate some infatuation.

But lurking beneath the humiliation was an even worse fear. Currently, the public mistakenly believed him to have failed in his duty as crown prince, but they were excusing it away with romantic notions of love. If he was forced to spend much time with Olivia, they might soon see missteps they couldn't so easily accept. He couldn't even imagine the errors he might make in the coming weeks. No one had ever thrown him out of his well-practiced role like she did.

And to begin it all, she was running them late. Not that he could show frustration at that. He was permitted only the mask of a man in love.

"You look...lovely," he managed to say in a straight tone. It wasn't the love-struck effusions of a besotted groom, but at least it didn't give away the turmoil within. "We need to leave immediately. The court will be waiting."

"Of course, Your Highness," Olivia's aunt said from behind her. The woman had been barely containing her glee since his arrival, and her excitement grated on his raw nerves. "I'll pack her bags and have them sent to the palace this afternoon."

"What? Bags?" Olivia tried to turn to her aunt, but Julius clamped down on her arm and pulled her inexorably toward the door.

Arriving at the palace a little late was forgivable, but if they didn't get moving, they would be late enough that it would reflect poorly on both of them. The court was waiting in the summer heat, and the new royal couple had enough obstacles to overcome without upsetting the court further.

"We don't have time," he said when she seemed inclined to resist.

She finally relaxed, accepting the necessity, and he immediately let her go. Stepping back, he ushered her through the front door ahead of him.

"You could try being polite about it," she muttered, making him frown.

But he decided it was better not to engage with that sally. He was already fighting hard to keep his emotions from snapping free of the tight hold he had on them.

She stopped outside the manor, blinking at the sight of the two saddled horses and the surrounding honor guard.

"We're riding?" she asked.

A fresh worry hit him. "You can ride, can't you?"

"Thankfully, yes." She sounded as close to snapping as he was. "But only because I grew up on a farm. Neither of my cousins can ride, so in this, at least, you are fortunate I'm not a girl of the capital. Please do try to stop making assumptions."

He nodded tersely before remembering the watching guards.

"Of course. I'm sorry for my oversight." He managed a smile which he hoped was enough to fool their audience as he tossed her up into the saddle.

Olivia's eyes narrowed as she settled onto the horse, but a glance at the surrounding guards made her flush.

"Thank you, Your Highness," she said in a soft voice. Combined with the flush, it painted a more convincing picture than his efforts.

Something shifted in his chest again, and he pushed it ruthlessly aside and swung into his own saddle. Had his compliment earlier sounded as insincere to her as her thanks did to him?

They took off through the streets at a sedate pace, a necessary restriction as they followed the wide road that led through the heart of the capital to the gates of the palace. Their way was lined with crowds on both sides, and the waiting people burst into loud cheers at the sight of the prince and his betrothed.

Olivia blinked, clearly taken off guard by their presence, and he wondered if that was something else he should have warned her about. He was totally unprepared for a bride who knew nothing of royal traditions or court life. And even he hadn't expected the crowds to be so large or so enthusiastic.

After her initial falter, however, Olivia took it in stride, smiling warmly and waving to the crowds. The people cheered even louder in response, and he reluctantly admitted that his parents had been right. The people loved the idea that he had chosen a bride for himself from among their own number. It was better than them thinking the royal family had been tricked into such a momentous decision.

As she waved, Olivia steered her mount close enough to his to allow for conversation beneath the shouts of the crowd. Despite the people around them, there was no one close enough to overhear their words since their guards had taken up positions ahead and behind, leaving enough room to give the crowds a clear view of the royal couple.

"Why is my aunt sending bags to the palace?"

Julius kept his own smile fixed in place, waving at a gaggle of small children who were enthusiastically throwing flowers into the road.

"If you're concerned your clothes aren't fit for the palace and would prefer a whole new wardrobe, I'm sure my mother will be happy to oblige. As my father said, you will receive appropriate care from us for the duration of our betrothal and beyond, if necessary."

Olivia's smile slipped for a moment before she pinned it back in place. "I'm not asking for new clothes! Are you telling me that I'm currently in the middle of moving to the palace? Permanently? Without so much as a by-your-leave—or even a chance to pack?"

"Of course you're moving to the palace." He fought the

frown that tried to creep over his face. "What did you expect? The prince fetches his bride the morning after the ball. That's always been the tradition. They've been readying a suite for you at the palace for weeks."

Olivia arched an eyebrow before waving at a group of young men who were whistling at her a little too enthusiastically. Julius glowered at them, making a group of girls just beyond the men break into sighs and giggles.

"It hasn't been prepared for *me*," she pointed out tartly.

"It wasn't personalized for anyone," he said impatiently. "Marigold's identity was a state secret until last night." He paused. "I suppose it's still a secret." He shot her a glance. "You didn't tell anyone, did you?"

"Of course not." Olivia's voice sounded brittle. "I was told to be a good girl and keep quiet."

Julius stared at her, forgetting for a moment to smile and wave. What was she talking about? Who had dared to talk to her that way after she had been publicly revealed as the future crown princess?

The sudden and unexpected surge of protective anger faded as it occurred to him she might have been talking about him. What had his exact words been at their parting the night before? With all the chaos of everything that had happened, he couldn't remember.

He rubbed the back of his neck. He had intended to counsel her not to discuss too many details of the evening's events in the few hours they were parted—not until they could get their stories straight. But he had hardly been in his usual state of poise. He might have worded it poorly.

He sighed. He had been talking to Olivia, so he almost certainly had worded it poorly. She had that effect on him.

"If you're talking about me," he said stiffly, "that isn't what I meant. I apologize for my poor communication. I'm sure you can understand that I was in a state of shock."

Olivia gave him a sideways look that he didn't like.

"Another apology," she said, as if that was a bad thing.

He frowned before swiftly turning the expression back into a smile and giving an extra enthusiastic wave to compensate. If only he could go back to their first meeting and start all over again. Or better yet, if only he'd never gone walking behind Manor Row at all. If Olivia had been a complete stranger at the ball, they would surely have gotten off to a better start—one in which the Legacy aided their connection instead of abandoning him completely. Maybe then, Olivia wouldn't make him so uncomfortable. Maybe she wouldn't have the ability to worm under his skin and make him behave unlike himself.

"The apology is sincere, whatever you may think," he said, wishing he didn't sound so stiff.

Olivia turned her large, luminous eyes on him, their expression clearly unconvinced. He bit back a retort. It was hardly the time or place to begin an argument with his new betrothed.

They finally reached the end of the road, passing through the great gates in the outer wall of the palace and riding into the enormous courtyard beyond. However, the walls provided no privacy. They were merely exchanging one crowd for another.

Members of the court stood gathered together in front of the palace steps, and they turned as one to watch the riders arrive. Unlike the people of the city, they didn't cheer or call to the prince and his betrothed, instead watching quietly as they rode through the courtyard. The prince led Olivia down the right side of the palace, grateful that they would have the chance to dismount away from the scrutiny, at least.

From the stiffness of Olivia's riding stance, she felt the same. She wasn't even attempting to smile at this crowd as she had done at the previous one.

Their honor guard melted away, and the two of them were alone when they reached the smaller courtyard between the back of the palace and the stables. Julius leaped from his mount and moved straight to Olivia's side, reaching up his arms to help her dismount. He would show her that he knew how to be charming, with or without the Legacy's help.

She accepted his assistance silently, sliding down the side of her horse until her feet hit the ground. When she looked up at him, the two of them were so close their clothes brushed against each other.

"Is there sincerity waiting for me here?" she murmured, referencing his earlier comment about his apology. "I'm not so sure about that yet."

He stiffened, unsure if it was her words or her proximity that put him on edge.

"We're all doing the best we can with a bad situation," he said, heat rushing through him. "A situation that was not of my or my family's making."

"Thank you for the reminder that this is all my fault." Her breath came sharper, her chest rising and falling and her cheeks flushing.

Julius stared down into her eyes, caught by their bright spark as the rising storm of heat between the two of them grew. He needed to calm the situation down—a skill at which he usually excelled. But as usual around Olivia, he couldn't find the right words. He couldn't find any words.

It was Olivia who broke the moment. "I'm already well aware of how you feel about having me as your betrothed. You don't need to keep reminding me."

For a strange moment, Julius wanted to tell her she was wrong. That she had no idea how he felt about their betrothal—sham or not. But then he remembered himself. He couldn't afford to be shackled to the girl from the hill for the rest of his life—too much rode on his ability to fulfill his role at all times.

At the same moment, he realized that she didn't even know the worst of it yet. He hadn't yet relayed his parents' orders about their supposed shared affection. She wasn't likely to receive the news well now. He should have been more careful about keeping the conversation amicable.

"Regardless of how either of us feel," he said carefully, "the public has formed their own impression of our situation."

"I heard," Olivia said, and he told himself the sensation in his chest was relief that he wouldn't have to spell it out and not hurt at her sour tone. She really didn't like the idea.

He skipped straight to the important point. "My parents informed me this morning that they intend to lean into the public perception rather than publicizing the case of mistaken identity. So they want us to..."

He trailed off, not quite able to say the final words.

"They want us to act the part?" Olivia asked incredulously. "Are you serious?" Her breathing sped up, her face growing panicked. "This is difficult enough for me as it is without adding anything more. I know nothing about life at court."

"I'm sorry it's so difficult to pretend any attraction to me," he said, the words coming out more coldly than he'd intended.

He almost flushed at making his offense so obvious. As if he didn't seem awkward enough already.

Olivia looked up at him, an arrested expression on her face.

"I didn't mean...That is...I wasn't trying to say..." Her face turned red, and she floundered to a stop.

Julius expected to feel a spear of triumph at not being the one flustered and stumbling for words for once, but instead he felt guilty and disappointed in himself. What had happened to his resolution to show her his famous charm? Wasn't he supposed to be capable of putting anyone at ease?

With yet another flush, he realized that he was practically standing with her in his arms, her back trapped against the horse. For someone who made him so uncomfortable, she fit neatly inside his arms.

He stepped swiftly back, putting some distance between them. She stepped away from her horse more cautiously, her movement a signal to the grooms who had been hanging back. They rushed in to take the horse's reins, and from the smirks on their faces, they hadn't missed the accidental embrace. Julius and Olivia were playing their part well enough already.

Julius cleared his throat and offered her his arm, remembering what still lay before them. "We need to walk through the palace and join my parents on the front steps. They will make the official announcement of the betrothal from there.”

He half expected her to protest or make some complaint, but she merely took his arm and walked silently beside him through the long length of the palace. From the surreptitious glances she kept casting left and right, he suspected it was their surroundings and not his presence that had inspired a mood of respectful silence. Unlike Julius himself, the castle never faltered in its royal bearing.

He winced. Jealous of his own castle now.

His mother threw a look over her shoulder at them as they approached, and Julius could easily read her relief and impatience. They were brushing the edges of unacceptable tardiness. He should have hurried Olivia along more effectively instead of getting caught up in…Whatever that had been outside the stables.

The two of them stepped up to stand on his father’s other side, and the murmurs of the crowd died down.

“Welcome!” the king boomed out in a great voice, losing no time in addressing the crowd. “It is with great pleasure that I announce the success of my son’s search. He has found his bride!”

The crowd cheered—playing their role with muted effort, a contrast to the genuine enthusiasm of the people who had lined the street. The ordinary citizens were delighted he had chosen one of them, but the court were more cautious, still waiting to see if they had cause for offense.

Julius gazed down at Olivia, letting every bit of his admiration show on his face. It was easier than he had expected to manage a proud smile. And when she glanced shyly up at him before blushing and looking away, the murmur that ran through the crowd was warmer. Apparently his parents had read the mood of their people correctly. At least for the moment Julius and Olivia would have to sell their charade.

Part of him feared it would prove too difficult. But a smaller, more terrifying, part feared it might be far too easy.

CHAPTER 12

JULIUS

Thankfully, there were no official functions organized for immediately after the announcement. The crowd hung around in gossiping clumps for a short time before dispersing completely. They were likely all still tired after the Midsummer Ball the night before.

But Julius and Olivia couldn't escape his parents. His father led the four of them into a small receiving room, reserved for more intimate gatherings, where his mother sank into a chair and began vigorously fanning herself.

"It's far too hot for so early in the morning," she complained, her eyes narrowing as they settled on Julius. "Or maybe that was just the stress of worrying that you might fail to arrive."

"I'm sorry, Your Majesties." Olivia sank into a deep curtsy. "That was my fault. It was another misunderstanding. I was unaware of the traditions for the morning after the ball and wasn't expecting such an early visit from His Highness, let alone the need to be ready for an official function."

His mother straightened and ran an assessing eye from Olivia's hair to her feet. "You did a good job in that case," she said with more knowledgeable admiration than Julius had been able to give.

Olivia smiled slightly. "My aunt helped me."

The door opened without a knock, and an unassuming man in palace livery entered. Julius recognized him at once as his father's most trusted aide.

The king stepped aside to conduct a quiet conversation with the man while his mother began a conversation with Olivia about the finer details of her dress. They moved quickly to a discussion of the dresses the queen intended to order for Olivia now that she was to reside at the palace and take part in court events. Despite Olivia's earlier insistence that she wasn't after a new wardrobe, she didn't seem to have any objection to the queen's plans.

When the aide disappeared, Julius's father rejoined them, a thoughtful look on his face. He directed his first words to his son.

"Are the reports exaggerated or was the reaction of the crowd on the street as enthusiastic as claimed?"

"I've never seen them like that," Julius said honestly. He glanced at Olivia and away again before adding, "They love her."

"They don't know me," Olivia said firmly, apparently determined to be part of the conversation despite her lack of status.

"They love having one of their own chosen as the future queen," his father said in a considering tone. "Perhaps there are more silver linings to this situation than we first envisaged."

His mother looked Olivia over with a new eye. "Perhaps this betrothal will be an opportunity for the people to see themselves represented at court. Olivia can not only represent the interests of the people but better help us understand their perspectives. I have been wondering for some time if we have raised Julius at too great a distance from his own city."

Julius shot her a surprised look. He hadn't known she was worried about that.

Could she be right? Was he disconnected from the common people? The sense of failure from his first meeting with Olivia washed over him again. Apparently he was even worse at his role than he had suspected.

"I don't think I can be much assistance there," Olivia said, cutting across both his thoughts and the conversation.

All three turned toward her, creases on both his parents' brows. "Unless you want to know what the people of the small town of Henton think," she added, "or perhaps my relatives in Manor Row. I'm not a native of the capital, and I've hardly even had a chance to explore it. I probably know less about the city and its inhabitants than Julius."

"I see," the queen said slowly, exchanging a look with her husband.

Irritation swept over Julius. Did Olivia always have to be so contrary? Was she trying to make her situation more difficult? They were all trying to do their best—even if Julius's best was apparently short of where it needed to be.

Olivia drew a deep breath. "There's nothing I can do about my past ignorance and inexperience. I can only improve for the future. I am well aware I have a lot to learn if I'm going to manage my role creditably—even if it is only a temporary role. So while I might not have much of value to bring, I am ready to learn and want to assure you that I will be a willing and enthusiastic student."

For a moment Julius let himself remember all the aspects of royal life that he did know well. In teaching Olivia, perhaps he would finally have a chance to show her his true capabilities. The pleasant image lasted for only a moment before she turned to his mother.

"I stand ready to be your pupil, Your Majesty."

His mother immediately softened. When she married Crown Prince Robert, she had known that the two of them would only ever have one child, and that the Legacy would ensure it was a son. But Julius knew she had grieved not being able to have more children—especially a daughter. She was delighted at the prospect of not only dressing Olivia but also training her to fill the same role she herself filled.

He tried not to let any disappointment show. He tried not to *feel* any disappointment.

But when his parents were called away, leaving him alone in the receiving room with Olivia, he couldn't stop himself speaking.

"You might find I have something to teach you as well, even if I'm just the prince." He heard the self-mocking note and changed tack. "And what of you? Don't you think you might be selling yourself short? Surely you have something you can—"

"Selling myself short?" Olivia, who had wandered to one of the windows, whirled around. "I have no idea what to do in this situation! Nothing in my life has prepared me for this. I suppose you think I'm just trying to be difficult, but I would far rather undersell myself than oversell. I have no desire to raise false expectations I can't possibly fulfill. I was only speaking the truth. I *don't* know the capital." She drew in an angry breath. "Don't you think enough damage has already been done from misunderstandings? I don't want to be the cause of any more."

Defensiveness surged in Julius, but the wild look in her eyes made him pause. He wasn't even sure if she was angry at him or just overwhelmed, and if he was honest, some of his irritability toward her had come from a similar place. Underneath it all, the two of them weren't so different. In the last week, he had also had reason to question if he was fit for his role, and the question had scared him as much as it seemed to scare her.

He gave a half bow. "My apologies."

"Those again," she muttered, making his brow crease.

They might be the same in some ways, but they were still a world apart. What did she have against his apologies? Her presence seemed to make him constantly misstep, and surely it was better that he apologized than not.

"Don't worry," he said after an awkward pause. "My parents have a whole team of scholars and historians scouring the kingdom's records and history books for any overlooked aspect of the Legacy that we might use to escape our...predicament."

A lovely way to describe a betrothal. But he knew she would think it was apt.

"So much trouble caused by one pair of glass slippers," she murmured. From her manner, his words hadn't inspired much hope.

His stomach twisted at the idea that any girl would

consider it a hopeless prospect to be tied to him. Even if he did feel the same way about being tied to her.

Mostly.

"Do you really think there's any chance they'll find something new about the Legacy after centuries?" she asked doubtfully.

Despite himself, he wanted to give her hope and see her smile again. "There are still parts of the Legacy that are unfamiliar," he offered. "Even after all this time, scholars are still debating what part of Sovar's history causes the Legacy to create treacherous ground anywhere there is particular natural beauty."

"That's true," Olivia conceded, perhaps remembering his own near fall, as he was. "But that's not exactly the same as an undiscovered aspect of the Legacy."

Julius shrugged, unable to think of anything to say that wouldn't sound depressing. Olivia turned away from him and pointed to a stack of paper and a pot of ink on a desk in the corner of the room.

"If I write a letter, will you see that it's delivered for me?"

Julius frowned at the sudden change of topic. "Of course."

She smiled at last, although he didn't feel he'd earned it with such a measly act of service.

"If I'm to live at the palace," she said, "I have a couple of requirements."

Julius's frown deepened.

She gave him a level stare. "I think that's fair enough given everything I'm being asked to sacrifice."

He considered pointing out that her sacrifice was exchanging the life of a servant for one of a princess but decided against it. He, of all people, knew that giving up your freedom was a sacrifice, regardless of what trappings of rank came with it.

"What are your requirements?" he asked instead. "I'll grant them if I can."

"Princesses have ladies-in-waiting, don't they?" she asked. "Or something similar."

"My mother doesn't call them that, but she has noble women of the court who act as her companions and assist her with social events and the like, so I suppose that's the same thing," he said.

Olivia nodded. "I want to select one for myself for as long as I'm living here and invite her to join me at the palace." She saw his raised brow and quickly added, "I'm not trying to bring anyone unsuitable to court. I just want to invite a member of my family to stay with me, and I want to be sure she'll be treated well. Surely that's acceptable."

"Certainly," he said, relieved her request was such an easy one to grant. He didn't even need to check with his parents. "I can see no possible objection to that."

She nodded. "I also have a...pet." His eyes narrowed at her hesitation, but she kept her chin raised defiantly. "I will only agree to live at the palace if I can bring her with me and care for her here."

"You want to bring your cat with you?" Julius asked, biting back a smile.

"Mildred is not a cat," Olivia said. "But the same prin-ciple applies."

Julius shrugged. "The palace has plenty of rat catchers and a number of dogs who run tame inside. I don't see how one more animal would cause any trouble."

Olivia smiled. "In that case, we have an agreement." She walked to the door but stopped partway with a grimace. "I think I'd better add a third request. I'm going to need someone to show me around for a while. The palace is enormous, and I already have no idea where I am right now."

Julius laughed. "Don't worry. You'll have plenty of maids and footmen at your service. In fact, I predict you won't be able to turn around without tripping over one. Everyone in Sovar is curious about you right now."

Her smile disappeared, and he kicked himself for once again saying the wrong thing to her.

"You can always order them to leave if you're uncomfortable," he said, trying to mend matters.

"Unfortunately, I suspect that's going to be all the time," she muttered, almost too quietly for him to hear.

Olivia spent the rest of that day and all of the next closeted with his mother and a series of experts chosen by the queen. Their role was to educate the new princess on various aspects of court behavior and court life.

Julius might have felt sorry for her if he wasn't similarly cloistered. Apparently his father's way of taking the temperature of his court and city was to have a private meeting with every noble of significance and a number of the more influential merchants. And he insisted his son join him.

The only saving grace was that for once his allocated role didn't require rigid restraint. He was playing the lovesick groom, so his father welcomed small signs of his impatience

—it gave the king an opportunity to insert a humorous remark about where his son would rather be. No one failed to chuckle in response to the suggestion that the prince would rather be with a certain beautiful young lady than stuck in a meeting.

He pretended to take the humor with good grace, despite his irritation at the entire situation, and at least he enjoyed the opportunity to look as bored as he felt. He expected the evening would bring an opportunity to check on Olivia, but they didn't even eat together at the end of their first official day as a betrothed couple. His father was hosting a select number of powerful guests, and his mother had sent word that Olivia wasn't yet ready to join such an illustrious group.

His father had neatly sidestepped the issue by making it a male-only affair. The adjustment allowed the queen to escape but didn't grant the same freedom to Julius. And by the time he was finally released, Olivia had already retired to her bedchamber, the external door to her suite firmly latched.

By the end of the second long day, Julius's patience was wearing too thin even for his father's false teasing to cover. It was only with enormous restraint that he maintained the necessary polite behavior. The day would come when he was king and such meetings would be unavoidable, but his mind was still in too much turmoil from his botched betrothal to bear the constraint easily. He longed to be among his own peers, discovering their reaction to the news—however painful those reactions might be—rather than spending every hour of the day shut up with his father's peers.

The last guest to be ushered in made him straighten with interest, however. Walter was the successful man of business

Olivia called uncle, and Julius examined him closely. He was unassuming in appearance, with no noticeable presence. But as the conversation progressed, Julius caught the keen light of intelligence in his eyes, and though he allowed the king to dominate the conversation, he responded with sense and insight.

"I can't say I'm a social man myself, Your Majesty," he said with a chuckle. "I leave that side of things to my wife."

"You are a man of business," the king said with a smile of his own. "And from what I hear a very good one. We cannot all be skilled in every area."

"You flatter me, Your Majesty." Walter looked pleased at the king's words, but after a moment's hesitation he straightened his back. "I was honored to be asked here today, just as my family is honored by your selection of our Olivia as the prince's betrothed." He bowed slightly toward Julius. "She is an excellent girl and has our full support and confidence." For the first time he held the king's eye, his back straight, and the subtle message was clear.

Julius raised his brows, pleasantly surprised. Apparently Olivia's family were willing to fight for her if it was needed. He had feared they held her in low esteem given her place in their household, but the situation must have been more nuanced than he realized.

Still, he wished the man had shown similar resolution when it came to his wife's treatment of Olivia when she first arrived with them. If they had treated her fully as family then, none of them might be in their current predicament.

He waited impatiently as his father concluded the meeting and finally—finally—released Julius, saying he would not be needed the next day. Julius hurried straight to his mother's favorite sitting room.

Stepping inside, he bowed politely to the queen, even while his eyes flicked around the room. Disappointment surged when he saw she was alone.

"Where's Olivia?" he blurted out.

His mother regarded him with a slight raise to her brows and a mysterious smile that wavered between amusement and curiosity. He winced internally. What was she reading in his face and bearing? Did she understand his reactions? Because he didn't understand them himself.

"Your father's meetings ran long." She gestured toward a small table still laden with the remains of a hearty supper. "Lady Olivia and I have already eaten, and she has retired early for the night."

"Again?" He bit out the word between clenched teeth.

His mother shook her head at him, her expression chiding, and he flushed as if he were once again a small boy being chastised for impatience.

"Your betrothed has a great deal to learn," his mother said in a firm tone. "And she has dedicated herself to her studies just as she promised. She is already making excellent progress, and I am greatly pleased with her. It's hardly surprising that she's exhausted by the end of each day."

"My apologies." Julius gave another shallow bow, and his mother softened.

"You were always a dedicated student as well, my son. Don't think I'm unaware of the sacrifices your position requires of you."

Julius's shoulders straightened, and she smiled at him, her eyes gleaming.

"While Olivia still has various intricacies to master, she has now covered enough of the basics that she can be trusted outside this room. Her lessons will continue at a gentler pace and without my supervision. I have given her the morning off tomorrow." She paused, her smile growing. "I'll inform your father that you also need to be released so you can show her around in a more informal capacity."

Julius strode over and dropped a kiss on the top of his mother's head.

"Thank you, Mother. If I have to attend another meeting without a break, I might lose my patience completely and disgrace the family. You always could read me best."

"Can I?" she asked lightly, her eyes glowing.

He stepped back warily, but whatever she was supposedly reading in him now, she kept it to herself. And as he departed to find his own supper and bed, he walked with a buoyancy to his step. The next day he would finally have a chance to see his friends and discover what they thought of Olivia.

CHAPTER 13
OLIVIA

Olivia woke with a feeling of relief. The bed and room no longer caught her by surprise, as they had the first morning, and she was finally going to be given some space to breathe. Her lessons didn't start until the afternoon.

She spread out, letting herself luxuriate in the softness of the sheets and the perfect tension of the mattress. At home in Henton she had enjoyed the luxury of her own bed only because all five of her siblings were brothers. The bed itself hadn't been near so fine. And at her aunt and uncle's house she had been given a guest room that was pleasant in appearance but possessed an overly firm mattress and sheets that were worn thin from long use.

Sunlight streamed through the window since she had left the curtains open the night before, wanting to watch the stars as she fell asleep. Given she was on the second story of the palace, she didn't have to worry about privacy, and she was determined to enjoy something about her new position. There had been little else to enjoy so far.

She propped herself up on her hands and surveyed the room, admiring the green velvet, gold highlights, and the repeated motif of twining vines. If she was honest, her room wasn't quite the only positive. The food was even nicer than at her aunt's house, and the nightgown she currently wore was the softest she had ever owned.

But she hadn't expected the lessons from the queen to prove more exhausting—to both body and mind—than a full day's work in her aunt's house. Perhaps she hadn't truly appreciated how much the Legacy helped with her chores. She certainly hadn't realized how mentally exhausting it was to try to absorb so much new information at once. She felt as if her head was bursting.

She slipped out of bed and wandered to the window. She suspected that if she'd left the outer door of her suite unlatched, she would have woken to fresh wash water and a hot breakfast. But she had no desire for strangers to come creeping through her room while she slept. The ability to lock herself securely away from everyone and everything at the end of the day had been the only thing keeping her sane through the whirlwind of the last forty-eight hours.

Gazing across the large grounds at the back of the palace, she drew a deep breath. As overwhelming as it had all been —from endless curtsies, to the dress fittings, to the etiquette lessons, and the charts of the major noble families and important businesses of the capital—she had to admit she felt more prepared for what awaited her in the palace than she had when she rode through its gates.

Of course, she had only learned the most superficial level of correct conduct. She wouldn't make the mistake of thinking she was ready to hold her own amidst the intrigue and social hierarchies of court. But at least she was no longer in danger of bumbling into a mistake that would reveal a shameful level of ignorance.

And the lessons would continue until she was fully confident. Eventually she would even be able to reach for the correct fork without needing to peek at her dining companions—a practice the queen had kindly assured her was more common than she might have thought.

She leaned on the windowsill, watching the distant gardeners moving through the grounds. Apparently, it was too early for the court to be out strolling the carefully laid paths. Maybe she would spend her morning outside, exploring the gardens from the ground level. She only wished she had a companion to explore it with.

Her letter to Daphne had been sent by royal express, so it should reach her soon. But would her cousin agree to come? And if she did, how long would it take her to arrive? It was no small thing to travel between kingdoms.

Olivia had written the letter out of desperation, knowing it wasn't a small request. Being so close in age, she and Daphne had corresponded for years, despite Daphne living in Glandore. But while Daphne might live in Glandore, she was no stranger to travel, having been born in Oakden.

Like everyone except the small band of roving merchants, Daphne and Olivia were both tied to their birth kingdoms by their kingdoms' Legacies. They could physically leave, but the Legacies would extract a price for the duration of their absence—one that varied from person to person and Legacy to Legacy. But the cost was high enough that it put most people off the idea of travel between kingdoms. Most merchant trains met at specified border locations and exchanged goods with their counterparts from the kingdom on the other side of the border.

The Legacy's price was the reason the king and queen of Sovar never chose foreign royalty for their son's bride, and it had kept Olivia and Daphne from spending time together in person, with a single exception. When they were seven, Daphne's parents had brought her through Henton en route between their decade-long sojourn in Oakden and their original home in Glandore.

But their flight home—necessitated by a decade of struggling under the Legacy's burden—had transferred that burden onto their daughter, who had been born during their years in Oakden. Even as a child, Olivia had thought that unfair. It was Daphne's parents who had chosen to move in the first place, and they were the ones who had made the decision to move home, though Daphne paid the price.

But Daphne had taken it in her stride. Even at seven, she had been a calm, unflappable person. And fortunately, her individual burden wasn't one of pain, merely inconvenience.

Knowing Daphne wasn't in her home kingdom anyway was the one reason Olivia had been willing to write and ask her to come. Daphne would suffer no more in Sovar than she already did in Glandore.

The last time they had spoken, Prince Julius had reminded Olivia that he had a whole team of scholars on his side. He had a whole palace—a whole kingdom—behind him. But Olivia was alone at court.

But that didn't mean she was truly alone. Aunt Helen had reminded her that her family, at least, would be on her side, and the family member Olivia most wanted in the palace with her was Daphne. Daphne would be far better equipped to handle the environment than Nell or Hattie, and she had the added advantage of not being a subject of Olivia's husband-to-be. Daphne, alone, had little to lose if she angered the royal family. If it came to it, she could simply return home to Oakden, as she had always planned to do once she reached adulthood.

Olivia shook herself. She trusted Daphne would eventually arrive, but for now, she had no companion for a morning outing. And she should be doing something more productive with her time off, anyway. Her aunt had sent Olivia's clothing and other belongings to the palace, but when packing up her room, she had missed Olivia's most prized possession.

Olivia couldn't blame her for doing so since Olivia had kept its existence a secret and even hidden it within her room. But she was eager to visit her old home to retrieve it—especially since the item might prove to be an excellent assistance in her new role.

If she didn't go that morning, she didn't know when she'd have another opportunity. And she needed to collect Mildred as well. Given the mouse's new size, Olivia feared that every day she wasn't under Olivia's protection put her at risk.

Olivia unlatched the external door in her sitting room before retreating to her bedchamber to dress for the day. Her new wardrobe from the queen hadn't been delivered yet, but her aunt had included some of Nell's nicer gowns along with Olivia's practical dresses, and after some hesitation, she chose one of those. While her planned activities didn't include mingling with the court, she couldn't be sure who she might run into. After all her hard work of the last two days, she didn't want to disgrace the queen the first time she was left to her own devices.

After struggling into the chosen gown without assistance, Olivia was pleased to find a breakfast tray had been delivered to the small table in her sitting room. Breakfast had arrived quickly on the previous morning as well, and she was half-convinced the servants had someone on watch to check when she unlatched her door.

She ate in the pleasant room, her amused glance dwelling on the single glass slipper displayed in a prominent position, protected by a glass dome. Apparently, that was why the prince had needed it that night after the ball. Anyone who entered her suite needed to be reminded of her role in the Legacy.

She had just polished off the last bite of the delicious repast, when the door to her sitting room swung open, making her start and spill her hot chocolate. She turned an annoyed frown on Prince Julius.

"Don't you know how to knock?" She looked around for something to mop up the spilled drops of chocolate.

The prince—she really needed to think of him as Julius now they were formally betrothed—stepped forward, looking like he intended to take over the task, but she gestured for him to keep his distance, and he stopped. She wiped up the spill while he sighed, presumably with impatience.

"Have I come too early?" he asked. "You struck me as an early riser."

She put down the cloth and stood to face him. "Early or late, you can still knock."

He raised a brow. "It's not as if I entered your bedchamber. This is a room meant for visiting, and I am your betrothed."

"In name only," she snapped, trying to control her rising indignation. None of the court would treat her with respect if her own betrothed did not.

He ran a hand through his hair. "How about we start again? I'm sorry for startling you. I'll make sure to give you warning of my entrance next time."

"Thank you," she said stiffly. "But what are you doing here? Queen Elsinore said I had the day off."

Surprise showed in his eyes, and something almost like hurt flashed across his features, quickly suppressed. Olivia frowned. What was she missing?

"Yes," he said carefully, "she said you had the day free of lessons so that I can show you around the palace and introduce you to some of the younger members of court."

Olivia's horror must have shown in her eyes because he quickly added, "I don't mean any formal functions, of course. It's supposed to be a day off. Just an informal tour and a few introductions. They're all dying to meet you, I'm sure."

Olivia opened her mouth only to close it again. She didn't think it would be a good idea to say any of the things running through her mind. And she was surprised to find that she didn't want to cause that look of hurt to return to his face. What he was describing sounded more stressful than the difficult two days of lessons—but he clearly had no idea that was the case.

Had she misunderstood Queen Elsinore entirely? Olivia

had thought she was being offered a break, but perhaps the queen had always intended the morning to be an initial test of her lessons. If so, Olivia had promised to devote herself to her studies, and she didn't want to make trouble over something that had to happen eventually.

She sighed. "I suppose I'll have to find another time for my own plans, then."

Julian's brows drew together. "Your own plans?"

"Yes," Olivia said tartly. "I do have those, you know. I had a whole life before I made the terrible mistake of wearing glass slippers to your ball."

She bit down on her tongue, annoyed at herself. She had resolved to keep her irritation to herself and had immediately failed. She was going to have to show better control if she wanted to survive at court.

"I had intended to visit my aunt's home and collect a few of my items that were left behind," she said in a politer tone.

Julius continued to gaze at her silently, so she didn't attempt any further explanation. Instead, she crossed to a mirror to check her hair. Now that she knew about the actual plans for the day, she wished she'd rung for someone to help her put it up instead of doing a simple style herself.

"Don't worry," Julius said. "It looks nice."

Her hands stilled against her head, and she threw him a look. He finally looked away from her, and she frowned. He must be impatient to get going.

But when she walked over to join him, he didn't move, instead looking down at her with an expression she couldn't read.

"I'll talk to my mother," he said, "and make sure she doesn't schedule any lessons for tomorrow morning. I believe she's planning a more sustainable schedule going forward anyway."

"Thank you," Olivia said, touched by his thoughtfulness. She had attributed his steadfast gaze to annoyance over her outburst, but he had been thinking about how to fix the problem he had created.

He smiled back at her, and her breath caught. Why did he have to look so attractive when he smiled? And what was wrong with her feelings? One minute she was forgetting his true status and snapping at him as if he were nothing more than the stranger on the hill. The next minute she was all too aware that he was the handsome prince who featured in many girls' dreams.

It was hard enough to stay on guard without him confusing her with unnecessary smiles and small acts of consideration. Olivia couldn't afford to get too involved with either Julius, the man, or Julius, the crown prince. His parents were actively seeking a way to dissolve the betrothal, and when they succeeded, Olivia would never see Julius again. She just needed to get through that time without making a fool of herself—or the royal family—in front of the court.

Julius's smile dimmed when she didn't return it, but he nodded and led her through the palace, moving along an unfamiliar route. Despite it being her third day of residence in the palace, she had still seen little of the building beyond the ballroom, the queen's receiving room, and her own suite.

The path they walked still felt familiar, however, thanks to the consistent white marble of the corridors with accents of aquamarine to match the tower roofs. It was more airy than such a large building had any right to be, aided by internal courtyards and long stretches of corridor with only pillars to support the roof instead of full walls.

Julius walked with purpose, and Olivia had to extend her stride to keep up. The further they went, the more he radiated a subtle, tense excitement. On both the last two days, the queen had mentioned he was busy in meetings with the king, and for the first time it occurred to her that he might have spent the time since their betrothal feeling as trapped as she had.

"Where exactly are we going?" she asked as they rounded another corner.

He slowed. "I thought we would start by introducing you to my closest friends. The most likely place to find them at this hour is in our courtyard."

"You and your friends have your own courtyard?" Olivia asked before she remembered he was the one and only prince. He could probably have as many courtyards as he wanted.

He chuckled. "It doesn't officially belong to us. But the guards train in practice yards behind the palace, next to their barracks, and traditionally this courtyard has been used for the same purpose for the young men of court—at least the ones with families powerful enough to keep suites in the palace as well as houses on Manor Row."

"And those are your friends." Olivia tried not to sound dismayed.

Julius shrugged. "Growing up, they were the only boys my own age that I knew. Since there are only five of us, we grew accustomed to always being together."

Hearing him describe friendship that way made Olivia feel a reluctant twinge of pity. But it wasn't really that different from her own experience growing up in Henton. There had been a limited number of girls her own age, and she had considered herself friends—or at least friendly—with them all, even if she'd had no particular close friend beyond her distant cousin. Apparently growing up in a palace or a small town wasn't so dissimilar after all.

"It was the same for me in Henton," she ventured.

She had just been lecturing herself on keeping an emotional distance from Julius, but she couldn't distance herself too effectively. They needed to establish some small sense of rapport before their stumbling, awkward interactions alerted the court to the true state of affairs between them.

"Do you miss your friends and family there?" he asked, but she couldn't tell if he was truly interested or just being polite.

"Sometimes," she answered truthfully. "And sometimes I feel guilty that I don't miss them more. But while I'm fond of my five younger brothers, they are high-energy and exhausting, and I never got any space to myself. Besides, my closest friend is actually a cousin who lives in Glandore, so I've been able to correspond with her from the capital as easily as I could from Henton."

"You have a cousin in Glandore?" Now the prince was definitely interested. "That's unusual."

Olivia nodded. "Daphne is actually the one I've asked to come and stay with me. Since you said I could have a family member to keep me company here."

"If she's from Glandore, she'll attract interest from the court," Julius said. "At least among the younger members. Even here at the palace it's rare for us to get foreign delegations, and they seldom stay long. They find it too uncomfortable."

Olivia had no chance to reply before they turned into a large courtyard, more sparsely decorated than the ones they had previously passed. A large clear area gave room for the casual sparring session currently taking place between two young men. Decorative greenery ringed the courtyard, however, and in one corner a small fountain was positioned next to several seats. Two more young men lounged on the seats, calling occasional jokes or encouragement to the sparring men.

All four of them were tall, well-dressed, confident, and imposing in Olivia's eyes. She fell back a couple steps without meaning to do so, bracing herself for their unknown reception to her and Julius's supposed romance.

One of the seated men—a dark-haired, good-looking young man with a friendly face—spotted the new arrivals first. He leaped to his feet with a glad cry of "Julius" before his eyes fell on Olivia, slightly behind the prince.

His brows quirked, and he looked blankly shocked for a moment. But he recovered quickly, his easy smile returning as he bowed low in her direction. His movement caught the attention of the others, and the sparring match broke off, all three men turning curious eyes on Olivia.

"Well, well, well," drawled a second dark-haired young man, wiping the sweat off his brow with one arm as he slid his sword back into its scabbard. "This is an unexpected pleasure."

Olivia, who had given the first young man a friendly smile, gave this second one a more wary look. His lazy tones hid a mocking hint that she didn't know how to read.

"You've been released from your punishment, then?" the first asked Julius with a chuckle, ignoring the sally of the fencer.

Looking between them, Olivia noted a resemblance that was strong enough to mark them as brothers, although their manner was entirely different.

Julius clapped the first man on the back with a smile even broader than his friend's. "They couldn't keep me shut up forever."

"I never thought I'd live to see you defy your parents, Julius," the second man said, a gleam in his eyes as he surveyed Olivia. "But then I only got back from my trip to Marleston yesterday. Now that I've seen her beauty for myself, it all becomes clearer."

Julius stiffened, stepping back toward Olivia, and she had to stop herself shrinking behind him.

"Her name is Olivia," he said sternly. "Lady Olivia to you."

"*Lady* Olivia?" the other member of the sparring pair asked, raising one eyebrow.

Olivia shifted slightly, her initial discomfort at the false title returning in full force. But the open curiosity on the face of the second fencer was at least easier to read than the subtle tone of his opponent, and there was no point trying to hide her situation.

"According to King Robert, the betrothed of the crown prince needs a courtesy title, at least." She smiled at the fair-haired young fencer.

Both his brows shot up, and he threw his head back and laughed. "You're not like I imagined. But I can see why our friend here was captivated." He gave her a shallow bow, still smiling when he straightened.

Olivia grinned at the fair-haired man's laughing compliment, feeling none of the discomfort she'd done at his opponent's earlier comment.

"My apologies, Lady Olivia," the dark-haired fencer said smoothly, mimicking his opponent's bow. "Naturally I meant no disrespect."

Olivia returned his smile with less ease, although she scolded herself for being overly sensitive. She had no understanding of the dynamics between these men, let alone between their important families, and she wouldn't do herself any favors by imagining offense where there was probably none intended.

"The graceless one is Zane," Julius said to Olivia, nodding in his direction. "He's Lord Strathmore's eldest and was away on business for his father, so he missed the ball."

He nodded at the fair-haired fencer next. "And that one is Ashton, the baby of the group."

Lord Ashton rolled his eyes. "I'll be twenty-one next year! I'm only a year younger than you and Cade, and less than three behind Zane and Kasper. I even beat Kasper in our match yesterday—if he's man enough to admit it since the other two weren't here."

"Of course I admit it," said the fourth young man, finally rising from his seat by the fountain.

His expression was guarded, giving nothing away, and Olivia found him even more intimidating than Zane. He bowed respectfully in her direction, however.

"I'm most interested to make your acquaintance, Lady

Olivia," he said, and she finally saw a gleam of emotion in his eyes, reflecting the truth behind his words.

Julius stepped closer to her again, a warning look on his face as he gazed at his friend.

"She's my betrothed, Kasper," he said.

His incongruous warning made Olivia examine Kasper again, her eyes lingering on his burnished bronze hair with its hints of red. She stiffened as she realized what she should have recognized at once.

The youngest of Marigold's three older brothers was called Kasper, and she shouldn't have needed the flash of familiar red to remember it. Unlike the others, his interest in her stemmed from knowing the truth of the original arrangements and at least something of the mix-up that had followed.

She wanted to ask Kasper about Marigold's current whereabouts—surely she had returned home by that point —but she didn't dare say anything in front of the others. As far as she knew, only Marigold's family and the royal family knew the truth of the original choice of betrothed for the prince.

"Welcome to the palace, Lady Olivia," said the final young man—the first to have greeted Julius. He smiled and bowed in her direction. "Ignore the rest of these fools. We're delighted to see Julius meet his match at last."

He might be the younger brother of the mocking Zane, but Olivia could find no trace of mockery in his words. He seemed sincerely pleased on his friend's behalf. She smiled back at him, finding him even easier to like than Lord Ashton.

"That's Cade," Julius said, something unspoken passing

between him and his friend that Olivia couldn't decipher. "We were born three days apart and have been stuck together ever since."

But from the way he said it, Olivia could tell he saw Cade as a true friend—perhaps the closest out of the group of his peers. She just hoped Cade's welcome really was as sincere as it seemed, and that perhaps he might prove friendly to her for the duration of her stay at court.

She could certainly do with some allies.

CHAPTER 14

JULIUS

Julius looked around at his friends. "Olivia is unfamiliar with court and life at the palace. I hope you'll all help her to adjust quickly."

Ashton and Cade nodded quickly, murmuring their willingness to assist, as he had known they would. Zane merely inclined his head in one of his usual careless gestures, but Julius trusted Cade to keep his older brother in line if necessary. Zane was too aware of his elevated rank to warm quickly to a future princess who had once been a servant.

But while Julius hadn't liked the tone of his comment about Olivia, his admiration of her beauty had been real—as it could hardly fail to be. If they could win Zane over, they would be well on their way to winning most of the court.

Kasper, however, gave a formal response, his voice stiff as he said, "I and my family stand ready to assist the crown in all matters."

Julius nodded acceptance of the words even as his mind whirred, separating out their layers of meaning. Kasper, the third son of Lord Emerson, must know the truth of what had happened—or at least some of it. He must resent seeing Olivia in the place that should have been his sister's, but apparently he was also aware that the exchange had been instigated by Marigold. His unusual response indicated he was keenly aware his family had been plunged into great, if secret, disgrace with the king and queen.

Julius just wished he knew how Kasper viewed Olivia herself. Did he understand she was also a victim, or did he think of her as complicit in the scheme?

"I knew I could rely on you all," Julius said lightly, hoping his words were true. He would have to keep an eye on Kasper.

"I'll be very grateful for any assistance you can provide," Olivia said in her musical voice, turning her smile on each of his friends in turn. "You'll probably find me wandering lost through the corridors at some point since they all look the same."

Something tightened in his chest at the way even Zane and Kasper smiled instinctively back at her, unable to resist the combination of her fresh beauty and self-deprecating charm. He wanted to step in front of her and shield her from their admiring gazes. Or, even better, cancel the visit entirely and sweep Olivia off to find someone else to help her.

But Julius had no one else he could trust to watch over her. He had always maintained a careful distance with the young women of court, not wanting to set the gossips talking—an ironic goal as matters had turned out. But consequently, he wasn't sure which of them could be trusted with the task of helping him guide Olivia through her first weeks at court. He might not like the appreciative gleam in his friends' eyes—especially when he remembered his mother's words about finding her a husband from the men of the court—but they were the only ones he could turn to.

"Lord Kasper," Olivia said, addressing his tawny-haired friend. "I believe my aunt and uncle's manor sits next to your home."

Zane's brows rose, and Julius threw a concerned look at Olivia. She shouldn't mention her connection to Marigold— or give any hint of her friend's scheme—in front of anyone, but especially not in front of Zane. Lords Emerson and Strathmore were long time political and economic rivals, and unlike his brother, Zane had never entirely shaken off his animosity toward Lord Strathmore's sons, even in front of Julius.

When they were younger, it had caused Julius a great deal of distress to see Cade and Zane at odds with Kasper, and so Cade had not only adjusted his own attitude but also worked to keep his brother in check. But, as the older son, Zane was far more interested in politics than Cade, and Cade's efforts had only muted his antagonism, not entirely overcome it.

Since the planned alliance with Lord Emerson had fallen through, Julius didn't want Lord Strathmore to get wind of his parents' failed plans. Lord Strathmore would resent the king and queen choosing his rival's daughter for their son, even while he delighted at seeing Lord Emerson in disgrace. If the crown didn't have the advantages of the alliance, they couldn't afford to wear the disadvantages either. The last thing Julius's father needed was to be at odds with more of his court.

Julius kicked himself for not warning Olivia beforehand about the necessity of not mentioning Marigold. But it was too late for him to say anything. If he attempted to cut her off, it would only draw attention, the opposite of what he wanted. He would have to trust that she possessed some good sense, despite her ignorance of court.

"We used to be neighbors," Olivia continued, "but while your mother and sister sometimes walk on the hill behind the manors, I don't think I ever saw you there. Do you all spend most of your time at court?"

She kept her voice light, and Julius hoped the others didn't notice the tightness in her stance, betraying how much she cared about the answer.

"My mother sometimes attends court," Kasper said warily, "although she has many duties. My sister would no doubt be fascinated to meet you—and even more eager to show you around than any of us could be—but she is currently on a visit to relatives in the southwest of Sovar."

Julius eyed his friend speculatively. So Lady Marigold had been packed off to relatives, had she? Keeping her out of sight for a while was a sensible move.

"Perhaps I'll have a chance to meet her when she returns," Olivia said lightly, although he saw the way one of her hands had balled into a fist within the folds of her skirt.

Julius couldn't share her dismay, though. He was utterly relieved at his narrow escape where Marigold was concerned. At least one good thing had come out of the accidental betrothal. Whatever happened with Olivia, he wouldn't let his parents instigate a second betrothal with Lord Emerson's daughter.

The thought reminded him that he had a bone to pick with Cade. He sent a glare toward his closest friend. Kasper wasn't the only one who knew the truth about the original choice of bride—and Cade had lied straight to Julius's face. That was a betrayal, even if he had been trying to calm Julius's supposed nerves. Not disappointed in his mother's choice, indeed!

But just like Olivia, he had to bite his tongue for the moment and wait for a more private opportunity to speak freely.

"It's been days since you were here, Julius," Zane said suddenly. "So it's your turn for a match. Who do you want to face?"

Julius glanced at Olivia, expecting her to protest that he was supposed to be showing her around. But she raised a challenging brow at him, almost making him laugh aloud.

"See," Zane drawled. "Your bride wants to see your prowess. You can't confess to being chicken-hearted in front of her."

"Zane," Cade's warning was quiet, and his brother ignored it completely.

Julius laughed. "Chicken-hearted? I think days cooped up in my father's meetings have made me reckless, rather. Should I take on two of you at once?"

"Careful, Julius," Cade said, although he sounded amused this time, "or you'll be embarrassed in front of your lady."

"I've always wanted to see a duel," Olivia said. "Do please have a match. Just try not to get hurt."

"How sweet." Zane's eyes laughed at Olivia in a way that made Julius's skin itch.

"Her Majesty wouldn't be happy with me if the first thing I did after she released me was to endanger her son," Olivia added, making all four of Julius's friends burst into surprised laughter.

She looked around at them in innocent surprise, leaving Julius torn between frustration and amusement. But when her eyes fell on him, she winked.

His mouth almost fell open, and Cade laughed.

"I think you really have met your match," he murmured to Julius. "And you behold me positively agog with curiosity to hear how it happened." He gave Julius a significant look, reminding the prince that his friend would have some questions of his own when they finally found the opportunity to talk without listening ears.

"I haven't sparred yet this morning," Kasper offered.

On any other day, Julius would have easily accepted, knowing the two of them were well-matched. But given his friend's formal behavior earlier, he feared Kasper meant to lose to the prince as another gesture of apology. As little as Julius wanted to lose in front of Olivia, he would look even more foolish if she could tell Kasper was going easy on him.

"Cade looks equally fresh, and I have a score to settle with him," Julius said with a laugh, clapping Cade on the shoulder and squeezing harder than was necessary.

Cade just grinned back. "Challenge accepted."

Kasper stepped aside, not protesting, his subservient behavior only confirming Julius's earlier impression. Usually Kasper was almost as inclined to haughtiness as Zane and would have insisted on his challenge being accepted.

Julius hadn't intended to join in their usual morning sparring, so he had come without his sword. But Kasper offered him the use of his, and Julius happily accepted, glad to be able to accept one of Kasper's overtures. Within seconds he had stripped off his jacket and vest, rolled up his sleeves, and taken his place across from Cade.

When he glanced at Olivia, she was seated beside the fountain, watching him with wide eyes. He looked back at his opponent to find Cade also watching Olivia, a soft smile on his face. Julius's enthusiasm hardened into determination. He had always been well-matched with Cade, but he hadn't practiced since before the ball, which put him at a disadvantage. But he refused to be defeated in front of his betrothed. He was suffering enough humiliation as it was, allowing the entire court to believe he was foolishly infatuated.

Kasper called for the bout to start, and Cade leaped nimbly forward, lunging into a picture-perfect attack. Julius jumped backward, out of reach, parrying before launching a counterattack of his own.

With the match begun, all other thoughts faded from his mind as he focused all his attention on the cadence of the parries and ripostes, his eyes glued to Cade for the telltale movement of his muscles that would signal a coming attack. It felt good to stretch his mind and body in unison, pushing himself instead of sitting around idle.

Finally, the perfect opportunity appeared. As Cade launched a complex attack aimed at disarming his opponent, Julius brought his sword up at an angle, sliding the attack away before twisting back again. Cade's sword flew from his hand, the resistance to Julius's blade instantly disappearing.

It was a new move, and Julius had only ever performed it on the visiting swords master who had taught it to him, so he was thoughtlessly expecting Cade to jump back immediately as the master had always done. But Cade stood motionless, caught by surprise, and the tip of Julius's blade caught on his wrist, skipping upward as it tore a light gash up his forearm.

Julius wrenched his arm back, his eyes widening. He might have won the bout, but part of the challenge of the practice matches was in not injuring your opponent, and Julius had a near perfect record in that regard. He'd let his determination overtake his caution. Once again, Olivia's presence had scratched Julius's surface, proving how little he resembled the perfect prince beneath.

"I didn't mean—" he began, his words cut off by Zane's admiring whistle.

"Nice move," Zane said in a more enthusiastic tone than usual. He didn't seem in the least worried by the injury to his younger brother.

"Very nice!" Ashton agreed with even more enthusiasm. He bounded over and clapped Julius on the shoulder. "I haven't seen that particular trick before. When were you planning to teach it to the rest of us?"

Julius grinned back, despite his underlying unease. "Only after I've defeated you all at least once, naturally."

Ashton laughed, but Julius turned back to Cade.

"Is it deep..." he started to ask, the words dying as he saw Olivia wrapping Cade's arm in a length of white cloth—presumably Cade's discarded neckcloth.

Julius had wanted to impress her for once, but given how quickly she had run to Cade's side, it looked like he'd managed the opposite. Again.

He strode over, intending to take over the task, but she had already completed it neatly and efficiently.

"It didn't look too deep," she said to Cade, answering Julius's earlier question and easing his guilt.

"Of course it's not." Cade laughed and gave a charming smile in Olivia's direction. "It was a mere glancing blow, barely a scratch." He turned to Julius. "I hope now that I've been duly beaten, you'll be willing to teach that move to me. Preferably before you teach any of the others."

"My apologies," Julius said, wincing. "I should have been more careful. I haven't used it with an opponent who didn't know it was coming before, and I should have considered the danger."

Cade scoffed. "It's hardly the first time one of us has been scratched, and it won't be the last. Kasper barely even mentions the time I accidentally skewered his arm." He threw a laughing look in Kasper's direction and received a snort in response.

Cade's voice lowered. "When facing each other across a blade, we're all the same. We decided that from the beginning. You don't have to wear the weight of your role in this, too."

Julius grimaced and sent Cade a light glare in response, not risking looking in Olivia's direction. His friend was talking too quietly for the other men to hear, but Olivia was much closer.

"Even if it's a minor wound," Olivia said, changing the topic and easing some of his tension, "it would still be wise to see a doctor. There must be one here in the palace—probably more than one. Let me help you to the closest."

Julius leaped in before Cade could accept such an appealing escort. "It was my error, I'll take him myself."

He expected Olivia to protest, but she merely nodded.

"You're right, that would probably be better. They'll see him more quickly if you accompany him."

Her words had sense, and that consideration should have been at the forefront of his own mind.

"I don't need any escort at all," Cade said with a laugh. "It was my arm that was *barely* injured, not my leg."

But Julius was determined. He had hurt his friend, and if Cade would be seen more quickly in Julius's presence, then he wasn't going to abandon him and return to a morning relaxing with Olivia.

Olivia.

He was supposed to be showing her around the palace. But he couldn't be in two places at once. He would have to trust Olivia to one of his friends.

His eyes skipped straight over Zane, who was watching the three of them with far too much interest, and lingered on Ashton. The youngest of his friends had always reminded him of the best qualities of a puppy—loyal, enthusiastic, and endearing. But Ashton's eyes lingered on Olivia with far too much admiration. He was just the sort of noble Queen Elsinore might think a good match for Olivia—wealthy and well connected, but not too influential. That thought sat uncomfortably for some reason, so he turned his eyes to Kasper.

Kasper was the obvious answer. Olivia was clearly desperate for a private word with Marigold's brother, and it was better to give her the opportunity sooner rather than later—before she slipped up and said something in front of the wrong person.

"I'll take Cade to the doctor," Julius called across the courtyard to Kasper. "I'm trusting the rest of Lady Olivia's palace tour to you."

Kasper's eyebrows rose, but he immediately strode over to join them.

"Don't forget what's due her new rank," Julius said more quietly, giving his friend a warning glance.

Kasper stiffened. "Naturally. I wouldn't make such an error."

"I hardly think that's necessary," Olivia said softly from his side, reproachful eyes fastened on Julius. "I'm sure Lord Kasper doesn't need such reminders." Her lips tightened. "And he may have other plans for his day. I'm neither a child in need of watching nor a parcel in need of safe delivery."

Julius gave a soft sigh. They were hardly selling their supposed love story. But he couldn't blame Olivia. The whole problem would have been avoided if only he'd been more careful during his match.

"Please humor his company for the sake of my conscience," he said, giving his words a teasing edge while his eyes tried to signal a warning. "I wouldn't want you to get lost on the way back to your rooms."

She blinked up at him for a moment, clearly confused by his silent message, so at odds with his light tone. Then her face relaxed, and she smiled. Apparently, she had understood his reminder that they had an audience and must keep up appearances.

"It won't be the same as getting the tour from you," she said, as both Ashton and Zane strolled over to join them. "But I appreciate the thoughtfulness."

Kasper bowed to her, his face once again an unreadable mask. "I know I'm a poor substitute for your betrothed, but you will be in safe care in my hands." He smiled slightly. "I haven't been lost in the palace for ten years."

Ashton slung an arm over Kasper's shoulder. "There's a story there, Lady Olivia. And since Kasper never indulges my curiosity, you'll have to be the one to ask him to tell it."

"Not even a lady could coax it from me," Kasper replied with a straight face.

"You should ask me to tell it instead," Cade said with a mischievous smile. "I was there, too, but I lack Kasper's self-consequence."

"More's the pity," Zane muttered in a sour tone.

Julius restrained the impulse to whack Cade's brother for disrespecting Cade while he was injured. But the rest of them ignored Zane, and Olivia's smile didn't dim.

Kasper held out his arm to her, and she took it with a polite smile. Something twisted in Julius's chest. It shouldn't have, but it did anyway.

He wasn't jealous of Kasper in the normal way—Olivia's interest in him wasn't personal. But even so, he didn't want to send her off on the arm of one of his friends. He wanted the chance to show her around himself, although it was his own fault he'd lost that opportunity.

"Relax, lover boy," Zane murmured with a grin. "She's already yours, remember?"

Julius turned narrow eyes on him, but Zane merely laughed.

"I do hope you're going to tell us how you managed to convince your illustrious parents, by the way," he drawled. "I wouldn't have thought they had it in them to accept a servant girl in the name of love." One eyebrow quirked. "Didn't think you had it in you either."

"Watch it, Zane," Cade growled, making Julius sigh. The

last thing Cade needed was a brotherly tussle when he hadn't even seen a doctor yet.

"It's past time I got you to a doctor," Julius said to Cade with a weighted look, firmly shutting down the other discussion. He glanced at Zane. "Are you coming?"

He hoped not—he would prefer to talk to Cade privately. But if Zane wanted to accompany his brother, he couldn't deny him.

"I'm sure you have the matter well in hand," Zane said with a nod. "Our family has always appreciated your favor to my baby brother."

Cade bristled but subsided at a warning look from Julius. Even more than their ages, the difference in temperaments was exactly why he had always been closer to Cade than Zane. Zane was too interested in politics and his family's honor, and he could never resist casting slights at his brother.

Zane gave a respectful nod before wandering off, sweeping Ashton along with him.

Julius turned to Cade with a wry grimace. "My apologies. You must be in pain and that all took far too long."

Cade laughed. "And you're making far too big a fuss about a minor scratch. How many times do I have to say I'm fine?"

Julius sighed. "I shouldn't have been so careless. Even a *scratch* as you call it could become infected. I haven't made such a mistake in two years."

"No," Cade agreed in a thoughtful tone. "You're usually far too serious and responsible for that. Should I assume it's the effect of your beautiful bride?"

Julius stiffened, but a moment later he relaxed and

sighed again. Cade was the one person Julius could be open with, so the last thing he wanted to do was ice him out.

"I was angry with you at the start of our bout," he said, "but given I skewered you, I'm not sure I can take the right-eous high ground anymore."

"Angry at me?" Cade sounded genuinely confused. "Whatever for?" He took a step closer and lowered his voice. "What is going on, Julius? Who is Olivia?"

Julius didn't answer, his eyes catching on a servant passing down one of the corridors bordering the courtyard. Cade followed his gaze, stepping forward to flag the footman down.

"We're in need of a doctor for a minor matter." He gestured at his arm with an easy grin. "Could you please fetch the royal physician to the prince's sitting room?"

The footman glanced at Julius, waiting for his nodded confirmation before he bowed and hurried away.

Cade turned his grin on Julius. "Clearly you have a story to tell, and I don't have the patience to wait on the doctor's leisure before I hear it. We'll let him come to us, and if it takes a bit longer, that will just give you time to confess all."

Julius glanced uncertainly at Cade's arm, and his friend rolled his eyes.

"If you say one more word about my deadly wound, I'll draw my sword again and see how you like being stabbed."

Julius laughed reluctantly and let Cade lead him to his private sitting room. It was probably better that they saw the doctor in private anyway. There were enough rumors about him currently circulating without adding talk of his doing violence to a nobleman of the court.

As soon as they were safely shut away from curious ears,

Cade whirled on him. From the look on his face, he must have been working hard to restrain his rampant curiosity all morning.

"Why has Lady Marigold been sent off to visit relatives?" he asked before Julius could even take a seat. "What happened? Who is Lady Olivia? If the citizens of Sovar were surprised to discover your great and secret love for a commoner, you can only imagine how I felt! And while I hate to agree with Zane on anything, I would very much like to know how you convinced your parents to humor you on a matter of such significance."

His expression dropped. "And why didn't you tell me about her? I thought you trusted me. We even talked about it all before the ball, and you never mentioned Lady Olivia."

Julius dropped into a chair and groaned, covering his face with a hand. "Actually, I did."

"Impossible." Cade seemed too animated to sit. "If you ever admitted something so shocking, I wouldn't forget it in a hundred years. You never go against your duty."

Julius wished for a moment that Cade had truly forgotten their earlier conversation. But it had only been a matter of days, and his friend wasn't likely to forget such a tale.

"I never said her name because I didn't know it," he admitted with a sigh. "But I do recall mentioning she was very beautiful..."

He looked up at his friend, waiting for the moment of realization. He wasn't disappointed.

Cade's eyes widened, and he gave an involuntary crack of laughter before staring at Julius. "Not the girl from the hill? The one who stopped you walking straight off a cliff? The one who didn't know who you were but probably thought you were lacking some or all of your mental faculties? But you said you weren't in love with her!"

"I'm not!" Julius cried. "What happened at the ball was a terrible misunderstanding, and now I'm stuck. Stuck betrothed to the one person I hoped never to see again."

"So you're not in love with her?" Cade said slowly. "And I suppose she's not in love with you either."

He had a strange look on his face as he said it, and Julius's brows drew together, although he couldn't put his finger on his discomfort.

"That is the least of my worries."

"But what happened to Lady Marigold, then?" Cade was clearly trying to puzzle it out and getting nowhere. "I never even saw her at the ball, although I was naturally on the lookout."

Julius stood up, his brows lowering further. "Yes, about that. You told me I wouldn't be disappointed! You lied right to my face! If my mother asked for your opinion, you should have talked her out of an ill-judged start like that." He shook his head. "Choosing Lady Marigold of all people."

Cade's mouth fell open. "Was I supposed to talk Her Majesty out of it? I admit Lady Marigold is a very different style from Lady Olivia, but she's just as beautiful. The young men of court all admire her."

"They might admire her beauty, maybe," Julius said darkly. "But at least half of them are also terrified of her."

"Some of them, maybe, but you never seemed to have a problem with her," Cade protested. "She often used to follow us around when we were young, and you were usually willing to let her join in. I thought you would be happy to have a bride who was both beautiful and a friend. It seemed a better beginning with your mystery bride than you were fearing."

"Yes, Marigold is an excellent companion in any hare-brained adventure," Julius said shortly, "such as the kind we engaged in when we were ten years old. But can you really imagine her presiding over court? Managing all the subtleties of precedence and alliances and...who knows what else my mother helps my father manage?"

"Oh." Cade blinked, clearly struck. "When you put it like that..."

"Yes." Julius shook his head. "Exactly. Marigold always showed my parents her sweetest self, so I think Mother is convinced she merely has a...a cheeky side or something. She probably expects her to outgrow it. Marigold saved her true disregard for both convention and sense for her peers."

"She isn't that bad," Cade protested, but his voice sounded weak.

"Of course, her family must know her true nature," Julius added, once again considering Kasper's unusual manner. "So they bear some of the blame. They agreed to the alliance without warning my parents, and now it has blown up in all our faces."

Cade frowned. "Are you saying this apparent misunderstanding was somehow the Emersons' fault? Is that why Kasper was acting so oddly this morning? Are your parents blaming Lord and Lady Emerson?"

"They should never have agreed to Marigold's selection," Julius said, "but the majority of the blame rests squarely on the shoulders of Marigold herself."

"Marigold?" Cade paused and huffed out a frustrated breath. "Didn't I already tell you I'm dying of curiosity? Stop dropping nonsensical hints and tell me exactly what happened!"

Julius told him as brief a summary as he could, but it was still a complicated tale. By the end of it, Cade's mouth was hanging open.

"So Marigold has been sent away in disgrace? But…" He fell back into a chair behind him, shaking his head. "What a trick to play."

"And against her own friend as well," Julius added, his already dark thoughts about Lady Marigold turning darker.

"But…why?" Cade asked, still shaking his head.

"Apparently I'm as unappealing a prospect to her as she is to me." Julius tried to keep his voice light.

"I—" Cade stood up, looked around the room, and sat down again. "I have nothing to say." He sounded bewildered, and the admission made Julius laugh.

"Is that a first?" he asked. "You're usually quite ready to give me your counsel—whether requested or not."

Cade smiled back ruefully, although the shock hadn't entirely left his eyes.

"I don't think I have any advice for this situation. I suppose you'll just have to hope the scholars find a way out of the betrothal. Who would have dreamed you'd find yourself betrothed to someone without wealth or connections?!"

Julius sat forward, leaning on his knees. "I don't know that I'd say she's entirely without connections," he said slowly.

Cade raised his eyebrows. "A servant?"

"She wasn't actually a servant but a niece of the household," he said, uncertain why he felt the need to defend Olivia. "She was always acknowledged as family, her aunt just pushed her to fulfill the duties of a servant because of the way the Legacy assisted her. Since the ball, my father has made some discreet inquiries. It seems her uncle has never had much interest in the court, but he's a canny and successful businessman with an extensive network and solid connections through the city. Father thinks there may be some advantage there."

One of Cade's brows shot up. "Do you mean your parents are starting to actually favor the match?"

Julius sank back against the chair. "I suppose they are hedging both bets, mentally speaking. She's still hardly their first choice. She could barely be considered on the list."

"And what about you?" Cade asked, speaking with the frankness no one else ever dared use toward the crown prince. "You don't approve of Marigold as first choice, so is it Lady Olivia instead?"

"No, of course not," Julius said quickly. A little too quickly.

"Interesting." A small smile played around Cade's mouth, making Julius narrow his eyes. Whatever his friend was concluding, he had a feeling he wasn't going to like it.

But a knock at the door announced the arrival of the doctor and the end of private conversation with the one person who now knew the full truth about what had happened at the Midsummer Ball.

CHAPTER 15

OLIVIA

Olivia restrained her impatience until she and Kasper had walked far enough from the others not to be overheard. She wasn't even attempting to pay attention to where he might be leading her, only waiting for the opportunity to ask the questions that plagued her.

"What do you know of me?" she asked abruptly, uncertain how to ask the question more subtly.

"That depends what you mean," Kasper said cautiously. "About you personally I know very little—as much as the rest of the court, I presume. But if you mean, do I know what happened the night of the ball, then...yes." He sighed heavily. "I actually heard my sister mention you a couple of times before that night, although she was careful never to say anything in front of our parents. And of course I had no idea what she was planning. We all knew Marigold disapproved of the planned match, but she seemed to go docile and compliant shortly before the ball. Our parents thought she had capitulated to the inevitable, but they should have known better." He groaned. "We did know better, but none of us dreamed she would do something so completely outrageous."

Olivia assumed the *we* he referenced was Kasper and his two older brothers.

"Then you know I wasn't involved in her scheming?" Olivia asked anxiously, still not sure if he might blame her, at least partially. "I truly knew nothing about it."

Kasper hesitated before speaking slowly. "I'll confess I wish you had been a little more wary in dealing with my sister. But I can hardly blame you for missing something that her own family also missed."

"And what of your parents?" Olivia asked. "Do they share the same view?"

He hesitated again, and she winced.

"I believe they'll recognize the full truth once they've had a chance to calm down," he said eventually. "They're currently frustrated with everyone involved. But they aren't fool enough to think you were the instigator of the scheme."

"I'll confess I was angry with Marigold myself at first," Olivia said slowly, voicing something that was only half-formed in her own thoughts. "But I've also been...worried." She turned to fix her eyes on the side of Kasper's face as they continued strolling down a corridor. "Is it true that she's gone to stay with relatives outside the capital? Are you sure she's really there? I heard..." Her voice dropped lower. "I heard she might be missing."

Kasper stopped, pulling her to a halt beside him and fixing her with a sharp look. "What? Where did you hear that? Are there rumors in the palace? Father is convinced he succeeded at keeping that quiet."

Dread rose inside Olivia. The slow tendrils of worry that had been weaving through her anger grew thick and strong, crushing the other emotion entirely.

"It's true, then?" she gasped. "Is she actually missing? The story of the visit to relatives is just to cover her disappearance?"

"Of course she's still missing," he said morosely. "Would you come back in a hurry if you knew what a mess you'd left behind and what you would be facing on your return?" He grimaced. "I suppose that's difficult to answer since you would never have played such a shocking trick in the first place—no one but Marigold would."

He started walking again, but Olivia dug her heels in and remained in place, forcing him to drop her arm. He stopped and turned back to her.

"I was very angry with her as well at first," she said. "And I'm sure the storm that's waiting for her is intense, but..." She trailed off as she tried to think of the right words to express her growing certainty.

"You've known Marigold a lot longer than I have, so I'm sure you've seen her do all sorts of things. She's certainly prone to making impulsive and sometimes rash decisions. But has she ever failed to own up to what she's done? Have you ever seen her try to shirk responsibility for her actions? I know I haven't known her as long as you, and I'm sure I don't know her as well, but she always struck me as brave."

Kasper stared at her in silence, his dazed response to her torrent of words making her flush.

"I just think," she added, forcing herself to speak more calmly, "that Marigold always seemed more likely to throw herself in front of someone else to shield them than she was to leave them to take the blame in her stead. That's why I started to worry—and the worry has just kept growing ever since my shock and anger died down. The whole business seems just like Marigold, except for one glaring element. The Marigold I know wouldn't have run away and left me to deal with the situation alone."

"No," Kasper said slowly. "I've never known her to do such a thing."

He ran a hand through his hair, his expression growing more and more perturbed.

"In truth, I agree with you," he said. "But Father is still furious with Marigold. He's convinced she ran off and left us to deal with the consequences of her trick, and I guess it has been easier to fall in line with his thinking than to push against it." His mouth twisted ruefully. "There's a reason he's so wealthy and influential at court. He's always been charismatic. And he's going to be even more furious now that whispers of the truth are leaking out."

"I haven't heard anything at the palace," Olivia said quickly. "I actually tried to visit Marigold at your manor the morning after the ball—before the prince came to collect me. I heard it there."

Kasper's eyebrows rose. "I can well imagine what sort of reception you would have received the morning after the ball. I'm surprised I didn't hear anything about it, though."

"I went to the back door in the wall," Olivia admitted. "It was answered by a gardener's apprentice. He told me more than he probably should have."

"Ah." The knowing amusement in Kasper's face and voice made Olivia flush again. She hadn't purposely flirted with the lad to encourage his confidences, but she knew he had been impressed by her.

"Hopefully the rumor hasn't reached anyone else, then," Kasper said thoughtfully. "Father had a stern talk with the servants the day after the ball. Anyone who spreads word of what really happened will lose their positions. I don't think any of them will talk now. He's spent time cultivating loyal servants—although apparently he should spend some more time on the outside staff."

He ended on a wry note, but Olivia had the impression he wasn't likely to report the lad to his father. She hoped he didn't since she didn't want to be the cause of the boy losing his position.

"So what do you think could have happened to Marigold?" Olivia asked, returning to the central issue. She clutched her skirts in an effort not to wring her hands together. "I'm worried she's been abducted. It was my first thought when she didn't turn up at the ball, but I let my initial shock and anger distract me." And Julius. But she didn't add that part out loud.

The prince had been the one to convince her away from that line of thinking at the ball. And as far as she knew, he still didn't suspect foul play, so she was going to have to raise the issue with him again. If Marigold's family weren't looking for her, then Olivia and Julius needed to do so in their stead.

"Have your parents done anything to look for her?" she asked Kasper, still hopeful it wouldn't be left to her.

He grimaced. "Nothing substantial. My father talks as if he's ready to wash his hands of her, but I know he doesn't really mean it. He's just worried that word will get out about what she did. Mother has begun some discreet inquiries, though."

"Does your mother think she might have been abducted?" Olivia asked hopefully. Marigold's family had nearly as much influence as the crown, so if they were searching after all, she wouldn't be needed.

"No, she's only looking in places where she thinks Marigold might have hidden herself." Kasper gave a heavy sigh. "My sister has run away twice before, you know, so they're not entirely unjustified in their assumption." He seemed to be pleading with Olivia not to think too badly of his family. "I can suggest the possibility of abduction to my mother, but I suspect she'll discount it immediately. I don't think she believes that anyone would dare cross Father in such a way."

He straightened. "But you shouldn't be worrying about my family's business. You have enough to deal with on your own behalf. If you would be willing to keep the truth to yourself, you will have done as much as my family can expect of you."

He offered his arm again with a gallant smile that didn't reach the strain around his eyes. "Are you sure you don't want me to give you a tour in Julius's place?"

Olivia shook her head. "I would prefer to return to my rooms, if you know the way." She already had plenty to think about before her afternoon lessons.

J ulius had lived up to his word. The footman who brought the tray with her evening meal informed Olivia that she would once again be released from lessons the following morning.

Eager for some time away from the palace, she rose early and dressed herself for a trip into the city. If she asked for a horse or carriage, the palace staff would surely oblige. But it would take time and would lead to inevitable fussing. She preferred to walk. It wasn't far.

As she approached the smallest of the palace gates, sudden doubts seized her. What if the guards tried to prevent her from leaving? But the two men on duty merely bowed and opened the door to usher her through.

Stepping onto the street, she felt a weight lift from her. And stretching her legs felt almost as good as the release from pressure. She took a meandering route that led her to the hill at the back of Manor Row instead of to the front of her uncle's manor. As she walked over the grass, she watched for Mildred, but there was no sign of the mouse.

Olivia's worry for the creature spiked, but the mouse was often busy foraging in the early mornings, so she headed for her aunt and uncle's house instead of searching for Mildred immediately. The door in the back wall was already unlatched, thanks to the early work of the gardeners, and she slipped inside without trouble.

But her quiet entry was foiled by the head gardener who immediately spotted her. He called out in welcome, and the gardeners converged on her. Several of the inside servants trailed further behind—all of them smiling and bowing and calling her Lady Olivia.

Olivia tried to respond with equal good cheer, ignoring

her discomfort. She had always occupied a strange role in the household—viewed as a family member by the staff, despite her work. She had taken her meals with her aunt, uncle, and cousins and stayed in a guest room, so she didn't know the other servants particularly well.

She had always shared a fellow feeling with them, however, and they had treated her as a strange sort of aberration—a servant when she was with them and a guest when she was with a member of her family. Apparently, they viewed her as one of the household either way and were overcome with delight at one of their own being chosen by the prince. From their comments, she gathered her new position had already elevated her family's status in the capital and their staff along with them.

Finally, Hattie appeared and waded through the small crowd to extract Olivia.

"You've come!" She grabbed hold of Olivia's wrist and pulled her toward the house. "We weren't expecting you."

"Sorry," Olivia said, immediately feeling guilty. She should have thought to write ahead and inform her family of her coming.

But, wait. Why should she write, as if she were a friend coming over for tea? The manor had been her home for a year and was her true home still. Her stay in the palace was merely temporary—she hoped.

Thankfully, Hattie kept up a stream of bright chatter, informing Olivia that Uncle Walt had already left on his usual business activities and that Nell had gone shopping with Aunt Helen. While Olivia would have enjoyed seeing her family, she was grateful for their absence on this occasion.

She had visited to retrieve the last of her belongings, not to socialize, and since she had other errands to complete as well, she preferred to keep the visit brief.

"Is it amazing at the palace?" Hattie asked breathlessly once they were inside the manor. "Do you have a whole suite to yourself?" She gazed wide-eyed at Olivia until Olivia nodded and then immediately continued talking. "But of course you would. You're basically the crown princess!" She gave a squeal at the thought, making Olivia wince.

"The rooms are lovely," Olivia offered, glad they were one thing she could praise unequivocally.

"Almost as lovely as the prince?" Hattie asked with a giggle, and Olivia barely managed to keep her face steady.

"I've come to fetch something from my room that Aunt Helen missed," she said, hoping Hattie wouldn't press her about what the item might be.

But Hattie's mind was focused on Prince Julius, not fetching mundane belongings.

"I'm sure I'd make a terrible queen," she said with a dramatic shudder, "but I do wish the prince had danced with me at the ball. I'm sure I would have treasured the experience my whole life." She clasped her hands together and sighed wistfully.

"I'm sure you can dance with him at my wedding," Olivia said without thinking as she hurried up the stairs.

Hattie gripped her arm with both hands, nearly unbalancing her.

"Really?" she gasped. "Do you mean it? At your wedding? So we really will be invited? Mother said she was sure we would be—we're your only family in the city after all—but

Father said not to be counting chickens, eggs, or even baskets."

Olivia wished she'd kept her mouth shut. She couldn't meet Hattie's eager eyes. If she did marry the prince, she would certainly invite every relative she had. But she wasn't planning on actually marrying him, which meant she had little chance of following through with her thoughtless offer.

"Of course you'll be invited to my wedding," she said which was true, regardless of the identity of the groom. "But I'll arrange a dance for you with Julius sooner if there's an opportunity."

"*Julius!*" Hattie sighed, her eyes shining. Apparently she was impressed merely by Olivia's use of his first name without a title attached.

Olivia's gratitude at Nell and her aunt's absence grew. Fielding Hattie's enthusiasm so early in the morning was difficult enough.

Thankfully Hattie didn't insist on accompanying Olivia into her bedchamber, and Olivia was even more grateful to see the room looked undisturbed. She'd been a little afraid that her aunt might have ordered a deep clean following her departure, resulting in the discovery of what she had hidden.

Closing the door firmly behind her, she collected a few odds and ends and a book she had been halfway through reading, placing the items in the small bag she had brought. But those things were inconsequential and wouldn't have inspired a trip into the city. What she had really come for was hidden beneath her mattress.

She withdrew the small, flat object. It was wrapped in soft, uncolored linen, and she hesitated for a moment before unwrapping it with quick fingers. The material fell away to reveal a tiny mirror, adorned with an elegant silver frame and handle.

She looked down into the polished surface and saw her own face reflected back, barely able to fit, given the mirror's small size. Olivia appeared just as the larger mirror at the dressing table showed her to be—a little pale but otherwise giving no indication of the dramatic transformation in her life.

For once, she was almost relieved at the mirror's failure to show any fantastical properties. Avery had warned her that it didn't always work—it had been made by an apprentice and was faulty. So while it sometimes showed a person's true emotions, sometimes it only worked as a regular mirror. Not that Olivia minded. It was the only reason she'd been gifted such a rare and valuable item.

The Auldana Legacy allowed people in the distant kingdom of Auldana to make mirrors with all sorts of fantastical properties, but they didn't easily part with them in trade. She had never even seen an Auldanan mirror before receiving the gift from Avery, and she suspected her cousins had never seen one at all.

But as she gazed down at her reflection, the image rippled slightly, her expression changing although her actual face never moved. Worry lines sprung up around her eyes, along with shadows that suggested either a lack of sleep or deep distress. Her mouth turned down, her overall visage shouting her internal disquiet.

She quickly turned the mirror over, working to calm her rapid breathing. She had feared she didn't have the ability to project a calm mask, but apparently she was better at it than she had ever suspected. And it was a good thing, too. If the people of court saw her true emotions, they wouldn't be sighing to each other over the prince's dream romance.

Not bothering to wrap the mirror properly, she thrust it and its cloth wrapping into her bag. As unnerving as the mirror's effect could sometimes be, it would be a useful tool at court.

Hattie suggested she stay for a belated breakfast, but Olivia had already eaten at the palace. Despite her early waking time, the meal had appeared as soon as she unlocked her suite door, just as usual.

She did tarry long enough to look over Hattie's new dresses, however, amazed at how quickly her aunt had gotten to work. Hattie's pure excitement was contagious, and Olivia didn't mind losing some time to humor her. Her sweet young cousin didn't resent Olivia's apparent good fortune in the least, and she was brimming with excitement about the possibility of attending court functions—although Olivia caught the note of anxiety as well.

She wanted to reassure her cousin, but Olivia was anxious enough herself about court functions, so she wasn't sure how to achieve the feat. And she needed to leave before any more members of the household could return. Using the excuse of her day's lessons, she extracted herself and escaped outside.

Standing in the manor's front courtyard, Olivia glanced toward the back gardens. She still needed to find Mildred, but she had one more visit to make, and she didn't think a giant mouse would be of assistance in making a good impression.

Gathering her courage, she exited the courtyard and walked the short distance to the neighboring courtyard. Last time she had approached Marigold's family home, she had done so from the back. But her status had changed since then, and she wasn't looking for a conversation with a gardener.

Olivia clanged the great door knocker with more confidence than she felt, waiting on the ponderous footsteps she could hear inside. In the past, she might have fled from the tall butler who answered the door. But she hadn't spent two days with a queen for nothing.

Raising her chin, she met his eyes, silently daring him to send her away. The man froze, clearly unsure how to handle the unprecedented situation.

"Who is it?" called a tired, strained voice from inside.

An elegant, middle-aged woman came into sight, her face wan. As soon as she caught sight of Olivia standing awkwardly in the doorway, a stream of emotions flashed across her face.

It was immediately obvious to Olivia that if she had been standing there as her old self—as the niece of the upstart merchant next door—she would have had the door shut in her face. But it was harder to shut doors in the face of a future princess. Especially when it had been the woman's own daughter who had elevated Olivia to that status.

"How...lovely to see you, Lady Olivia," the woman said at last. "Do please come in."

CHAPTER 16

OLIVIA

Lady Emerson seated Olivia in an enormous formal sitting room in the front of the house.

"My apologies," the noblewoman said in a stiff voice. "I wasn't expecting visitors and so have nothing prepared. However, if you'll give me a moment, I will ring for tea and—"

"Please don't put yourself out on my behalf," Olivia said quickly, well aware that she wasn't welcome. The household was clearly closed to visitors of the regular sort. "I merely wanted the chance to briefly speak with you."

"And why would you want to speak with me, Lady Olivia?" Lady Emerson's clasped hands trembled slightly.

Olivia leaned forward. "I'm worried about Marigold. She was always a good friend to me and—"

"Too good a friend, it would seem," Lady Emerson said quietly but with bite. "I fully understand Their Majesties' fury toward our family. That is to be expected, and no more than Marigold has brought down on our heads. But I hardly see what you can have to complain about. My daughter elevated you beyond what anyone could have imagined—beyond reason.”

Olivia sat back, thrown off by the unexpected attack.

“I didn’t ask for this *elevation*,” she said with as much dignity as she could muster. “I certainly did not seek or even want a betrothal to the prince. I don’t belong in the palace.”

Lady Emerson watched her, her brows creasing as the silence stretched between them.

“You really mean that,” she finally said, her tone incredulous. “I’ve always been good at reading people.” Her voice dropped even lower. “All except my own daughter, apparently.”

Olivia leaned forward again. “I do mean it. I had no idea what Marigold was planning, and when I found out what she’d done, I was furious. But I don’t want her to come to any harm. And I’m afraid she has come to harm. It doesn’t seem at all like her to run away in this situation, and—”

“Unfortunately,” Lady Emerson said, cutting her off with sorrow this time instead of heat, “it isn’t at all unlike Marigold to run away. She’s done it before.”

“Yes, I know,” Olivia said, fighting down her rising frustration. “But what I mean is that she wouldn’t—”

“After pulling a stunt like hers, can we really say that anything is beyond her?” Lady Emerson’s voice was heavy with the same sadness. “Believe me, I don’t want to believe any of it. Marigold’s father and I are desperate to find our daughter and bring her home.”

Olivia perked up at those words, but Lady Emerson continued. “But if you truly care about my daughter, the best thing you can do is to stay away from this house and keep her name off your lips. If others learn the truth she will be shunned and disgraced." Her words finished on a suppressed sob.

Olivia's heart twisted. Lady Emerson might believe the worst of Marigold's behavior, but she clearly still loved her daughter and wanted to see her home and safe. If only she would let Olivia finish what she was trying to say.

Olivia tried again. "So there hasn't been a ransom demand or anything like that? I'm worried that—" But Lady Emerson didn't even seem to hear her, instead standing and gesturing toward the door.

"On that note," the noblewoman said, "I must thank you for your continued kindness to my daughter and ask you to leave."

"But I—"

Lady Emerson's stern expression made Olivia falter into silence. On impulse, she thrust her hand into her bag and closed her fingers around the handle of her mirror. Ignoring how odd she must appear, she pulled it out and examined her reflection, twisting so that her back was to Marigold's mother.

With a subtle angling of her hand, she was able to capture Lady Emerson's face in the reflective surface. A second ago, the noblewoman had been looking impatient, but in the mirror's reflective surface, she appeared haggard and desperately worried. Olivia leaped to her feet, an instinctive reaction when confronted with someone on the verge of collapse. But when she spun around to view Lady Emerson directly, the noblewoman looked merely irritated and confused.

Olivia swallowed and thrust the mirror back into her bag. Shaken by the glimpse of what lay beneath the noblewoman's surface, she allowed herself to be ushered toward the door. By the time she had thought of a fresh argument, she was standing outside facing nothing but a closed door.

Should she knock again? She strongly suspected the door would not be opened to her a second time. Closing her eyes, she groaned. The visit hadn't gone well. She should have been better prepared.

But from the true emotions of Lady Emerson, Olivia wasn't sure the noblewoman would have been receptive to anything Olivia could say. She was clearly already on the edge—teetering where any further burden of worry and fear might push her over. Was it any wonder she wouldn't allow herself to consider the possibility of foul play? Such a fear might sink her under completely.

Olivia's dejection turned to determination. If Marigold's family weren't chasing down every possibility, then Olivia had to find a way to search herself. Mere weeks ago she would have had little hope of success. But for the moment she was living in a palace, practically a princess—surely she could use that position to search for her friend.

Before she reached the street, a tall male figure turned into the courtyard, his head down and gait hurried. As he passed her, Olivia seized his arm, halting his progress and spinning him back toward her.

"Lord Cade?" she asked as they came face to face.

He met her eyes, his own going wide. "Lady Olivia!" He forced a smile and executed a hasty bow. "How lovely to run into you. I'm just stretching my legs and—" He cut himself off as his gaze swept their surroundings, and he recognized the foolishness of his words given they were standing inside Lord Emerson's courtyard.

"Well," he said awkwardly. "That is to say, I..." But apparently he couldn't think of an explanation because his words trailed off.

Something snapped into place in Olivia's mind, and she seized his arm again, attempting to give him a knowing look. He blinked back at her.

"We need to talk," she said. "But I don't think this is the place."

"Talk?" Cade's eyes shifted toward the manor behind her. "I actually need to—"

"There's no point going in there," Olivia said firmly. "They probably won't even open the door when you knock, since they'll suspect it's me again."

One of Cade's eyebrows rose. "Again?"

Olivia shook her head. "Come on. I know a better place to talk."

She tugged him out of Lord Emerson's courtyard and into her uncle's. To her relief, no one saw their arrival, and she was able to lead him straight through the gardens to the back of the manor. Cade didn't protest, following under his own steam as she led him to the back wall and out onto the hill.

"This is a nice spot." He looked across the grassy incline and then back at the row of manors. His eyes lingered on the Emersons'.

Olivia nodded and pointed at the building directly behind them. "That's my aunt and uncle's manor. Until a few days ago, it was my home too. And it's up here, on this hill, that I first met Marigold."

Cade's eyes snapped to her face, his involuntary response only confirming her suspicions.

"I heard she played a...trick on you," he said carefully. "Julius told me about what happened."

"She did fool me," Olivia said, "and I intend to have stern words with her about it. But I still consider her a friend."

Cade's tense posture relaxed slightly.

Olivia fixed her eyes on him. "What I really want to know is whether Julius is aware that you're the one Marigold is in love with."

Cade flinched backward, the guilty look on his face providing the final confirmation. After meeting him outside Marigold's house, clearly worried and distracted, Olivia had been nearly certain. But his response made it feel shockingly real.

"You and Marigold are secretly in love?" Her voice rose higher than she'd intended. "And you haven't even told Julius? She didn't even tell me!" Olivia shook her head. "But why keep it a secret?"

Cade collapsed into himself. "I've known Marigold most of my life—like I know all the others our age at court. But our families don't get along. They're rivals in every area that matters. Marigold insisted we stay quiet about our feelings because her father would never approve. She said that if he found out, he would keep us apart. I wanted to face his wrath and prove the strength of our love—to argue for the benefits that could come from uniting our families—but Marigold..."

"She's hard to resist," Olivia said sympathetically. "And I'm guessing she loved playing the role of star-crossed lover in a secret romance. She probably arranged clandestine rendezvous and stolen kisses in all sorts of silly locations."

Cade flushed, and Olivia feared she had overstepped. She

had forgotten for a moment that while she knew Marigold well, she hardly knew Cade at all.

But instead of showing offense, Cade straightened his shoulders and drew a deep breath as if choosing bravery in the face of something fearsome.

"I suppose that's all it was on her side, and that's why she's abandoned me now. She did delight in the situation, just like you described." He looked away. "I've even wondered at times if she loved the role more than she loved me specifically."

Olivia's heart squeezed at the pain in his eyes, and she bit her lip, unsure how to answer. The mirror had shown sincerity beneath Marigold's dramatic manner, but Olivia couldn't be sure how well Marigold knew her own heart. She had no idea how to judge if her friend's feelings had been lasting and deep. Olivia didn't even know how to judge such a thing for herself. Marigold wouldn't be the first girl more in love with love than she was with the man.

But if Cade's conclusion was drawn solely from Marigold's disappearance, she could at least offer another possible explanation for that. Even if the explanation wasn't likely to find favor with him. She just hoped he didn't reject it outright as Marigold's mother had done.

"I can't see into Marigold's heart," she said. "But I do believe she was always sincere toward me. I can't accept the idea that she tricked me and then abandoned me to deal with the consequences alone. And neither do I think she would have declared her love for you and then run off without a word. If she found her love had disappeared, the Marigold I know would have told you to your face."

Cade winced and then laughed. "That's the Marigold I

know as well. She's no coward." His brows contracted. "But what are you saying? Do you think she's being held captive by these unknown relations? They would have to turn their home into a prison to successfully prevent Marigold from escaping if she desired to do so."

"She isn't with relatives at all," Olivia said, relieved he was taking her concerns seriously. "I've confirmed that with both Kasper and Lady Emerson."

"What?" Cade's jaw clenched, his muscles tensing. "What do you mean she's not with relatives?"

"They think she's run away," Olivia said. "But I'm not convinced. It just doesn't sound like Marigold to me."

Cade's face settled into rigid lines. "You think she's been abducted?"

Olivia swallowed and nodded. "That's the only conclusion I can come to. Kasper seemed to think it was a possibility, but I'm not sure how much influence he has with his parents. Lady Emerson wouldn't listen to me at all. She basically kicked me out of the house when I tried to suggest it. So I can't imagine you'd have any more luck." She cocked her head to the side. "I assume you were going there to ask about Marigold?"

Cade nodded. "I was going to beg them to tell me where she is so I could at least send a letter." He looked down. "She might be in danger right now, and I've been sitting in the palace, doubting her! She may even..." He swallowed convulsively, unable to finish the sentence.

Olivia shook her head vehemently. "No, we mustn't think like that! If there's anyone who can stay alive, it's Marigold. And you mustn't blame yourself for doubting, either. You thought her safe at home with her family, so it was reasonable to question her sudden silence."

"I should have trusted her." Cade sounded tormented. "But I always thought her love for me seemed like a dream. How could someone so vibrant and beautiful and brilliant love me? And then I heard she'd been chosen to wear the glass slippers..." He shuddered. "It seemed only natural they'd choose her—all the other girls at court faded beside her. And of course Julius would easily fall for her once she appeared at the ball. He probably would have already if he didn't always hold himself so aloof—waiting to do his duty and marry his parents' choice."

Cade stopped and swallowed. "Marigold tried to fight it, of course. She never liked being dictated to. But Lord Emerson was adamant that she accept the betrothal, and how could I stand in the way of her becoming queen? If I truly loved her, I had to stand aside and let her step into a bigger life. It was easy enough to believe that she would forget me and learn to love Julius. I suppose I was trying to protect my own heart by telling myself she must have already fallen out of love with me..."

Olivia's eyes moistened. Cade had been ready to step aside and watch the woman he loved marry his best friend, believing they would be happy with each other. And he didn't even speak as if he had resented Julius. Every look and word confirmed he truly cared about both Marigold and his friend.

But even so, she slipped out her mirror just far enough to angle it toward his face. She truly thought Cade was sincere, but she had to rule out the possibility that he was merely a good actor. If Marigold had seen his true face and fled from him, it might offer an alternative explanation to abduction.

For several seconds, the mirror showed nothing, and she pressed her lips together. It was an unfortunate moment for it to stop working. But then the surface rippled, showing her a visage even more devastated and lovesick than Cade's actual face.

Her heart softened even further, and she slipped the mirror away, placing a gentle hand on his arm.

"We have to find out what happened to Marigold. Will you help me? Surely together we can convince Julius to—"

"To what?" asked a cold voice behind her. "I'm here, so you can ask me directly."

Olivia dropped her hand from Cade's arm, turning to see Julius striding toward them, jaw clenched and eyes narrowed.

CHAPTER 17
JULIUS

Julius stood outside Olivia's sitting room door and drew a breath. He'd arrived a little later in the morning this time, but he didn't want to arrive too late. She might be annoyed at him for making her wait.

But when he knocked, there was no answer. He frowned and knocked again, this time louder. Was she still in bed? It didn't seem likely. But perhaps she was in her bedchamber and couldn't hear the knock on the sitting room door.

He tried the handle, pushing the door open when he found it unlatched. On the other side of the door, he discovered an empty room, save for the tray of breakfast—long since consumed from the look of the leftovers.

His eyes strayed toward the door that led to her bedchamber. If she didn't answer a knock on that door, he would have to find a maid to go in and check on her. If she was still in bed after all her plans for the day, she might be ill.

But the door stood wide open, allowing him a clear view of the equally empty room beyond. Olivia wasn't asleep— she was gone.

Julius's mind went blank for a moment. Where was she? She couldn't be in lessons. His mother had specifically given them both the morning off so he could escort her to her old home, as Olivia had requested. Was she wandering the corridors trying to find his suite?

He hurried back out, prowling through the wing that held both their suites. But he could find no sign of her. And the servants he passed claimed not to have seen her either. Had she wandered into a different section of the palace by accident?

When he stopped yet another servant to ask after her, he was finally met with something other than a blank stare.

"Lady Olivia? Oh yes, I saw her leaving the palace first thing this morning."

"Leaving?" Julius asked with a sense of foreboding.

The servant shifted uncomfortably. "Well, I can't say for sure, of course, Your Highness. I didn't follow her or anything." The man threw him an uncertain look. "Should I have done so? She didn't look lost."

"No, no, I'm sure she would have asked for assistance if she needed it." He hesitated. "She will have been on her way to her aunt's house. She had business there this morning."

The man's face cleared. "Aye, that makes sense, Your Highness, since she was headed outside."

Julius produced a smile—the court smile that he had long ago learned to manufacture regardless of his mood.

"Thank you."

His thoughts spun as he hurried toward the stables. Olivia had left the palace without him—without even leaving him word of her departure. If she was impatient and thought he was taking too long, she could have sent for him, or at the very least left a note. Then he wouldn't have spent so long searching for her and worrying.

When he called for the stable master, the grizzled older man appeared promptly, bowing before the prince and grinning from beneath bushy eyebrows. But when Julius asked whether Olivia had requested a horse or a carriage, he frowned.

"She hasn't been here this morning, Master Julius," he said, using an informality that was permitted him as the man who had taught a young and eager princeling how to ride. "We're ready when she does come, though. I've picked out the perfect mare for her. I got a good look at her seat when you brought her to the palace, and I think this mount will be a perfect fit."

"That's very good of you," Julius said, trying to hide his dismay.

Had she walked into the city?

He extricated himself as quickly as possible, hurrying from the palace grounds using the same route he had taken on the day of his first meeting with Olivia. Had she also taken the back way, or had she walked through the city streets? She was used to being an anonymous face in the capital, but that had all changed now. She might be accosted by a crowd and—

His steps quickened.

His path took him to the hill behind Manor Row, but he was too agitated to care whether he arrived at the front or back of Olivia's old home. He just wanted to be free to move quickly—he was almost as likely to draw attention on the streets as Olivia given all the current excitement about their recent betrothal.

But as he hurried along the grassy hill, his eyes found two people instead of the manor he sought. They were engaged in an intense conversation, and even from a distance, he easily recognized them—Olivia and Cade.

Neither of them had noticed his approach, and as he watched, Olivia leaned toward Cade, placing a familiar hand on his arm. A knot formed in Julius's gut, and he strode faster.

Olivia's words reached his ears. "Surely together we can convince Julius to—"

"To what?" he asked, his voice sounding harsh in his own ears. "I'm here, so you can ask me directly."

He wasn't sure he actually wanted her to answer, though. Everything about the scene made him deeply uncomfortable, and he had no desire to help with whatever plan they were hatching. He knew his mother intended to find a man of the court for Olivia to marry instead of him, but Julius found the whole concept increasingly distasteful, and the idea of that man being Cade was unthinkable. Even if Cade knew the truth of Julius's engagement to Olivia, it would still be a betrayal of friendship and loyalty for him to court her while she was Julius's betrothed. If Cade thought he could win Julius's blessing, he was sorely mistaken.

Olivia turned startled eyes on him, but her face showed no guilt. She did, however, throw a quick look at Cade. Something significant and unspoken passed between them, and Julius's stomach clenched again.

"I suppose this is why you didn't wait for me," he said, stopping in front of the two of them but looking only at Olivia. "You already had an escort."

Olivia tipped her head to the side, looking confused.

"What do you mean? Did you want me to wait for you? I didn't know you were coming this way."

"You didn't know I was..." Words failed him, and he ran a hand through his hair, needing some outlet for the frustration boiling inside him.

Olivia exchanged another look with Cade, this time one of obvious bewilderment.

"I always stand ready to escort Lady Olivia anywhere she needs to go." Cade gave Olivia a warm smile that seemed to carry a wealth of meaning. "But on this occasion, we met by chance, here on Manor Row."

Julius frowned, his understanding of the situation only growing more tangled.

"If you didn't have an alternative escort," he asked Olivia, "then why did you leave without me?"

Olivia shook her head. "I don't know what you're talking about. Were you expecting me to go somewhere with you this morning? I'd made plans to visit my aunt's house, remember?" She gestured at a small bag by her feet.

"Of course I remember. That's why I'm here." He ran his hand through his hair again, wondering if they were speaking a different language. "I especially asked my mother to give us both the morning off so that I could take you to your aunt and uncle's."

Olivia's eyes widened. "You asked for the morning off as well? You were planning to accompany me?"

"Of course! That's what we discussed."

Olivia shook her head, a stubborn light coming into her eyes. "You never said anything like that. I'm sure I would have remembered."

Julius's brows drew together. "But I said..." His words

trailed off as he tried to remember exactly what he'd said. Now that she was asking, he couldn't remember actually saying the words.

Cade cleared his throat with what sounded suspiciously like a suppressed chuckle. "You'll have to excuse him, Lady Olivia." He leaned closer, talking in an exaggerated whisper that easily reached Julius's ears. "You have a way of disabling his usual eloquence."

Julius's brows snapped together, but he couldn't deny it. Would he never stop misstepping when it came to Olivia? How could he ever succeed as future king if he was so easily thrown off balance?

He turned to Cade, trying to mask his discomfort. "What about you, then? What are you doing here?"

"Pure chance," Cade said cheerfully, seeming amused by Julius's discomfort. "Lady Olivia and I ran into each other on Manor Row, and she was kind enough to show me this spot." He glanced across the hill. "She was trying to enlist my help because she knows I have your ear." He grinned broadly at Julius who glowered back.

"It's about Marigold," Olivia jumped in quickly, and Julius groaned. Marigold again. Was the dratted girl going to plague him forever?

Olivia ignored him and continued, her eyes urgent. "I'm worried about Marigold, but her family are convinced she's run away and are too angry to look for her. I think she's been abducted, and I have to try to find her. You will help me, won't you?"

Julius was silent, not wanting to commit himself, but not wanting to reject her earnest plea either.

"I think Lady Olivia might exaggerate my influence,"

Cade said dryly, his eyes on Julius's face. "But of course I'll lend my voice to hers." He bowed in her direction. "Anything to assist my future queen."

Julius sighed. Olivia was his betrothed, and he could hardly offer her less assistance than Cade—even if he didn't think they owed Marigold anything.

"If it's so important to you, of course I'll help." He drew a deep breath. "And my apologies for the misunderstanding. I should have clarified our plans more clearly. But please don't go off alone again."

Olivia's eyes narrowed, so he continued quickly, not wanting yet another misunderstanding. "I know you're used to moving around the city alone, but your status has changed. Our betrothal has generated a great deal of interest, and half the population now knows your face, so it isn't safe. That doesn't mean you can't leave, just that you should take an escort with you. If I'm not available, there will always be grooms and guards who you can call on."

The indignant light in Olivia's eyes softened. "I'm sorry. I wanted to stretch my legs and didn't want to cause a fuss. It didn't occur to me that you might be worried as a result. I'll make sure I don't leave without an escort in future."

"Don't forget I stand ready to assist you if Julius isn't available," Cade said in his usual good-natured way.

But on this occasion, Julius wished he was a little less helpful and friendly. Julius wanted to be Olivia's escort himself. But he said nothing aloud. He could hardly complain when he had just told her to find a replacement when he wasn't available. As prince, his time was rarely his own, so there would be many times when he wasn't available.

But he was there now. He looked at Cade. "I can escort Olivia back to the palace myself on this occasion."

Cade laughed. "I can recognize a dismissal when I hear one." He turned to Olivia. "Consider me always at your disposal, my lady."

Julius watched his friend stroll away with a frown. Julius had told Cade he wasn't in love with Olivia, but surely his friend couldn't be developing feelings of his own for her so quickly. Julius wasn't sure what he was going to do if Cade was.

When Cade disappeared from view, Julius turned to Olivia. "Did you get everything you wanted?" He peered at her small bag. She couldn't have collected much.

"Actually…" Olivia gave a grin that filled him with foreboding. "There's one more thing." Her smile somehow grew broader. "Something you've already agreed I can bring to the palace."

She turned and called loudly across the hill. "Mildred. Mildred!"

Julius looked around in bewilderment. Wasn't her cousin called Delilah, or Daphne, or something like that? And what was she doing hiding on the hill behind Manor Row? She shouldn't even have been in Sovar yet.

A loud squeaking sounded across the grass, and a mouse the size of a miniature pony scurried into view. Julius gave an undignified exclamation and instinctively leaped backward. The palace had too much Legacy power for mice of any kind to be tolerated there, and he'd only seen one a couple of times. He'd certainly never seen one so large.

"What is that?" he breathed.

The creature raced over to Olivia and leaned against her, nearly knocking Olivia over.

"This is Mildred," Olivia said, still grinning. "And if you remember, you told me I could keep her with me at the palace. I've been terribly worried about her."

"I thought you meant a cat!"

"Well, you didn't specify in your agreement, so you can't take it back now." Olivia sounded smug, but the eyes she turned on him were pleading. "I won't be able to rest easy if I have to leave her out here. She's too big to hide herself now, and it's all my fault."

With a sigh, Julius accepted the inevitable. The Sovaran palace was about to acquire a horse-sized mouse.

He watched Olivia gently pat the soft fur of the enormous creature, remembering her words at the ball about feeling her own sense of responsibility. Whether it was working hard at her lessons, rescuing Marigold, or saving a mouse, Olivia had already proven the truth of her words. She might not have the connections expected of a royal bride, but Olivia clearly had the necessary character—more so than plenty of the girls at court.

But that didn't mean he wanted to marry her. She was still almost a stranger, and one neither he nor his parents had chosen.

OLIVIA

Their arrival back at the palace caused a small sensation, thanks to Mildred's presence. Stares and whispers followed them through the grounds, and Olivia tensed, worried she was doing damage to Julius's royal image. But he didn't falter, and she watched the way his confidence affected those around them. It was a clearly abnormal situation, but Julius made it ordinary and acceptable with his manner alone. Would she ever be able to do the same thing?

He flagged down first a gardener, then a groom, then a guard, and finally the castle steward. On each occasion, he introduced them to Mildred and instructed them to spread the word about her protected status. And every one of them accepted the palace's newest resident without batting an eye.

Mildred kept up with them easily, trotting along trustingly at Olivia's side. It had been a relief to see her come over the hill, her soft ears twitching. Olivia was just grateful she had managed to stay hidden for so long.

"She must eat an enormous volume of seeds and grains," Julius murmured, eyeing Mildred dubiously. "Or does she prefer something else?"

Olivia gave him an amused sideways look. "I know there aren't many mice in the capital, but didn't you learn about them in lessons on the Legacy? They are a part of Sovar's unique landscape, after all."

Julius said nothing, and she shook her head. He must have been taught by tutors rather than attending school like most Sovarans, and she could only assume mice weren't considered as necessary to the education of a prince as to a farmer's daughter.

"They might be enormous," she explained, "but their size is sustained by the Legacy's power. They don't eat much more than a regular mouse. Naturally speaking, the anatomy of a mouse isn't designed to sustain the pressures of such a large size. She's definitely smarter than normal mice, too. I've heard even our normal, cat-sized mice are smarter than regular mice in other kingdoms. A little like the parrots in Glandore, I suppose. Although Mildred doesn't talk. Sadly."

She gave Mildred an affectionate look and a pat, her face softening as it always did when she interacted with the sweet creature. Julius quickly glanced away, clearing his throat.

She eyed him, wondering if he was more upset than he was letting on about her adoption of Mildred. But it didn't matter since she wasn't willing to back down on that point. She wasn't going to leave the mouse to fend for herself.

"Do you want to house her in a stall in the stables?" he asked, no longer showing any hint of annoyance.

Olivia considered her options. "I would prefer to have her

sleep in my sitting room if it wouldn't upset the servants too much."

Julius chuckled. "I'm sure we can unearth at least a few palace servants who aren't afraid of mice."

Olivia snorted. "You have no idea how tough some servants are. But that doesn't mean they appreciate extra cleaning."

To her surprise, he only chuckled again at her reference to her previous status. "I defer to your greater experience, my lady. Feel free to request as many servants as you feel the job needs."

Olivia huffed. "Please, just call me Olivia. You, at least, should be able to do so safely. I feel like a ridiculous fraud every time someone calls me *lady*."

Julius gave her a piercing look that made her heart skip a beat. "You have no reason to feel like a fraud. You've been working hard since the moment you arrived to earn that title." His mouth twisted. "From what I understand, you're back in lessons this afternoon."

Olivia sighed. By the time she finished with all the lessons, she would know the etiquette of court better than someone born to the position.

Julius didn't leave her until servants had arrived to begin making arrangements for Mildred. At that point, she had to leave herself or risk running late for her lessons, so they parted at her door in unexpected amity. She returned in the evening to find Mildred settled on a giant nest of straw tucked into one corner of her sitting room.

But her warmer feelings toward him evaporated when she tracked him down the next morning. She managed to make it all the way to his personal courtyard with only one stop for directions, and she arrived just in time to catch him and Cade finishing their final bout. None of the other three were in sight, so she dove straight into the topic of Marigold after the briefest exchange of morning greetings.

Julius clearly didn't share her enthusiasm.

"I'm not convinced this is necessary," he said with a deep frown. "You have quite enough to do here without wasting time trying to work out where Marigold is hiding herself."

He cast a long-suffering look at Cade, but when he saw Cade's expression of serious concern, he huffed and looked away.

It would be easier if they could tell Julius the truth about Marigold and Cade. It would not only bolster their claims but provide Julius an incentive to help find her. Surely he would want to help his best friend if he knew. But it had to be Cade's decision to tell Julius, not Olivia's. She wasn't going to betray the confidence she had forced out of him.

"We can't just abandon her, Julius," Olivia said instead. "How can I enjoy my new life in the palace when my friend might be in serious danger?"

Julius wiped the back of his neck with a cloth and began replacing the various items of clothing he had discarded for the bout. "I know you feel responsible for everyone around you," he said as he buttoned his vest. "But extending that to the friend who stabbed you in the back and then ran away is going unnecessarily far. We don't actually know she's in danger, and for myself, I have no desire to see Marigold again any time soon."

Olivia cast a despairing glance at Cade who grimaced and shrugged.

"But what if she didn't run away?" Olivia asked, trying again.

"Oh, what if she only stabbed you in the back, you mean?" Julius shrugged into his jacket.

"If I'm not upset about that, I don't see why you should be!" Olivia shot back.

Julius tugged his clothing into place as he looked up and met her eyes. "Maybe because she stabbed me in the back too? I've known Marigold far longer than you, remember?"

"I thought you didn't even want to marry Marigold," Cade said quietly.

Julius shot him a look, and Olivia was instantly consumed by curiosity. They had clearly discussed the situation of Julius's betrothal, and she wanted to know what else Julius had said.

But neither of them gave anything else away, an uncomfortable silence falling between them all. Marigold's betrayal of Julius might not have been personal, but she had done more damage to the royal family than she had done to Olivia, so Julius's point was still valid.

"Perhaps we can convince Kasper to assist in the search instead?" Cade murmured.

Julius groaned. "Let's not make this any messier than it already is. I said yesterday that I would help you, Olivia, so if you're fully committed to this then of course I will. I just wish you would reconsider. You're already tackling one monumental task here at the palace."

Was he worried about her or worried that the search would distract her and her role at the palace would suffer as a result?

Determination filled her. If Julius didn't want to be

involved, she would find a way to search for Marigold without him. Despite their early interactions, Olivia knew Julius took his role as the gallant prince very seriously. The last thing she wanted was to use that to manipulate him into doing something he didn't want to do. Knowing Marigold had betrayed the royal family only made it worse. Olivia couldn't use their resources when the whole search was based on nothing more than her hunch.

Olivia might not be able to give the resources of a princess to the search, but she could still give her own time. She just hoped that would be enough to find some sign of Marigold.

Julius seemed relieved that Olivia didn't push further, although Cade looked concerned. She would have to find a private opportunity to let him know that she hadn't given up on Marigold. It would be even better if she had some progress to report to him when she did.

But despite her best intentions, it was two days before her packed schedule presented her with an empty afternoon to make a start on her plan. Remembering her promise to Julius, and not wanting to be reckless, she approached the stables first and was directed to the stable master.

The older man was delighted at her request for a horse, producing a lively mare who won Olivia over instantly with her perfect lines and cheeky attitude. The stable master was equally as proficient at providing a groom to accompany her, so Olivia rode into the city with the satisfaction of knowing she had followed royal protocol for once. Julius would have nothing to upbraid her for this time.

For a while she had to give her full attention to navigating the flow of traffic—a very different experience on horseback than on foot. But as she became more comfortable with the city from the back of a horse, she put more attention into the direction of her path. She hadn't been sure of her destination when she'd left the palace, but the salt in the air pulled her toward the sea, and she followed her instincts. When the vast expanse of shimmering blue came into view, she smiled, pleased with her choice.

She had reached the shore to the south of the docks, where a long stretch of grass met the sand and provided the perfect spot for picnics. As usual on a bright, sunny day, the grass was littered with small pockets of people enjoying a few leisure hours.

Olivia dismounted, handing her reins to the groom, and walked among the picnicking groups. The ordinariness of the scene refreshed her, but she hadn't come to the shore to enjoy an afternoon off. She was searching for information, and she needed to consider where she had the best chance of obtaining it.

Her eyes drifted over a number of couples, all of them too wrapped up in each other to welcome interruption. Some youths were laughing and splashing in the shallow water, and several clumps of either mothers or nannies watched gaggles of small children. None of them seemed like ideal candidates.

But finally she noticed a group of girls playing a complicated game of handball—one she remembered from her own youth in Henton. Sidling up to them, she waited until the small sack filled with dried beans flew off course, in danger of falling to the ground. Intercepting its fall with the back of her hand, she propelled it straight upward. As it fell back toward her, she whipped her hand around and hit it for a second time, this time with the heel of her palm. It flew across the small circle to the girl directly opposite.

The girls acknowledged her inclusion in their circle with grins but didn't break their movements, continuing to pass the ball between them. Olivia received it twice more before it finally flew wide, plopping to the grass before anyone could reach it.

The girls relaxed.

"One hundred and twenty," one of them said with a smile. "That's our best effort in a long time." She turned to Olivia. "I didn't know noble girls played handball too."

Noble girls? Olivia blinked before suddenly remembering what she was wearing. When had she gotten so used to wearing finery that she forgot all about it? She should have changed into one of her old gowns before venturing into the city.

"Wait," one of the girls whispered to her neighbor, "isn't that the new princess?"

Overlapping murmurs spread through the group until one of the more confident girls spoke. "You are Princess Olivia, aren't you?"

The others fell silent to hear her answer.

"Yes, I'm Olivia," Olivia admitted. "But I'm not a princess yet."

Fresh murmurs broke out among the girls, this time even more excited.

"That doesn't matter," said the speaker. "You will be one soon. We all think it's terribly romantic. But what are you doing here?"

Olivia glanced at her accompanying groom. He was some distance away, occupied with walking both their horses back and forth along the street that bordered the grass. The street ran parallel to the shoreline, and the far side of it was lined with a mix of shops and houses, all facing toward the sea. The traffic was heavy enough that she lost sight of him for a moment before he circled back. But she was hardly at risk from a group of fifteen-year-old girls.

"I came to see the ocean." Olivia hesitated. "And because I want to ask you a question."

"Ask us?" one of the other girls asked, shock making her bolder.

Olivia nodded. Her theory was that if Marigold had been abducted but no ransom demand had been made, then she couldn't have been the only young woman to go missing. And girls the age of the ones in front of her tended to pay attention to the girls a few years older as they anticipated their own arrival into adulthood.

"Have any of you ever heard of girls my age going missing?" she asked. "Perhaps being abducted?"

"Did someone try to abduct you?" the boldest girl asked, a gleam of excitement in her eyes.

Olivia's hands flew up in repudiation, her head shaking urgently. She couldn't risk such a juicy piece of false gossip spreading through the city.

"No, no," she rushed to say. "Nothing of the sort. Everyone I've met has been most kind." Or at least, mostly everyone. She wasn't counting Lady Emerson. "I was just curious because I heard a story about something similar, and I wondered if it might be true. And I'm betting girls like you know everything that goes on around you."

The girls exchanged pleased grins at her assessment of them.

"Adults always think they know better," the main speaker said, "but they have no idea how much we see and hear."

Olivia nodded. "I know because I was you not so long ago. Girls like you listen and watch everything going on—with both the adults and the children."

Several heads nodded agreement.

"See," one of them whispered to another, "the prince really is marrying one of us."

Olivia flushed slightly, feeling like a fraud on every front. These girls thought she'd been welcomed into the palace with open arms, not realizing the royal family were working for a way to free themselves from her—and that she was encouraging them to do so.

"I haven't heard of any abductions, though," the main speaker said thoughtfully. She glanced around the cluster of girls. "Have any of you?"

Most shook their heads, but one girl pushed herself forward from the back of the group.

"I've heard of one," she said.

Olivia's heart lifted. "You have? When? Where? Do you know what happened to the girl?"

"Really, Bess?" one of the other girls asked. "I never heard about that. Who was it?"

Bess shrugged one shoulder. "I don't remember her name. It was at least two years ago. I only heard about it because my father worked for her father, and I overheard them talking about it. I don't know if anyone outside the business even knew."

"Why did the girl's father keep it a secret?" Olivia asked, frowning. "Didn't he want help from the guards?"

"The abductors demanded he keep it quiet," Bess said. "They wanted a ransom, and they told the girl's father that if he reported it to anyone, they would kill his daughter."

Several of the girls gasped, but the topic was removed enough from them that their horror was edged with an excited thrill.

"What did they demand for the ransom?" Olivia asked. The situation Bess was describing differed significantly from Marigold's, but it might still be connected in some way.

Bess shrugged. "I didn't hear that. But I know the father paid, and his daughter was returned safely. So I suppose it was a happy ending."

"Depending what he had to give up to save her," Olivia muttered, mostly to herself. "You said you don't remember the name of the girl, but could you direct me to her father? I'd like to ask him some questions."

"Sorry," Bess said. "They moved away from the capital as soon as they got her back. My father said they wanted to get as far from the city as possible. They completely abandoned their plans to expand their business and everything. I guess the owner lost the heart for business matters. He hired my father to manage his existing contracts and walked away from it all." A brief look of guilt passed over her face. "So our family ended up benefitting from what happened." She looked down. "I think of them sometimes because of that."

"Don't feel bad, Bess," another girl said firmly. "Your family has only profited because your father is a trustworthy and dependable person. There's nothing wrong with that. It's not like you abducted the girl."

The other girls chimed in, echoing their agreement, and Olivia nodded along. Another abducted girl was intriguing, but she had no way of knowing if it had any connection to what had happened to Marigold. And apparently there was no way for her to follow the incident up to find out further information, either. But it was something that the girl had been returned unharmed. That, at least, was encouraging.

"Thank you for telling me," she said to Bess. "I appreciate your help."

Bess glowed, curtsying prettily and flushing. "My ma is never going to believe I helped a princess today."

Olivia didn't attempt to correct her on the title a second time. She had a request to make, and she wanted them as receptive as possible.

"Actually," she said, "I would prefer if you didn't mention the details of our conversation to anyone else. I wouldn't want anyone to think—"

"Umm," one of the girls interrupted, "about that…" She gestured at the grass around them, her face apologetic.

Olivia scanned the surrounding groups, her dismay rising. She had been so focused on Bess that she hadn't noticed a couple of the girls slip away. Apparently, they had been so eager to share the news of her presence that they had already begun the task, flitting with glee from group to group. Many of the other people on the grass were already making their way in her direction.

Olivia stepped backward and looked again for her guard. He was down the far end of the road, only just turning back in her direction.

"Your Highness!" A group of men and women hurried over, curtsying and bowing politely.

Some of Olivia's nervousness abated. These people didn't

wish her any harm, quite the opposite. They all looked excited to see her.

Another group arrived and another. Olivia kept smiling and nodding at them all as they called her name and shouted excited questions. One woman patted her arm in a motherly way, but it unleashed a flood of hands reaching for her. They patted her arms and her hair or grasped at her hands.

She tried to look for the groom again, but she could no longer see through the wall of people. Panic rose up in her throat. She was trapped, and the growing crowd kept pressing closer and closer. No one was trying to harm her, but her overwhelmed senses received it as an attack, screaming at her to get away.

She ripped her hands free of the reaching fingers and flung her arms up to shield her face. Pushing blindly, she struggled through the throng, bursting free onto the edge of the street.

But the crowd followed, still calling to her with so many overlapping voices that she couldn't catch the individual words. She plunged blindly across the street, weaving through traffic. Ducking behind a moving wagon, she put herself momentarily out of view of the people coming behind her, but the cover wouldn't last long.

With a burst of speed, she reached the other side of the street. Before she could call for the groom, a hand shot out from an alley between two shops and seized her arm. With no time for more than a squeak, she was yanked off the street and into the dark shadows beyond.

CHAPTER 19
JULIUS

Julius wanted to find Olivia and ask about her afternoon plans, but his mother had her on an even tighter schedule than Julius himself. So instead he directed his steps to the palace library. The airy space, with its reassuring rows of solid shelves, had been a haven for him in his younger years, but he hadn't visited in some time.

On this occasion, it wasn't the library itself that attracted his interest, but a private study room located near the back. Inside, he found three men and a woman seated at a table covered in haphazard piles of books. All four were engaged in a lively debate.

They stopped talking abruptly at his entrance, standing to bow deeply. He waved them back into their seats, dropping down to sit beside them.

"I've been meaning to come and check on your progress for some time," he said. "Have you discovered anything?"

The small team of scholars and historians had been working nonstop since the Midsummer Ball to devise a strategy to release him from his betrothal. In all that time, he had yet to hear anything about their progress.

The woman exchanged a look with one of the men, and Julius's stomach swirled. What did that look mean? And what did he want it to mean? He wasn't even sure he knew anymore.

"We have found nothing conclusive, Your Highness," she said cautiously.

Julius frowned. Did that mean they had found a possibility or not? Or had his mother already instructed them not to give him any details? If so, he wasn't likely to get anything out of them.

"I see," he said slowly. "So there's been no definitive progress."

"There's no need to despair yet, Your Highness," the oldest of the men said. "We remain hopeful. But we've agreed not to share anything with your family until we can come to a consensus between us." He nodded at the others and chuckled. "We have some differing opinions, thus the enthusiasm you witnessed earlier."

It wasn't much in the way of reassurance, but at least his parents weren't concealing the truth from him. He stood again, pretending not to notice the relief on their faces at his swift departure.

"Thank you for your efforts," he said. "I look forward to hearing your conclusions once you reach agreement."

He walked more slowly back through the library, his mind heavy. Near the door, he encountered his mother, for once not accompanied by her usual bevy of court ladies.

She greeted him with a glad cry, and he quirked an

eyebrow at her. "You're here for an update as well? I can save you the bother. They still have nothing conclusive to report."

His mother sighed. "The same as always, then. And yet I can't seem to stop myself from checking every day. I'm probably driving them to distraction."

She looped her arm through Julius's and let him lead her out of the library. He glanced down at her quizzically.

"Are you so desperate for them to succeed? I thought you and father were coming around to the advantages of my marrying a commoner."

His mother sighed. "It is our job to examine every eventuality and plan for each to the best of our ability. The fact that we are considering how best to utilize the current situation doesn't mean it's our first preference. Olivia is a dear girl, but there's so very much for her to learn." She gazed ahead of them, her eyes appearing distant and unfocused. "Do you think she could ever be comfortable here in our world? It was difficult enough for me, and I was raised in one of the most prominent court families."

Julius frowned, wishing he could reassure her, but not confident in his answer. Olivia had impressed him in the days since her arrival at the palace, but that said nothing about her own comfort and happiness. And, somehow, that consideration had grown in importance in his mind. He had initially opposed the match for the sake of himself and the kingdom. Now he wondered if he should be opposing it for Olivia's sake, as his mother seemed to be.

"If she's not able to fit in here," his mother continued sadly, "then it will make your life very difficult. You already have such a challenging role, and your father I want to help you with our choice of wife, not hinder you. There are other ways we can secure the goodwill of the populace."

He glanced sideways at his mother. Apparently, it wasn't Olivia's well-being that concerned her after all. Not that he should be surprised—she had always been a very doting mother.

"Olivia seems to be adjusting quickly," he said lightly, hoping his mother wouldn't read too much into his words.

She turned to examine his face, and he kept his expression neutral. Whatever she saw there must have satisfied her because she nodded and smiled.

"We've certainly been fortunate. The situation could be a lot worse. You would never guess she was a servant from her quick wits and level of education."

Julius frowned. "She wasn't a true servant, Mother. You know that. She's a farmer's daughter, and the niece of a successful businessman. And I'm sure even true servants are sufficiently educated. Sovar requires decent wages to be paid for the job."

"Yes, yes, but you know what I mean," his mother said. "I've been asking about her history, and she sat in on many of her cousins' lessons since her arrival in the capital. So that will explain some of it. Servants just don't have much opportunity to broaden their horizons."

"Well, she's certainly having them broadened now," Julius muttered. "Whether she wants it or not."

His mother's words didn't sit comfortably, and he suspected he knew the reason why. It wasn't long since she had lamented about his own lack of experience outside the court, a strange mimicry of her words now about servants. Maybe it was Julius who had failed to broaden his horizons.

"In fact, Olivia is doing so well," his mother continued, oblivious, "that I've decided she's ready for social functions. I've already started planning a soiree as her first event. After that she can join court life freely."

"That's excellent news," Julius said. Olivia had been sequestered long enough, and the people of court were growing impatient to properly meet her. "I'll let her know. Is she in lessons at the moment or in her suite?"

His mother's brows rose slightly, but she accepted his offer without question. "In her suite, I would assume. She only had morning lessons today. She can join us at the evening meal tonight where it will be just the four of us. A rehearsal, if you will."

"Thank you, Mother." Julius threw her a final smile as he disentangled his arm and turned down the corridor that would lead him to Olivia's suite.

When he glanced back his mother was watching him with an expression he couldn't read. His quick steps soon took him beyond her view, however, and he was knocking at Olivia's sitting room door within minutes.

For the second time there was no answer, and he was forced to let himself in. When he was once again greeted with an empty suite, he rocked back on his heels, considering where she might be. She hadn't had the opportunity to make friends at court yet—unless he counted Cade, and he preferred not to count Cade. It was a beautiful day, however, and his eyes were irresistibly drawn to the row of windows with their view of the grounds below.

He could see no sign of her from the window, but if she had gone for a ride, she would be out of view. He hurried straight for the stables, where the stable master greeted him with good humor and confirmed that Olivia was out riding.

"The mare can be trusted to keep her head in traffic," the old man remarked, clearly seeking to assuage any concern Julius might feel for his betrothed. Instead, his words awakened the first stirrings of Julius's alarm.

"Has she gone outside the grounds?" he asked.

The stable master nodded. "Requested an escort as pretty as you please, Your Highness." He gave a gruff chuckle. "I suspect there's not many as could gainsay a young thing like her." He gave Julius a reassuring smile. "I sent one of my steadier lads."

Julius nodded absently, relieved.

"Did she mention how long she expected to be with her aunt and uncle this time?" he asked, playing with the idea of riding out to meet her.

"Aunt and uncle?" The stable master rubbed his chin. "I don't know about that. She sounded as if she was planning an excursion into the city."

Julius's eyes snapped to the man's face. "The city? She went into the city with just a groom? No guards?"

The stable master frowned. "She didn't say anything about guards, Your Highness." The creases on his brow deepened. "Are you expecting trouble, Prince? You often ride out with a single escort."

Julius bit back a low growl. The words were true enough, and the situation wasn't the stable master's fault. A rush of anger toward Olivia filled him, but he recognized it for what it truly was—fear.

This time he wasn't going to rush to blame her. She had followed his instructions exactly—he was the one who had failed to be clear about what escorts she would need for what activities. Worst of all, he had a sinking feeling that he knew what had sent her into the city. If she was poking around looking for hardened criminals known to abduct young ladies, he would have liked a whole battalion at her back.

"Saddle my horse as quickly as possible," he bit out, turning on his heel without waiting for the stable master's acknowledgment.

Racing across the open yard between the stables and barracks, he snapped out an order for an escort of guards. The sergeant on duty didn't waste time with questions, bellowing for his chosen men to fetch their mounts.

As Julius mounted his own stallion, he told himself he was probably overreacting. He hoped he was. If Olivia was merely riding around the city for some fresh air, she would probably be fine, even with a single groom. But he didn't believe his own reassurances. Olivia had been too passionate about finding Marigold for that, and he should have questioned her sudden quiet on the topic.

Riding out of the palace, at the head of two rows of brightly dressed guards, he tried to think where to start his search. In the end, at a loss, he directed his horse toward the city's central market.

On main market days, people would come from the surrounding countryside to set up stalls, but even on a non-market day, the permanent stallholders would be there. Julius headed straight for a small stall in one of the far corners, keeping his horse to a walk as he wove through the milling customers.

He had never openly approached that particular stall

before, but his father's aide—the one whose name wasn't known to most of the court—had once pointed out the stall. Julius wasn't supposed to approach it openly, but his worry was too great to allow for caution.

He stopped in front of the stall and pointed silently at one of the barrels of cider.

"Yes, Your Highness!" the man inside the stall cried, leaping to his feet. "At once, Your Highness!"

He dipped a tankard into the cider and carried it to the prince, who remained astride. Handing it up, the man bowed obsequiously, but his manner was belied by the light in his eyes, which was intelligent and knowing.

When he straightened, he murmured too quietly for even Julius's guards to hear.

"If you're interested in the location of Her Highness, I've heard word she was headed for the seaside—the popular beach south of the port, I believe it was."

"My thanks." Julius took a long draft before handing the tankard back to the man and tossing down a coin.

The man accepted the tankard with another bow, catching the coin with a practiced movement.

"My stall is honored by your visit, Your Highness," he said, but Julius was already moving again, his guards behind him.

The man provided a flow of information to the palace on the state of the populace, and he could now see why his father valued him so highly. Julius might face the king's displeasure for openly interacting with the man, but he didn't regret it. He would never have tracked Olivia down without some direction.

As he rode, the panicked feeling in his gut slowly

subsided. If Olivia had gone to the popular section of waterfront, it was good news—much better than imagining her poking around in the underbelly of the city. She must have been seeking information from the general populace rather than seeking the abductors directly.

And if she wasn't in direct and immediate danger, he needed to rethink his approach. The southern beachfront was one of the places where the people of the city mingled freely, regardless of their usual occupations and ranks, and it was always a popular location when the weather was favorable. If he rode up with a squad of guards and plucked Olivia from the people's midst, he might create the sort of stir that was certain to anger his father. Better to approach with a little more circumspection.

He pulled up short of the beachfront street, directing his men to remain there out of sight. Dismounting, he crossed the final distance alone.

CHAPTER 20
OLIVIA

Yanked off the street, Olivia was too shocked to fight or scream. Just keeping her feet under her was a struggle as she stumbled across the cobblestones. Before she knew what was happening, her back was against one of the shops, and her captor had angled his body to block her from view of the main street beyond, his arm against the wall beside her.

But his other hand cradled the back of her head, ensuring it didn't crack against the stone behind, and his face was familiar.

"Julius," she breathed, her panic subsiding, replaced with an unexpected feeling of security.

His drastic action suggested she had been right to fear the crowd, and yet she felt infinitely safer than she had a moment before. The sound of running feet and the murmur of voices made him tense, but he didn't pull back. Instead, he pressed closer, dipping his head toward hers.

Olivia froze, all thoughts fleeing her mind as his lips hovered just over hers, his body pressing her back against the wall. The crowd and street beyond faded, Julius filling her awareness completely. She couldn't blink, could barely breathe. What was happening to her?

But he stayed there, just out of reach, his breath brushing her face, but his lips never touching hers. A heartbeat passed and another, his steady hand still cupping the back of her head, his fingers soft on her hair.

Olivia's hands instinctively found the front of his jacket, clinging to him, and the ridiculous thought flashed through her mind that she could tip onto her toes and close the remaining distance between them herself.

But a breath later, Julius pulled abruptly back, his eyes dark and impossible to read. He dropped his arm from beside her head and looked toward the mouth of the alley.

"They didn't see you," he said. "And hopefully they'll have dispersed now. I don't think they meant you any harm."

"No," Olivia sounded more breathless than she would have liked. She cleared her throat and tried again. "I didn't realize a crowd of people would behave like that."

Julius turned back to her, a frown on his face. "Crowds can be unpredictable. Which is one of the many reasons why you shouldn't have embarked on this foolish errand with only a single groom."

His voice rose toward the end, and somehow the distance between them had closed again. When she didn't say anything, he continued.

"You should have talked to me before leaving the palace." His brows drew further together. "You were looking for Marigold, weren't you? Must you insist on being so reckless?"

Olivia's temper flared, her emotions still overwhelmed

and seesawing wildly. She took a step toward him, her skirt brushing against his boots.

"And what if I was? I was trying to consider you—your resources, your feelings—by not involving you. Is that a crime now? I was trying not to use any resources except my own time, but I still respected what you'd said about bringing an escort. If I needed a larger escort, you should have made that clear. How was I supposed to know?"

She was almost vibrating with the force of her anger by the time she finished. Distantly she recognized she wasn't being fair, but the aftermath of her recent flight was still coursing through her, roiling her emotions in its wake. Not to mention whatever that had been between them when he had held her so close.

Julius didn't back down, meeting her gaze fiercely as sparks leaped from his eyes to hers and back again.

"Do you really think I was worried about using the palace's resources?" he asked with none of the usual princely polish in his voice. "I was trying to protect *you*!"

Olivia wanted to scoff at the suggestion, but she couldn't entirely dismiss it. Even so, she wasn't ready to let him off the hook.

"But that's my choice to make," she snapped, "not yours. If you truly wanted to protect me, you should have accepted that this is important to me. We could have worked together to find a safer way. I won't let you stop me from doing what I believe is right. If I let you control me in the name of keeping me safe, where does that end?"

Her breaths heaved in and out, and there was no space left between them. Their eyes locked as something intense

and charged bound them together, too much emotion overflowing the small alley.

Distantly, behind her anger, she wondered how he had
found her. He must have ridden across the whole city in her
wake. What had driven him to do so? Was it really only his
sense of responsibility toward her?

The tension built, and unconsciously Olivia swayed even
closer to him, her eyes dropping to his lips.

"You're right." Julius stepped back, breaking the tension.

Dazed at his sudden movement, Olivia blinked at him.
"What?"

"I shouldn't have dismissed your determination to help
your friend—even if I was doing it for your sake. And by the
same token, you shouldn't have acted alone in the name of
protecting me. You're right that we'll do better if we work
together and not at cross purposes."

Olivia drew a steadying breath, nodding her agreement.
She had blamed him for trying to protect her when she had
been doing the same thing to him.

"On that note," he added, "if you're going to start
roaming the city, interrogating the populace, you would save
me a great deal of stress if you take a squad of guards with
you."

Olivia glanced toward the street and shivered. "Yes, I can
see now that it was naive of me," she said quietly. "But I've
seen your father riding through the city, and I didn't think
there was any danger." Her lips twisted.

Julius sighed. "If you'd stayed on horseback, there probably wouldn't have been. And honestly, in a few years' time
—when the excitement of both the betrothal and the
wedding is past—you can probably visit the beach with a

single groom and be fine. But right now, you're a novelty. The city is intensely interested in you, but no one is used to seeing you yet. You need to give them time to adjust."

Olivia nodded slowly, trying not to place any weight on his phrasing—the assumption that their wedding would proceed. It gave her a fluttery feeling inside that she wasn't ready to analyze.

The rest of his words made sense. But nothing in her life had prepared her to even consider such matters. It was yet another reminder how out of depth she was in her new role.

"Thank you for coming for me," she said softly. "I know they weren't trying to hurt me, but I was truly frightened back there."

Julius's face softened. "You're my betrothed, Olivia. If I think you're in danger, I'll always come for you. Just as you are doing your best to protect me and my family with those endless lessons."

Olivia smiled at him, but her heart wasn't in it. His words depressed her a little instead of providing the reassurance he obviously intended. It wasn't Olivia he had ridden out to save but the public figure of his betrothed.

She turned her thoughts to more practical matters. "So if I take a squad of guards in the future, I'll be safe?"

"You should be."

She sighed. "They won't help me when I'm trying to talk to the people of the city, though." She hummed to herself as she considered the possibilities. "What if I took Cade with me as well? He could stay at my side while I talk to people, and the guards could hang back a little, ready to step in if needed."

"Cade?"

She frowned, confused by his sharp response. "He said he was happy to be my escort whenever I needed one, remember? As a younger son, he has more free time than a crown prince. And then I'll be safe without needing to bother you at all."

"Not bothered?" Julius almost growled, running a hand through his hair. "When did I say I didn't want to be bothered?"

Olivia's frown deepened. "But back at the palace, you said—"

"I said that I didn't want *you* bothered. It's not the same thing." He sighed and let his hand drop. "If you're determined to come out with a squad of guards, of course I'll accompany you. I'm sure I can find some windows of time in my schedule. If you run into trouble, I'll be more use to you than Cade."

"Thank you," Olivia said, surprised at his insistence.

She hadn't expected him to use all his limited free time on her project—especially when he disapproved of it. But secretly she was pleased. Between her lessons and his responsibilities, they'd been seeing much less of each other than she'd expected. And the less they saw of each other, the more likely they were to keep miscommunicating.

"Your Highness?" The voice of a concerned guard pulled their attention back to the main street.

His guards had found them, along with Olivia's groom.

Julius helped her mount before swinging himself into his own saddle, positioning his horse beside hers as they turned back toward the palace.

"So, was your attempt at information gathering successful?" he asked lightly. "Did you find anything?"

Olivia told him Bess's tale, and he frowned in response.

"It's a concerning occurrence, if true," he said. "I'll check the records kept at the guard's barracks to see if there's any mention of it. But I don't see any connection to Marigold's situation."

"Perhaps not," Olivia said lightly, not wanting to fight with him again. Logical or not, it felt like a start to her.

"I was actually looking for you with some news of my own," Julius said after a long minute of silence.

He gave her an update on the scholars' efforts—which seemed to amount to no progress, from what she could understand. She should probably have felt something about that news, but her emotions were so disordered from the afternoon's events that she couldn't be sure what she was feeling.

"And I ran into my mother," he added. "You've officially graduated to royal meals and court events now, so you're to join us for dinner. And I should warn you that she's planning a soiree."

It turned out Olivia did have room inside for more anxiety, after all. But there was some anticipation as well. She was ready to spend more time outside the classroom, putting what she'd learned into practice.

Later that evening, when she approached the small private dining room used when the royal family were eating alone, she found Julius waiting in the corridor. He smiled reassuringly at her.

"I know you haven't spent much time with my father," he said softly, "but I promise he's quite friendly in private."

Olivia's brows rose. "To his own son, perhaps."

"And for the moment, you're family as well," Julius said lightly.

"For the moment," Olivia murmured under her breath, but she took his offered arm, relieved to have him at her side as she entered. It was thoughtful of him to have waited.

Thankfully, Julius's claims turned out to be accurate. The atmosphere over the meal was casual, and King Robert treated her with genial good humor. Like Julius, it seemed he had a public and private facade.

Most of the conversation was taken up with the queen's plans for the upcoming soiree, and Olivia began to feel some enthusiasm for the event. The queen had treated her with kindness, and she wanted to repay those efforts by performing creditably. But it would be more comfortable if she had some friends of her own, instead of relying only on those Julius had introduced to her. If only Daphne had already arrived.

A sudden thought made her put down her fork.

"May I make a request for the guest list, Your Majesty?" she asked the queen.

Queen Elsinore smiled, but Olivia thought she detected a hint of caution lurking behind the expression. Hopefully the queen's fears would be allayed when she heard Olivia's small request.

"Would it be possible to include my aunt and two cousins on the guest list? I know they aren't usually invited to court functions, but it would be a great relief to me to have them there."

The queen immediately relaxed, her smile widening. "My dear girl, of course we can invite them! I should have thought of it myself. It's true that they haven't previously moved in court circles, but as your family, they have every right to join us.”

Olivia smiled in relief at the queen’s warm response. Nell and Hattie would be over the moon to receive the invitation, and enjoying the event through their eyes would make it much less nerve-wracking for her.

The days before the soiree passed quickly and without any opportunity for Olivia to return to the city in search of further word of Marigold. But she did fall into the habit of meeting Julius and his friends every morning in their private courtyard. Sometimes she arrived in time to watch their bouts, cheering for first one young nobleman and then another. Other times she arrived at the end, missing the actual fighting and contenting herself with exchanging a few words with Julius.

She had spent long hours of darkness lying in her grand bed and considering what had passed between them in the alley. Her conclusion was that she needed to be wary of him. Her resolution to guard her heart had wavered for a moment, and she couldn’t let it do so again. But if they were going to act as a team, they needed regular contact. She only hoped that daily conversations would inoculate her against his handsome face and princely charm. As the population would one day grow used to her, so repeated exposure would enable her to grow used to Julius’s proximity.

On the morning of the soiree, Ashton bounced to her side the moment she appeared and assured her earnestly that she could count on him. Olivia regarded him in surprise until Cade approached more sedately and grinned at her.

“Julius has enlisted us to make sure your cousins have a good time. Helen and Harriet, is that right?”

Olivia threw a look of surprised gratitude toward Julius who was in the middle of a bout with Zane.

"Oh, that's kind of you," she said. "They actually go by Nell and Hattie. No one ever calls them by their full names."

"Excellent information," Cade said. "Any other gems to impart?"

Olivia laughed. "I'm sure they'll be utterly swept away by you both." She considered. "Perhaps you could introduce them to some of the younger girls at court? The ones who've only just started attending grown-up functions? Both Nell and Hattie are a bit younger than me."

Cade looked to Ashton. "There you go, youngster. It's your moment to shine."

"One year," Ashton grumbled. "I'm one year younger." He gave an elaborate shudder. "The girls you're describing are my younger sister's friends, and I normally avoid them like the plague."

Cade raised his eyebrows, and Ashton turned quickly to Olivia.

"But of course I would be more than happy to assist you in this matter, my lady! Your cousins are safe in my hands."

Olivia thanked him gravely while privately worrying that neither of the girls would be safe at all. She would be much surprised if they didn't both fancy themselves in love with the young lord by the end of the soiree.

But she wasn't going to interfere. Now that Nell and Hattie were to gain royal approval and entrée into court circles, she didn't think a court match was out of the question for either girl—not given their father's wealth. She had no interest in taking advantage of the queen's matchmaking offer on her own behalf, but when the time came, she would

gladly request that her cousins receive the honor in her stead
—if either girl was interested.

All of that would have to wait until they were a little
older, though, and for the moment, Lord Ashton seemed a
safe option for their girlish flights of fancy.

Julius won his bout and strode over to her, wiping his
brow with his forearm. She waited until he reached her side
before speaking.

"Thank you, Julius," she said softly. "I appreciate your
consideration for my family."

Julius shifted uncomfortably. "It was nothing, just a
word with my friends."

Olivia shook her head. "It was thoughtful, and I appreciate it."

Kasper and Zane strolled over to join them, and the
conversation shifted. All five young men would be at the
soiree that evening, and they joked with each other about
people she'd never met—although she recognized many of
the names from her lessons.

A flutter of nerves erupted in her belly, but Julius sent her
a reassuring look that steadied her. He wouldn't abandon her
that evening, and she would have her cousins and aunt as
well.

"If there was to be dancing, I would ask you to save me a
dance," Zane drawled. "But since there will only be music
and conversation, I will instead ask you to stand ready to
rescue me. If the inane chatter becomes too much to bear, I
will escape to your side and demand at least ten minutes of
sensible conversation."

Olivia laughed and agreed. She didn't feel as comfortable
with Zane as she did with his brother, but she was deter-

mined to make an effort for Cade's sake. And she liked the idea that at least one person at the ball would view her as an oasis and not like a bug under glass.

But even that thought wasn't enough to steady her as she waited to enter the soiree, her arm gripping Julius's far too tightly. Since the soiree was in honor of their betrothal, their entry had been carefully managed by his mother, meaning they were left to wait, the buzz of voices reaching them through the closed door.

A voice called, "His Royal Highness, Crown Prince Julius and Lady Olivia," and the doors swung open.

Julius stepped forward, and Olivia managed to keep pace despite her shaking knees. The initial hush gave way to a rush of murmurs, but to Olivia's relief, the majority of the staring eyes soon turned away, the normal ebb and flow of conversation resuming. She released a breath and looked around properly.

She had discussed the queen's plans for the event extensively, but it was different to see the results of Queen Elsinore's efforts in person.

The receiving room was smaller than the full ballroom, but like the ballroom, it also contained a wall lined with double glass doors. Unlike at the Midsummer Ball, however, they were all thrown open, giving free access to the broad stone terrace beyond. Only a few steps led down from the terrace into the gardens, and the event flowed freely between indoors and out. The small orchestra had even been set up on the balcony outside so the volume wouldn't overwhelm conversation inside.

To enhance the integration of the two spaces, vines had

been twined around the balcony railing and throughout the ballroom, along with a plethora of vibrant blooms.

"How lovely," Olivia breathed.

Julius smiled down at her. "Mother's aim is to host all three of the summer's best events—every year."

Olivia laughed. "How exhausting. But I'm sure she always succeeds if she puts on events such as this."

She continued to look around the room, wide-eyed, until she caught Julius's gaze. He was watching her with a smile that made her duck her eyes and will herself not to flush.

"Since the soiree is in your honor, I'm glad you approve," he said.

Olivia smiled back and tightened her grip on the small bag that dangled from one wrist. She had slipped a certain mirror inside, feeling that its presence might give her a last-minute confidence boost. She was certainly in need of any insight it could give her.

As it was, she had been fighting the urge to use it on Julius ever since he had appeared in his party finery. She longed to know what was truly behind the friendly smile on his lips. But she had to wait for a surreptitious moment, and none had yet arrived.

"Olivia!" Hattie's glad cry gave her a second's warning before both cousins launched themselves at her, full of giggles and happy exclamations.

Her aunt smiled over their heads, clearly also happy to be present, although she showed more reserve than her enthusiastic daughters.

"Now, now, girls," she chided. "Your cousin is a princess, and you must treat her with more deference at court."

Nell and Hattie immediately let Olivia go, although they continued to giggle as they dropped into deep curtsies.

"I'm not a princess yet," she said to her aunt. "I am, however, very glad to see you."

"Thank you for inviting us, niece," Aunt Helen said in reply. "The girls have been in raptures ever since the invitation was delivered."

"I hope they have a lovely time." Olivia smiled at her cousins affectionately. "I've asked some friends of mine to make sure you're well looked after."

As if on cue, Ashton appeared, dragging Kasper in tow. The two young men bowed to Nell and Hattie, sending the two girls into a fresh round of giggles.

"If you'll allow us to escort you to the refreshment table, my sister is most eager for an introduction," Ashton said with his particular, engaging charm.

Both Nell and Hattie flushed red and glanced at their mother for permission. She waved them off with an indulgent smile, and the girls accepted the arms offered them.

As soon as they were out of earshot, Olivia turned to her aunt, intending to reassure her as to the young men's identities. But her aunt was watching the two retreating couples with a knowing eye.

"That's the first time one of our neighbors has given a single one of us the time of day," she murmured. "Our status truly has changed."

Olivia winced. Her aunt clearly recognized Kasper, at least, without her assistance. But she just as clearly still knew nothing of Olivia's history with Marigold.

Queen Elsinore swept over to them, embracing both Julius and Olivia before exchanging polite greetings with

Olivia's aunt. When she finally bore Aunt Helen off to meet some of the court's matrons, Olivia let out a breath of relief.

"Maybe we've been a little too welcoming to your family," Julius said with a wry note. "Weren't they invited to keep you company?"

"Just having them present makes me happy," Olivia said. "And I'm relieved to see them starting to make their own acquaintances here. Besides, we have company of our own." She nodded toward Cade and Zane who were approaching them, both bearing a glass in each hand.

Cade handed one of his glasses to Julius, leaving Olivia to accept one from Zane.

"Don't tell me you're already overcome with inane conversation, Lord Zane," she said with a smile. "We've only just arrived."

"*You* have only just arrived," he said with a sardonic smile. "I've been here for more than half an hour."

Cade rolled his eyes. "And spent that whole time talking to two of Father's allies. If I hadn't pulled you away, you would be talking business for the next two hours. You are allowed to be young occasionally, Zane."

"I thought you were being young for both of us," Zane said lazily.

Cade protested strenuously, and the brothers' banter distracted Julius. Their group had drifted into a corner, and Olivia finally saw her chance. Slipping her hand into her bag, she closed her fingers around the mirror's handle.

She pulled it out and turned it toward her own face, as if she was taking a moment to check her appearance. But she didn't stop there, subtly angling it further until she caught a flash of greenery and bright flowers and then someone else's face. But it wasn't Julius's features reflected in the mirror.

Zane's expression was amused, and his eyes looked straight back at her through the reflection. Olivia's eyes snapped to his real face and, sure enough, he was watching her, a single brow slightly raised.

Olivia flushed and pushed the mirror back into her bag. She should never have brought it. There was no subtle way to use it at the soiree, and she was only going to look foolish trying.

"Is my hair straight?" she whispered to Zane, trying to cover for her odd moment.

The amusement that she found so difficult to read still lurked on his face, but he reassured her with perfect solemnity of her neat appearance. Leaning close, he murmured, "I believe young ladies usually take such actions in the ladies' dressing room provided for the purpose." He indicated a plain door on one side of the receiving room.

Olivia mumbled almost inaudible thanks and threw herself into the general conversation, resolving not to risk taking the mirror out again. She had wanted to use it so she could learn how to read and understand people as the roving merchant, Avery, did. But now that she was at the palace, perhaps she needed to rely more on her own intuition and less on the mirror.

CHAPTER 21

JULIUS

As Julius had known they would, his friends played their parts perfectly. Olivia's cousins were soon part of a circle of laughing girls, and Olivia herself looked far more relaxed than she had when they were waiting outside the doors. He would have preferred a more informal event for Olivia's first official appearance, but his mother had assured him it would cause great offense if any member of the court was excluded. Since the soiree had become the crown prince's betrothal party, he had been forced to concede the point.

Unfortunately, that meant every member of court wanted a chance to congratulate the happy couple and introduce themselves to Olivia. At first, he feared the endless parade of new faces would be too taxing for her, but she remained at his side, smiling politely and remembering every name. His mother had drilled her well.

But as he watched her chuckle brightly at a joke made by one of the oldest members of court, he knew it was more than that. The tiny line of concentration between her brows told him how hard she was trying, but she seemed utterly natural in her manner.

When Julius had scratched the façade of charm provided for him by the Legacy, he had found awkwardness and ignorance beneath. But with Olivia, it was the opposite. In their early interactions, she had been ignorant of etiquette, direct to a fault, with no veil over her emotions—a rough, unchiseled version of herself. But her time at the palace had polished her natural shape, revealing beneath someone who was charming, personable, and utterly appealing. He predicted that half the court would be under her thrall by the end of summer.

When he caught her muttering a stream of adjectives under her breath—singular features that she seemed to be using to remember which face belonged to which name— she flashed him a conspiratorial smile, good-natured amusement at her own expense in her eyes. His heart turned over. If he wasn't careful, he would be the one in thrall before the summer ended.

Eventually, the stream of people died down, and they were able to take a moment to breathe. Julius left her against the wall while he went to fetch them both drinks. If her throat was as dry as his, she would need one.

But when he returned, she was gone. He could see no sign of her inside, so he strode out onto the terrace and scanned its length. He spotted her at the far end, her head bent close to Cade's as they examined an unusual flower nestled among the vines of the balcony railing.

Julius's fists clenched around the drinks as he took in the image of the two of them. Olivia looked so relaxed and happy, smiling up at Cade. Had he ever seen her look that way beside him? He feared not. To her, he was a millstone, weighing her down with responsibilities and duty.

"They make a lovely couple," his mother murmured quietly beside him.

His eyes jerked to her face, but she was looking at Cade and Olivia, a satisfied smile on her lips.

"I hadn't noticed," he said stiffly.

He tried to think of something to say to redirect her thoughts. He was already uncomfortable with the idea of his mother matchmaking Olivia with a member of the court, but it would be unbearable if she tried to pair Olivia and Cade. Cade was the brother the Legacy had denied to Julius—the only reason he hadn't had the lonely life that should have been his as the only child of a king. He relied on Cade's cheerful presence and loyalty.

And lately, he had been coming to rely on Olivia in a similar manner. Even with Cade's company, Julius had always stood apart and alone—until the moment Olivia blazed her way into his life. She had demanded they work together, coming to find him each day, and he had started to look forward to those interactions as the brightest part of every day. And at the soiree, for the first time, he had completed his royal duties with a companion at his side— someone to share stolen smiles and hidden moments of humor. It was a gift he had never expected.

He didn't think he could bear it if the two people he now relied on most for company and support turned to each other and cut him out.

But before he could find the right words for his mother, she had floated away again, the pleased smile still on her lips. Julius was dimly grateful for the drinks in his hands—

without them, he might have punched the stone beside him.

Instead, he strode the length of the balcony and presented Olivia's glass to her. She smiled up at him.

"Cade rescued me and brought me out here for some fresh air. Have you ever seen this flower before? Do you know what it's called?"

But the smile faded from her face as she took in the glower on his. "Is something wrong?"

"I don't know," he said in a soft, defeated voice. "You tell me. Is it?"

He turned his eyes on Cade, and Olivia frowned, looking between them. Julius hoped for reassurance from his best friend—for Cade to laugh at him and chase away the lowering fog. But for once, Cade didn't act to lighten the moment. He stayed in his place at Olivia's side, his expression challenging Julius.

Julius's hand tightened into a fist, but he forced himself to relax it. Olivia was enjoying her first true moment of repose at an event that was supposedly in her honor, and he wasn't going to ruin it with his foolish starts.

He rubbed his eyes. "My apologies," he said curtly. "It's been a long evening, and I'm tired." The words were true, even if they were only the tip of the iceberg hiding beneath.

Olivia's expression turned sympathetic, and she murmured support, asking if it was too soon for them to respectably retire from the event. Her assumption that they would either stay or go together soothed his nerves far more than his own efforts to lighten his mood.

Cade's stance relaxed as well, although his knowing eyes remained pinned on Julius, and he didn't back away from

Olivia. But what could Julius have said anyway? His friend knew Julius's betrothal to Olivia was temporary, an illusion for the sake of the Legacy, so there was no true betrayal. And Julius himself had asked Cade to help keep an eye on Olivia during the soiree.

He couldn't even blame Olivia if she preferred Cade's company to his own. She had been told to prepare for another match among the men of the court, and he could acknowledge that Cade was the best of them.

Pain lanced through Julius—an anticipation of loneliness that was hard to fight. He couldn't shake it off, although he longed to let it go and enjoy the current moment. He didn't know how many more court events he would be able to enjoy at Olivia's side. Having experienced one in her company, he knew future events without her would be cold and draining by comparison. And if his mother succeeded at her scheming, he might have an endless number of such painful events stretching before him.

CHAPTER 22
OLIVIA

Olivia had the whole day after the soiree free—a reward for her success the night before. Apparently, the queen had been pleased with her performance.

Olivia had even enjoyed the event more than she expected, making a game of finally putting faces to all the names she had learned. She was just sorry Julius had found the event so draining. Even the prince deserved to relax and enjoy himself sometimes.

When a knock sounded on the door of her sitting room, she called a hopeful welcome. And sure enough, it was Julius who strode into the room, making her smile and push away the last of her breakfast.

Unlike the night before, he smiled back. A night's rest must have done him good. He did give Mildred's nest a wide berth, though, which made her laugh.

"She's not going to hurt you," Olivia laughed. "She's sleeping after a big feed, so she's not even going to wake up. I was worried about her feeling too confined at the palace, but

I don't think she's left my suite even once since we arrived. She seems to love it."

"For the sake of the other palace residents, I suspect that's a good thing." Julius eyed her with misgiving. "Is she bigger than when we brought her here?"

Olivia winced. "She looks that way to me, too. There's just so much Legacy power here given our recent betrothal. But at least she's safe—even if she eventually grows to the size of a fully-grown horse."

Mildred opened an eye and squeaked at Julius, making him flinch. Olivia laughed again.

"I heard you have a whole day off," he said, finally reaching the small table where she was sitting. "And it just so happens to be a full market day as well, which gives us a good excuse to go into the city. So would you like to visit the central market?"

"Oh yes!" Olivia leaped to her feet. "Just let me get organized."

Julius laughed. "You can finish your breakfast. We have the whole day."

"No, no, I'm ready." Olivia was too excited to sit sedately and eat, and she'd been mostly finished anyway.

Julius's gaze saddened as he watched her. "I'm sorry you've had to wait so long to get into the city again."

Olivia stilled, worried by his tone. Did he think she resented him for her busy schedule?

"I'm not totally unreasonable." She kept her voice light. "I know we have no evidence that something bad has happened to Marigold, and I know my first responsibility is to my current role here at the palace—Marigold herself ensured that. I just want to be allowed to search for her in my free time."

Julius hesitated. "I want you to know that if we do find any solid evidence of foul play, everything will change. If we can prove to my parents that she's been abducted, then finding and retrieving her will become a matter of utmost importance to the crown—despite her most recent actions."

Relief flooded Olivia. Finding evidence was a much less daunting prospect than actually finding and freeing her friend. Everything considered, it was a most reasonable compromise.

Riding out of the palace, she practically bounced in her saddle. A visit to the market was appealing even without an ulterior motive. She had often found an excuse to head into the city on market days when she lived with her aunt and uncle.

The bustle of the crowds reached her ears before the central square came into view, and the smells followed close behind—the delicious scents of roasting food and sweet buns mixed with the less appealing smell of livestock—a combination potent enough to override the pervading smell of the ocean.

Olivia and Julius dismounted, half the guards dismounting with them while the other half took charge of the horses. Olivia feared the guards would serve as an invisible wall, scaring the populace away from them, but to her surprise the royal couple were approached by a slow but constant trickle of people.

Most wanted to congratulate them on their betrothal, but a few had questions about Olivia's background or complaints to raise with the crown. Olivia answered the questions about herself honestly, and Julius fielded the complaints with easy poise. And each time he was forced to do so, she was grateful again for his presence. Without him, she would have struggled to answer.

"The people don't seem at all put off by our guards," she murmured after a middle-aged merchant bowed and disappeared back into the crowds. She reconsidered her words. "Or perhaps they're put off just the right amount since no one is crowding us this time." She shivered involuntarily at the memory of her previous excursion, and Julius stepped closer, the pressure of his shoulder against hers reassuring.

She tried to shake off the mood. "It's admirable the way your family have made the crown so accessible."

"Actually," he said slowly. "I think they're approaching us because of you. I've never had this experience before."

Olivia turned to him in astonishment. "But you must have been to the market before today!"

"Of course. But when I came, no one approached to talk to me. Not like this."

"No one?" It didn't seem possible given their experience thus far.

Julius shrugged. "It seemed normal to me, and I never questioned it. Not until my mother made that comment after our betrothal."

Olivia frowned, trying to think what comment he might mean. It had obviously made more of an impression on him than on her.

"I thought I'd mastered my role as crown prince—as Prince Charming," Julius continued in a low voice. "But it turns out I had only learned how to manage at court." He forced a laugh. "I'm not nearly as charming as I thought I was."

The sound of his flat laugh twisted Olivia's heart. In her time at the palace, she had seen how much Julius dedicated himself to his position. And she had experienced firsthand the power of his charm—even when he was being Julius, not the prince. It pained her to think he doubted himself so much.

But when he looked at her, his face lightened, and he gave a more natural-sounding laugh. "I used to be quite secure in my own brilliance, you know. Until I met a girl on a hill who didn't find me charming at all."

Olivia laughed, thinking how much her perception of him had changed since that day. "It wasn't your fault, you know," she said. "At least not at first. I just didn't want you looking for my slipper! Although I'll admit that walking off a cliff was an excessive reaction to my rejection."

Julius's lips twitched as he looked down at her. "Everyone says you're beautiful, but you're not that beautiful, I'm afraid."

She snorted. "I should hope not!"

"But I'm sure you're far too kind to leave me curious a second time." He grinned at her. "What was the great mystery of the missing slipper?"

Olivia flushed and mumbled the answer in a hurry, under her breath.

"Pardon? What was that?" Julius's lips twitched, despite his solemn expression.

Olivia sighed and repeated it more slowly and at an audible volume, making Julius break into unrestrained laughter.

"No wonder you wanted to get rid of me as quickly as possible," he said when his mirth subsided.

Two matrons approached them, and they broke off their conversation to accept the women's greetings and congratulations. When they walked away again, Olivia watched Julius from the corner of her eye.

"It's true I didn't find you charming at first," Olivia said after a moment of silence between them. "But I also misjudged you, and I'm sorry for that."

Julius raised a quizzical eyebrow, and she sighed. "In the beginning, I thought your apologies were insincere—that they were all self-serving. But I'm sure now that you did mean them. You might not be perfect, Julius, but you try harder than anyone I've ever met."

"A compliment, of sorts." He gave her a twisted smile.

Olivia shook her head stubbornly. "It's a very high compliment. You never got to choose your role, Julius, and yet you still dedicate yourself to it. I admire that." She was silent for a beat. "And I think you underestimate yourself. Every person who has approached us today has left with a smile. Prince Charming seems to be perfectly well received by the regular citizens."

"Yes, because you're here. You make them more comfortable."

Olivia shrugged. "And I'm able to be comfortable at court because I have you beside me. Why do you think you have to be good at everything alone? No one is good at everything— not even Prince Charming." She grinned. "You have to leave something for me, or else why am I even here?"

He stared at her, as if struck by her words. When he remained silent, she looked away. It would have been nice to hear some words of reassurance—to hear that he saw value and purpose in her presence as she did in his. But perhaps that was too much to ask when he hadn't asked for his betrothal any more than he'd asked to be born crown prince.

She stumbled, clutching at his arm as her toe landed on something small and sharp inside her boot. Sighing, she limped toward the large fountain in the center of the market. She could sit on its rim and fish out the stone that had wormed its way into her shoe.

"I'll just need a minute," she told Julius, sending him to line up for sticks of roasted meat.

Removing her boot, she shook out the stone and placed the shoe on the fountain edge beside her. Twisting up her foot, she examined the hole the stone had made in the toe of her stocking. It was located in an annoying position, but there was nothing she could do about it until she returned to the palace.

Turning to retrieve the shoe, she found the fountain beside her empty.

"Drat!" She looked around for it without much hope. It had been her fault for letting it out of her grip. She should have known better. It was too tempting an opportunity for the Legacy.

And thanks to the Legacy, she was unlikely to see it again. Most people never did find the single shoes the Legacy caused them to constantly lose. It was a wonder the whole kingdom wasn't littered with piles of discarded, pairless shoes.

"Are you looking for this?" A now familiar voice asked from beside her.

She looked up to find Julius grinning down at her, her

lost boot in one hand and two sticks of fragrant roast meat in the other.

"You found it!" she cried in surprise, happily accepting the shoe and slipping her foot into it.

"Of course I did." He grinned smugly at her. "Don't tell me you've forgotten that I'm the one person in the kingdom more prone to finding shoes than losing them."

"You should set up a business reuniting people with their lost shoes," she said. "It would be a great boon to the whole city."

"I'm not sure my parents would consider that the best use of the advantages I've been gifted by the Legacy," Julius said dryly.

"That's just because they've always had you around to find their missing shoes," Olivia muttered under her breath, getting back to her feet. "You could be the most popular prince in history."

"I think I might already have achieved that." Julius's smile turned warmer, making her chest tighten, and she quickly took one of the sticks of meat and resumed walking.

She led him to one of her favorite spots in the market—a glassblower's stall. She had never been able to afford any of the wares, but she loved to look at the fantastical products that could only be made in Sovar.

Glancing across the rows of slippers, heat-resistant flexible gloves, shatter-proof pieces of armor that were stronger than steel, and all manner of more frippery baubles, she looked in vain for a mirror.

In the past, she had only ever gazed at the glass creations, not wanting to pester the stallholder with questions when she wasn't a true customer. But with Julius at her side, she was emboldened to engage with the man.

"Do you have any mirrors?" she asked, unable to remember any lessons on Sovaran mirrors in school, only Auldanan ones.

The stallholder, who had perked up at the appearance of the royal visitors, looked crestfallen. "I'm afraid not, my lady. Sovaran glassblowers can only make standard mirrors. The Sovar Legacy doesn't help us at all—I guess it leaves that to the Auldana Legacy."

Olivia tried not to look disappointed. "Do any of the stalls here carry Auldanan mirrors, then?"

The stallholder's brows rose. "Is Your Ladyship after an enchanted mirror?"

Olivia quickly shook her head. "I was merely curious. I've heard stories about their various powers, and I was hoping to see for myself."

"Aye," the stallholder agreed, seeming to accept her explanation. "The stories are certainly fantastical. It's enough to make you wonder if they've been exaggerated." He looked at his own wares and huffed a laugh. "But then who would imagine armor made from glass? I'm sure it sounds just as fantastical to other kingdoms as the stories of the mirrors are to us."

"Then you've never seen an Auldanan mirror for yourself?" Olivia asked.

"More's the pity," the man said. "I reckon I could fetch a pretty penny for one. But those Auldanans don't like selling 'em outside their own kingdom. If you don't mind my saying so," he added as he suddenly remembered his audience.

"It isn't forbidden," Julius added. "Not like it is in the

case of those Oakdenian weapons that they infuse with their sleeping herbs or with our own glass armor." He rapped a knuckle on a breastplate in front of him. "But they refuse to sell their mirrors to regular merchant trains, so we only have a few that were sold to us by roving merchants."

The stall keeper nodded. "It doesn't help that we're so far from Auldana, either. The roving merchants rarely have mirrors left by the time they reach us." He leaned out of his stall and pointed at another one further down the row. "You could try asking there. Those two are Halburan, so you're in luck that they're here today. They don't spend much time in Sovar, as you can imagine. But it's possible they might have a mirror—for such illustrious customers as yourselves."

Olivia thanked him and moved quickly in the direction he had pointed, curious to meet a Halburan, even if they didn't have any mirrors. She had never met someone from the eastern kingdom of Halbury.

"Welcome! Welcome!" the man and woman called when they approached the indicated stall.

There was nothing in their appearance to mark them as foreigners, but their stall was full of unfamiliar wares. Olivia could see no sign of any mirrors, but she examined the displayed items curiously. They all appeared to be woven from straw, but she could only guess at their special properties.

The male stallholder looked from the two of them to their guards and smiled broadly.

"Surely I don't have the pleasure of addressing His Royal Highness, Prince Julius and his lovely Lady Olivia?"

Julius smiled and confirmed their identities, making both the man and woman bob into a series of enthusiastic bows.

"A great honor. A great honor," they repeated over the top of one another.

"I'm Snuffelslidefoot," the man said.

"And I'm Handelboatlobe," the woman echoed, her smile broadening at the startled look on Olivia's face. "We're siblings, and our parents are highly traditional. Believe in keeping up the old ways, they do—especially when it comes to proper Halburan names."

Olivia giggled and then immediately felt guilty, but the woman didn't seem offended.

"I'm impressed you've traveled all the way here," Olivia said, wishing it wasn't rude to ask what price their Legacy extracted while they were in Sovar.

"We never could stay in one place," the man said. "Which means we're a great trial to our traditional parents."

The woman smiled and winked. "Although they do like the presents we bring back. There's nothing like Sovaran glass for making bargains in Halbury."

"I don't suppose you have any Auldanan mirrors?" Julius asked, and they both looked disappointed, shaking their heads.

"Everything we have comes from Halbury, Your Highness. But we can keep our eye out for one for future visits, if you're interested."

Julius hesitated, glancing at Olivia. "By all means, I would be most curious to see anything you could find. And naturally I would pay more for a special commission."

The siblings beamed at his words, once again falling into a series of bows.

When they had exchanged final well wishes with the unusual two, they strolled further down the row of stalls.

"Are Auldanan mirrors really so valuable that you would request one without limitation?" Olivia asked, surprise and unease stirring inside her.

Julius nodded. "I'm sure my parents will be willing to purchase any mirror the Halburans can find."

Olivia worried at her bottom lip, thinking of the mirror she had tucked away in her room back at the palace. When Avery had gifted it to her, she had claimed to still have it because it was faulty. Olivia had accepted the gift under the assumption that it was a defective product—one the merchant girl wouldn't be able to sell. But now she suspected Avery had phrased it that way so Olivia would feel free to accept it. And as a consequence, Olivia hadn't realized the value of the gift she had been given.

"Is something wrong?" Julius asked her quietly, concern in his eyes.

"No, nothing," she said quickly, not ready to confess to the mirror's existence.

But her mind lingered on the conversation, uneasiness still roiling in her gut. If her mirror was much rarer than she had supposed, was it right for her to hoard it for her own use? Shouldn't she offer it to Julius to be used for the good of the whole kingdom?

She glanced at him, reluctance staying her tongue. It wasn't that she feared he would misuse it. She was just reluctant to part with something that was so precious to her. The mirror had given her the last bit of courage to leave home and seek a new life for herself. If she handed it over to Julius now, she would lose it completely when their betrothal was dissolved.

Julius was still watching her with concern in his eyes, so

she pushed the thought aside. She didn't have to make a decision immediately.

"Look, cider!" she cried, spotting her favorite stall. She turned to Julius with a broad smile. "Wait until you taste it. He gets the spice mix perfect."

Julius looked much more surprised than her enthusiasm for a common market drink warranted, but he followed her over to the stall without protest.

"Olivia!" the stallholder called as soon as he saw her, his face breaking into a welcoming smile. "Lady Olivia, I should say now." He gave her a deep bow, and she protested.

"That's not necessary, Markus. Here at your stall, I'm merely another customer."

The man's eyebrows rose, his eyes darting briefly to Julius. "Is that right now? In that case, you'll be wanting two tankards of my cider?"

"Of course." She grinned at him. "It wouldn't be a trip to the market without one."

Markus ushered them to two rough stools he kept along the far edge of his stall as a convenience for customers who wished to enjoy their drink at a more leisurely pace. Olivia sat in one with alacrity, settling in for a comfortable chat with the unusual man, as she always did.

His manner was odd, at times almost bordering on foolish, but his observations were witty and astute. She had learned many an interesting piece of capital gossip at his stall.

"This is Prince Julius," she said as she gestured for him to sit beside her. "Julius, this is Markus, the maker of the city's best cider."

"You flatter me!" Markus's obsequious manner was even

more pronounced than usual. "But it does a man's heart good to see his hard work appreciated."

He filled two tankards and handed them each one. Olivia glanced at Julius, hoping he would see past Markus's off-putting manner.

To her relief, she could see no trace of distaste on the prince's face. But the intensity of the look he was directing at Markus threw her off guard. It was almost as if Julius was trying to signal something to the man without words. Had they already met?

"I'm not sure there's much gossip I can relate to you today, lass," Markus said with a grin. "Most of the gossip these last weeks has been about you, and I hope I know better than to repeat gossip to its subject." He chuckled. "But you've nothing to be ashamed about, I'll say that much. The city has rallied behind you."

Julius shifted slightly, leaning infinitesimally toward the man. "Nothing at all, sir? Are you sure? Not even the smallest tidbit to occupy us while we drink?"

Olivia stared at him, her eyes narrowing. There was definitely something going on she didn't understand.

"Well, now." Markus scratched his chin. "I might be able to think of the odd bit of news." He glanced between them. "Perhaps something related to the new princess if not actually about her, per se."

"Related to me?" Olivia asked.

Julius tensed beside her, as if anxious to hear Markus's news. She gave him another odd look, but his full focus was on the stallholder.

"Word reached my ears that Her Ladyship was interested

in kidnapped girls," Markus said, busying his hands as he wiped down his stall.

Olivia's mouth fell open. But Julius gave a small, satisfied smile before taking a sip of cider.

"When I heard that," Markus continued. "It got me curious, it did. As it might have done for anyone. So I asked around a bit."

"And did you hear anything?" Julius asked.

Olivia also leaned forward. She had come to the market intending to ask Markus about that very topic—since he always seemed to know something about everything. But she couldn't believe they had started on the topic without her needing to say anything.

"Well, now, that turned out to be mighty interesting," Markus said. "Mighty interesting."

He fell silent as another customer approached. The woman was seeking wares to take away with her, and she didn't linger, leaving them alone again with Markus.

"Well?" Julius asked, clearly struggling to contain his interest.

"Rumor has it," Markus said, "that in the last five years there has been a whole string of abductions—always girls between ten and eighteen."

Olivia gasped, and Julius put a hand on her knee, out of sight of the general marketgoers. She looked down at it and then back at him. He wasn't looking at her, but from the tension in his frame, he was clearly trying to warn her of something. But what? Was she not permitted a dramatic reaction to such a shocking piece of news?

Schooling her face into a calmer expression, she nodded with polite interest. Julius's hand lifted from her knee, and she had to stop herself staring at the spot where it had rested.

"How many have been taken exactly?" Julius asked, although his tone and face suggested they were talking about the merest commonplace.

"Now, that's hard to say." Markus fetched a new cloth and began wiping the stall again. "Hard to pin down details, it is, since the families have all left the city."

"What, all of them?" Julius asked. "Are you sure?"

Markus threw him a sharp look, and Julius murmured a hurried apology. Olivia looked between them again, her bewilderment growing.

"Why have I not heard of this before?" Julius asked instead. "If girls are being steadily spirited away from beneath our noses, surely my father has been informed."

"As to that..." Markus hesitated. "I think you might find it hasn't come to the palace's ear. Even I hadn't heard enough to join the dots together until I started looking."

"But how is that possible?" Julius asked, taking another distracted drink.

"Perhaps because all the girls have been safely returned? Not a scratch on them, I heard."

"They were returned?" Olivia forgot her confusion in her relief at that piece of information. "All of them? That's very good news." She was thinking of Marigold as she said it, although she was glad for the other girls as well.

"Depends who you ask," Markus said cryptically, unconsciously echoing her own response to Bess on the beach.

"Were they all ransomed, then?" she asked. "What did their families have to give up?"

Markus gave her an approving smile. "I always thought you were a right one, lass. Good instincts. Aye, that's the question." He looked at Julius. "It was no easy feat getting answers, but my curiosity was well and truly awakened by the time it got that far, so I'll confess I chased the matter down, despite no exact orders, so to speak."

Orders? A startling possibility occurred to Olivia—one that might explain the strange mismatch between Markus's manner and the intelligence she had recognized underneath.

"What did you find?" she asked, keeping her suspicions to herself for the moment.

"It's what I couldn't find that interested me," he said. "There was plenty of talk of ransoms, but not a single account did I hear of any coin changing hands."

"What sort of ransom could the abductors have demanded if not gold?" Julius wondered aloud.

"No one would tell me direct," Markus said. "Most of them probably didn't know. But I have a noggin of me own." He tapped his head. "Every one of those poor girls was the daughter of someone running a small to medium-sized business—successful ones, mind you. Ones on the verge of expansion."

Julius's brows drew together. "And after the abductions?"

"Every one of the families moved out of the capital, leaving managers to run their businesses, and all thought of expansion was forgotten."

Olivia's eyes widened. It matched Bess's story exactly.

"A business rival, then," Julius breathed. "But why didn't they make their complaints to the palace? I can understand if they were afraid to do so while the girls were still missing—

I'm sure all sorts of threats were made. But after they had been recovered, they could have gone to the guards. With such a specific ransom, they must have had some suspicion who was behind the abductions."

"Perhaps they had more than a suspicion." Markus didn't meet Julius's eyes. "Remember, these families weren't yet wealthy or influential enough to have the ear of the king. And mayhap they knew their adversary was someone who did have that ear."

Julius put down his tankard, his voice turning to ice. "If you mean to suggest my family had anything to do with—"

"Now, now," Markus said with alarm, wiping even harder. "Of course I wasn't suggesting any such thing. But there are powerful people who have the king's ear, are there not? Is it impossible to imagine one of them might have dealings below the law? Dealings he would do much to keep concealed."

Julius let out a breath and picked his tankard back up. "My apologies. Of course I can't deny the possibility of such a thing. Although I can assure you that if it is the case, my father knows nothing about it."

"Aye, he's always been a fair dealer, King Robert," Markus agreed. "But when it comes to a man's children, there are some risks a man isn't willing to make."

Olivia took a small sip, unable to enjoy the burst of flavor in her mouth. Was it only good fortune that Nell or Hattie hadn't been taken, back when Uncle Walt's business was less established and his influence less substantial? The abducted girls had been returned safely, but they must have been traumatized by the experience.

"So someone has been abducting girls at key moments throughout the last few years," Julius muttered. "And whoever it is has enough influence to send the families fleeing the capital rather than point any fingers."

"And because they all stayed quiet," Olivia said, "no one connected the threads."

"There are only a handful of families with that sort of power," Julius said. "And all of them are far too powerful for us to start making accusations based on a hunch. Even I would need some sort of proof before I started pointing fingers. Although if I at least had a name, I could start digging."

He glanced at Markus, who silently shook his head. He had no more information.

"It's a compelling case," Julius said. "I'll grant you that. But I can't see the connection to Lady Marigold. Her family is far too powerful for anyone to threaten in such a way. And you said there's been no ransom?" He looked to Olivia for confirmation.

She nodded silently, wishing she could think of something that might definitively link the cases.

"Oho!" Markus accepted Julius's empty tankard back and dunked it in the tub he kept for washing. With a start, Olivia realized she had stopped drinking hers.

"Oho," Markus repeated. "So you're looking for someone in particular. And the daughter of Lord Emerson? Now that is a tasty tidbit."

"You mustn't tell anyone," Olivia said quickly, glaring at Julius. "She's missing, but we have no proof she was abducted. Her family are keeping it quiet, thinking she's run away, so please don't spread any rumors. If you were to hear something, though…"

"Don't worry, Your Ladyship." Markus smiled at her with the light of genuine affection in his eyes. "I always know which bits to pass on and which to keep to myself." He glanced at Julius. "And which to pass on only to very specific ears."

Olivia relaxed at the reminder that the man clearly worked for Julius. She finished her tankard and passed it over.

"Excellent cider," Julius said as he stood. "You can be sure we'll be back for more next time we're at the market."

"Of course." Olivia smiled despite the whirring in her thoughts. "I never miss Markus's stall when I come here."

The man smiled proudly, bowing again to them as Julius tugged Olivia away.

"And an excellent thing that you're an established customer, too," he murmured in her ear. "Now we won't need to worry about anyone noticing we've started visiting his stall."

Olivia stared up at him. "So he really is one of your spies?"

Julius frowned at her use of the word, and she bit down on her tongue.

"Not mine," he said shortly. "I've only met him once before. But he's an excellent source of information for my father. But we don't normally visit in person."

"So does that mean he's a credible source?" she asked. "Can we take this tale to your father?"

Julius hesitated, and Olivia's heart sank.

"Until we can find a link to Marigold, I don't think it's

worth the risk of telling anyone about this," he said. "Except Cade, if you feel the need to confide in someone."

The last words seemed wrenched out of him, but Olivia didn't have time to consider such oddities.

"But why not?" she asked hotly, drawing him into an alcove in the far corner of the market, away from the general flow of traffic. "What risk is there?"

Julius glanced over her shoulder at the bustling square. "That my parents might forbid us to come at all if they learn what we're attempting to do."

Olivia tensed but didn't speak her dismay, and he continued.

"They would almost certainly forbid us from directly approaching Markus again."

"And if they don't believe there's any connection, they may even tell him not to pursue the matter." Olivia heard the defeat in her own voice.

Julius gave her an encouraging smile. "We have no need to tell them at this stage, anyway. We already have the crown's best man on the case. If he tracks anything down about Marigold specifically, or any tangible proof of the other kidnappings, we can go to my father at that point."

Olivia nodded, unable to fault his logic. Visiting Markus and waiting on news wasn't much, but she was loath to have even that taken from her.

"Very well," she said. "We wait, and we visit the market again as soon as we can."

Julius gave her another smile, clearly hoping to cheer her up. "And we celebrate the one bit of good news."

Olivia stared at him, unable to think of anything good.

"All those girls were returned unharmed, remember. So

we have good reason to hope that if the same villains have Marigold, they won't be harming her either."

Olivia finally smiled. That was one piece of good news, and she would cling to it through her protocol-filled days like a lifeline.

CHAPTER 23

JULIUS

Julius walked through the market with Olivia on one side and Cade on the other. Some of the stallholders called greetings, and Olivia waved back to each of them with a sunny smile. He met Cade's wondering look over her head, shrugging his shoulders.

"They love her."

He breathed in the cooler, crisper air. Autumn had arrived, and with it, the court had shifted from its social summer season into a different rhythm. According to his mother, that meant a whole new round of lessons for Olivia, and for him it had meant an endless series of meetings.

Had it really been a whole week since he had stepped outside the palace? That was far too long. He much preferred the weeks when he and Olivia managed to escape not only on market day but on other days as well—sometimes visiting Markus's permanent stall, but sometimes going to the sea or paying a visit to her family in Manor Row.

The only shadow on their stolen hours was the lack of any word about Marigold. He had watched the toll it took on

Olivia each time Markus reported no news. The man had managed to uncover two more stories of past abductions in the weeks since their first conversation, but there had been no whisper of Marigold.

He had seen Cade's eyes also lingering on the lines of worry on Olivia's brow, and he suspected those lines were the reason his friend had decided to join them. And from Olivia's glad welcome, he assumed she had taken Julius up on his permission to keep Cade informed of their search. He just hoped his father never found out that both Olivia and Cade knew about Markus.

Well—he hoped other things as well, but he kept a tight lid on those thoughts.

Olivia wove through the marketgoers, stopping first at their favorite food stall before heading to Markus to wash the food down with tankards of cider. Julius prepared to introduce Cade, but Markus spoke before he could.

"Lord Cade! How lovely to see you again. My clientele has become quite highbrow these days. Maybe soon I'll be able to afford a stall in the center of the market instead of tucked back here."

Julius snorted softly, knowing it wasn't a lack of customers that had led Markus to choose the secluded position of his stall. But as he sat, he looked with dismay between Cade and Markus.

Cade had been to visit Markus before? Had he come with Olivia? She was sometimes free when Julius was not, but he hadn't realized she was visiting the market on those days, nor that she had done so in Cade's company. It had never occurred to him to ask her if she had gone into the city without him.

He looked down at his tankard, his hands gripping it until his knuckles turned white. Something burned down his throat although he hadn't yet taken a drink. It shouldn't have mattered, and yet it changed everything to know that the market trips weren't something special between them but something she shared with others as well. Did she prefer to travel with a non-royal escort? Did she gather more information that way?

Markus produced an extra stool, joking comfortably with Olivia and Cade as they sat down. Julius, however, remained silent, wrestling down his unwelcome emotions.

"Heard a new one this morning," Markus said quietly, jolting Julius from his own head. "The Larkins' girl has gone missing, and her parents are sure she's been abducted."

"She's currently missing?" Julius asked, his attention fully captured. "Has there been a ransom demand?"

Markus shrugged. "That's all I've heard."

Olivia leaped to her feet. "We have to go see them. Do you know where they live?"

"Sit down, lass, and finish your cider." Markus said the words with a chuckle, but the expression in his eyes was commanding.

Olivia promptly sat down and picked up her tankard with an apologetic expression. They had to act normally while visiting Markus, and Julius had never seen Olivia abandon an unfinished cider.

Satisfied, Markus gave them directions to the Larkins' home, but he also issued a warning not to go there straight from his stall. Once the information was imparted, he changed the topic, chatting about innocuous things until they had all finished their drinks.

Walking around the market afterward was an exercise in patience. They didn't know exactly how long they needed to wait, and Olivia in particular was having trouble even pretending to focus on anything else.

But Julius had a different struggle. He found himself unable to keep his attention away from Olivia herself, no matter how many times he tried to wrench his eyes elsewhere. She glowed, her excitement at the potential breakthrough lighting her up from the inside out. He wasn't in the least surprised that people approached them constantly— her vibrancy and compassion certainly drew him like a moth to a flame.

Now that he had grown used to her presence in his life, he couldn't imagine how bleak and lifeless the palace would seem without her. She had taught him his own weaknesses and then showed him how much stronger they could be as a team—teaching him that it was all right for him to be both more and less than what the Legacy tried to make him.

And seeing the way people reacted to her, it was obvious she was just the princess Sovar needed. She was just the princess he needed.

She turned to him with a dazzling smile, and his heart stuttered. It was a good thing Cade was with them, or he might not have been able to resist pulling her into his arms and pressing a kiss to her lips.

Cade leaned over to him, a mocking grin on his face. "Still sure you want to break the betrothal?" he asked in an undertone.

Julius stared at him, struck silent. Of course he didn't want to break the betrothal. He wanted the wedding to happen tomorrow.

Sick dread crept down from the top of his head, swamping him completely. When had he forgotten that breaking the betrothal was the plan? In the weeks spent at Olivia's side, she had slowly grown to eclipse everything else in his heart. But the process had been so gradual and constant, he had forgotten the game they were playing.

Cade's brows drew together. "Julius? Are you all right?"

Julius shook himself, trying to force the chaos in his mind into order. He dimly remembered he had once told Cade that he wasn't in love with Olivia. It seemed an impossibility now—a lifetime ago, although it had been less than a full season. When had his distaste for the betrothal transformed into worry over Olivia's feelings? He couldn't pinpoint the exact moment it had happened—he just knew he couldn't remember the last time he'd wanted to be free of her.

"I'm fine," he managed to choke out, and Cade clapped him on the shoulder, although a faint line remained between his brows when he looked at his friend.

Was Cade worried that Julius had changed his mind and wanted to keep the betrothal after all? Was he concerned because he wanted Olivia for himself?

Julius's thoughts burned hot, but he remained silent. The question wasn't how he or Cade felt, but how Olivia felt. And while she seemed to have settled well into life at the palace, he worried that all their best times together were spent outside it. Did she spend her days putting a brave face on a situation she couldn't easily escape?

Even if she did care for him on some level, was it enough to outweigh the burdens of his rank? Olivia had never been interested in being a princess, so his rank was a count against him in her eyes.

From his earliest memories, he had known his life would be sacrificed to duty. He had long ago accepted that. But could he ask Olivia to sacrifice hers as well? And if he did ask it of her, would his parents agree?

If he truly wanted what was best for her, should he step back and let her connection with Cade grow? She might have a happier life with him than with Julius.

"That's the tenth group to approach us since we left Markus," Olivia murmured, breaking through his tortured thoughts.

Julius had barely noticed the excited greetings being exchanged between Olivia and the young family who had just walked away. Had they been the tenth? He hadn't been counting.

He nodded anyway because he was sure she had been paying close attention.

"Any of them could have said something that sent us to the Larkins' home, so surely we can go now?" Olivia looked first at Julius and then at Cade.

The two men exchanged a look. Julius shrugged and Cade nodded, his own face reflecting some of Olivia's determination. Olivia took their gestures as consensus, leading the group toward the edge of the market.

Julius tried to push his tumultuous thoughts into a compartment at the back of his brain. He could think about Olivia and their future later. For now, he was about to visit a family who had just had a daughter abducted, and he needed to keep his mind in the moment, no matter how hard that seemed to achieve.

When they reached the indicated street, Julius sent most of the guards back to the palace, keeping just two men to hold their horses. Two would be sufficient for the ride back to the palace.

At the door, Olivia hesitated, as if finally faced with the reality of what they were walking into. Julius stepped instinctively to her side, trying to brace her with his presence. She looked up at him and smiled tremulously before knocking.

The sound was greeted with a long silence. She exchanged another look with Julius before raising her hand to knock again. But before she made contact with the wood, footsteps sounded inside.

A moment later, the door was flung open.

"Elisabeth!" The middle-aged man in the doorway cried the name before he took in their presence, his face immediately crumpling when he did so.

Julius glanced sideways at Olivia who looked on the verge of tears herself. He cleared his throat and took a half step forward.

"We apologize for intruding on you at such a time," he said, "but we urgently need to ask you some questions about your daughter's disappearance."

The man's eyes flashed for a moment, as if offended by his words, but then they narrowed.

"You look like Prince Julius," he said gruffly.

"I am Prince Julius." Julius gestured to the others. "And this is Lady Olivia and Lord Cade."

The man's expression grew fearful, and he peered up and down the street before gesturing urgently for them to come inside. Julius and Cade exchanged a wary look, but Olivia plunged quickly forward, leaving the two men with no choice but to follow.

As soon as they were inside, Master Larkin shut the door behind them, breathing easier only once it was shut.

"I heard the door!" a woman's voice called sharply. "Is it—"

She broke off as she reached the hall and stopped, her eyes growing round. The man shook his head at her and ushered them all ahead of him into the room the woman had just vacated, which turned out to be a prettily furnished sitting room.

"My dear," he said to the woman, "Prince Julius and Lady Olivia have come to visit. They want to know about Elisabeth."

The woman's mouth gaped open, swinging shut and then falling back open several times. She finally sank into an overstuffed armchair and looked at her husband in bewilderment.

"I don't understand?" she said. "Why are the prince and his betrothed visiting *us*?" She stiffened. "Does this mean the authorities have heard of Elisabeth's abduction? But the note said—"

Julius, who had taken a seat as directed by Master Larkin, leaned forward, resting his elbows on his knees. He hoped his casual pose came across as reassuring.

"So you have received demands from your daughter's abductors?"

Mistress Larkin exchanged a worried look with her husband, and Olivia spoke quickly.

"We aren't here in any official capacity. As far as we know the guards are unaware of your daughter's situation."

"I see." Master Larkin looked like he didn't see at all. "Then what brings you here?"

"We—" She began to answer, but Julius intervened, afraid her compassion might lead her to tell them the full truth.

"We heard a whisper of your situation in the market," he said, "and we guessed you would have been instructed not to go to the guards. We want to help you find your daughter."

Mistress Larkin immediately burst into tears, sobbing out something that was too garbled to understand. Her emotions wrung Julius's heart. He could only imagine how desperate and alone the couple must have been feeling.

"Whispers in the market?" Master Larkin seemed much less grateful for their offer. "I feared as much." He sent his wife a reproachful look, and she flushed, her sobs subsiding.

He looked back to Julius. "The note warned us not to tell a soul, but of course my wife had already told anyone who would listen that she was sure Elisabeth had been abducted."

"They should have delivered the note more quickly if they didn't want us to say anything," his wife said defensively. "I haven't said a word to anyone since. I haven't even left the house!"

"I know, my dear." Her husband spoke in a softer tone, reaching over to pat her knee.

"We don't want to do anything that could put your daughter at risk," Julius said carefully, "but could we see the note?"

The couple exchanged a look. "You can if you like," Master Larkin said, "but if you're hoping for some clue as to where she is or who took her, I fear you'll be disappointed."

He crossed to a desk, opening the top drawer and

retrieving a folded slip of parchment. He returned and handed it to Julius.

Olivia and Cade crowded close behind him, reading over his shoulder as he scanned the words.

The note was addressed to Master Larkin, but there was no signature. It informed the man that his daughter had been taken, but that she would not be harmed if he complied with the kidnapper's demands.

"Do you think they mean that bit about not hurting her?" Mistress Larkin asked as the three silently regarded the paper. She sounded close to tears again.

"Oh yes." Olivia sat beside the woman and took one of Mistress Larkin's hands in hers. "Your daughter is not the first to be taken, and from what we've heard, all the other girls were returned safely and unharmed."

The mother gave a small squeak and threw her arms around Olivia. Julius looked up, ready to intervene, but although Olivia looked startled, she gave Julius a small smile over the woman's shoulder, gently patting her on the back.

Julius had been hoping to avoid mentioning the other abductions, but he could understand what had compelled Olivia to speak. It would be cruel to do otherwise in the face of a mother's distress.

"What's this?" Larkin asked. "Other girls have been taken?"

Julius shrugged. "That is what the rumors say. But we need hard evidence to take it further."

The man leaped to his feet, lunging forward and taking Julius's wrist in an iron grasp. Julius was barely able to keep hold of the note as Larkin's eyes speared into him.

Cade stepped forward, his posture menacing, but Julius waved him away.

"If that's what you want the note for, you can't have it," the man said. "I won't allow anything that puts my Elisabeth at risk."

Julius spoke gently, putting as much sincerity into his voice as he could muster. "I understand. We also don't want to see harm come to your daughter. But what about once she is safely recovered? Would you give testimony then?"

Larkin hesitated, glancing at his wife, who sniffed and nodded. He released Julius and stepped back.

"I suppose that would be another matter. Naturally I want to see the villains who would hurt an innocent girl brought to justice." He cleared his throat. "And I hope Your Highness will excuse..." He trailed off and gestured at Julius's arm. "A desperate father will dare anything to protect his child."

Julius nodded, and Cade finally sat back down, nodding at the note in Julius's hand. "The note is obviously a test—to see if you will obey their orders and keep quiet before they reveal further information. It says that if you obey them, they'll contact you again in a few days with details of the ransom and how to safely recover your daughter. How long ago did you receive it?"

"Two days almost exactly." A determined look had replaced Mistress Larkin's tears. "When we heard your knock, we thought maybe..."

Julius sighed. "You're right that there is very little information in this note to go on. Especially since we can't take it for analysis. But there will be more clues in the next one, and you should hear from them soon."

"Assuming they don't hear these rumors and think we've disobeyed their command," Larkin said in a worried voice. "If the rumor is freely circulating the market..."

"Not freely," Olivia said quickly, giving Julius an apologetic look. "I don't think it's as bad as you fear."

Larkin frowned, but Olivia didn't say anything else, and he didn't press her.

"I have only one request," Julius said. "Please inform us when you hear from the abductors again."

Larkin's brows rose. "And how am I to do that, Your Highness? And without alerting the abductors to your involvement?"

Cade leaned forward. "Do you ever buy bread from the stall in the southwestern corner of the market?"

"Bread, my lord?" Mistress Larkin asked.

Cade nodded. "From that particular stall. Do you ever shop there?"

"All the locals use the market baker," she said. "He's even better than the baker with the shop on Hayder's Way. I've told him many times that his bread is worthy of a bigger establishment than a market stall."

Cade smiled. "That's easy, then, and you needn't worry about alerting anyone. Once you've received the note, attend the market yourself and buy a loaf of bread and four rolls from that stall."

Julius nodded approval, easily grasping Cade's plan. "We'll have someone watching the stall. They'll let us know when you make the purchase, and we'll come as quickly after that as possible."

With Markus located in the same corner of the market, they wouldn't need to assign a watcher.

Having agreed on the arrangement, the only thing left was to hear the story of Elisabeth's disappearance. Unfortunately, there were no clues to be found in that either. She had gone out to the market one day and never returned. When her parents quizzed the local stallholders, they all agreed that she had never arrived at the market. She must have been snatched from the street before she got there, but if anyone had witnessed it, they had not come forward.

Julius sighed as they exited the house.

"I had hoped to find out a little more than that," Cade said, voicing Julius's own thoughts.

"But the ransom demand will tell us more," Olivia said, clearly determined to take an optimistic view of their first real clue in weeks. "And if we can tag along for the exchange, we'll have a real chance of tracking the abductors back to wherever they're holding Marigold."

Julius's brows drew together. "*We* won't be tracking anyone. Once it gets to that stage, we'll have to bring in my father and at least some of the guards."

He half expected Olivia to argue, but she merely nodded agreement. Relief filled him. He didn't want Olivia anywhere near the abductors. Not even to rescue Marigold.

CHAPTER 24
OLIVIA

Olivia floated through the palace. She had grown increasingly comfortable in her life as a temporary royal—due in large part to Julius's constant and reassuring presence. But as her happiness in her new life grew, so had her guilt at not having found any hint of her missing friend.

But now they had a lead, and her hope had brightened anew. She felt sure they were on the cusp of uncovering her friend's location.

And to make matters even better, she had received word that Daphne was finally due to arrive that day. She didn't know what time, but she intended to wait on the front steps until her cousin's carriage rolled in.

As it turned out, she had barely arrived at the front doors when a carriage entered at the distant gates. Olivia hurried down the stairs, waiting with bated breath to see who would emerge.

The carriage pulled to a stop in front of her, and a royal footman stepped past, moving at a much more dignified pace than her own excited rush. He opened the door and pulled down the steps, but no one emerged.

He waited, hand held out to assist any occupants to alight, but still no one appeared. Olivia, abandoning patience completely, rushed forward and peered through the open carriage door.

For a second, the interior appeared to be empty. Then her vision adjusted to the dim lighting, and she spotted a small figure huddled in the corner. The young woman's dark dress allowed her to blend in with the shadows inside the carriage, and she was slumped with her head against the wall, almost as if she was—

"Sleeping? Really, Daphne?" Olivia laughed because she should have known. Thanks to the Oakden Legacy, Daphne was always sleeping. "You've arrived, you know. It's time to wake up."

Daphne slowly opened her eyes and smiled calmly at her newly royal cousin. "Olivia? Have I reached the palace, then?"

"Of course you have!" Olivia reached in and pulled her cousin out, ignoring the footman.

The two girls embraced.

"I would ask about your journey," Olivia said, "but you clearly slept the whole way."

"It was most relaxing," Daphne agreed. "I haven't had such a long stretch of time without someone pestering me to hurry since..." Her mouth pursed. "Possibly ever."

Olivia laughed again, full of delight just from her cousin's presence. "I'm glad my invitation could provide such a respite for you." She held Daphne at arm's length and examined her. "I haven't seen you in person for more than a decade, but I would have recognized you just the same."

"You, on the other hand, look much fancier." One side of Daphne's mouth twitched up. "You were knee-deep in dirt last time I saw you. But are you really a princess now?"

Olivia rolled her eyes. "No! As I keep telling everyone. And as you very well know! I wrote you all about it."

"Did you?" Daphne yawned, turning to watch the footman unloading her trunk. "Your letters are so long that you can't possibly expect me to read the entire thing every time. It's far too fatiguing."

"Daphne!" Olivia shook her head and linked arms with her cousin, pulling her toward the stairs.

Daphne eyed the flight distastefully but ascended without complaint and without losing her breath.

"So how long until I have a chance to feast my eyes on the handsomest prince in six kingdoms?" Daphne asked. "You perceive me positively agog."

Her words, paired with her placid expression, made Olivia snort. "What in the kingdoms are you talking about, Daphne?"

"Me?" Daphne turned a wounded expression on Olivia. "You were the one who informed me of that vital piece of information. You tried to hide it in the second of three post-scripts, but my keen awareness drew me straight to the most salient point."

They reached the front door, and Olivia propelled Daphne through.

"See! You do read my letters all the way to the end. I knew it." Olivia wrinkled her nose. "Your replies are far too astute for someone who skipped half of what I said."

"It's all the napping." Daphne looked around the white marble interior of the palace with interest. "It sharpens the brain."

Olivia gave her an impulsive hug. "I'm so glad you're here. It's nice to have one of *my* people here."

"Yes, it sounded like you'd gotten yourself into quite the fix." Daphne's eyes settled on Olivia. "I could hardly fail to respond to your desperate plea for an ally."

Olivia bit her lip, her eyes sliding away from her cousin's. "I may have been a tad emotional when I wrote that first letter from the palace," she said. "But I'm still delighted to have you here."

Daphne looked away, a small smile on her face. "So the handsome face has worked its magic. I did suspect as much. Not that I wouldn't have come sooner if I could, mind. But there were things I couldn't miss back home."

"Have you really left Glandore for good?" Olivia asked. "You'll return to Oakden after this?"

Daphne hesitated before shrugging. "That's the plan for now. But Glandore feels like home, whatever the Oakden Legacy thinks, so I haven't quite made up my mind to stay in Oakden forever. We shall see."

"Well, you'll always be welcome here if I have anything to say about it," Olivia declared.

"Your letter didn't exactly reassure me on that head." Daphne followed Olivia around a corner. "So I think I should meet this prince of yours to be sure I really am welcome to stay as long as I like—or rather as long as you like."

"Do you really want to meet him immediately?" Olivia asked. "You don't want to freshen up first? Or have a rest?" As soon as she said the word rest, she knew it was a silly suggestion, given Daphne had napped the whole way there. But Daphne responded immediately.

"Of course I'd far rather rest. In truth, your prince is only third on my list behind both rest and the famed and enormous Mildred." She turned curious eyes on Olivia. "Is she really as big as a small horse? Have you tried riding her?"

Olivia giggled. "Yes, she is that big, but no, of course I haven't tried riding her!"

Daphne nodded. "Very wise. It sounds far too fatiguing to ride without a saddle." She heaved a sigh. "But I wouldn't want to offend royal sensibilities by allowing your prince to find out he rates below a giant rodent."

"And a nap," Olivia interjected, but Daphne ignored her.

"So you might as well take me to your prince now and get it over with."

"You don't have to keep calling him that," Olivia said with a laugh that didn't sound quite natural.

Of course, it was true in a technical sense, given their betrothal. But Daphne said it in a tone that made it sound real, and the vulnerability of that made Olivia uncomfortable.

Because she did want Julius to be hers—not just in name but in reality. And if Daphne had been able to read Olivia's heart from only a letter, how many other people—including Julius himself—could plainly read it on her face?

"I don't mind if she calls me that," said a deep voice, bringing a flush to Olivia's cheeks.

She spun to see Julius striding toward them. He smiled first at her and then at Daphne.

"Welcome to the palace, Daphne. As Olivia's cousin,

you're basically family. You can call me whatever you like—
at least in private."

Olivia's flush faded. It had been a mere politeness? She
tried to ignore her disappointment.

"However, I'm not so sure how I feel about being ranked
below a rodent." He flashed Daphne a grin. "Even if Mildred
is a...*magnificent* creature."

Olivia leaned toward Daphne and spoke in a clearly
audible whisper. "Julius is afraid of her."

He straightened, assuming a look of offense, although his
eyes were still laughing.

"I'll have you know that if it came to her or me in a dark
corridor, I'm confident in my ability to send her running."

Olivia snorted. "That's not hard. Mildred runs away from
everyone except me." She looked at Daphne. "Mildred is even
more wary of people than Julius is of her. I don't think she's
left my suite once since she arrived."

"Very sensible," Daphne said. "Suites are comfortable places
full of beds and armchairs. I highly approve of them myself."

"You would." Olivia shook her head. "Since Julius is here,
why don't we give you a tour of the palace? Not that you
need to remember your way around. I'll stick to your side like
glue until you have it all straight. It's a big place. When I first
arrived, I needed a guide, too."

Olivia paused, startled to realize that it had been a long
time since she had gotten herself turned around in the palace
corridors. Until Daphne arrived, she'd almost forgotten how
overwhelming the palace had been at the beginning. In just a
couple of months she had grown so used to it that it felt like
home. So how would it feel to leave it and never return?

She shook off the momentary melancholy, determined not to ruin her reunion with Daphne.

"Come on!" she said. "It's an incredible building. You're going to love all the courtyards."

She propelled Daphne along the corridor. "And don't tell me it sounds too fatiguing," she said, cutting off her cousin's complaint before she could make it. "You just slept all the way here. You can manage a little exertion."

"Slept all the way here?" Julius's eyebrows shot up. "Is that even possible? It's a long way from Thebarton to the Sovaran capital."

"No one sleeps like Daphne," Olivia responded. "But thankfully she's too good-natured to say no to me." She threw her cousin a grin, but Daphne just sighed.

"Here I thought I was finally going to get a break, but you're just like Rosalie."

Olivia laughed, flattered by the comparison, despite the small pang of jealousy at the mention of Rosalie. She had always been a little jealous of Daphne's Glandorian best friend. Not just because Rosalie got to see Daphne in person every day, but because Olivia had wanted a friend like her in Henton. But from the stories in Daphne's letters, there was no one quite like Rosalie.

They reached the first courtyard, and Daphne expressed suitable admiration, immediately lifting Olivia's spirits once again. Her cousin had lived far from the Glandorian capital and had never been inside a palace before, so she was interested in everything they saw. The swell of pride inside Olivia grew at the chance to show her cousin her new home. It might be temporary, but she had come to feel a sense of connection to the palace and belonging with the whole community who lived and worked there.

When they reached the courtyard where both Julius and Olivia now started their mornings, they found Cade and Zane in the middle of a bout.

Olivia smiled, pleased to have run into the brothers so quickly. She sat beside the fountain, and Daphne sat with her, while Julius strolled closer to watch the bout from the sidelines.

"Fighting." Daphne sighed. "The most fatiguing thing of all."

"I think it's interesting," Olivia said. "Julius said he'll teach me when things slow down in the winter." She paused, wondering if she would even still be at the palace in the winter. She hadn't thought of that when Julius was at her side, talking of future lessons while his eyes shone with warmth.

A shout from Cade drew her attention. She looked up in time to see him skip backward, barely escaping an attack from Zane. She cheered when he regained his footing and launched a counterattack, earning an enigmatic look from Julius. But she didn't mind playing favorites when it came to Cade. Not only was he Julius's closest friend, but he had been suffering for weeks under the weight of Marigold's continued disappearance.

Zane threw a glance their way, his eyes lighting with curiosity when he saw someone new beside Olivia. But his inattention nearly cost him the bout, and he was forced to focus again on Cade's attacks.

"That's Lord Zane and Lord Cade," Olivia said for

Daphne's benefit. "They're the two sons of Lord Strathmore, who is—" She glanced sideways, and her words died.

Daphne was leaning against a small potted tree, to every appearance asleep.

Olivia shook her head wonderingly. How could Daphne possibly sleep through the sounds of the bout and her own cheering and chatter?

The bout finished with a neat move from Zane, ending with his sword point hovering lightly over Cade's heart. Cade took the loss in good part, strolling toward Julius, his breath still coming hard. Zane followed more slowly, dipping his head in Julius's direction.

"I'm glad you're both here," Julius said. "Olivia's cousin has come to stay with her, and I wanted to introduce you before the reception tonight."

The reception would be smaller than Olivia's first soiree —held for the select group of nobles who maintained apartments in the palace. However, the guest list meant that despite its size, it would still include the most influential segment of Sovaran nobility. Thankfully that included the two brothers.

Between the queen's lessons and the string of summer entertainments, Olivia had become familiar with every face in the Sovaran court. But she still felt most comfortable with the four men who made up Julius's inner circle.

The girls her own age were invariably polite but kept her at a distance. She had sometimes wondered if they guessed her betrothal might not last, and they were reluctant to open their inner circles to an outsider until it was confirmed she was there to stay. Whatever the reason, she hadn't pressed the matter and so was delighted to finally have Daphne for female company.

Julius led Cade and Zane over to the fountain. "This is Daphne." He gestured at her before looking at her properly and letting out a crack of laughter.

Both Cade and Zane stared in silence.

"Is she...asleep?" Zane asked, shaken out of his languid drawl for once.

Daphne straightened, stretching her arms and yawning. She blinked several times and looked around.

"Is the fighting over?" she asked. "Good."

Olivia choked down a laugh. "This is my cousin, Daphne," she said. "She's originally from Oakden."

Immediate comprehension filled both men's faces. Everyone knew the link between the Oakden Legacy and sleep. Cade gave Daphne a respectful bow, and Zane followed a beat later.

"It's a pleasure to meet any relative of Olivia's," Cade said, and Zane murmured agreement.

The brothers didn't linger long due to a scheduled meeting with their father, and after their departure, Olivia finally took pity on Daphne and led her to Olivia's suite to meet Mildred.

Daphne was suitably impressed with the mouse, showing more enthusiasm than she had for Olivia's human friends. And Mildred responded to her admiration, acting quite unlike her usual shy self.

"Did you know mice nap throughout the day and night?" Daphne said. "Very sensible creatures."

Since the part of the palace that had most impressed Daphne was Olivia's suite, Olivia was a little concerned that her cousin would protest the need to spend the evening at a royal reception. But Daphne accepted the scheduled event without comment, taking great joy in choosing herself a dress from Olivia's now extensive collection.

"You look stunning!" Olivia declared when she saw Daphne dressed in a new formal gown she hadn't yet worn. "It's a good thing Aunt Helen is right about the women in our family all having similar proportions."

"I might be willing to marry a prince myself for a wardrobe like that," Daphne said with a wistful sigh.

Olivia grinned. "But just think how fatiguing it would be to be a princess!"

Daphne shuddered. "You're right, of course. It doesn't bear thinking of." She admired herself in the mirror a final time before turning to Olivia.

"Will Cousin Helen and her girls be at the reception tonight? We didn't pass through the capital when I was seven, so I still haven't met them."

Olivia shook her head regretfully. "But I'll take you to visit them as soon as I get the chance. You'll like Nell and Hattie. They're hard not to like."

"And Marigold?" Daphne asked. "Will I meet her? She's their neighbor, isn't she? You were always writing about her when you lived with Cousin Helen, but since you moved to the palace, you haven't mentioned her once." She eyed Olivia, clearly aware there was something Olivia hadn't told her.

She was right, of course. Olivia's letters had been vague since she had been careful not to put anything about Marigold's trick or her subsequent disappearance into writing.

Olivia gestured Daphne closer and lowered her voice as she quickly filled her in on the full story of how she had ended up betrothed to the prince and about Marigold's suspected abduction. She even confided Marigold's connection with Cade and the recent kidnapping of Elisabeth, although she swore her cousin to secrecy on all of it.

"Well," Daphne said blankly when Olivia finally finished, "I knew something must have happened, but I can't say I dreamed of that tangled web."

"Who would!" Olivia shook her head. "I just wish we could find Marigold and make sure she's safe. Then we might have a hope of untangling it all."

Daphne shot her a perceptive look. "Are you sure you want it all untangled?"

Olivia looked away, busying herself with putting a late rose in her hair. "I certainly want to know my friend is safe."

"Yes," Daphne murmured softly. "There's definitely that."

As a result of their conversation, Daphne showed far more interest in Cade at the reception than she had done on first meeting. Before long, she was engaged in a light but humorous conversation with both Cade and Zane, leaving Olivia free to think her own thoughts.

Her eyes skipped around the receiving room, taking note of how light the decorations were compared to the more elaborate social events of the summer. The change of season hadn't affected the clothing of the attendees, however, and their silks and satins filled the room with color.

Her sweeping gaze fell on Lord Emerson, and to her surprise she found him gazing back at her. When their eyes met, she inclined her head respectfully before looking quickly away. But when she risked a glance back at him, his eyes were still trained on her. He held her gaze, gesturing with a subtle wave for her to approach him.

Olivia blinked, glancing behind her. Was he signaling to someone else?

But there was no one behind her. He gestured again.

Bemused, she moved toward him. She had greeted him before at Julius's side, but she couldn't remember a single proper conversation with the influential lord. He had certainly never sought her out.

Apprehension and hope battled within her, swirling in her stomach in a nauseating dance. Was it possible Marigold had been found? Olivia would gladly be wrong about her friend's abduction if it meant Marigold was safe.

"Lady Olivia." Lord Emerson said her name in a gruff voice as soon as she reached him.

She nodded, waiting for him to say more, but he remained silent for several awkward seconds before clearing his throat. He still didn't speak, however.

"My lord?" she asked, her concern growing.

Was the news of Marigold too terrible to relate? She looked around for Marigold's mother, hoping to gain some clue from her countenance, but Lady Emerson wasn't in the room. Olivia's concern grew even larger.

"Has something happened to Marigold?" she asked breathlessly, giving in to the pressure.

A flash of something crossed Lord Emerson's face—a rare outburst of emotion from a man who was usually tightly controlled, at least in public.

"Is she all right?" Olivia asked, her voice higher.

"That's what I was hoping you could tell me," he said.

"Me, my lord?" Disappointment seeped through Olivia. "I don't know what you mean."

"I understand you were my daughter's friend," he said.

"I'm still her friend," Olivia said staunchly.

His eyes narrowed, and she immediately wondered if she'd given the wrong impression.

"Wherever she is," she added. "I just mean that I haven't given up on her." She hesitated, but Lord Emerson had been the one to initiate the conversation. She decided to be bold. "I heard she was missing. She hasn't contacted you?"

Slowly he shook his head. "I was angry with her after the Midsummer Ball. She has always been a...challenge." He almost growled the last word. "But that trick she played was too far even for her."

Olivia nodded. She couldn't dispute the point, no matter how worried she was for her friend now. The Midsummer Ball had been Marigold at her most outrageous and feckless.

"I was certain she knew she'd gone too far and had run off afterward." He gave Olivia a keen look from under his brows. "She really didn't go to you? You haven't seen her since?"

Olivia shook her head. "I swear I haven't seen her since I left her carriage to enter the ball."

Lord Emerson gave a heavy sigh. "It's been so many weeks. I thought she would have returned by now—reappeared in a whirlwind, trying to charm us all into forgiving her. She probably would have succeeded given her track record—as long as she left us enough time to calm down and begin to worry. But it's been too long. She wouldn't have waited this long. I started checking with every relative, every friend. You're the last one."

He hesitated, glancing around. "My wife said you visited once. She said you mentioned…abduction?" He almost whispered the word.

"Yes," Olivia said breathlessly, her mind racing as she tried to decide how much to say. She hadn't expected a second chance to talk to Marigold's parents. "I'm convinced she was abducted. I know she was prone to outrageous and dramatic actions, but she wasn't the type to abandon her friends to face her consequences for her. I don't believe she would have abandoned me."

Lord Emerson looked down and away. Did he feel guilty for not having had the same faith in Marigold as Olivia had? Sympathy welled in Olivia, quick and strong. His worry for his daughter had to be even greater knowing he had left it so long to look for her.

"It's been challenging finding evidence to corroborate my theory," she said. "But I haven't given up searching."

Lord Emerson's eyes flew to hers. "You've been looking for Marigold?"

Olivia nodded, wanting to reassure him. "I was hoping that if I couldn't find her, I could at least find evidence to support my theory of an abduction." She hesitated before pressing on. "In fact, I believe I've finally found some evidence. I'm hoping that in just a few days, I'll be able to—"

"Evidence?" Lord Emerson's voice grew sharper than she had ever heard it. "You have evidence that my daughter was abducted?"

"Well…" Olivia faltered before the blaze in his eyes. "I need a few more days before I can completely confirm it. I don't have anything concrete yet. But we think we're on the verge of finding out where she's being kept, as well as who took her."

"I can tell you right now who took her," the lord said through his teeth, his body rigid and his face furious.

Before she could respond, he stormed across the room.

Olivia watched him go in astonishment. What was he talking about and where was he going? He hadn't even seemed to believe in an abduction two minutes ago. Was he going to the guards to demand a proper search?

But Lord Emerson stormed directly across the room to a small cluster of noblemen. Two of them turned to greet him, but he ignored them both. Striding up to Lord Strathmore, he seized the front of his clothing in an angry fist and jerked the other man toward him.

"Where is my daughter?" he roared. "What have you done with her?"

CHAPTER 25
JULIUS

Julius's conversation with Zane and Daphne was shattered by an angry shout—an incongruous sound for the setting. It only took him a second to find the source of the disturbance, and his eyes widened, shock holding him momentarily immobilized. Lord Emerson had Lord Strathmore by the front of his shirt and was shouting in his face.

"Release my Marigold at once!" he bellowed.

Julius's eyes shot toward Zane, but the man at his side looked equally frozen with shock at the abrupt and absurd attack on his father—and by a man who was usually the epitome of careful control. Julius had never seen Lord Emerson lose control of anything but his daughter. He'd certainly never lost control of himself.

"She's been abducted," he ranted, "and I know it was you. Who else has motive to take her without even a ransom? Give her back!"

"What is this?" Julius asked Zane, his mind struggling to make sense of what he was seeing and hearing. "Why would

Lord Emerson make such an accusation? This is taking rivalry too far!"

Zane shook his head slowly, but in the wake of the initial shock, he looked less surprised than Julius.

"It's that worthless son of yours," Lord Emerson shouted. "You never could control him, and now he's gone and taken my daughter. I won't have it! I won't have it, do you hear me? I told you as much when you dared to come to my home—groveling on behalf of your offspring. As if I would ever stoop to ally myself with your conniving family!"

Julius turned slowly to stare at Zane, hardly able to believe what he was hearing. Zane had flinched at the word groveling but otherwise seemed to have recovered his countenance.

"Zane?" he asked, his tone a mixture of query, astonishment, and warning.

Zane threw him a sardonic look, his eyes half-lidded. "I'm sure Lord Emerson has called me many names over the years, but *worthless* isn't one of them."

Julius's world tilted on its axis.

"Cade?" he breathed. "Cade and Marigold?! Cade is in love with *Marigold*? Wants to marry her?" His voice rose at the end, as he struggled to assimilate the information. "Why didn't he tell me?"

"He certainly fancied himself in love," Zane said sourly. "I have no idea what he thinks now. I can only hope he's come to his senses given I haven't seen the girl in months. As to why he kept it a secret, that should be obvious." He looked toward the two lords, still locked together, both of their faces red.

"But…"

Cade attempted to join the altercation in defense of his father, but Kasper leaped in to block him, preventing Cade from prizing Lord Emerson's hands from Lord Strathmore's jacket. Julius knew his parents weren't in the room, and that it was up to him to intervene before the situation grew any larger. But his legs were frozen in place.

"Your father approved of the match?" he asked, wondering why that was the most surprising aspect of the affair.

"Hardly." Zane's lip curled. "We didn't know anything about it at first. Apparently Cade has just enough sense to know he was disgracing his family by running around with Lord Emerson's daughter."

Julius raised an eyebrow. It seemed a hypocritical perspective, given Zane and Cade both sparred with Lord Emerson's son every morning and talked with him at social events. But Julius remained silent, wanting to hear anything Zane would tell him—anything to make sense of such a nonsensical situation.

"But when Cade heard there were talks of choosing Marigold for your betrothed..." Zane shook his head. "He grew desperate. Our mother has always coddled him, and if my father has one flaw, it's his soft spot for her. No matter how ridiculous her requests..." His lips tightened. "She begged him to intercede on Cade's behalf, and so Father went to see Marigold's parents. Lord Strathmore himself—one of the most influential and respected nobles at court—lowered himself to plead with his greatest rival. And he was laughed out of their house."

Despite the rancor of his words, Zane's tone and face teetered on the edge of boredom—as if the events from the summer were so distant as to no longer greatly interest him.

Julius stared across the room at Cade who was still trying to shake off Kasper in order to go to the defense of his father. From the look on Kasper's face, he had no idea what was going on but had leaped in blindly in support of his own father. The whole thing was a mess.

Zane sighed. "It looks like it's up to me to stop this farce. As usual." He began to move toward his father and brother, progressing at his usual languid stroll.

"That is an interesting man," Daphne said, reminding Julius of her presence for the first time. He turned to find her watching Zane walk away. "A most interesting man."

Despite his overwhelming shock—or perhaps because of the numbness it had caused—Julius felt a small spurt of amusement at the thought of two such languid persons forming an attachment. Despite his current irritation with Zane, he recognized that he would be a good match for Daphne.

But he shouldn't be thinking of such things. He needed to take control of the situation. He needed to join Zane and stop—

"That is enough!"

His head snapped up at the crisp voice. Its calm authority cut through the chaos of the room, bringing quiet in its wake.

Olivia. She faced the two struggling noblemen—both decades older than her—radiating offended dignity.

"Cade and Kasper, step back at once."

The younger men reacted instinctively to the command

in her voice, releasing each other and stepping away with shamefaced expressions. She turned to their fathers next.

"Lord Emerson! You shame the crown with this public attack."

She had chosen the right words. Lord Emerson—who had seemed oblivious to the involvement of Cade and Kasper—stiffened at her mention of the crown. When she said public, he crumbled completely. Releasing Lord Strathmore, he stepped back. His eyes remained wild, however, and he hardly seemed aware of his surroundings.

Lord Strathmore immediately swelled, and Julius braced himself for the man's outrage. But Olivia spoke before he could get a word out.

"You will both join me through here. At once." The command in her tone left no room for disagreement as she swept them toward a door that Julius knew led into a small waiting room. "Their Majesties are on their way and will adjudicate this matter." When both Lords looked like they were about to speak, she added firmly, "In private."

They both subsided and fierce pride filled Julius. Had he ever thought Olivia out of place in the palace? In that moment, she was every inch the royal.

Finally finding his legs, he hurried to her side. He reached her as she swept the two lords the last of the way into the waiting room. Once they were through, she hesitated in the doorway.

Julius put a light hand on her back and felt the tremble he hadn't been able to see across the room. She threw him a look of relief.

"Are my parents really coming?" he asked.

Her mouth twisted slightly. "I hope so. I sent a footman

running for them the moment Lord Emerson started shouting."

"You're incredible," Julius murmured, still awestruck by her.

She laughed self-consciously. "Hardly. But I have been watching you for months."

"Me?"

She nodded. "I told myself that I just needed to copy you —that if I acted with enough confidence, people would respond to my words without thinking. It was all a show, though. My legs were shaking so hard I could barely walk."

"But you did walk." Her confession had done nothing to diminish his admiration. "I was too shocked to do anything but stand and stare along with everyone else."

"Yes, well." Her mouth twisted further. "Since it was my fault for setting him off, I knew I had to do something."

"You told him Lord Strathmore abducted Marigold?"

"No, of course not! I barely said anything before he stormed off and—" She sighed. "I knew they were rivals, of course, but I had no idea Cade's father had gone to Lord Emerson before the ball and pleaded on Cade's behalf."

She threw a pained but sympathetic look in Cade's direction, and he met her gaze with an apologetic grimace. Another explosion went off inside Julius's brain.

Olivia had known. She had known about the information that was still robbing him of coherent thought.

Cade loved the missing noble girl, and Olivia knew it. Which meant there had never been thoughts of love between Cade and Olivia. Their connection had always been because of Marigold.

The lightness of extreme relief made it hard for Julius to

think clearly. Knowing he wasn't in danger of losing the woman he loved to his best friend changed everything. And seeing Olivia step fully into her royal role only confirmed it. She was clearly more than capable of taking on the crown at his side. Even his parents couldn't doubt her now.

A door on the other side of the waiting room opened, revealing the king and queen. Olivia let out a small sigh of relief, and he could have echoed it. He had no desire to be responsible for sorting out the conflict between the two powerful lords.

His father dismissed them with a small gesture, and Julius closed the door with alacrity, shutting them off from his parents and the two lords.

"I know you have every right to be in there," he said to Olivia, "but I get the impression you're just as glad as I am not to be."

"More than glad," she assured him. "I'm sure Their Majesties will have better luck navigating that delicate situation without us."

"I had no idea life at court was so exciting," Daphne said wryly from behind them.

Olivia gave a shaky laugh. "It isn't usually."

"No." Julius grimaced and glanced around the room. "This reception will be talked about for years, I warrant."

Olivia bit her lip. "Should we send everyone away?"

Julius considered. "There's no stopping them talking," he finally concluded. "It's probably best to let them get some of it out of their systems now."

The three of them were silent for a moment before he burst into speech again. "But I still can't believe it. Cade, of all people, in love with *Marigold*!"

"Why not?" Olivia sounded defensive. "Marigold is stunning and kind, and I've never met anyone so full of life."

"She really does sound exhausting," Daphne muttered.

Olivia threw her an amused look. "You have no idea."

"All right," Julius conceded. "Maybe someone might love Marigold—there are all kinds of tastes. But why did Cade never say anything?"

"Marigold didn't want me to," Cade said simply from behind him.

Julius turned a hurt expression on his friend, but Cade only shrugged.

"As Sovar's prince and future king, you have the loyalty of my sword," he said. "As a friend, you have the loyalty of my time and care. But when it comes to my heart, my loyalty lies with only one, and it isn't you, old friend."

The two young men stared at each other silently for a moment before Julius relaxed and clapped his friend on the shoulder. "I suppose I can't argue with that."

Cade looked relieved at Julius's acceptance, and Olivia even more so. He felt like a fool for worrying about the two of them. And even more of one for never guessing what Olivia had apparently worked out with ease.

"But what happened?" Cade asked, clearly still bewildered. "What made Lord Emerson think *I'd* taken Marigold?"

Olivia briefly related her conversation with Lord Emerson, repeating exactly what she'd said.

"I never dreamed it would set him off in such a way. He was clearly much closer to the edge than I realized."

"It isn't your fault," Julius said quickly, and Cade nodded agreement. "You barely said anything. He was the one who decided Cade's father must have abducted Marigold on Cade's behalf."

Cade frowned, anger dancing in his eyes. "He's a fool to react that way if he believes that's true. Shouldn't he be relieved to think his daughter was taken by someone who would cherish and care for her—someone of her own choosing? At least it would mean she was safe. His rigidity and his foolish pride are exactly what drove his daughter away in the first place."

"I even got excited for a minute," Olivia said despondently. "I thought he was going to throw his resources into the search. But all he did was jump to another ridiculous assumption. We can't possibly risk telling him about the Larkins." She dropped her voice for the final two words, and Julius looked questioningly at Daphne.

"Don't worry," Olivia said. "I've told her everything."

Julius wasn't sure that confession alleviated his worry, but he had to trust Olivia knew her cousin well enough and that he could trust Daphne too.

Daphne must have caught him looking at her because when Cade and Olivia began to speculate about when they might hear from the Larkins, Daphne shifted in his direction.

"Don't worry," she murmured to him. "You don't need to worry about me doing anything to hurt Olivia. It's far more likely Olivia will try to do something to help and get herself into trouble."

Julius's chest tightened at hearing someone speak his own fear aloud. Apparently he wasn't the only one who cared about Olivia, although the relationship between the two girls confused him.

"I know you and Olivia are cousins," he said, "but haven't

you been living in Glandore since you were seven? How do you know Olivia so well?"

"My cousin writes long letters."

Julius chuckled, but his amusement quickly died. "What can I do to make sure that when we hear from the Larkins, she doesn't put herself at risk? Between us there has to be something we can do."

"Do something?" Daphne eyed him in surprise before sighing languidly. "I suppose such delusions come from being a prince. Convincing a determined person not to follow their course is a hopeless endeavor. So I, for one, don't bother trying anymore. Believe me, I have a lot of experience in this area."

"But we can't do nothing!"

"Can't we?" Daphne sounded mildly surprised. "I think you'll find we can indeed do just that. We do nothing until the time comes to do something. And then we do the right something."

Julius blinked at her as she stepped away to rejoin Olivia and Cade's conversation. He had expected Olivia's cousin to be a little unusual thanks to the Oakden Legacy, but he was increasingly unsure whether she was oblivious or brilliant.

She spoke so confidently, but for himself he just hoped that when the moment she spoke of came, he knew the right course of action. Because that night had only sealed his determination to win Olivia's heart properly. He might not have realized it at their first meeting—or second, or third— but she was the perfect person to help him guide and protect Sovar.

CHAPTER 26

JULIUS

J ulius, Olivia, and Cade headed into the market again the next afternoon, this time with Daphne in tow. Ostensibly they were taking Olivia's cousin sightseeing, so her presence was essential. But he suspected she wouldn't have accepted being left behind anyway.

They went straight to Markus's stall, and as soon as they had received their tankards of cider, he spoke in a low murmur. "Mistress Larkin showed up this morning. Bought a loaf of bread and four rolls from the baker's stall, just like you said."

"This morning?" Olivia looked ready to jump up, but Julius put his hand over hers, and she settled, lifting her tankard quickly to her lips.

"Mmm," Daphne said. "You're right, Olivia. This really is delicious cider."

Markus grinned. "Thank you, my lady."

"Oh, I'm not a lady. Just Daphne."

Markus grinned. "Well, I always appreciate praise for my cider—whether it comes from a commoner or nobility."

"With cider this good, I'm surprised your stall isn't teeming." She took another long drink.

Markus leaned forward, his eyes shifting from side to side. For the first time, he actually looked as if he were about to impart a secret, a break from his usual subtle manner.

"I don't give everyone the good stuff," he said in a hoarse whisper. "I'm very discerning about who gets to enjoy it." He patted the barrel their drinks had come from.

Julius sat back and laughed. "Consider us honored in that case. Although I suppose it's Olivia we have to thank, since she was the first one to win you over."

Markus smiled at Olivia. "I can recognize an overwhelmed, homesick expression when I see one. And I'm willing to offer a bit of cider-flavored comfort to those that need it."

Olivia laughed. "How long ago that seems! I remember my first visit—I couldn't believe how enormous the market was. I was wishing I had convinced my cousins to come with me instead of braving it alone when I sat down at Markus's stall just to escape the crowds." She smiled at him. "I'm glad you took pity on me as I can't imagine my time in the capital without your delicious cider."

"Have we waited long enough?" Cade murmured, clearly struggling with the task of looking calm and relaxed for enough time to finish a tankard.

Julius threw him a sympathetic look. His respect for Cade's self-control had grown considerably since learning about his connection to Marigold. He had shown remarkable self-restraint in appearing so normal for the last months.

"I think we can go now." Julius drained the last of his drink in one long swallow. "Ladies?"

"Oh, yes! I'm done." Daphne stood up with a satisfied sigh. "And you can be sure I'll be back, sir."

Olivia laughed. "Cider appreciation runs in the family, apparently."

Julius caught the intensity of the glitter in her eyes. Her laughter was the only outlet she was allowing herself, but her emotions were running high.

They left their two grooms at the market in charge of the horses, walking the short distance to the Larkins' home on foot. They hadn't bothered to bring any guards since they couldn't risk taking them anywhere near the Larkins' anyway. And Julius was no longer concerned about the need for a guard in the market. The people had already grown used to his and Olivia's frequent visits, and he no longer feared they might be crushed by an enthusiastic crowd.

Thanks to the new hint of cool in the air, they had been able to get away with bringing cloaks, and all four of them donned the garments and drew up the hoods shortly after leaving the market. Julius looked around keenly as they walked, searching for any hint of watchers. He could see no one.

His heart beat quickly anyway as they waited outside the Larkins' door, the seconds after their knock seeming to stretch impossibly long. Were the Larkins not home?

Finally the door swung open. The young maid on the other side fell back with a gasp at the sight of four cloaked figures on her doorstep. But there was no time to reassure her. Rushing forward, the four of them pushed their way into the house, the maid staggering back out of their way.

"But who...who are you?" she gasped.

Olivia pulled off her hood and Julius quickly followed

suit. The girl gave a squeak of delight as soon as she got a good look at Olivia, reassuring Julius that she wasn't too upset at their abrupt entry.

"Your Highness!" She dropped into an exaggerated curtsy.

"What's this?" Master Larkin's harried voice came from further down the hall. "Is it—?"

He caught sight of Julius and hurried forward. "Back to the packing now," he told the girl. "I'll see to our guests."

The maid obeyed slowly, looking disappointed. She threw frequent glances over her shoulder until she was out of sight, but Larkin waited patiently for her to disappear before speaking again.

"We don't have many staff," he said, "and we haven't mentioned you to any of them. It seemed safer that way."

Julius nodded. "Very wise. And you've received the ransom demand?"

"That we did." Larkin led them into the sitting room from their previous visit. "And we're nearly packed and ready to go. You came just in time."

"Packed?" Julius asked blankly. "How much coin did they demand?"

"None," Master Larkin said grimly. "Their demand is that we pack and leave the city immediately, collecting our daughter on the way."

"The abductor wants you to leave the capital?" Cade asked. "That's all? But why? What does he stand to gain from that?"

"Or she," Daphne murmured, but Cade didn't seem to hear.

"That's not quite all," Master Larkin said with a note of

resignation. "I'm also to drop my current business plans. I assume he wants me to leave the capital to make it harder for me to ever pick them back up again."

"And what are your business plans?" Julius asked, tension knotting deep in his belly. Would they finally get a clue to the identity of the abductor?

"I'm not a skilled man myself," Larkin said. "Not in the way of making things anyway. But I can recognize quality when I see it. I found several smaller glass workshops that produced quality products but were struggling to distribute their wares effectively. I've been negotiating a deal to pool their products and managed the sales and distribution as combined stock. We were planning to focus on Glandore to begin with as I have a good merchant contact there who would take possession of the goods at the border."

"And someone sees your deal as a threat," Julius said. "It sounds like the abductor works with glass in some way."

Master Larkin's lips pressed into a thin line, his eyes darting around the group before he shrugged, not speaking.

Cade shifted uncomfortably beside Julius. "I take it there was no direct responsibility taken by anyone?"

"No, my lord." Master Larkin looked down, seeming nervous.

Julius frowned. Was he hiding something? But why would he want to hide something from the people who were trying to help him?

He glanced at Cade, wondering if he had some insight, but from the tightness of his muscles, he was too on edge to think clearly. They would have to make do with the clue they had been given and hope the father wasn't holding anything back.

When he looked for Olivia, he found her a few steps away, fumbling with something in her pocket. When she caught his eye, she nodded reassuringly.

"I know this must all be very terrifying for you and your wife, Master Larkin," she said in a gentle voice. "But we intend to help you retrieve Elisabeth safely."

"Thank you, my lady." The man didn't seem very reassured, despite his words.

Julius's brow creased even further, but when Olivia gave him a second small nod, he accepted her judgment. He didn't know what made her so certain about Larkin, but she was silently asking him to trust her, and he was willing to do so.

"Do you really intend to flee the city, even with our support?" he asked. "We can protect your family."

Larkin's head jerked from side to side. "Thank you, Your Highness, but as long as my daughter's abductor is free, I won't sleep a wink in the capital. We will obey our instructions to the letter."

"Can we at least have the two letters?" Julius asked. "They can serve as proof of the abduction after you've left."

Larkin hesitated. But after another glance at each of their faces, he retrieved two folded parchments and handed them over to Julius.

"We truly do appreciate your support, Your Highness, but all we want now is to have our daughter safe back in our arms again and to take her far from any future danger. If I have to give up a new business opportunity, I'll do so without a second thought."

"You're a truly loving father," Olivia said softly, "and that is to be admired. I hope you have your daughter safe at your side again soon."

Larkin cleared his throat. "Thank you, my lady." He hesitated. "I don't wish to be rude, but we're currently in a frenzy of packing. If we're to make the rendezvous on time, we'll need to leave in half an hour. I'm afraid I have to ask you to leave now." He nodded toward the letters. "I hope those can be of some use."

"We will do all in our power to make sure they are," Cade said earnestly, and Larkin smiled although it didn't reach his worried eyes.

"Will you not let us accompany you?" Julius asked, shocked at their sudden expulsion. "We could stay back out of sight when you approach the rendezvous."

"No!" Larkin said sharply. "We were directed to come alone, and we intend to obey all instructions. To the letter."

"But—" Julius started to protest, but Cade laid a restraining hand on his arm.

"Come on," he murmured. "We can talk outside."

Julius frowned, wanting to argue further, but Olivia approached on his other side.

"The Larkins have helped us. We can't do anything to put their daughter in danger."

Meeting her eyes, Julius sighed and capitulated.

As soon as they stepped outside, the door was shut firmly behind them. Julius hesitated, but Cade moved swiftly, hauling him down the narrow lane that ran between the Larkins' home and the house beside it. The two girls followed on their heels, everyone's faces creased with worry.

"We couldn't stay and harass the poor Larkins," Cade said breathlessly. "But I don't intend to leave it at that, and I'll warrant none of you do either." He threw a slightly doubtful look at Daphne, but when she didn't protest, he continued. "Let's see the letter. It might give us a clue."

Julius unfolded the top parchment, holding it out so that everyone could read at once. Four heads bowed close to peer at it in the dim light of the laneway.

The note was brief and to the point—addressing the Larkins by name but giving no signature, just like the first one. The straightforward demands aligned exactly with what Larkin had told them, the only new piece of information being the rendezvous location.

"Is it far?" Daphne asked, clearly unfamiliar with the listed spot.

"It's near the northeast gate." Julius pulled up a map of the city in his mind's eye. "I suspect the abductor intends to hand over Elisabeth and then lurk nearby to observe their departure for himself. It's a perfect location for that since he wouldn't need to follow them for long."

"I entered the city through that gate," Olivia said. "And I remember this square. We stopped there for a drink from the public fountain, and I was so excited by everything I saw that I still remember the name plaque. It's a small square, yes, but it still seems a very public place for a handover of this sort."

"The square itself is public," Cade said, "but it has a number of dark alleys and lanes that feed into it. I think it would work for the purpose. I'm sure they wouldn't be planning any sort of dramatic meeting. They'll probably send Elisabeth in to meet her parents alone—with a warning to pass on to them, most likely."

"What kind of warning?" Olivia asked, her face pale.

Julius grasped Cade's point instantly, answering for him. "A warning that they're being watched, and that if they do anything but progress straight to the gate, they'll be shot. There could be archers hiding in second stories or down alleyways easily enough to make the threat real."

"They wouldn't even need real archers," Daphne added. "We've already seen that fear alone will achieve their ends."

"But what if the Larkins had gone to the guards?" Julius asked, thinking aloud. "At a location like that, it would be easy to surround every alley and lane from the rear and catch the watcher that way. At least that's what I would have planned to do if we'd had time for elaborate plans. But there's no time for that now, which I suppose is why Larkin was willing to hand the letter over."

"I think the Larkins know the identity of the abductor, even if we do not," said Daphne thoughtfully. "And I think it's someone powerful enough that he doesn't fear such an eventuality."

"Do you really think Master Larkin lied to us?" Olivia didn't sound convinced. "I looked at him *closely*, and he looked sincere." She gave her cousin a significant look, one Julius couldn't interpret.

"I looked as well," Daphne said calmly, "and I saw sincere fear. Deep fear. The kind that comes from an enemy who far outmatches you. I'm not saying he lied outright. The note doesn't include a name, so he doesn't know for sure. But I think he's guessed it anyway. He must know his own business rivals."

"I have an idea," Cade said abruptly. "But we have to move fast."

"You want to go to the rendezvous ourselves?" Olivia asked, sounding torn. "That would mean breaking our promise to Master Larkin, but it might be our only chance to identify and follow the abductor."

Julius frowned. If he was alone, he would have planned to do just that. But he had no desire to put Olivia at risk.

"We need guards for such an endeavor," he said, "and we didn't bring any with us. We'll have to detour and fetch some."

But Cade was already shaking his head before Julius finished speaking. "There's no time for any of that. Even if we leave now and hurry there by the most direct route, we still may not make it in time. If we happen to pass any guards on city watch, by all means, order them to join us. But we can't take the time to divert in search of them."

Julius frowned. "Time isn't quite as tight as that. We won't have time to set up a proper surveillance operation, of course, but we have plenty of time to reach the rendezvous point, even if we divert for troops on the way. In fact, when we reach the guards, we should trust the matter to them and not go ourselves at all." He threw a quick look at Olivia who frowned in response to his words.

Cade shook his head again. "You may do what you like—in fact, as crown prince, I encourage you to keep yourself safe. But I will be going myself."

Julius hesitated, torn. Of course he couldn't let his best friend go haring into danger alone. But if he said he was accompanying him, then he was willing to bet that—

"Agreed," said Olivia before he even spoke. "I intend to go regardless of what you do, Julius." She gave him a defiant look, and he groaned.

Cade sighed. "I would honestly prefer you all keep yourselves safe, but I don't mean to waste any time on a losing battle. The key point is that I'm not thinking of going to the rendezvous. Its location—along with the clue about glass-blowing—has given me a theory. There's an old, disused warehouse close to that square. It used to house glass wares, but a water leak on the second floor caused part of the ceiling to collapse, smashing a large section of stock on the floor below. It still hasn't been repaired, so it's not in active use and would be the perfect place to stash an abducted victim—or two."

Julius immediately understood the urgency visibly vibrating through Cade. After all this time, he had a possible location for Marigold.

"But surely they won't have been keeping Marigold in one place all this time," he said.

"If they had, she would have found a way to escape by now," Olivia said with a grin.

Cade nodded once. "Agreed. The neighbors could also become a risk if they stayed anywhere too long. I suspect they've been moving around, and it's likely that after the exchange this afternoon, they'll move again. They won't risk staying where they are in case Elisabeth reports them after all."

"Marigold might be at this warehouse right now!" Olivia bounced on the balls of her feet. "What are we waiting for?"

"Precisely." Cade didn't wait for agreement, taking off for the entrance of the lane and jogging down the street.

Both girls took off after him, and Julius brought up the rear. He hadn't even been given the chance to voice his concerns—including that they didn't know how many men the abductor might have guarding the kidnapped girls.

While he understood Cade's desperation, he didn't want to be part of leading any of them to their deaths.

But he couldn't restrain all three of them at once. And he knew when a royal command would do no good. All he could do was accompany them and do his part—and keep his eyes peeled for guards along the way.

They didn't pass a single pair of patrolling guards until they reached the northeast corner of the city, and he'd almost despaired of any appearing. Putting on a burst of speed, he overtook the others and stopped in front of the armed men.

"You're with me," he barked out. "We have trouble and there might be fighting. There's no time to explain."

"Excuse me?" one of them asked coldly, but his companion elbowed him hard, his eyes wide.

"Yes, Your Highness," the second man said. "We're at your disposal."

The first speaker's eyes also widened, and he gave a deep bow. "My apologies for not recognizing you, Prince Julius."

"Never mind that." Julius's breath came fast after his dash through the city. "For now, follow me. We're being left behind."

The others hadn't slowed or stopped, although Olivia was looking back for him over her shoulder. But he knew they would slow to a walk soon. They had only made it so far by alternating jogging and walking since none of them were professional runners.

When the group did slow, Julius quickly caught them up before dropping to a walk himself and quickly filling the two guards in on the bare bones of the situation. He didn't mention

Marigold by name, but both men were incensed and ready to assist, although they respectfully suggested that Julius himself should stay back and allow them to take his place.

"I thank you, but no," he said. "And that's not up for debate," he added when one of them looked inclined to argue.

Cade led the small group through a maze of back alleys, amazing Julius with his sense of direction. If it had been up to Julius to lead them, he would have been hopelessly lost by that point.

His friend finally stopped beside a building that gave every appearance of still being abandoned. The windows had been boarded up, and weeds grew around the back door, broken bricks scattered among them.

"We should wait for the abductors to leave," Julius murmured in an undertone. "We can lay an ambush and take them by surprise in the open."

Cade shook his head, stubbornness radiating from every line of his body. "If she's not in there, I have to know it now. There's still time for me to make the rendezvous point if I was wrong about this warehouse."

"And what?" Julius whispered, exasperated. "Find the abductor yourself? On your own?"

"If I have to."

Julius sighed. There was clearly no talking Cade down. Julius now had two guards on his side and could order for the young lord to be restrained, but he didn't think Olivia and Daphne would just accept it if he did. And in truth, now that they were there, he could feel some portion of Cade's eagerness coursing through his own veins. If Marigold was really on the other side of that wall, it was time they rescued her.

Cade tried the back door, rattling the latch, which didn't open.

"Maybe we should try—" Julius began, but Cade had already picked up half a broken brick and thrown it through the window.

The sound of breaking glass made everyone except Cade flinch. He was already in motion again, knocking out the remaining glass shards using the other half of the brick.

"Really?" Julius hissed, but there was no time for him to get angry at his friend's reckless haste. Cade had just announced their arrival, and they needed to act quickly.

Cade reached through the now empty window frame and unlatched the door. As soon as he'd done so, he wrenched it open and rushed through. Julius ran at his heels, one of the guards right behind him. The second guard had been instructed to remain at the rear, keeping Olivia and Daphne in the center of the party.

The two girls both wielded daggers, although he had no idea where they had come from. Had they been carrying them in their boots?

The door opened directly into a large, empty space. On the far side, he could see a couple of doors that likely led into offices, but the wreckage of the collapsed upper floor partially blocked both doors. The fallen ceiling still lay scattered across half the warehouse, along with smashed shelves and broken glass, making it unlikely their quarry was in the blocked rooms.

He swung around to examine the other half of the warehouse.

"Cade!" a piercing voice screamed, and his eyes settled on Marigold.

She was shackled to a heavy table but had somehow removed the gag that now hung limply around her neck. A short way away, a second girl, perhaps a little younger, stood staring at them, each of her arms restrained by a burly man. Apparently they had arrived just as Elisabeth was being led from the room.

One of the men abandoned Elisabeth and faced off with the newcomers, three other men appearing to join him. One of them ran past Marigold's table, and she gave a loud scream and tried to sweep his legs out from under him.

He responded with a vicious blow that she only partially dodged.

Cade immediately let out a wild bellow and ran for the man, seeming oblivious to the three others standing in his way. Julius shouted as well, waving for the guards to join him in distracting the remaining three.

Two of the men had turned aside, moving to intercept Cade, but they wheeled back at Julius's shout, each of them drawing a sword. Julius faced the man, putting himself between the abductor and Olivia, who had dashed after Cade. He wasn't giving the armed men an opportunity to go after a weaker target.

The two guards surged forward valiantly, each engaging one of their attackers in a desperate struggle. Julius lunged for the remaining man who skipped backward, away from his blade. Julius remained in place, unwilling to be lured into a dangerous position.

The man changed tack, abandoning his strategic retreat and rushing Julius with a yell. Julius stepped back, expertly parrying the man's attack. But he nearly misjudged the force of his counterattack, too accustomed to the careful bouts he engaged in with his friends.

Pulling back, he adjusted, his next lunge catching the man off guard. The man gave way before the force of Julius's blow, his sword slipping away as Julius carried the thrust all the way through.

His opponent threw himself backward off Julius's blade but immediately collapsed to the ground, both hands clutching his wound. Julius raised his sword again, panting as he looked toward the other two fights. One of the guards had subdued his man, but the other had somehow lost his blade, as had his opponent, and the two were pummeling each other with their fists.

Julius watched the cadence of the fight, ready to intervene when an opening presented itself, but a piercing cry of "Julius!" made him swing around.

CHAPTER 27
OLIVIA

Olivia gripped her dagger in a sweating hand, but she wasn't foolhardy enough to take on a man armed with a sword. She would leave the guards to handle them.

Instead, she ran along the inside wall of the warehouse, following behind Cade. By the time she got a clear view of him, he had Marigold's attacker lying at his feet and was attempting to free Marigold while she sobbed noisily.

Something wound tight inside Olivia loosened. Her friend was all right. The tears sounded more like a natural overflow of emotion than the deep wail of someone badly injured or in extreme distress.

Olivia started to move closer to the pair when she remembered that the warehouse held another captive. And the second captive didn't have a desperate lover to rush to her rescue.

Olivia swung around, searching for Elisabeth and her remaining captor. But Daphne was ahead of her. Before

Olivia had done more than visually locate the abducted girl, Daphne was shouting for Elisabeth to duck.

Elisabeth obeyed promptly, and Daphne hurled a broken piece of plaster at her captor. Olivia wasted no time in following suit. Swapping her dagger to her left hand, she seized a piece of loose debris from the floor and aimed it at the man.

He had successfully dodged Daphne's plaster and was attempting to haul Elisabeth back upright again. The girl was stubbornly resisting, however, and her captor wasn't prepared for Olivia's chunk of wood. It hit him on one shoulder.

He bellowed and swung around just in time for Daphne to catch him in the side of the head with part of a brick. He swayed and crumpled to the ground.

Daphne hurried to Elisabeth's side, helping her to her feet and talking in a soft, reassuring flow. Energy coursed through Olivia, and she breathed hard, despite her relatively minor exertion.

She couldn't relax yet, however. Spinning around, she searched for Julius, hoping to find he had already completed his fight.

For a second all she could see were swaying, shouting figures, but her eyes latched onto Julius, a point of calm in the chaos. He appeared unharmed, his focus on two men locked in a rapid fistfight.

Before she could release a sigh of relief, however, her eyes caught on another man. Whatever Cade had done to incapacitate Marigold's attacker, the effect hadn't been permanent. He was back on his feet, unnoticed by Cade, who was still working to free Marigold, and was approaching Julius from behind.

He no longer had his sword—if he had ever had one—but he held a brick raised high, ready to bring it down on the back of Julius's head.

"Julius!" Olivia screamed, throwing herself forward in a desperate lunge.

She slid forward across the ground, her wild, screaming approach distracting the man. As she slid all the way to his side, she stabbed her dagger—still clutched in her left hand—awkwardly into his foot.

Julius turned, his sword coming up as he instinctively ran the man through. The attacker gave a soft, surprised grunt and dropped the brick, his hands going to the sword now protruding from his middle.

The brick fell toward Olivia. Trapped in an awkward position, she tried to roll away, but there was no time.

She braced herself for the strike of the brick, but instead a heavy weight fell over her as Julius threw himself across her. Bracing himself with his arms, he took the blow of the brick against his back.

"Julius!" she cried again, her words muffled this time.

But while the brick must have hurt, it had missed his head, and he was able to scramble easily to his feet. He pulled her up after him, his eyes roaming over her.

"Are you all right?" He sounded frantic with worry. "You weren't hurt?"

Olivia shook her head, letting him pull her into his arms and feeling his relieved sigh all the way through her. As she rested against his chest, she remembered there was still one fight unfinished.

She peered toward the guard who had been wrestling

with his opponent. The man had both hands propped on his knees, his back hunched as he sucked in breaths, clearly winded from the fight. His opponent lay at his feet. Daphne stood beside the downed man, a brick in her hand.

She looked up, met Olivia's eyes, and shrugged. "Someone had to do something," she said matter-of-factly.

Olivia laughed shakily, her eyes roaming over the men scattered across the ground. The other guard had already secured his opponent with a length of rope and was moving on to the most lively looking of the other prone men.

She relaxed into Julius again. It really was over.

"Are you sure you're all right?" Julius asked again, and she forced herself to pull away from him.

"Yes, just a little shaken. But what about you?" Her eyes roamed over him, looking for any sign of injury.

"I'm fine." He looked like he wanted to say more, but with a shake of his head, he also stepped back and surveyed the chaos of the room.

Cade had finally succeeded in freeing Marigold, although Olivia didn't know how he'd managed it. She was wrapped in his arms and had stopped sobbing, at least.

But when she caught Olivia's eye over Cade's shoulder, she launched into motion, wriggling free of his grip and flying across the room to throw her arms around Olivia.

"Cade said you're betrothed to the prince in my place? And that you were the first to guess I was abducted. He said you never stopped looking for me. I'm so sorry, Olivia," she wailed.

Olivia patted her back, meeting Julius's eyes over her shoulder with a silent laugh. The reaction was so very

Marigold—sincerity wrapped in the most noisy and dramatic shell possible.

Now that she understood being a royal involved constant restraint and a lifetime of doing and saying the right thing at the right time, she couldn't imagine Marigold in her place.

"Right now I'm too relieved you're safe to be angry," Olivia said when her friend finally let her go. "But I intend to have stern words with you later. How could you trick me like that! It was an abominable thing to do!"

"I never intended to trap you into a betrothal, let alone a marriage!" Marigold dashed the tears from her face. "I didn't think they'd actually go through with it! I just wanted them to see how ridiculous the whole thing was."

"Well it didn't play out like that," Olivia said with what she felt was admirable restraint.

"Of course, I expected to be there the next morning to explain it all myself," Marigold said in subdued tones. "I never meant to leave you to face everyone alone."

Olivia squeezed her arm. "Yes, that much I knew almost immediately. It wasn't at all like you to disappear like that."

Marigold threw her a grateful look. "You had more faith in me than my own family."

Olivia thought of her interaction with Lord Emerson. "I don't think your father truly understands you. But I do think he loves you, in his own way."

Marigold heaved a sigh. "I know. But really!" She fired up again. "To not even look for me!"

"He did start looking after a while," Olivia said, before adding, "But he was looking thinking you'd run away, so he was looking in all the wrong places."

"He would," said Marigold darkly. "But I truly am sorry, Olivia. I've had plenty of time to reflect on what I did." She wrinkled her nose. "And I can see that it was too much. You're a true friend, and I never should have done that to you."

She sighed. "It wasn't my first plan. At first I was going to ask you to conspire with me and go to the ball in my place knowingly. I knew you shared my frustration at the royal family's stance on the Legacy and the way they let it control matters rather than finding ways to fight it. I wanted us to show them how ridiculous the whole situation was and force them to let Julius choose his own bride."

"How selfless of you," Julius said wryly.

Marigold threw him a look. "Don't pretend you wanted to marry me any more than I wanted to marry you!"

"So why didn't you tell me everything?" Olivia asked, refusing to be distracted from the point—or to imagine Marigold and Julius married.

Marigold's lips twisted, guilt suffusing her face. "You mentioned your misconception about needing glass slippers before I said anything, so I decided on a whim not to tell you. I thought it would shield you from any blame that way," she hurried to add.

Olivia regarded her steadily, brows raised, and Marigold winced.

"I did think that! But fine, I was also a little afraid that I wouldn't be able to convince you to go along with it. I thought that if I just didn't go to the ball, my parents would find me and force me there and it would happen anyway. I'm sure the royals would have thrown another ball if necessary."

Olivia felt frustration and anger rise up inside her, but it was mixed with a thread of relief. Her friend had wronged her, but if she hadn't, Olivia would never have known Julius as anyone but the strange man on the hill. Marigold had done wrong, but she had already suffered for it—for months.

Olivia's anger melted away.

"I forgive you," she said. "As long as you never play such a trick on me again. As far as I'm concerned, you've already paid for your trick, and I don't intend to try to extract further punishment." She looked back at the shackles lying abandoned by the table. "Did they harm you?"

Marigold's face crumpled, and Cade appeared to wrap one arm around her.

"They provided me with basic necessities," she whispered, "and they didn't hit me, if that's what you mean. But I'll admit I wasn't an easy prisoner at first, and they weren't afraid to fight back if I initiated it."

"And of course you had to fight them," Cade breathed against her hair. "You wouldn't be Marigold if you didn't."

"I had company for a while at the beginning," Marigold said. "But then the other girl was released. I was on my own after that until Elisabeth arrived a few days ago."

She smiled at the girl who still stood alone in the middle of the warehouse. She didn't seem to have yet recovered from the shock and confusion of her abrupt rescue, and she could have done with another hug from Daphne.

"Wait, where's Daphne?" Olivia spun around, looking for her missing cousin.

When she found her, her heightened emotions bubbled out into laughter.

"Who is Daphne?" Marigold asked, peering in the same direction. "Is she…asleep?"

Daphne was perched on a pile of stacked bricks, her head resting on an even taller pile beside her. Her eyes were closed.

"That's Daphne, Olivia's cousin," Cade said. "She's from Oakden."

"Even so!" Marigold shook her head. "Sleeping here?"

"I'm sure she'll wake up soon," Olivia said. "She always does wake up at just the right moment."

Marigold narrowed her eyes, clearly suspicious of the newcomer. But after everything Marigold had put them through, Olivia wasn't going to let her question Daphne.

"Why did you never tell me about Cade?" she asked instead. "Didn't you trust me to keep it quiet?"

Her hurt shone through in her voice, and Marigold's face fell. "It wasn't that." She looked guiltily sideways at Cade. "To tell the truth, I enjoyed playing the role of star-crossed lovers with a secret romance. It was the most thrilling thing in my life."

Cade's arm tightened around her, but his expression froze.

"I was afraid of that," he whispered. "I worried that you'd never really cared for me at all. That's why I didn't start looking for you sooner."

Marigold's face twisted further. "That's not true! I was having fun with the role, but loving you was never playacting. I wouldn't have started if it was. I really do love you, and I did since the beginning. I got my just desserts for keeping it a secret, too. If I'd told my parents sooner, I might have been able to convince them to approve our betrothal. But I didn't tell them about you until they told me about the arranged betrothal to Julius. And it was too late by then. Letting me marry one of their most bitter rivals would have been hard enough, let alone losing the prospect of becoming queen."

She looked at Cade. "At least your parents were willing to put aside their pride to argue on our behalf. My parents weren't. I'm glad I'll be joining your family when we're married."

"My family have their faults as well." Cade sounded constrained.

The external door crashed open with a dramatic bang. They turned to see four guards and a medic race inside. The new arrivals were all breathing heavily as if after a run.

"Apparently our fight was noisy enough to alert the neighbors," Julius said lightly.

He stepped forward to greet the guards, and they must have recognized him because all five men bowed. The two guards who had been in the process of securing the injured men called for assistance, and Julius nodded for the new guards to join them. Three of the men did so, and the medic ran immediately for the nearest injured man, but the leader of the small troop approached Julius.

"What happened here, Your Highness?" he asked. "Were you attacked?"

"We rescued two young women who had been abducted." Julius indicated Elisabeth, who had shrunk back from the new arrivals, and Marigold.

"Lady Marigold!" The sergeant bowed again, his eyes growing even wider as he saw Cade's arm around her. "And Lord Cade!"

Whatever Marigold's parents thought about her choice,

they were going to have to deal with rumors of it flying through the capital soon. Given her rank, manner, and appearance, Marigold had always attracted attention and was a favorite with the public. It was probably the reason the queen had thought her a reasonable choice for Julius despite her casual manner.

"I need you to send one of your men to the closest garrison for horses," Julius told the sergeant. "We've obviously attracted attention here, so a crowd will likely gather. I want us on horseback for the trip back to the palace. Five mounts, if you can manage it." He glanced at Olivia. "Daphne can ride?"

"Passably." Daphne sat up on her improvised sofa. "Are we finally leaving, then?"

Olivia stifled a laugh at the bewildered face of the sergeant.

"Ah yes, Your Highness," the distracted sergeant managed. "We should be able to provide five horses, though they might not be of the same quality you're used to."

"Any horse trained to take a rider will be fine," Julius said. "The rest of you should secure these men and escort them to the palace as soon as possible." He eyed the medic who was shaking his head over one of the men. "Those who are able to be moved anyway. We'll want to question them without delay."

"Of course, Your Highness." The sergeant saluted him before turning to bark orders to his men.

Olivia put a hand on Julius's arm. "Have the horses meet us at the rendezvous point. The first thing we have to do is get Elisabeth there to meet her parents. They'll be desperately worried if she's not there at the appointed time."

Elisabeth burst into tears at the mention of her parents, and Daphne hurried back to her side, taking her arm in a bracing way.

Julius eyed her warily but agreed, clearly having no desire to prolong the Larkins' suffering unnecessarily.

After relaying the revised order to the sergeant, he led the group of six out of the warehouse. The sergeant tried to send guards with them, but Julius refused. As it was, they were only leaving five guards and one medic to deal with five severely wounded but hostile men.

Outside, only a small crowd had gathered, and they drew back at the sight of the nobles, whispers breaking out in every direction. Julius hustled the others along quickly, and they reached the rendezvous point only a few minutes late.

"Mother! Father!" Elisabeth shouted as soon as her parents came into view. She broke away from Daphne and sprinted across the small courtyard to throw herself into her parents' arms.

The rest of them followed more sedately.

"Your Highness, what is the meaning of this?" Larkin asked as his wife held their crying daughter.

Julius's mouth twisted. "We were able to use the information you provided to guess where the abducted women were being held, so we decided to move at once and stage a rescue."

"Women? There were more taken than just my Elisabeth?" Larkin asked sharply, his eyes surveying the group and fixing on Marigold. They grew wide and then wider again as he took in Cade's protective arm around her. "I don't understand," he said weakly.

"For now, all you need to know is that your daughter is safely returned to you," Julius said.

"Elisabeth didn't fight them," Marigold said in a subdued voice, "so they didn't hurt her. I told her they wouldn't as long as she didn't resist her imprisonment."

"Thank you!" Elisabeth cried from the safety of her mother's arms. "I would have been terrified without you." Her voice dropped. "More terrified, anyway."

Marigold smiled. "I consider us sisters in captivity, and I hope once you've recovered, you'll visit me."

Both Larkin and his wife's brows rose in unison, and they exchanged a look.

"There's no longer any need to flee the city," Julius said. "The perpetrators of this crime will be uncovered and brought to justice. I swear it."

"I see…" Master Larkin's eyes lingered on Marigold, nestled in the circle of Cade's arm. "In that case, we'll take our daughter home." He bowed low, gesturing to his wife and daughter, who let go of each other to drop into curtsies.

"We're so sorry for the ordeal you've endured, Elisabeth," Olivia said. "We'll be sure to keep you all updated on any developments."

Two guards entered the courtyard, leading a string of five horses. Julius signaled to them, and goodbyes were said quickly as the five bound for the palace quickly mounted.

Cade and Marigold looked reluctant to separate, but at a look from Julius they did so, each mounting their own horse.

Just before Cade swung onto his, Julius clapped him on the back. "That was an excellent guess, by the way. I don't think I've congratulated you on it yet. Just try not to get us all killed alongside you next time, please."

Cade gave him a tight smile as he mounted, not bothering to answer. Olivia couldn't imagine he felt any regret for his rash actions given how everything had turned out.

She just hoped they would be equally successful at identifying the culprit behind the abductions and ensuring there were no more victims.

CHAPTER 28

OLIVIA

Somehow, word of their rescue reached the palace ahead of them. When they rode through the front gates and across the long courtyard, they found Lord and Lady Emerson waiting on the front steps of the palace, along with King Robert and Queen Elsinore. The two monarchs looked tense, and Olivia suspected their hands had been full preventing Marigold's parents from racing into the city in search of her.

As soon as Marigold tumbled off her horse, her mother scooped her into a hug, and her father turned a furious face on Cade. But Julius leaped down and inserted himself between the older and younger lord.

"We have just rescued your daughter from a warehouse, where she was shackled and held in captivity with another abducted girl. Lord Cade was part of the group that fought to free her and was responsible for working out where she was being held. Without him, she would likely still be in captivity right now. I will not permit any more of the baseless accusations you spewed last night."

Lord Emerson drew himself up, his eyes flashing, but Julius held his gaze, his face steadfast. Lord Emerson finally relaxed, throwing a single vitriolic look at Cade before turning to his wife and daughter.

But when he tried to embrace Marigold, she thrust him away. "All this happened because of your stubbornness! I wouldn't have been abducted to stop me marrying the prince if you hadn't insisted on the betrothal in the first place!"

"That's why you were abducted?" Olivia asked, realizing that in all the chaos, no one had clarified that point.

Marigold shrugged. "As best I could work out from the occasional comments dropped by my captors. They didn't bother with a ransom demand because they were planning to hold me until the prince married someone else."

"I'm relieved you were rescued but devastated you were in captivity for so long," King Robert said gravely. He turned to Julius. "Well done, son. From what I hear, tales of your bravery are already spreading through the city."

Julius raised his brows. "And the bravery of the others, I hope." He indicated Olivia, Daphne, and Cade. "I didn't do it alone."

"As to that—" Whatever the king had been about to say was interrupted by the appearance of a man in palace livery.

Olivia recognized the man as one of King Robert's most trusted aides—the same man who had reported on the response of the crowd the day of her betrothal announcement. She watched as the man whispered in the king's ear, and whatever he was imparting must have been significant because she could see the traces of strong emotion on King Robert's face, despite his lifetime of royal training.

When the man finished, the king nodded before turning to the people before him.

"Son, Lord and Lady Emerson, I must consult with you at once."

"Have the men we captured been questioned?" Olivia asked eagerly, unable to keep quiet. "Have they identified their employer?"

"That is a matter for the guards," the king said. "I'm sure we will receive a report in due time."

Olivia's brows drew together. "But—"

"I'm afraid you will have to excuse us," the king said inexorably. "We need to deal with a matter of both urgency and sensitivity."

Before Olivia could think of anything to say, Lord and Lady Emerson, Marigold, and Julius had somehow been swept inside, leaving Olivia, Daphne, and Cade to wait with the horses until the approaching grooms arrived.

Olivia's mouth dropped open. She turned to Daphne, incensed. "The abduction of girls from across the capital—and even of the daughter of one of the richest and most influential families in the kingdom—isn't a matter of urgency and sensitivity?"

Daphne's eyes narrowed. "What do you think, Lord Cade?"

But when the two girls turned to Cade, he was already halfway up the stairs to the palace door.

Olivia's mouth fell open again. "Is he going after them? What is happening right now?"

"I don't know," Daphne said, her voice uncharacteristically grim. "But I don't like it. The abductions should be their top priority right now. Unless there's been an invasion we haven't heard about or something."

Despite everything, Olivia laughed. The idea was impossible to imagine. There had been peace between the kingdoms far beyond living memory.

"Come back to my suite," Daphne said when the grooms finally reached them, and Olivia had given instructions for returning the horses. "You'll just worry yourself sick if I leave you alone."

Olivia reluctantly agreed, but she only ended up pacing Daphne's suite instead of her own.

"Sit down," her cousin complained. "I'm tired just watching you."

"You're always tired." Olivia paced to the end of the room and back again. "Maybe we should go to the guards' barracks ourselves. Julius ordered the prisoners brought there as soon as possible, so the first ones might have arrived. We could—"

"What?" Daphne asked dryly. "Conduct the interrogation ourselves? I suppose you're trained in the skillful questioning of hostile prisoners, are you? I didn't realize that was part of the crown princess's duties."

Olivia sighed and finally collapsed into a chair. "When you put it like that, I do sound ridiculous, don't I?"

Daphne smiled, but the expression didn't last long. "I understand your concern. There is definitely something strange about this situation. They should be hailing you as a hero right now, not leaving you here, excluded and alone to worry." Her voice dropped. "I expected more from your prince."

Olivia frowned. "It isn't Julius's fault. His duty as crown

prince is heavy, and if there's a legitimate matter of concern to the kingdom, then of course he must attend to it."

"*If* being the crucial word in that sentence," Daphne muttered.

Olivia rubbed her neck. "It's nearly time for the evening meal. We're scheduled to eat with Julius and his parents, so let's wash up and dress appropriately. Hopefully we'll have a chance to hear what's going on over the food."

Daphne looked skeptical, but she didn't protest, allowing Olivia to leave for her own suite.

The corridors of the palace were abuzz, but no one stopped her—if anything, they seemed to be avoiding her—and she reached her suite quickly. Inside, she found Mildred out of her usual nest, cowering behind a sofa. It was a comical sight, given the mouse was much larger than the back of the chair, but Olivia hurried to her side, murmuring quiet reassurances.

"Did you pick up on the atmosphere of the palace, girl?" she whispered, patting Mildred's soft fur. "Don't worry, you're safe." Determination hardened in her voice. "I'm about to find out what's going on."

The mouse finally calmed and returned to her nest, and Olivia moved to her bedchamber. But as soon as she opened the door and stepped inside, she froze.

The entire room lay in ruins. Her bed curtains had been pulled down and the bedclothes thrown across the room. All her drawers had been pulled out and their contents piled haphazardly on the floor. The wardrobe doors stood open, and a figure leaned inside, in the process of rifling through her dresses.

"What?" Olivia gasped, too shocked to avoid the loud exclamation.

The man immediately straightened and turned to look at her. Their eyes met across the room, and Olivia's mouth dropped open.

"Zane!? What in the kingdoms are you doing right now?"

Of all the unexpected happenings of the day, finding Julius's friend destroying her room was the most unexpected and inexplicable.

Zane sprang into motion, sprinting toward her. Skirting the bed, he leaped over the piles of her discarded belongings.

Too late, Olivia tried to flee. She didn't make it more than a few steps before he caught her, grabbing both her arms in an iron grip.

"Let go of me!" She kicked at him and opened her mouth to scream.

He dodged, twisting her around and restraining her with a single arm across her middle, her back to his chest and both her arms trapped. It left his other hand free to cover her mouth.

Olivia struggled wildly, but her efforts did little to loosen his hold.

"Where is it?" he growled in her ear. "Where have you stashed it?"

Olivia shrugged, trying to indicate that she couldn't answer with a hand over her mouth. He seemed to get the point because he slowly removed his hand, although his arm still hovered ready to silence her again.

"Zane, seriously!" she cried. "What are you doing? What are you even looking for? I haven't stashed anything anywhere!"

But even as she said the words, a thought made her stiffen. She did usually have something stashed in her room. Something she had slipped into her pocket that morning, just in case.

"That's right," Zane said. "Where is that Auldanan mirror of yours? And what does it do?"

Cold seeped through Olivia. In all her calculations on whether or not to keep the mirror, she'd never envisaged this scenario. She should have handed it over to Julius long ago.

"I don't know what you're talking about," she said stiffly, but Zane only laughed.

"If it isn't in the room," he said, "then perhaps..."

He used his free hand to tap at her pockets, quickly finding the bulky shape of the mirror in the second one.

"Aha!"

Olivia broke into fresh struggles, but she was too weak to overpower him, and he wrestled the mirror free.

He held it up in front of him, gazing at his own face. "Now, what does it do?" he asked. "What does it show? Will it reveal places and people far away? Does it let you spy on others?"

"What? No, of course not," Olivia cried, shocked.

The way Zane was restraining her meant she could see into the mirror as easily as he could, and it showed a face inflamed with anger and furious pride, the emotions overlaid with fear. It was nothing like the languid mask he usually showed the world.

The sight shocked Olivia and made her question every interaction she had ever had with him. Did Cade know of his brother's true nature?

Several things came together in Olivia's mind, all at the

same moment. Cade's odd behavior ever since they learned the details of Elisabeth's ransom demand. The information she had learned in her lessons about the Strathmores' business interests. And the truth she had just seen in the mirror. Her heart sank all the way down to her toes. She didn't want to believe it, but she couldn't resist the words that came out of her mouth.

"Doesn't your family own the largest glassblowing workshop in Sovar?" she asked quietly. "I don't suppose you're in the process of expanding that business? Perhaps even trying to obtain a monopoly on glass distribution?"

Zane's arm tightened convulsively around her.

"Be quiet!" he snapped.

Energy spiked through Olivia's system. Lord Emerson had accused Lord Strathmore of taking his daughter, and he had been nearly right. It had been Lord Strathmore's son who had taken Marigold. But not Cade. It had all been Zane. The abductions. The ransom demands. Did his father and brother know?

But, no. There was no way Cade had known of his brother's scheme. Even before Marigold had become a victim, he wouldn't have acquiesced in such a strategy. He certainly wouldn't have agreed afterward.

But he had grown up alongside Zane. He must have known something of his brother's true nature. And he would know his family's business plans better than the rest of them. At some point in the afternoon, he had guessed the whole truth—probably as soon as he heard the ransom demand. Was that how he had known of the abandoned warehouse? It was probably one of the Strathmore properties. No wonder Cade had been both desperate and subdued.

And no wonder the Larkins had assured them so many times that they meant to follow the demands to the letter. They had guessed which family it was and knew Cade was one of the Strathmore sons.

But did the king and queen know? Was that the news the aide had brought?

One of the captives might already have talked. If King Robert had just learned that one of the most trusted and influential families in the kingdom was responsible for kidnapping the daughter of someone as powerful as Lord Emerson, she could understand his wanting to deal with it as quickly and sensitively as possible.

She could even understand Julius's continued absence. Lord Emerson wouldn't be easy to placate.

"What have you done, Zane?" she whispered.

"Be quiet!" he snapped, giving her a small shake along with the words. "With my foolish brother too weak to advance the family's interests, it was up to me to advance the Strathmore fortune. I've only done what I had to. And then the news that an Emerson would sit on the throne." The arm holding Olivia trembled. "Unthinkable. I couldn't allow it to happen."

"But you were willing to let me marry Julius?" Olivia asked, curious despite herself.

Zane laughed, but it was an unpleasant, cruel sound. "Of course. If the crown is weakened, the Strathmores will rise even stronger. It's just a pity Cade wasn't born a girl. He might have done some good for us then. Or if my useless mother could have had another child. We could have seen a Strathmore on the throne instead, and my father could have seen his grandchild as crown prince. But no more equivocating. What does the mirror do? I could have been out of the palace and free by now if I hadn't stopped to look for it. But if it's a spy mirror, it will be worth the delay. They'll never catch me then."

"It shows the true emotions behind your mask," Olivia said, unable to keep her voice from shaking. "And it was made by an apprentice, so it doesn't even always work. It clearly didn't work the last time I saw you reflected in it. It isn't as valuable as you think. You've delayed your flight for no reason at all."

"Oh, I don't know about that," Zane said in a voice that sent fresh chills down Olivia's spine. "The mirror might not be what I hoped it was, but I think I've found something valuable anyway."

Olivia swallowed.

"Don't worry," Zane said, "if you don't fight me, there's no reason for you to get hurt. You know all about the other girls, so I'm sure you already know that. Don't resist me, and as long as my demands are met, you'll be freed without any harm. I'm not a monster."

"I think that's exactly what you are," Olivia snapped. "And you must be a bigger fool than I ever dreamed if you think Their Majesties will give you anything in exchange for me."

"Oh, I'm not thinking of Their Majesties." Zane's voice held smug amusement. "I've seen the way you and your gallant prince look at each other. I'm willing to bet that Foolish Julius would give up his kingdom to keep you safe."

Olivia swallowed again, chiding herself for the ridiculous bubble of hope that rose up despite her situation. His words couldn't possibly be true, could they?

Zane let go of her, and Olivia was so surprised by the unexpected move, that it took her a full second to remember to flee. By the time she tried, he had his sword drawn and the tip hovering at her back.

"I promise I'm faster than you are," he growled. "Remember, if you cooperate, you'll come to no harm."

Olivia nodded meekly while her mind raced. She had no intention of allowing Julius to sacrifice anything to save her.

Zane prodded her lightly, propelling her through the door of her bedchamber and into her sitting room. Mildred was cowering behind the sofa again, squeaking frantically, and Olivia wished fleetingly that she'd befriended a tiger instead of a mouse. But she couldn't blame Mildred for her nature. It was what had kept her alive for years.

She still looked longingly at the mouse, though, and called her name. But Zane pushed her roughly forward.

"Ignore the ridiculous mouse," he said. "If she tries to come to your rescue, it will be the last thing she does."

Olivia gulped and went silent as Zane swapped his sword for a dagger and pressed close behind her, keeping the concealed point against her back. As they stepped into the corridor, Olivia cast a final glance backward, meeting the beady black eyes of Mildred and hearing a final squeak.

CHAPTER 29

JULIUS

J ulius fought to rein in his temper. The more he gave in to emotion, the more his father would dismiss him. The king had often told him that personal emotions were inevitable—even helpful at times—but they had to be set aside when making decisions for the good of the kingdom. But Julius could not accept this decision as good for Sovar.

"The idea that I should set aside Olivia after months of betrothal and marry Marigold instead is absurd," he said for the third time.

He threw a look at Marigold. She was sitting in the corner, her body quivering with the effort to remain silent. She had raged and screamed and refused the betrothal loud enough for both of them at the beginning.

But her father hadn't achieved his position and wealth because he was a fool. He had known the one argument that would persuade his daughter.

He was wielding her love against her, threatening Cade. And since it turned out that Cade's family was behind the abductions, Lord Emerson had the ability to follow through with his threats. He had promised to see Lord Strathmore and both his sons suffer to the full extent of the law—as well as being utterly annihilated both socially and politically.

The only way he would stay his hand was if Marigold agreed to marry Julius. If she did so, Cade and Zane would be spared and even allowed to keep a portion of the Strathmore wealth. They would have a chance to build their family anew.

Given Julius was certain Cade had never been involved, he had almost exploded with fury when his parents sat back and allowed Lord Emerson to threaten his daughter with the destruction of Cade's future.

He didn't think his parents believed Cade was involved, but they were clearly in favor of his marrying Marigold. They probably thought it was a neat way to placate Lord Emerson after the grievous harm done to his family while also turning his wrath away from the innocent Cade—all while achieving their original goal of marrying Julius to Marigold. The entire thing was brilliantly devious and utterly infuriating.

But he needed to restrain his fury. Both his and Marigold's best hope lay in presenting his arguments logically and convincing his father not to go through with the ridiculous plan.

"Olivia has proven herself to be a fast learner and a natural royal. You didn't see her when Lord Emerson attacked Lord Strathmore, but she handled it with more command and dignity than I did. The court have accepted her. And you yourself said that the people of Sovar love Olivia and love having a commoner princess," he said. "How will they react if I abandon her now?"

"That is why we must act immediately, son." His mother's voice was pleading. "The story of Marigold's suffering and your brave rescue of her is already spreading through the city. She was popular before and will be exponentially more so now. It's the optimal moment for you to free yourself from your current betrothal."

"There's no need to free myself from it at all!" Julius exclaimed, unable to keep some of his emotion from leaking through.

His mother moved closer and put a sympathetic hand on his arm. "I know," she said in a quiet voice, too soft to be overheard by the Emersons, who stood at the other end of the room with their daughter. "I've long suspected you weren't blind to Olivia's charms. I'm fond of her myself."

"It's not just her charms," Julius snapped. "I've worked my whole life to be the perfect Prince Charming I have to be, but recently I've realized how far short of that ideal I actually fall. But Olivia fills in the gaps I lack. Together, working as a team, we're far more effective than the empty illusion I was managing on my own. I don't just want her, Mother. I'm better with her at my side."

His mother shifted uncomfortably, but she refused to accept his points or back down.

"If you truly care for her, then you should think of her well-being, Julius. She wasn't born into this life. She wasn't trained for it as you were, and to her credit, she has never coveted the crown. You may think you love her, but I've seen no proof she feels the same way. If you truly care for her, would you trap her with the burden of a royal position? Surely she would be happier without it."

Julius froze, dismay seeping from the top of his head to

his belly. He had feared the exact same thing himself and now his mother—the one person who had once been in Olivia's position—was confirming it. Could he ignore her words?

His father must have sensed his weakness because he pressed his advantage, his voice equally low.

"The criminal behavior of Lord Strathmore has put the kingdom in a dangerous position," he murmured. "We are on the cusp of a political crisis. If Lord Emerson turns against the crown, we will be in true trouble. Many in court will feel he has just cause, and the whole kingdom will be thrown into turmoil. You've heard his feelings about Marigold marrying Cade."

He spoke in a dry tone since they had all heard Lord Emerson's feelings on the matter—loudly and repeated several times. He would not even consider the possibility of Marigold marrying the son of her abductor, and he wanted her safely married to Julius instead as soon as possible.

He was claiming it was for her own good, naturally, and even her mother had pleaded that Marigold would agree with them eventually. She thought that marrying Cade would only serve to constantly remind Marigold of her traumatic experience.

Julius clenched his teeth, his mind spinning. If Olivia wanted to be released from him, he would do it—no matter the pain it caused him. But he would not rush into marriage with Marigold in her stead. Their parents were the ones who were mistaken—that was the direction true disaster lay.

"Olivia seems very fond of Cade," his mother said, clearly thinking she was being helpful. "And he of her. He'll have to withdraw from court for a few years at least, so that will be perfect. I'm sure the two of them will be able to mend any hurt feelings with each other."

Julius was going to be sick.

He was silent for a moment as he desperately fought to keep his stomach from expelling his last meal.

"But what of the Legacy?" he tried desperately once he had regained control. "That was the reason for my betrothal to Olivia in the first place. Do you really want to risk losing its power by swapping brides?"

"Of course we won't just swap them without any ceremony about it," his mother said. "The scholars have finished deliberating, and they believe that it will be fine as long as we have another ball and do the whole thing over again."

Julius frowned. The scholars had reached a consensus? Why hadn't he been informed? Had his parents purposely kept the information from him given his mother's awareness of his feelings toward Olivia?

"We'll expand on the story of your rescue of Marigold," his father said. "We'll say that the two of you are in love and that she was intended as your betrothed from the beginning, but she was abducted on the night of the ball. We'll tell them that Olivia is a close friend of Marigold and stepped in to placate the Legacy, intending only to help her friend and the kingdom. That's very close to the truth, anyway. The people will understand that your and Olivia's ruse was intended to fool the Legacy, not them. We'll say the two of you have never been more than friends, but that you've been working together this whole time to locate Marigold. You finally succeeded at locating her, and you were so desperate to rescue her that you rushed in yourself. It's a romantic tale and won't do Olivia any harm in the public's eyes, so you needn't worry about that. She will be a selfless hero who worked tirelessly to save her friend. And you will be a desperate lover, doing your duty to protect your kingdom, even while you worked in the shadows to find your true betrothed. We're already organizing the new ball for tonight."

"Tonight?" Julius and Marigold cried in unison.

"It doesn't matter if it's not as fancy as the last one," the king said shortly.

The queen's mouth twisted, clearly pained by the necessity of putting on a less than stellar social event.

Julius's mind raced to find the flaws in his parents' plan. He was sure they must be there—they had put the whole thing together under pressure and at unbelievable speed. There had to be flaws.

But Julius's growing desperation didn't help him to think clearly. He wasn't as convinced as his father that the public would accept the story the king had concocted. But by the time that became clear it would be too late. Olivia would have been sent away—with Cade, no less, apparently—and he would be tied to Marigold. Given the current mood in the room, he wouldn't be surprised to hear the wedding was already being planned for the following week. Autumn was the traditional season for weddings, after all, given all the betrothals that began during the summer social season.

"Father," he began, having run out of arguments. He had no options left except to refuse to participate in the outrageous scheme—and to keep refusing no matter what they threatened.

But before he could state his refusal, the door of the small receiving room burst open, and Daphne stormed in, an enormous mouse trotting behind her.

"There you are!" she exclaimed. "Why is this palace so enormous?"

"Excuse me," the king said coldly, "but this is a private meeting."

"I don't care," Daphne said calmly. "I need to speak to Julius."

Julius ignored his parents, hurrying to Daphne's side. "What is it?" he asked, alarm spiking through him. "Where's Olivia?"

"That's just it," Daphne said, clearly concerned. "I can't find her. Mildred came to my room and—"

"Mildred walked to your room? Alone?" Julius cried. "But she never leaves Olivia's suite."

"Exactly!" Daphne said, clearly gratified that he understood the enormity of what had happened. "So I went back to Olivia's suite with her to try to find my cousin, and she was gone."

The queen cleared her throat awkwardly. "I didn't expect her to respond so promptly, but it's most considerate of her."

"What do you mean, Mother?" Julius asked, his voice icy. "What have you done?"

"While Lord Emerson was…explaining the situation to Marigold, I thought it would be best to send Lady Olivia a note," his mother said. "You were probably too distracted to see me slip out for a moment."

Cold fury ripped through Julius. Before he had agreed—before they had even finished discussing the situation—his mother had attempted to preempt his decision.

"How dare you," he said, his low voice so loaded with his fury that his mother turned white and fell back a step.

"Your mother was perhaps a little precipitate," his father said in a measured tone, "but there's no harm done. If Lady Olivia has already left the palace, she obviously doesn't mean to cause trouble, which is a relief. We must all work together if we're going to see Sovar safely through this crisis."

"Excuse me," Daphne said with as much icy dignity as Julius had ever displayed. "I wasn't finished speaking. Olivia wasn't only missing from her suite, but her bedchamber was in chaos. Her possessions were thrown everywhere, like someone had searched the room in a hurry—or there had been a fight."

"What?" Julius asked sharply, stepping back toward Daphne.

The queen shifted uncomfortably. "If she's already gone, she must have packed in a hurry. I can understand if she didn't feel the need to worry about the state of the items she was leaving behind. It's reasonable she might feel a little hurt."

"Someone will need to track her down and smooth any ruffled feathers," his father said, his brow creasing. "We don't want her causing trouble. But that can wait for after the ball. Once the new betrothal is official, we can have someone—"

"It absolutely cannot wait," Julius said, his voice and stance as implacable as stone. "If you will not search for Olivia, I will do so. Do I really have to remind you that you've already made this mistake once before?" His eyes flicked to Marigold.

"I assure you she hasn't been abducted by Lord Strathmore," his father said in a tone of strained patience. "We already have him in custody."

"If you mean to suggest my cousin might have been offended and flounced off without Mildred *or me*," Daphne said, "then you obviously never knew her at all. I've never heard such a ridiculous theory."

"Nevertheless," the king said, "our focus for now must be on the ball. It is mere hours away. Guards can search for Olivia after that."

Julius shook his head, hearing what was behind his father's words. He should be an obedient prince and play the role his father decreed. If he did that, then resources would be put into finding Olivia. But he was done playing an empty role. The woman he loved didn't need Prince Charming. She needed him—the real Julius beneath the role. And he wasn't going to let her down.

"Sorry, Father," he said. "But I'm finding Olivia now."

Before his father could move to stop him, he left the room, Daphne and a giant mouse at his heels.

CHAPTER 30
JULIUS

Julius had only made it a few steps down the corridor when Cade pounced on him.

"What's happening in there?" Worry laced his voice.

He looked as if he meant to rush into the receiving room, so Julius restrained him with a hand on his arm. "I'm afraid you won't find a warm welcome in there." He met Cade's eyes steadily.

Cade looked away, sinking into himself. "Everyone knows, then?"

"Walk with me." Julius wasn't willing to stop, even for this conversation.

Cade fell into step at his side, his shoulders still hunched, and Julius spoke again.

"You knew, didn't you?"

"Not before today," Cade cried. "I swear it. I had no idea."

"Don't worry," Julius said. "I never thought that. You would never have let Marigold be taken. I assume it was the mention of the glass trade that tipped you off? That was your family's warehouse, wasn't it?"

Cade nodded miserably. "I was going to tell you, I swear. I was just so ashamed, and my focus was on rescuing Marigold." His voice turned earnest. "And I hope you know that I would never have been part of such a thing, even if Marigold wasn't involved. Zane's behavior is outrageous and criminal. I could never condone—"

Julius stopped, turning to stare at Cade. "Zane? Are you saying your brother is behind this? Not your father?"

"This has Zane's fingerprints all over it, I'm afraid." Cade's brows drew together. "I should have seen it earlier, but I never thought…" He shook his head. "My family's holdings are so diverse that it didn't strike me that all the businesses Markus mentioned crossed with ours in some way. But I did notice one of the names. It's been bothering me ever since, wondering where I'd heard it before. I remembered today after everything became clear. Zane had a petty dispute with the man two years ago. Zane didn't think the man had shown him sufficient respect, given their respective positions, and so Zane…"

Cade broke off, pressing his lips together. "My father has his faults—he's done plenty of less than praiseworthy things over the years. And he raised Zane to place far too much stock in his rank and the family name. But my father would never have come up with such a criminal and cruel scheme." His mouth twisted. "It would disappoint Mother, and Father loves her too much to ever do that. A trait that Zane sees as a weakness, of course."

Julius swallowed. He had heard Zane say something similar with his own ears.

"But one of the captives talked," he said, still struggling to believe it. "He said they got their orders from Lord Strathmore. So my father has arrested yours. He's in custody now."

Cade's hands fisted, his arms trembling. "Why am I not surprised to hear that Zane did it all in my father's name? He probably already thinks of the title as his."

"So where is Zane right now, then?" Daphne asked, reminding them she was there with the single most relevant question.

"If he's taken Olivia out of revenge, I'll run him through myself," Julius said in a voice he barely recognized as his own.

Cade shook his head. "That isn't Zane's way, thankfully. Even cornered, he'll be thinking strategically. Olivia is a valuable hostage."

"A hostage?" Julius was still furious, but he clung to the hope that Olivia might survive long enough for them to rescue her.

Cade nodded, his face lined and tight.

"So where would he have gone?" Daphne asked. "He could hardly walk out the front door with Julius's betrothed as hostage."

"Our courtyard!" Julius and Cade said at the same time.

They broke into a run, Daphne and Mildred racing behind them. "Why the courtyard?" Daphne called.

"We never showed Olivia all its secrets," Julius called back, but he didn't explain further, saving his breath for running.

They careened down corridor after corridor, finally sliding into the courtyard. A man in Strathmore livery turned to meet them, a surprised look on his face.

Cade and Julius drew their swords in unison, and the man went white and tried to flee. He didn't make it far.

"Maybe we should have kept him conscious," Cade said doubtfully when the man lay at their feet.

"No need," Julius said shortly. "We know what he was doing." He pointed at the bench seat by the fountain.

"I don't know, however." Daphne said, puffing as she reached their sides.

"We chose this courtyard when we were boys for a reason," Cade said. "It has a little-known entrance to the tunnels beneath the palace."

"Tunnels?" Daphne's brows flew up.

"Look at all the scuffed dirt." Julius crouched down beside the potted tree next to the bench seat. "The servant must have only just got the pot back in place when we arrived, which hopefully means we aren't far behind them!"

He and Cade worked together, grunting, their muscles straining as they lifted the pot and rolled it away. The tree and pot had both been smaller when they were younger.

"Phew," Cade breathed. "I'm glad we were armed and he wasn't. That brute must be as strong as an ox to move this thing on his own."

Before them, a cunningly concealed trapdoor lay in the ground. Julius pulled it up, revealing a dark hole beneath.

Daphne looked into it and shivered. But she didn't protest when Julius dropped into the hole. Cade eased her down after him and then, at her insistence, half-lifted, half-dropped Mildred down as well. He brought up the rear himself, leaving the trapdoor open behind him.

"Where does the tunnel go?" Daphne asked, as they

hurried along the smooth floor in the near darkness. "Isn't it a security risk?"

"It ends inside the grounds," Cade explained from behind her. "It doesn't lead beyond the walls. It comes out in the kitchen gardens by the west gate."

"The west gate is the most isolated gate," Julius said grimly. "Zane will know it's his best way out."

The traces of light from the trapdoor behind them eventually faded into pitch blackness, but it wasn't long before the air gradually started to lighten again. They were approaching the other end of the tunnel. Julius broke into a jog up the mild incline, the square of light at the end of the tunnel soon becoming visible.

The floor sloped up to join the door-like opening, and the four of them raced out, blinking in the sunset light. They stood in the middle of a pumpkin patch filled with enormous produce.

Julius's eyes immediately caught on two figures halfway between them and the western gate.

"Zane!" he shouted, his furious cry tearing through the air and making the people ahead of them freeze.

"Julius!" Olivia's voice cried, and his heart lifted, only to crash again when Zane seized her arm and shook her roughly. He was clearly making some sort of threat that didn't carry back to them.

Julius hesitated, trying to work out the best avenue of attack—one that wouldn't put Olivia at risk. But Mildred—unhampered by strategy—charged forward. With a resounding squeak, she thundered toward Zane and Olivia, looking surprisingly fearsome thanks to her unnatural size.

Zane turned to meet the threat, attempting to push Olivia between him and the mouse, but he moved too slowly.

Mildred rammed him, knocking him off his feet, and Olivia jerked free of his hold. Running from him, she zigzagged through the pumpkins. Julius charged toward Zane, but his former friend was already back on his feet. Dodging Mildred, Zane dashed after Olivia. He knew that Olivia was his only hope of escaping Julius's wrath.

The pumpkin patch extended up a slope, and Olivia had fled uphill instead of down, away from Zane, but also away from Julius. When she reached the top of the incline, where the ground leveled out again, she turned right and ran along the top of the slope. Zane changed the angle of his run, looking to cut her off, but his new path took him nearer to Julius than he had taken into account.

With a final, desperate burst of speed, Julius caught up with him just as he crested the slope, a short way ahead of Olivia. She had already stopped running and was backing away as Zane turned toward her. Zane tried to move to close the gap between them, but Julius tackled him from behind, sending both of them crashing to the ground.

Zane kicked out at Julius, catching him in the midriff. The blow temporarily winded the prince, giving Zane a chance to wriggle free. He reached for his dagger, and Julius only just managed to grab him again, preventing him from drawing the blade.

They rolled across the ground, Julius's blow to Zane's nose being returned with an elbow to the sternum. The pain of the blow made Julius flinch instinctively back, only to freeze as his head rolled out over empty space.

He risked a half second's glance sideways and down.

Blast! When had a miniature cliff appeared behind the pumpkin patch? He was sure it hadn't been there a month ago.

The pain subsided enough for him to roll forward, but Zane was already bearing down on him, an ugly light in his eye. Apparently, he had decided that he could take on the prince even without a hostage.

Julius scrambled to his feet, relieved that Zane was still coming after him rather than chasing after Olivia. He couldn't see her any longer, but he hoped she had already fled for the relative safety of Cade and Daphne.

Zane lunged for Julius's neck, both hands outstretched, and Julius only just evaded him, seizing his forearms and holding the other man at arm's length. The two struggled, swaying in place, until Julius's foot slipped on the dirt at the edge of the cliff, nearly plunging off the edge.

Zane tried to push him further in that direction, but Julius let go and ducked away at the last second. Zane cursed and spun, ready to lunge at him again. Julius danced backward out of reach.

With a second's breathing room, he shot a quick glance behind him, trying to catch sight of Olivia and make certain she was safe.

She hadn't run as he had hoped. She still stood further along the top of the slope, although now she held a dagger. Her eyes were fixed on something behind him, and as he watched, they widened in shock.

He swung back around, realizing his mistake a moment too late. While he had used the momentary space to look for Olivia, his opponent had used it to arm himself.

Julius had stood across from Zane's blade a hundred

times before, but never like this. Despite his fury, he couldn't entirely shake off the dissonance—the history of all their shared mornings in the courtyard overlaying the current moment.

Zane lunged toward him, dagger out, and Julius jumped backward. But his retreat had taken him too near the cliff's edge. He dodged again, this time moving along the cliff, parallel to its edge. He couldn't go far in that direction, though. He couldn't risk letting Zane drive him too close to Olivia.

Julius wished he still had his sword—or even his dagger. In a fair match, he could have disabled Zane with or without an adjacent cliff. But Zane's blade unbalanced the scales, and Julius had no choice but to dodge for a third time.

His movement swung him briefly toward Olivia, who had placed herself behind a pumpkin that had grown at the very top of the slope. As soon as his gaze fell on her, she gestured wildly for him to get down.

He only had a second to grasp her intentions and respond, but it was enough. He dropped low and threw himself under Zane's blade, aiming for his ankles. Zane hastily sidestepped, taking himself nearer the cliff just as Olivia gave a final shove on the pumpkin and set it rolling. It careened wildly along the top of the slope, bouncing as it came.

Julius—still on the ground—rolled sideways out of the way. But Zane, too focused on his opponent, caught sight of the incoming threat too late.

Like a ball hitting a skittle, the pumpkin collided with him at full speed. He fell backward straight off the cliff.

His shout sounded briefly before being cut off by a solid

thud. Julius lay still for a second, his own breath harsh in his ears as he listened for sounds of life. A low groan floated upward. Zane had survived the fall.

Julius slowly stood and dusted himself off. Olivia met him at the edge of the cliff, both of them peering down at Zane's prone body.

After confirming he was still alive, although apparently unable to stand, Julius looked in the opposite direction, searching for Cade. How would he react to his brother's fall?

But Cade had moved, and it took Julius a moment to spot him. When he did, he realized that Cade had found a place where the cliff leveled out, sloping down more gently and giving access to the lower ground below.

Julius followed him as swiftly as his tired body would go, the two girls on his heels. None of them spoke.

They reached Cade as he stood over Zane, staring down at him.

"Brother," Zane said, his voice edged with pain. "Help me."

"You must be out of your mind if you think I'll help you now." Cade's voice was ice cold, despite Zane's injuries. "You held Marigold for months, Zane. *Months*! And you made me complicit in doing it. It makes me sick to think I've been benefitting for years from your criminal behavior."

"You never did value your family." Zane managed to put poison in his voice, despite his pained, gasping breaths.

"No, you're the one who didn't value your family." Cade's ice had melted, and he just sounded sad. "Look at how you always treated Mother and me. The only thing you ever valued was the family name."

Zane stared at his brother, but he must have realized he

had no hope of convincing him because he turned his head to look toward Julius.

"Julius." His tone was conciliatory, although it looked like the effort pained him. "We've been friends our whole lives. And what have I done that was so very bad? I've never killed anyone. I think one of my legs is broken, and isn't that punishment enough? Let me leave the capital quietly, and you'll never see me again."

"You speak of our friendship," Julius said, "but you ended that the second you attacked my betrothed." His eyes narrowed. "No, you ended it the first time you abducted one of my subjects for your own gain. You traumatized *children*, Zane, just to grow your own, already vast, wealth. You destroyed families and businesses—people who had never done you any wrong. You've clearly never cared who you hurt, and now you can face justice just like anyone else. You're no friend of mine."

"It should have been me born the prince," Zane burst out. "You've always been too soft. You waste the endless opportunities before you."

"Because unlike you, he isn't selfish," Olivia snapped. "And that's why he's exactly the person who should be prince."

Warmth spread through Julius's chest, but he directed a final comment at Zane. "You are far from the kind of leader Sovar needs."

The kind of leader Sovar needed wasn't in front of him—she was at his side. He was sure of it. Olivia had expressed her belief in him, and he had just as much belief in her. She would do a far better job than Marigold, and one day she would help him do a better job than his own parents. His mother and father's response to Marigold's rescue had shown they didn't have the flexibility of thinking that Sovar needed—the sort of flexibility that would lead the kingdom away from people like Zane and Lord Emerson and toward a more just future.

A guard jogged up to them, looking concerned. He had obviously seen them from his station at the nearby gate and had come to investigate, leaving his companion behind to guard their assigned position.

"Your Highness?" he asked breathlessly, bowing.

"Bring more guards and arrest Lord Zane," Julius said, hoping the arrests of the day were finally finished.

The man looked from one to the other of the small group, eyes wide, but no one else spoke, so he bowed again and raced off.

"We'll need to stay until the guards arrive," Julius said quietly to Olivia. "The other guard can't leave the gate unguarded to assist us."

"I'll watch Zane," Cade said stonily. "It isn't as if he can run. He's not going anywhere."

"Mildred, on the other hand, has already fled back to the palace," Daphne said, a note of amusement in her voice. "I think she's run straight back to your suite, Olivia."

"She deserves a medal!" Olivia's voice shone with wonder and gratitude. "I never dreamed she'd do something like that for me."

"She's the one who alerted us to your abduction," Daphne said. "It's only thanks to her loyalty that we were able to follow you so quickly."

"What a wonderful, excellent mouse!" Olivia's face fell. "I should have thanked her properly before she ran off."

"Since Cade has matters in hand here," Daphne said, "why don't we go and check on her?"

Julius was grateful for her prompting. He wanted to get Olivia away from Zane as quickly as possible. Daphne seemed to have other matters in mind, however, because she gave him a knowing look and took off without waiting for the other two. Although they followed promptly, she quickly outpaced them, showing more energy than he'd yet seen from the sleepy Oakdenian.

Olivia watched her with amazement. When Daphne disappeared into the palace before them, she called out her cousin's name, but received no response. Olivia clearly didn't understand why Daphne was giving them privacy, but Julius didn't mean to miss his chance.

The moment they reached the first corridor of the palace, Julius whisked Olivia into a convenient alcove.

She stared up at him, her mouth still open in an adorable circle after calling for her cousin. "What are you doing?" she asked breathlessly.

He pressed her against the wall, concealing her from passersby with his own body as well as the sheer curtain that hung across the alcove.

"That depends," he said, a soft tease in his voice. "What do you want me to do?"

Olivia immediately blushed a glorious pink, and his heart rate took off. She said nothing, but her body spoke for her, swaying toward him as her luminous eyes dropped to his lips.

His heart soared, and he closed the last of the distance between them, pushing her up against the wall.

"I'm going to do what I should have done a long time

ago," he whispered and bent the final distance to crash his lips against hers.

She responded, her hands running up his chest to grip the front of his jacket and meld them together. His arms tightened around her.

But the moment was over too soon.

The clang of racing guards made him pull reluctantly away from her. Turning, he watched two rows of guards run past, presumably on their way to arrest Zane. But four of the men broke away and stopped in front of Julius.

He remained still, blocking their view of Olivia behind him.

One of the men bowed respectfully. "Their Majesties are searching for you, Your Highness. Your presence is urgently required."

Julius sighed but thanked the man for the message, expecting the guards to rejoin their fellows. They didn't move, however.

"We've been instructed to escort you to His Majesty immediately."

Julius growled under his breath. He wanted to refuse, but it didn't seem like the right moment to publicly defy his father. The situation with Zane and Lord Strathmore was too tangled, and it would be better for his father to hear the truth from Julius directly. As much as he wanted to forget all his responsibilities and remain in the moment with Olivia, he had to face up to his duties.

He glanced back at her, ready to explain, but she was looking at him with affectionate amusement.

"I know," she murmured. "Go. I understand."

Gratitude filled his chest. He didn't deserve her.

"I'll come and find you as soon as I can," he promised.

The guards made no comment as he stepped away and revealed Olivia behind him, although several cast surreptitious glances at her. It reminded him of all the people who had gawked at Marigold and Cade in the city. Even if he'd been willing to go along with his father's concocted story, there were too many witnesses to the truth for it to go down smoothly.

Julius strode through the palace toward his parents' receiving room, the guards struggling to keep up. All he wanted was to finish talking to his parents and get back to Olivia.

When he reached the room, they remained outside, leaving him to step in alone.

"Mother, Father," he said, "we need to release Lord Strathmore. It wasn't him. It was Zane."

But his mother was gone. Only his father remained there, a suit laid out on the chair beside him.

"I've heard," the king said. "But it changes nothing. It's time you got ready for the ball, son." He gestured at the waiting clothes.

Julius squared his shoulders, preparing for a fight. "I'm not going to the ball. Not unless you give up on the whole idea of breaking my current betrothal."

"And what of your mother's words?" His father watched him with an inscrutable expression. "Do you truly care so little for Lady Olivia's well-being?"

One side of Julius's lips curved upward as he remembered Olivia's enthusiastic kiss. Only a short time before, he had still been questioning if she could be happy with him, but she was the one to judge that, and she had already given him her answer.

"I believe in Olivia and her ability to choose for herself. It's not for me to decide what will make her happy."

"Very well, then," his father said. "We will allow the ladies to choose."

"Just like that?" Julius watched his father through narrowed eyes. It couldn't possibly be that easy.

"In exchange, I ask only that you do your duty. Get dressed, attend the ball, and play your role. We have roused the court from their homes to attend, and they expect their prince to be among them. So attend the ball, and we will see which girl turns up in glass slippers this time."

"And if they both come?" Julius asked, thinking of the threats made to Marigold by her father.

"Then you will choose," his father said.

"And does Olivia even know of this ball?" Julius asked suspiciously.

"Of course." His father regarded him coldly. "She was informed of it in your mother's note. If she truly wishes to remain here at your side—and has the strength of character and determination necessary for the role—she will fight for you, will she not? She knows of this ball, so if she wants you, she will surely come."

Julius hesitated. He and Olivia hadn't had time to discuss anything. But he trusted her. She would come. And if she didn't...

His heart turned away from that possibility. She would come.

"I want to speak to her myself," he said.

The king shook his head. "There's no time. Wild rumors

of all kinds are already flying through the kingdom and capital—including that you have been killed in the fighting. The three of us must be there to open the ball. The kingdom needs our strong, steady leadership today. One day you will be king after me, son, and this is what it means to be king. You must put aside your personal feelings and arrive at the ball with your mother and me."

Julius hesitated, but his father was right—the events of the day had been pivotal for him personally but also for the kingdom. It was his duty to do what he could to prevent harmful turmoil, and he was still committed to his duty. Marrying Olivia had never been a rejection of that—rather, it would be a deepening.

"How do I know you won't order the guards to arrest Olivia the moment I go into the ball?" Julius said, still suspicious. "You would only need to hold her for one night to achieve your purpose."

"A palace-wide order will be given," the king said. "No guard is to lay hands on Olivia, and neither should they bar the ballroom to her. There are guards waiting outside, and I will give the order in your presence and have them spread it immediately."

"So if I open the ball with you and Mother," Julius said warily, "you swear not to bar the ballroom doors against Olivia? And if she comes, you'll allow me free choice."

"I give you my word," his father said.

Julius reached for the outfit laid out for him. "In that case, just give me a minute to change."

CHAPTER 31
OLIVIA

Olivia floated through the corridors, her fingers tracing her tingling lips. Julius had kissed her!

They had been interrupted before words of love could be exchanged, but she had seen the truth in his eyes. Why had she doubted his feelings all this time? She had been too cautious of her own heart and had let that caution hold her back. But now there need be no more barriers between them and no need to break the betrothal.

She glided through the door to her suite, shutting it behind her. As expected, Mildred was back in her nest, still quivering with the stress of the last hour.

Olivia hurried over and flung her arms around the mouse's neck. "Thank you, girl," she breathed into her fur. "You saved me."

Mildred squeaked, and Olivia let her go. "Sorry," she said with a giggle, her joy and relief still overflowing. "That was too tight."

Olivia wandered toward the middle of the room, wondering how long Julius's parents would keep him. The situation with Zane was a complicated tangle, so it was possible it would take some time to sort out. But no matter how late it got, Olivia wouldn't go to bed. She was confident that Julius would come looking for her when he was finished, regardless of how long he took.

Her eyes fell on a silver tray on the low table between the two sofas, a folded note resting on top of it. Her heart leaped, her mind racing straight to Julius. But a moment's reflection was enough to realize it couldn't be from him. It must have been left in her room earlier and overlooked when she discovered Zane searching her bedchamber.

The note didn't take long to read, and only a few lines turned her idle curiosity into shocked horror. The swirling script tangled and shifted in front of her eyes. She had to be reading it wrong. Break their betrothal? Julius to marry Marigold? No! It was impossible.

Olivia collapsed onto the closest sofa and forced herself to read the note again, going more slowly this time. Every bit of her earlier joy soured, turning to jagged shards in her gut.

No matter how many times she reread it, the words were there in undeniable ink. The king and queen had released Olivia from her betrothal. There was to be another ball that very night. Julius was to marry Marigold after all.

But Marigold was no more likely to agree to such a scheme than Julius. There had to be some mistake.

Olivia leaped to her feet. She would find Julius immediately, and he would explain everything. Surely, it was all one big misunderstanding. That had to be it. She would—

The door to her suite wouldn't open. Olivia tried the handle again, rattling it loudly. When it still wouldn't budge, she banged on the wood and called out. No one answered.

Olivia stepped back, her stomach surging and her breath catching. She had been locked in. There was no other explanation.

She looked down at the note again. The word *ball* stared back at her. There was to be a second ball, and this time the king and queen weren't going to let Olivia interfere with it.

The soft tap of a knock made her startle.

"Is someone there?" she called, trying the door again.

Still locked.

The knock came again, but this time she realized it hadn't come from the door in front of her. It had come from behind her.

Olivia spun around in confusion and stared at the window. A mass of fiery curls was pressed against the glass, visible despite the setting sun.

Stumbling, Olivia rushed to the window and wrenched it open.

"Help me in," Marigold said between pants, reaching her hand toward Olivia.

Dazed, Olivia grasped her wrist and hauled her over the windowsill and into the room. Marigold collapsed on the ground in swirls of silk. She was wearing a full ballgown, her hair piled artfully on her head.

Olivia leaned through the open window and gaped at the distance below. "You climbed all the way from the ground on those vines?"

She pulled her head back into the room and shook her head at her friend. Apparently Marigold's time in captivity had done little to curb her wild streak.

"Actually, I only had to climb from the floor below," Marigold said. "It turns out my family's apartment is directly below yours. My parents think they've cowed me into submission, so they let me retreat into my room alone to get dressed for the ball."

"I just found this note." Olivia thrust the paper at Marigold. "What is going on?"

Marigold read the note in grim silence before telling Olivia all about the scheme concocted by her parents and the king and queen.

"Honestly, it's mostly my father's fault," she said with a scowl. "He's furiously angry at Lord Strathmore and talking like he's ready to burn the kingdom down over it. I think he'll be more sensible once he's calmed down. He isn't truly a heartless person, and he won't want to see all of Sovar suffer. But King Robert isn't willing to take the chance. Arresting Lord Strathmore has unleashed all sorts of chaos on the court—his wealth and support networks run deep. So the king wants to make sure there's a solid alliance between the crown and my family. So here I am, all dressed up and ready to be the sacrifice."

"And Julius agreed to this?" Olivia asked, struggling to breathe. "I know he takes his duty to Sovar seriously. I just thought..."

"Of course he didn't agree," Marigold said promptly, and Olivia's throat loosened.

"But I haven't seen him since he raced out of the room to find you," she added, "so they may have found a way to bully him as well. For me, my father is threatening to make sure Cade takes the fall along with Lord Strathmore. But for Julius, they were trying to spin some sort of tale about you being better off free from the palace." She shook her head.

"The king and queen must be blind if they can't see that you'll make a far better queen than me."

"Did Julius believe her?" Olivia asked. "Does he think I'd be better off without him?" She tried to hold onto their kiss, but what if she'd read it wrong? What if it had been a farewell kiss?

Marigold hesitated, sending ice through Olivia's veins.

"I'm not sure," she admitted. "I wasn't supposed to hear any of it, but I have excellent hearing." She grimaced. "I couldn't catch every word, though."

"Then we'd better hurry and get you dressed for a ball, Olivia," Daphne said from the bedchamber door. "It's past time you told Julius how you feel about him for yourself." She gave her cousin a knowing look. "You do think he's worth the sacrifice of being royal, don't you?"

Olivia gaped at her.

"Well?" Daphne asked.

"Of course I do," Olivia gasped. "But where did you come from? Were you in there the whole time?"

"Of course." Daphne stretched and yawned. "When I came back into the palace, I came straight to check on Mildred. She was fine, so I thought I'd have a little nap while I waited for you." She grinned. "I thought you might be a while."

Olivia flushed, thinking of that alcove and the stolen moment with Julius that had delayed her. Julius's kiss had opened a beautiful future for her, and she refused to believe it had been meant as a goodbye. She had to trust in Julius and his kiss. She would find him and tell him how she felt just like Daphne said.

Then she remembered the flaw in Daphne's plan. "Unfortunately, I can't go to the ball. They've locked me in." She glanced at the window doubtfully. "I don't think I'm as brave as you, Marigold. I can't climb down to the ground on unstable vines."

Marigold grinned wickedly and pulled several long hairpins from the elaborate arrangement on her head. "Fortunately, one of the Emerson servants didn't always lead such an upright life. He knows how to pick locks, and I convinced him to teach me when I was thirteen. I like to practice now and then to keep my skills fresh. You get dressed, and I'll get us out of here."

Daphne smiled. "I wasn't sure I liked you at first, but you've won me over."

Marigold grinned back, unoffended. "Same."

"I just hope I have a dress to wear," Olivia wailed. "Zane had just started pulling apart my wardrobe when I found him."

"Wait, Zane?" Marigold paused halfway to the sitting room door and looked back over her shoulder. "He did what?"

Olivia quickly told the other girls what had happened between her and Zane in her suite, and about being forced into the tunnel and out of the palace.

"It wasn't Lord Strathmore?" Marigold asked, incredulous. "It was Zane the whole time?" She shook her head. "If Lord Strathmore gets released, my father will be livid." She grinned slowly at the idea before quirking an eyebrow. "You know, I never did like Zane, even though he is Cade's brother. Something about him always made me uncomfortable."

"Always trust your intuition," Daphne murmured.

Both of her friends trailed Olivia into her bedchamber

and to her wardrobe. To her relief, most of her gowns were still untouched.

Daphne drew out a magnificent creation from the back, an elaborate, formal gown whose embroidery and layers of blue paid homage to the dress Olivia had worn for her betrothal announcement. "This is perfect," she announced. "You should definitely wear this one."

She helped Olivia into the gown, and all three girls nodded in approval. Daphne ushered Olivia to a seat in front of her dressing table and began quickly pinning up her hair.

"You'll have to wear my slippers, of course." Marigold kicked off her glass slippers. "I just hope you can walk in them since your feet are smaller."

Olivia met Marigold's eyes in the mirror on her dressing table. "No," she said. "Julius approached me at the Midsummer Ball because he thought I was his parents' choice. And then his parents accepted me to appease the Legacy. This time, I want him to choose me himself, freely. If he chooses his duty over me, I can't stop that. I won't trap him. Neither am I willing to allow such an important decision to be dictated by the Legacy. We both go in glass slippers, and Julius chooses between us himself."

Marigold wrinkled her nose. "That's very noble of you— but know I'm only agreeing because I'm confident in his choice. I have no interest in becoming queen."

"But where are you going to find a second pair of glass slippers?" Daphne asked, ever practical. "I can see they've put one on display in your sitting room, but you can't wear one slipper."

Olivia bit her lip. She hadn't even thought about what

had happened to her other slipper. But in some things, Aunt Helen was extremely reliable.

"My aunt packed my clothes for me, and one of the maids unpacked them into the wardrobe. I'm betting the other slipper is in the bottom somewhere."

Marigold hurried over and dove into the wardrobe, unworried about her own outfit. She emerged triumphant, one glass slipper gripped in her hand.

Within seconds, she had the other one out of its display and was kneeling to slip them onto Olivia's feet. Olivia wanted to protest that she could put them on herself, but the nervous knot in her belly made it hard to talk.

Marigold flashed her an encouraging grin and left the bedchamber, her lock picking hairpins back in her hands. Olivia stood and faced Daphne.

"Are you coming?" she whispered.

Daphne surveyed the remaining dresses, a gleam in her eyes. "I'll get myself ready and come behind you. The two of you should make your grand entrance alone."

Olivia nodded, swallowed hard, and joined Marigold.

"Success!" Marigold cried as the door lock clicked. She opened the door and peered outside. "And they didn't even leave any guards."

Olivia grimaced. "I'm sure they thought there was no way I could get out on my own. They were probably right, too."

"Never!" Marigold cried loyally. "You would have found a way."

The two girls wasted no time hurrying through the palace. The whole way, Olivia remained tense, watching for guards, but none crossed their path. They slowed as they approached the ballroom.

"Are you ready for this?" Olivia asked Marigold.

Her friend took her hand. "This is how it should have been from the beginning. I can see that now. The two of us entering together."

Olivia smiled back at her, but half her attention was on the ceremonial guards placed on either side of the ballroom door. One of them shifted slightly at the sight of the two girls together and sent his comrade a questioning look.

The second guard shook his head. "I heard His Majesty myself. Lady Olivia is free to enter the ball."

"Even in glass slippers?" the first guard whispered. "*Both* of them in glass slippers?"

His companion shrugged. "The king didn't mention footwear. He just said that she's to be allowed in."

Olivia drew a relieved breath. Just reaching the ball had felt like enough of an ordeal. She didn't fancy fighting off two guards to get inside.

Her heart beat faster as she and Marigold stepped into the doorway, the double doors allowing them to stand side by side as they surveyed the ballroom.

A fanfare sounded from invisible trumpets, and silence spread through the ballroom as every head turned to stare at the two arrivals. Eyes skipped from Olivia to Marigold, whispers breaking out as people caught the flash of two pairs of glass slippers.

A path opened through the crowd, revealing Julius, tall and regal. Olivia's breath caught.

She had already chosen Julius, and she would continue to do so every day, despite the difficulties that came with him.

But would he choose her over the duty his parents demanded?

Julius stood for a moment, staring across the ballroom at the two girls standing together. And then he was moving—running—toward them, his smile wide and his eyes bright.

Marigold squeezed Olivia's hand and tugged her gently down the shallow stairs to stand on the ballroom floor. They reached it just as Julius arrived in front of them. He gave no indication of even seeing Marigold, his eyes for Olivia alone.

He held out his hand to her.

"Will you dance with me, beautiful lady?" he asked, amusement dancing in his eyes and brightening his smile. "And then would you be mine forever?"

"Yes." Olivia put her hand in his willingly this time, giving him her heart along with it. "And yes. I will gladly do both."

Julius pulled her into his arms and onto the dance floor as the music swelled around them and the crowd broke into cheers. The crown prince of Sovar had made his own choice, but Olivia still felt the power of the Legacy giving wings to her feet. They would have their love and the future of the kingdom as well.

EPILOGUE

OLIVIA

"Do you really have to go?" Olivia stood at the palace's entrance, gazing disconsolately at the carriage waiting at the bottom of the stairs.

"I've been here for six months," Daphne said with an amused smile. "So I think we both know the answer to that is yes. It's past time I was heading for Oakden."

"Couldn't you just marry Ashton and stay forever?" Olivia wailed, giving her cousin yet another final hug goodbye.

Daphne snorted. "Appealing as that sounds, I think I'll leave that honor to Nell or Hattie. I wouldn't like to earn either of our cousins' enmity by stealing their favorite lord."

Olivia sniffled and chuckled weakly. "I'm sorry. I promised myself I wouldn't do this."

"It's already been three months since your wedding, Princess Olivia," Daphne said with a long-suffering look. "And I even let you twist my arm into being one of your attendants. And I thought Rosalie's wedding was exhausting! When it's my turn, I think I'll just run away to a beach somewhere and get married on the sand."

"Don't be silly," Olivia said. "You're on your way to Oakden. You'll no doubt meet some handsome, charming man there who will convince you to settle down in your birth kingdom and have twenty babies. You'll forget what exhaustion even is!"

"With twenty babies? You must be joking." Daphne stared at her in horror. "Legacy burden or not, there aren't enough naps in the world to cover twenty babies."

"You wouldn't have them all at once," Olivia pointed out, warming to the topic.

"I won't be having them at all," Daphne said firmly. "I'm going to Oakden because I have to know what life is like without the constant burden of the Legacy. I'm not going there for romance."

"That's what you say now," Olivia said, but in a small voice and with a cheeky smile.

"Stop harassing your cousin, love, and let her leave before the sun sets and the coachman refuses to set out at all." Julius's welcome voice lifted some of Olivia's sorrow.

She smiled at him as he reached her side and slipped an arm around her waist. But Daphne regarded her with a wounded look.

"Ah! Your plan has been revealed! That's why you're waffling on about twenty babies."

Olivia laughed. "We only just finished breakfast. You've got plenty of daylight left. But Julius is right; I should let you go."

Daphne stepped forward for yet another final hug, and Olivia clung to her tightly.

"Don't worry," Daphne said lightly. "Marigold and Cade get back from their wedding trip tomorrow, remember? You won't be lonely for long."

Julius's arm tightened around her waist. "She won't be lonely at all."

"Whoa, slow down there, lovebirds," Daphne said lightly. "Wait until I'm napping in the carriage, and then you can gaze passionately into each other's eyes for as many hours as you like."

"I suppose you really will nap all the way to Oakden." Olivia shook her head. "I can't imagine you without the tendency to sleep everywhere you go. It's hard to imagine an Oakdenian Daphne."

"Which is precisely why I need to go," Daphne said softly. "Even I don't remember anymore."

There was nothing to be said to that. Instead, Olivia gave the actual final hug and called repeated goodbyes as Daphne descended the stairs and climbed into her carriage. Her face didn't appear at the window, but Olivia still waved until the carriage had passed through the distant palace gates.

She lowered her arm with a sigh, and Julius pulled her around into his arms, her front flush with his.

"You'll miss her." It wasn't a question. "But we can hope she'll come back."

"To visit, yes." Olivia sighed. "But this isn't her home. If she ever decides to live outside of Oakden, she'll go to Glandore and Rosalie."

"You don't need to be jealous of Rosalie anymore," Julius reminded her. He now knew all about her complicated feelings toward Daphne's best friend. "You're not in Henton. Here you have your own best friend to make trouble with. And as Daphne said, that friend will be back tomorrow. We should probably brace ourselves. It's been unnaturally peaceful for the last month."

Olivia laughed. "Marigold isn't that bad! Especially once her father admitted defeat and agreed to let her marry Cade. I think he's a settling influence on her."

"We can only hope." Julius didn't sound convinced. "She may just be biding her time."

"I'm so glad Lord Emerson did relent," Olivia murmured, gazing across the front of the palace. "Marigold would have married Cade anyway, of course, but it's much more peaceful at court without having to manage feuding Emersons."

"Listen to you, talking like an old hand," Julius said with a teasing smile.

"After the eight months we've had, I feel like I am!" Olivia leaned into him and rested her head against his chest, letting herself draw comfort from the strength of his arms around her. "Were you surprised when Lord Emerson capitulated? I thought he would eventually, but I didn't expect it to happen so quickly."

"When it comes to court," Julius said wryly, "alliances are always subject to change. Lord Emerson claimed he opposed the match due to Cade's family, but his tune changed rather quickly when Cade became *the* Lord Strathmore instead of just a younger son."

"Meaning Marigold got what she most wanted and most dreaded at the same time." Olivia couldn't help chuckling. "Marriage to Cade and the central position at court that suddenly came with it."

She remained silent for a moment, thinking back on the upheaval of the previous autumn. It hadn't been surprising when Zane was stripped of his title and sentenced to prison. But she hadn't expected the panel of nobles convened by the king to rule that Lord Strathmore was at least partially complicit in his son's actions. The old lord had been a little too careful in avoiding all knowledge of his son's criminal activities—clearly he had known something was going on and had implicitly, if not explicitly, given Zane permission.

Since he hadn't been directly involved, he had merely been stripped of his position—both his title and the family's wealth passing to his second son. But Cade had immediately gifted his parents one of the more distant Strathmore properties, well out of the capital. The last Olivia had heard, the two were adjusting to a quieter and more ordinary life.

She would probably get a new update soon since Marigold and Cade had planned to stop by and see them at the end of their wedding trip before returning to the capital.

"I was more surprised by my own mother's speedy change of attitude," Julius said thoughtfully, resting his chin gently on the top of Olivia's head.

She slipped her arms around his waist and gave him a squeeze. Julius had forgiven his parents, but there was still work to be done to fully restore the relationship that had existed between them before. And she couldn't blame him for that. Trust was a slow thing to rebuild.

For herself, however, it had been easier. Without the complication of history and family between them, she had chosen to accept the queen's profuse apologies and put the incident behind them. Given all the work she still had to do to learn the role of crown princess and eventually queen, she couldn't afford to be at odds with her mother-in-law.

Olivia still had moments of crippling self-doubt, and perhaps that was what helped her view Queen Elsinore more softly. The queen was the only person who had stood in Olivia's shoes, and she suspected that even decades later, the queen had her moments of insecurity and fear.

Or perhaps it was merely that the queen was the only person who loved Julius with the same fierceness that Olivia did. From the moment of her repentance, Queen Elsinore had pleaded that she had acted out of concern for her son. She had feared that Julius would end up in a miserable marriage with someone who resented both him and the court and who didn't understand his life in the way a high-ranking girl would.

But after hearing exactly how Olivia had escaped her locked room, the queen had finally accepted Marigold's unsuitability, acknowledging she had been wrong. And with a wedding to plan for Julius and Olivia—who had wanted to get married as quickly as possible—she had thrown herself behind their match just as heartily as she had once opposed it.

The king had been less flexible, responding to Julius's accusations of treachery by pointing out that he had only said the guards would not impede Olivia's access to the ball. He had said nothing of not locking her suite—a task that had been completed by a servant, not a guard.

This argument had found no favor with Julius, and it had been up to his mother to plead on his father's behalf.

"Robert is in a unique position," she had said. "When he

took those actions, he wasn't acting as your father, but as your king. And while it may seem obvious now that he made the wrong choice—" A snort from her son made her adjust her words. "*Several* wrong choices, he was under immense pressure and acting for what he honestly thought was the good of the kingdom. Remember, he wasn't asking for a sacrifice from you that he hadn't made himself when he was crown prince. He truly believed it was your duty to do as he had once done."

Julius didn't accept his mother's words immediately, but Olivia knew he pondered on them. And while the king had still not directly acknowledged his errors—either through stiff pride or a mistaken belief that it would undermine his position as king—he did show increasing favor to Olivia, which she saw as his attempt to acknowledge his mistake and make amends.

Eventually, Julius told his mother that she could stop hounding him as he'd decided to forgive his father. His subsequent manner toward the king couldn't be considered warm, but it had at least grown a great deal less frosty. And Olivia noticed it thawing a little more with each passing month—a source of relief to both Julius's mother and his wife.

When his mother asked him what his father had done to convince him to relent, Julius had shrugged.

"Nothing at all. I just realized that the day will come when I sit on his throne and wear the burden of his crown. And as king, I'm sure I'll eventually make a wrong decision as well."

His mother had nodded slowly, pride in her son shining

in her eyes. And the same warmth had remained on her face as she looked at her daughter-in-law, sitting at her son's side.

"Everyone is fallible, so I agree that such a situation is inevitable," she said softly. "But I suspect that when that day comes, your queen will do a better job of helping you see your error than Robert's queen did."

After that, both women were in tears, and hugs were exchanged all round.

It also helped that Olivia now had her own family around her, not just Julius's. Her parents and brothers had come to the capital not only for the wedding but to move there permanently. Uncle Walt and Aunt Helen had opened their home to them, and Nell and Hattie were adjusting to life with five younger brothers—a situation that caused great amusement to Olivia, who had once stood in their place.

But at least when Nell and Hattie needed a break they could flee to court. Olivia's aunt and uncle now maintained an apartment in the palace, like the inner circle of nobles, and Olivia's cousins frequently used it as a refuge. Olivia's mother had firmly decreed that none of the boys were fit to even visit it yet. She was determined to wait until they'd grown up before unleashing them on the palace.

Thankfully, the boys seemed to think having the whole capital as their playground was good enough for the time being and had accepted her strictures. And Olivia could visit them on Manor Row whenever she wanted—something that she enjoyed less once she discovered that they'd brought two lizards with them from Henton in the hope they would grow to the size of dragons. And unfortunately, given the Legacy's approval of Julius and Olivia's wedding, the two creatures were well on their way to achieving the boys' aim, much to Aunt Helen's dismay.

"Are you really so sad to be left behind with just me?" Julius asked in an affectionate voice, clearly already knowing the answer.

Olivia pulled back so she could smile up at him. "No, of course not. I'll miss Daphne, but I always knew she had to leave eventually. And it's amazing how much easier it is to watch people go when there's one person who's promised never to walk away from me."

"Never," Julius vowed in a solemn voice, leaning down to capture her lips with his. When he pulled back, she sighed and put her head against his chest again.

"You are the best mistake I ever made," he murmured. "And I look forward to dancing at many, many more Midsummer Balls with you."

"And one day we'll watch our children dance there," Olivia agreed.

"Children...plural?" Julius asked cautiously.

Olivia lifted her head so she could see his face, giving him her most determined look. "I want more than one child. Our experience showed that the Legacy can be placated with a much less rigid approach, and the number of our children isn't something I'm willing to leave up to the Legacy."

Julius's brow creased, and he remained silent for a minute as he turned her words over in his head.

"I'm not sure how we haven't had this conversation before," he finally said, but Olivia knew.

They'd hardly had a quiet moment in the last six months.

Thinking about something as far away as children hadn't been at the front of their minds.

"I like it, though," he added, a grin growing over his face.

Olivia breathed a sigh of relief and relaxed.

"I always wanted a sibling," he added. "I'm glad our future crown prince won't have to suffer the same loneliness I did."

Olivia raised an eyebrow. "Are you so sure it will be a crown prince?"

"The Legacy isn't going to let us go completely," he told her. "But I can handle having a son first. And second and third, if that's what we get. Although a little princess would be just as acceptable."

"Three," Olivia murmured, leaning back into him. "That sounds nice." She was silent for a moment. "I want to invite Avery to visit Sovar as well."

"Avery?" She could hear the frown of concentration in his voice. "The peddler who gave you your mirror?"

She nodded against his chest. "I've heard she's been investigating the Legacies, and I want to ask her to include Sovar in her investigation. I think it's time we knew why cliffs keep appearing everywhere—our future king has nearly gone over two of them at this point."

The rumble of Julius's quiet laughter felt soothing against her cheek.

"If we're going to take a different approach to the Legacy during our reign," he said, "then I think it makes sense to learn everything about it that we can. After weeks of deliberation, our best scholars were only able to come up with the strategy of doing everything exactly the same for a second time. I think we're ready for some new ways of thinking."

"Exactly." Joy rose up in Olivia at the sense of unity she felt with her new husband.

She had never felt so excited for the future as she did in that moment, wrapped in his arms, making plans together. Her friends and family would come and go, but she would remain content, buoyed by a lifetime of such moments.

NOTE FROM THE AUTHOR

I hope you enjoyed Olivia and Julius's story! Find out what happens to Daphne when she finally returns to Oakden in Legacy of Thorns: A Sleeping Beauty Tale.

If you missed the story of Avery, the roving merchant who gave Olivia the enchanted mirror, you can read it in Ties of Legacy, a Kingdoms of Legacy companion novel.

To be informed of my new releases, as well as new bonus shorts, please sign up to my mailing list at www.melaniecellier.com. At my website, you'll also find an array of free extra content for my various worlds.

Thank you for taking the time to read my book. I hope you enjoyed it. If you did, please spread the word! You could start by leaving a review on Amazon (or Goodreads or Facebook or any other social media site). Your review would be very much appreciated and would make a big difference!

ACKNOWLEDGMENTS

I've been excited to write Olivia and Julius's story ever since the kernel of the idea for it came to me. But it also turned into my longest first draft to date, so I'm grateful to all those who helped me find the time and space to write and who then helped me shape the story into its final form.

So a big thank you to my incredibly supportive husband, Marc, and our little ones for letting me escape when I needed to in order to write for hours on end.

Thank you also to my writing tribe—you guys rock!—and to the awesome friends on my beta team. It is so awesome to be surrounded by people who love to read.

To my professional team—Lyra, Mary, my dad, James, Rebecca, Karri, Esther, and Nathaniel—thank you for bringing your skills and excellence to Legacy of Glass and helping me to refine the story and to bring it to visual and audio life. I'm incredibly grateful to have found you all.

And, as always, thank you to God for always being ready to walk beside us and to provide strength when we are weak.

ABOUT THE AUTHOR

Melanie Cellier grew up on a staple diet of books, books and more books. And although she got older, she never stopped loving children's and young adult novels.

She always wanted to write one herself, but it took three careers and three different continents before she actually managed it.

She now feels incredibly fortunate to spend her time writing from her home in Adelaide, Australia where she keeps an eye out for koalas in her backyard. Her staple diet hasn't changed much, although she's added choc mint Rooibos tea and Chicken Crimpies to the list.

She writes young adult fantasy including books in her *Spoken Mage* world, her *Mage's Influence* world, and her various *Four Kingdoms* and *Kingdoms of Legacy* series that are made up of linked stand-alone stories that retell classic fairy tales.